Angeline

For: Francis

Angelina Salvaggio

Secret Dwellings

A historical romance

Author's Note:

Thank you for buying my book!

While the majority of this tale is historically accurate, a few liberties were taken.

Please note that I wrote the English vernacular in a way that most resembles the Regency period for ease of reading.

For a detailed content rating and possible triggers, please visit my website:

www.angelinasalvaggio.com

I hope you enjoy reading it as much as I did writing it!

Reviews are always appreciated.

My debut is dedicated to my husband, Daniel.

I love you, I love us, I love who I am with you, and I love our boys.

Special Thanks

I offer my deepest gratitude to the Holy Trinity, the Blessed Mother, my Guardian Angel, and to St. Edmund Campion.

*

Daniel – Even though this isn't your typical genre, thank you for reading it more than once, for being my second eyes, comma Nazi, and for lifting me up all the times I needed it. You're an amazing husband; I couldn't have done this without your help and support!

*

Isaac – thank you for your vast knowledge of weaponry and for listening to me word vomit about my book. I love you!

*

Tristan – thanks for helping with that tricky scene and for being so patient while I worked on this. I love you!

*

Christina Stabinski – thank you for being my best friend for over 20 years, my fashionista expert, and my first Beta reader. That meant so much to me! Your advice, critiques, excitement, and encouragement were invaluable. Also, sorry for driving you crazy with blurb rewrites.

*

Bridget Fairley – you were my most thorough Beta reader! I'm so grateful for having gotten to know you. Not just for your extensive historical knowledge, but for our wonderful friendship too. Going through my book with you taught me so much and helped Secret Dwellings become what it is now.

*

Rachel Matatics, **author E.R. Magdalen**, **Magdalena Olechney**, and **author Brynn Nelson** – thank you for all the time you took to read my book in its editing stages, and for all the deeply valued input, critiques, and kind compliments too! I appreciate you all so much!

*

Mom and **Dad** – you've both always fostered my creativity, and inspired a deep love for my Faith. I'm so grateful for everything you've done for me throughout my whole life! Love you both so much!

*

Bernie Salvaggio (best big brother ever) – you've been such a huge help and support to me! Thank you so much for everything! I love you! I especially appreciate the awesome website you made for me: https://www.angelinasalvaggio.com/

*

Enormous gratitude to **Tim Guile**, Chairman of the English Catholic History Association and Fellow of the Royal Historical Society! Thank you for taking the time to pour over my Prologue to ensure its historical accuracy. I felt very privileged to learn from you. Thank you for your corrections, insights, and your patience. I appreciate you and your life's work more than I can say! I hope I can take you up on that offer for a tour of Oxford one day.

*

Immense thanks to **Allison Ramirez** – editor extraordinaire! You're so talented and patient. I'm very grateful to have found you! Thank you for giving Secret Dwellings the professional polish it deserved.

*

Special thanks to **Lily Dormishev Art**! You were amazing to work with and I'm so grateful for your artistic talents. You're a fantastic listener and I love the magic you create! Every time I admire my book, I'll think of you.

*

Shout out and thanks to, **With Love, Wyatt Photography** for my head-shot! You were so fun and professional to work with!

*

Thank you, **Mrs. Ferell**, for sharing your love of writing with me when you gave me that journal in 1st Grade. I've gone through so many since then.

*

Thank you to all of my family and friends who have supported, helped, inspired, and offered advice — I truly appreciate you all!

*

Shout out and special thanks to my ARC readers team!

Author Cara Ruegg

*

Evelyn Masters

*

Author Avelina Balestri

*

Mary Pancino

*

Cathy Bonham

*

G Bonham

*

Gloria Lopez

*

Heather Foster

*

Sarah Marstall

*

SECRET DWELLINGS

Author Alison Brown

*

Prologue:

In the 1500's, England began a journey that would place them at grave odds with the Catholic Church.

Contrary to what some may think, the king who began this historical spiral was once a loyal Catholic. To King Henry VIII's great pride, Pope Gregory XIII had even granted him the title *Defender of the Faith,* after writing a pamphlet against the rising swell of Lutheranism.

The king's ever changing taste in wives, however, caused England to split with Rome. Pope Gregory XIII refused to grant him an annulment. With Henry's departure from the Pope, the Church of England was born, also known as the Anglican faith.

The King was promptly excommunicated from the Catholic Church, thus officially losing his beloved title.

Much like a toddler throwing a tantrum, Henry demanded that Parliament give him that same title. Having no desire for decapitation, they were quick to bestow the now empty title upon him.

Having no need for Catholicism any longer, King Henry VIII closed down all the monasteries in hopes of making a nice profit. This left all of the monks, priests, and religious sisters homeless and caused a social upheaval, as the monasteries served many functions for the English people. They acted as schools, hospitals, shelters, places of rest for travelers, libraries, they provided jobs, and aided the local poor and orphans. The King gave no thoughts for the thousands of lives he had made harder, however.

A man named Thomas Cranmer served as advisor to King Henry VIII and was considered a master of theology for his time. Sadly, he was swayed by most of Martin Bucer's _{Luther's} Protestant ideologies and became the first Anglican Archbishop.

He also took it upon himself to begin composing the *39 Articles* that summarized Anglican beliefs. This was accepted by Convocation in 1563.

One of the changes he is responsible for was the rejection of transubstantiation – where bread and wine are turned into the Body, Blood, Soul, and Divinity of Jesus Christ and more.

Most Catholics didn't notice the changes in the beginning, as he was very careful to make the service and prayer book appear similar.

After the death of King Henry VIII in 1547, one could say that Thomas Cranmer was decidedly eager to replace the Catholic Mass with a communion service, and to adapt the Book of Common Prayer in 1549.

The crown fell briefly to Henry's son Edward at the young age of 9. Sadly, he was succumbed to an early death when he was only 15.

Briefly, England had a Catholic Monarch in Queen Mary Tudor. She was largely welcomed, especially by her fellow Catholics. A few months after becoming the first Queen Regent, she abolished the Act of Supremacy which King Henry had created to have Catholics swear their allegiance to him, both spiritually and patriotically, and threw out the Book of Common Prayer. While Queen Mary was not perfect, she had a most challenging life full of suffering and served her people well.

In 1558 after 5 years, Queen Mary Tudor passed away.

Elizabeth I became the next Queen of England. Under her rule was a man known as William Cecil, or Lord Burghley. Like many others, he was extremely power hungry and sought favor with his queen. He appeared to have more success at this than others. During her reign, he was appointed as her Secretary of State, Lord Treasurer, Chief Minister, and was an advisor to Queen Elizabeth on her Privy Council. His influence over her was possibly the most historically significant.

Cecil pioneered Francis Walsingham's creation of the spy network; it was filled with countless spies, hired assassins, and informants. Being a Catholic would become a dangerous battle thanks to them.

Changes to the Mass were made purposefully vague and confusing so as not to incur further rebellions. The most notable alterations that Queen Elizabeth ordered under Cecil's influence were:

- The host was not to be elevated during consecration.

- The name of the pope was removed from the list of sovereigns and was no longer to be prayed for during Mass/Communion services.

- She wrote her own Act of Supremacy and revived the Book of Common Prayer.

- She also had every Catholic Bishop who did not comply removed, imprisoned, or killed and replaced with newly ordained Anglican bishops. It was done in such an underhanded way, that once again, most didn't realize they weren't Catholic – at first. Word eventually spread. One can only imagine how horrified the people were by such trickery.

Before long, the Catholic Mass had been covertly replaced. People were now ordered to attend the Church of England's services. The queen demanded hefty fines for those who chose to ignore her Anglican substitute for the Mass. Too many absences would often result in imprisonment.

The persecutions of Catholics living in England were not an overnight occurrence, but happened gradually over time. Nor did it span the entire country; many areas were left largely unaffected due to sympathetic Magistrates or location.

In 1570 Pope Pius V issued a Papal Bull titled, *Regnans in Excelsis*, where he declared Queen Elizabeth I to be a heretic, excommunicated her, and released her Catholic subjects from any and all obligation to obey her.

Elizabeth was enraged by this. The following 30 years would show, in detail, the extent of her wrath. This anger coupled by fear of a rebellion, spurred her on to make being a Catholic priest, or harboring one, an act of high treason. She was particularly harsh with the Jesuits.

These prisoners were "asked" to take the Oath of Supremacy. If they refused to reject their faith and submit to the Church of England by reciting it, the punishment was often death.

Anyone caught attending a Catholic Mass in secret would be fined or imprisoned. "Minor infractions", such as possession of rosaries, holy water, or other Catholic contraband, would oftentimes only merit a fine or a few weeks in prison with moderate torture. However, all Catholic items were confiscated and immediately disposed of.

Brave Catholics, later dubbed recusants, would shelter priests in priest-hides — small secret rooms within their homes. Priests quickly became expert actors, always traveling in various disguises to bring the sacraments to their scattered flocks.

Despite their best efforts at concealing their faith, hundreds or thousands of souls were martyred with at least 180 of them being priests. The exact number of martyrs is debated as many were not officially recorded, or were recorded incorrectly. Some sources claim 300. Others say over 700 died during Elizabeth's reign alone. Many agree the number to be in the thousands, especially when taking into account those who died from various Catholic rebellions.

Priests, religious sisters, men or women – it made no difference. With some exceptions, Catholics found to be guilty of high treason were most often hanged, drawn, and quartered. For the sake of modesty, women were typically hung.

Many other Catholics succumbed to torture and poor prison conditions. Even more were left impoverished due to the excessive fines, and with no monasteries to help them, their families were often left homeless.

Not all of Elizabeth's subjects agreed with her treatment of Catholics; there were many Protestants who sympathized with their plight and who aided their fellow countrymen from detection. Some were killed for doing so.

How seriously Catholics were hunted greatly varied depending on who local Magistrates were, where they lived, and who was currently on the throne, however.

Queen Elizabeth I was arguably the most aggressive enforcer of these anti-Catholic laws.

It was not until January 1829, thanks to the Duke of Wellington winning the battle of Waterloo, that he was able to convince King George IV to allow Catholics to practice their faith without any fear of persecution.

Only recently, in 2013, was a royal permitted to marry a Catholic without being disqualified from the throne. As of 2025, a Catholic may still never be king or queen of England.

This is a fictional story based on actual events in the year 1588 during the Protestant Reformation and reign of Queen Elizabeth I.

May the English martyrs pray for us all, especially my favorite, St. Edmund Campion.

Chapter One

"*Isabel Dawson!*"

Gasping at my mother's shriek, the quill pen in my hand jerked, causing the inkwell to topple over.

No!

The dark liquid gushed across the parchment. With great haste, I picked the inkwell back up and tried to contain the blackening river with my handkerchief. In a moment, the white, delicate square transformed into a murky patch of ebony. At least the desk had been spared, though I could not say the same for my poetry.

She called out for me again as I stood, heart still pounding. My mind reeled at the innumerable offenses I may have committed recently.

I tried licking the ink stain from my finger. *Blech! How ill mannered of me...and rather unpleasant tasting.*

I smoothed out my blue dress, inspecting it for black spots. Miraculously, it had managed to stay clean, despite my clumsiness.

Mother opened the door to my father's old study with the speed of a hunter who had found her prey.

"Isabel, I have been searching all over the house for you! The servants have been scouring the gardens while your sister has been keeping our company entertained."

I hid my blackened finger behind my back. "I'm sorry, Mama, I didn't hear you until just now.

Her brow furrowed, "What is in your teeth?"

I tried deflecting her question, "What company is here?"

"Do not tell me you've forgotten? Only *Lord Drake*...the Earl of Aylesbury and his brother. You promised to go with them and your sister into town for the market fair last month."

By the time mother had finished reminding me, she had crossed the distance to my face and was lifting my lip to investigate the black mark on my upper right tooth.

A loud gasp proceeded from her delicate features. She glanced at the desk and back to me. "Isabel. Do I want to know how INK got inside of your mouth?" She spied again at the desk before allowing her eyes to roll. "Oh good heavens! What is Lord Drake going to think of you?"

She sighed the sort of sigh that only a mother can manage, which conveyed both frustration and disappointment simultaneously. I swallowed sheepishly as she continued,

"He's been so very attentive to you, especially since your poor father passed away. Could you perhaps *try* and not scare him off, my darling? I'm quite sure your brother won't want to take care of us forever."

"...Um, yes Mother."

"Do not say *um* like a pauper."

Her irritation with me was palpable. Taking a moment to regain her composure, her tone softened.

"Refrain from smiling too widely or talking too much today – we haven't time to try and scrub the ink off. Oh, heavens, don't let him propose today of all days!"

Propose? My mouth dropped. Surely not. My mind leafed through the last few years of visits and gifts and...well, maybe she *was* right. I felt a shade paler as I composed a response.

"Mama, I will be careful not to show my teeth, and while I appreciate the earl's kindness, I have no interest in marrying the man. He's..." *Old*. I wanted to say old.

Mama's eyebrow lifted as she paused to stare at me while I contemplated my next words carefully. I glanced towards her hesitantly. "He's just not someone who evokes a romantic feeling, is he?"

Puffing out a sigh, she looped her arm in mine and rushed me out the door. Reassuringly, she patted my hand.

"Isabel, love is not all feelings. It's making a choice about who is compatible. Not to mention that becoming a countess would be an honor and a promise of an easy life. Keep an open mind and a closed mouth!"

Once we came to the doors of the drawing room, Mother stopped and turned me towards herself. She fluffed my sleeves, pinched my cheeks, and smoothed away a stray hair.

"There! Beautiful." She smiled, quite pleased with herself.

I smiled back as she suddenly sighed, and stared disapprovingly.

I pressed my lips together. "I'll remember, I promise!"

A servant opened the door for us as mother apologized for my tardiness. "Beautiful but a bit absent-minded, I'm afraid, my Lord!"

Lord Drake was a tall man with dark features. The shade of his doublet matched his black hair almost perfectly. The only exception being the gold buttons and lining with a small white ruffle about his neck.

With a smile, he rose to greet me, "A worthy compromise, I'm sure!" Taking my hand to kiss it, I obliged him by expressing how kind he was, curtsied, and took a seat next to my younger sister.

Anna, who had recently turned eleven, looked positively pristine. As though she should have been born into royalty, or at the very least, marry into it one day. Every blond curl was perfectly in place and every fold of her pink dress lay evenly.

I do believe our mother often wished *I* had been the youngest child. Anna was so much more poised and graceful, like Mama herself.

My sister knew how I felt about the earl however, which explained why her gaze was so sympathetic towards me. She offered a reassuring smile.

I looked about the familiar room, keeping my eyes hidden from a certain guest. Our drawing room was larger than most; it contained several chairs, two cushioned settees, a lovely harpsichord, a card table, and even a writing desk.

A fireplace with a beautifully carved hearth was to the right with four generously sized windows to the left that let in a dazzling amount of sunlight during the day.

We have been quite blessed between grandfather's inheritance and my own father's successful business adventures. I am certain Lord Drake's friendship assisted with many of those favorable outcomes.

"I trust my youngest daughter has been good company in our absence?" Mother addressed Lord Drake and his younger brother. And when I say younger, I mean more than a decade my senior.

"She has been nothing but charm itself, Mistress Catherine!" Lord Drake assured her with his standard crooked smile.

Anna beamed at the compliment, sitting up even straighter than before.

His lordship turned his powerful gaze to me. "Shall we be off for the fair, Miss Dawson?"

His voice was deep, his stature proud, and his age nearly doubled my own. While this may be inappropriate to mention, dear reader, his scent was quite strong; a mixture of leather and musk. Perhaps the outdoors *would* be an improvement.

"Of course." I responded politely.

Anna was eager to grab her blue petticoat and gloves from the servant who had hers and mine ready by the door.

Lord Drake took my white petticoat from the servant and assisted me. I refrained from shuddering as I placed my arms through, and thanked him as I put on my white gloves to quickly cover the ink stain on my finger.

Lord Drake turned and faced his shorter brother. "Paul, didn't you say you've been wanting to go hunting? Why don't you go and find Jonathon in the woods? You might prefer that to the town today."

Paul was the fairer, clean shaven version of Lord Drake. Though perhaps not as bright. He looked confused for a moment as he shifted his weight from one foot to the other. Then, his eyebrows rose as though recalling previous instructions. "Oh – yes. Hunting *would* suit me better – what an excellent notion!"

The earl scratched his facial hair as he nodded his approval.

Mama smiled knowingly between the earl and Paul. "You are welcome to our horses and equipment as always, of course."

My stomach curled tightly at the awkward tension. The crawling sensation of anxiety began to creep up my neck. With Paul gone, this left only me, my sister, and Lord Drake setting off for Aylesbury's town center.

Lovely.

This would be the first time we'd be mostly alone. I had always been successful at avoiding this situation in the past; if only papa were here.

My only hope was that Lord Drake would have to receive permission from my brother – Jonathon – in order for a proposal to take place. Surely my brother would not approve...would he?

With Paul headed down to the stables, the three of us made our way along the dirt road.

"The weather is rather ideal, is it not, Miss Dawson?" Lord Drake commented as he smiled down at me, tucking his raven-like hair behind his ear.

Anna skipped ahead of us a little ways, and I called after her to keep pace with us before responding, "Yes. Quite sunny. A pleasant reprieve from all the recent rain."

Lord Drake extended his arm to me, "You don't have to worry about keeping your sister close... I assure you that I am quite trustworthy!"

In moments such as these, my stomach always felt ill at ease. Yet, he was a family friend and held much sway in our society. For reasons I will disclose later, it was important for me not to insult the man.

Hesitantly, I placed my arm in his which brought a satisfied smile to his elongated face. He wasn't unattractive – most referred to him as handsome even. I'm sure his wealth swayed many opinions, however.

Anna picked wild flowers that grew along the country road ahead of us. She would occasionally look back to check on me. It was not long before her arms were filled with bright yellow rattle shoots, purple hues of tufted vetch, and deep red ovals of great burnets.

"Out of curiosity," Lord Drake began, "where were you when my brother and I arrived?" He smirked. "Had you forgotten me completely?"

I could feel my cheeks burn. What an improper question to ask! Furthermore, how was I to answer him in a manner that did not offend him?

"Oh! My Lord, it isn't so much that I forgot you...rather that I'm afraid I lost all track of time!" I responded, careful to keep my black mark of shame hidden.

"We've known each other since you were a small child, I think it would be appropriate if you called me Elwood, don't you? And praytell, what were you doing that made you *lose all track of time?*"

My heart felt a tinge of panic. "I'm afraid I should find it rather challenging to call you something different now! – I shall tell you what I was doing as long as you promise not to hold it against me?"

He stopped and turned towards me. His hand folded over mine that was placed on his arm. "I hope one day that you might find it less strange to call me Elwood instead."

The ardent gaze with which he held my attention broke, and we continued walking as we had before. "I doubt anything you tell me could make me hold the smallest offense against you. What scandalous thing were you up to?"

Any doubt I had previously about his affections towards me – were now quite clear. I'll confess only to you, dear reader, that occasionally my heart was tempted to explore him further and cast aside my hesitations about him. My dearest papa hadn't liked him for me though, and perhaps that, more than anything else, held me back. It had been a subject of great contention between him and my mother.

"I'm afraid, my Lord, that one of my favorite pastimes is a bit of an oddity for a woman to have. Papa introduced me to books as a young child, and now I enjoy writing my own stories and poems as much as I like to read them."

"Oh my, indeed, Miss Dawson!" His feigned horror made me smile wider than I had intended as he continued, "Tell me it isn't so!"

Most gentlemen would have been put off by my confessing that; it was relieving to feel accepted. Without thinking, the smile grew larger as I met his gaze.

"Is that perhaps," he began, "why there is an ink smudge on your tooth? That is what it is, isn't it?"

My eyes widened as I immediately covered my mouth with my free hand; Mama was going to have my head herself!

"I have no idea what you mean," I said with as much pride as I could muster, putting my hand back down by my side. "That would be most unlady-like."

7

Realizing he had embarrassed me, he bent his head down to my height and whispered, "I shan't tell your mother, that is, if you will call me Elwood and permit me to call you by your given name."

Inwardly, I cringed; I strongly dislike being trapped into things I have no desire to do. Much like this walk to the fair that he had cleverly tricked me into agreeing to during his previous visit.

His face was uncomfortably close to mine; I removed my hand from his arm and took a step away. "Surely, you are not intending to blackmail such an old family friend?" I offered a coy smile.

Holding his arm out to me again, I could see the wheels turning in his head. "I wouldn't call it blackmail exactly, but rather a trade! One kind gesture in exchange for another?"

Reminding myself that it was improper for a lady to argue, I took his arm again and replied that I would think about it. Immediately, I changed the subject to the beautiful scenery around us.

The smell of a spring in full bloom was a beautiful distraction – sweet, crisp. The wind blew playfully through the long grass and wildflowers; it rustled through the occasional hawthorn and birch tree, even going so far as to send my brown curls twirling about my face. I regretted not wearing a coif to keep them under better control.

Crossing a small stone bridge that brought us over a rushing stream, Lord Drake proved to be singularly minded. "What can I do, *Miss Dawson*, to make you feel more at ease with me? Must I sneak you sweets while you hide under the tablecloth in your father's study again, as I did when you were a child?"

A smile played across my face at the memory. I had been quite frightened of Lord Drake's serious features and looming height as a child. When he did not give away my hiding spot and instead brought me tarts, it did go quite a ways in garnering my trust.

We passed under a large twisted oak at the end of the bridge, a favorite of mine to climb as a child. "A cherry tart, was it not?"

He grinned as he thought back, over a decade ago now. "Yes, they were cherry. — I say *they*, because you gobbled up four of them."

I gulped down my embarrassment, "*Four?* Was I really so greedy?"

"I never thought so for a moment," he answered with a kind expression.

"Why didn't you give away my hiding place all those years ago?"

"Oh, I suppose I thought it sweet that you seemed to want to spend more time with your father than with your own mother. You were rather too cute to tattle on as well."

"Ah, I see! I am not so cute now that you would indeed tattle on me if I do not *trade* for your good gesture?" My eyebrow raised as I studied his features. He was comely, in his own way.

"I think you know, *Miss Dawson*, that you are far more beautiful than you were cute in your childhood years. There is not an eligible man in all of England who would not readily lay his life down for you, myself at the top of that list."

"You flatter me, Lord Drake, quite more than I deserve, I am sure. And yet, I dare say you *would* tattle on me if I do not give in."

"Would it be so very terrible if you did? Are you as afraid of me now as you were as a little girl?"

"Before or after the tarts?"

Lord Drake laughed. "Must I buy you sweets when we arrive in town? Are they the only way to win your trust?"

I chuckled. "Well, it certainly helped then…" I called to my sister, "Anna, Lord Drake has offered to buy us sweets at the fair, what do you think of that?"

Anna's face brightened, "Strawberry tarts?"

I glanced upwards at the earl…

He sighed. "As if one could go to the market fair and not have a straw-berry tart!"

Anna skipped along ahead of us again with newfound energy to reach town.

"You are very kind," I said. "It is her favorite time of the year, save perhaps Christmas."

"I would do anything to please you and your sister."

I smiled graciously as we continued on.

The sun seemed to play with the clouds this afternoon. Rays beamed dramatically upon us as another cloud ran past.

Looking towards the road, to adjust my eyes, the reflection of the sun found me all the same. It played frantically upon the golden hilt of Lord Drake's blade.

Though it was tucked into a black leather sheath upon his belt, it was still easy to admire the hilt. It had intricate carvings and small red jewels pressed into the end of the hilt.

My brother always thought it was odd for an earl to have such a small weapon, (the blade being about two feet length), and yet the opulence of the craftsmanship boasted well enough of his wealth. I imagine that was rather the point.

Typically, market fairs are not held until the summer. However, Lord Drake had been fortunate enough to secure an earlier market fair the week after Easter, which would not detract from larger towns' festivities.

As we neared, the sound of music reached our ears. Fiddles, lutes, flutes, and shawms played lively tunes, beckoning us to the heart of town.

"We are nearly there!" Anna exclaimed with a large grin etched in every corner of her face.

A small sigh escaped me. "It's a shame our brothers did not wish to accompany us to the fair, it's only held but once a year! Mother I understand not coming, of course, as her knee quite bothers her."

Lord Drake smiled down at me. "I must confess, I'm rather relieved it is only us."

"–Oh?"

"It isn't that I do not enjoy their company, Miss Dawson... It's only that I am eager for the opportunity to enjoy yours more intimately."

My stomach summersaulted as I tried to think of a response that did not reveal the panic I felt. *Oh, dear Guardian Angel, help me, please!*

"—What a kind thing to say, my Lord."

He sighed with a hint of a smirk. "Elwood is not difficult to say, you know...some might even say that it rolls off the tongue a might easier than *Lord Drake*."

"Old habits are rather hard to break, are they not?"

He straightened his posture, "Apparently so."

The road changed from dirt to flattened rocks with tufts of grass trying to break free of them. We were nearly there now. Surely this would become an easier outing when surrounded by a crowd of people?

Following the road onto the main street, there were many colorful flags strewn across the houses and shops. Dozens of tables, carts, and small tents were set up, filled with food, goods, clothes, and other fineries. A group of men and women danced zestfully, with women holding colorful ribbons winding round from a pole.

From here you could see the bell tower from what was once a Catholic Church. Its gray stones arched higher than any other building in the town.

The musicians began a new song; the melody grew louder as we approached.

Anna spotted her friends playing with ribbons in another circle and begged me to allow her to join them. As much as I did not wish to lose my little chaperone, I could not bear to deny her that joy. In a moment, she was dancing within the ribbons and throwing the flowers she had gathered all around her and her friends. Hearing her squeals and giggles was worth the loss of her presence.

Walking through the bustling town, arm in arm with the earl, we received many glances of curiosity. This only doubled the apprehension I felt.

"You are so lovely and fair, Miss Dawson, that no one can help but admire you!"

"Really – I was sure it was because I was on the arm of *Lord Drake*."

"Perhaps it is both."

"Perhaps." I conceded.

We passed by several tables, "Do you see anything that pleases you?" He asked, "I will happily buy anything you desire."

"There *is* a woman who bakes the *most* delicious gyngerbrede every year. I am extremely fond of them; hers are very soft and the spices are balanced perfectly. Papa would always buy me three pieces whenever he would bring us here. And of course, the strawberry tarts for Anna and Jon. And of course, a cherry tart for himself." I realized I was talking far too much. "Forgive me; I'm prattling on like my little sister."

"Not at all, those sound like fond memories."

I nodded.

"Now, we shall have to find this famous baker! We musn't let such a wonderful tradition die. Is there nothing else you would like, though? A new coif or petticoat, perhaps? More ribbons to decorate your hair?"

"You are most generous, my Lord, although I think the cookies will please me well enough."

"I could be even more generous to you *and* your family if you would allow me."

My breath quickened at the tone of his statement. "I'm sure I don't know what you mean, my Lord. You have already demonstrated your generosity so much to my family and I. I could hardly ask for anything more."

"I don't think you are as naïve as you'd have me believe, Miss Dawson."

"No?"

Turning, he paused to read my countenance. "No, quite the opposite, in fact. I can see by the blush on your face that you have a very good idea of my intentions. You must sense them, do you not?"

I was suddenly trapped looking into his dark, pulling eyes without being able to form a reply. A peculiar fluttering sensation nestled in the pit of my belly.

The corner of his mouth curved. "Am I right?"

Chapter Two

I BLINKED AND LOOKED away for a moment as we continued on. "I cannot fathom why, my Lord, but yes. I sense your feelings."

"How can you be so modest? Are you not the fairest creature God has ever made?"

I chuckled. "I daresay, God has created many things far more beautiful than I."

"Are you saying that I am deceived? Is your auburn hair not smooth and lush? Is your complexion not that of the angels themselves? And your eyes, Miss Dawson...they are the most beautiful thing about you." He stopped and turned to look into them. "They are so piercingly blue, it's as though the heavens rest in them."

"I fear, Lord Drake, that you insult the angels and indeed the heavens by comparing me so."

He smiled broadly as we began walking again. "Regardless of whom I may have insulted, your blush tells me it was worth it."

I turned my glance back to the street, unsure of how to respond.

Lord Drake brushed his hand against my fingers. "I do enjoy seeing you blush, you know? Do not be embarrassed – it should not offend me if it never left your cheeks."

Just then, Anna came running up to us. "Isabel! You've walked past our favorite baker, come quickly with Lord Drake – there is no line at the moment!"

"Oh...so we did. I must not have been paying attention."

Lord Drake fought against a grin. "I am eager to try these famed baked goods. Lead the way, little Miss Dawson."

Elated with being charged with the task of leading, Anna promptly directed us to the table filled with various sweets and breads of all kinds. The baker's table always smelled delicious.

Lord Drake proceeded to buy a dozen pieces of gyngerbrede, six strawberry tarts, and a few small spiced cakes for himself. Gyngerbrede is a rather expensive treat, due to the saffron. I could hardly believe the price, which he paid without any hesitation.

Anna's eyes lit up with delight as she took Lord Drake's free hand to continue to lead him on. "Come this way!"

Surprised, Lord Drake looked confused; I attempted to explain as we walked together. "Our father would take us to sit on the stone wall up the road there to eat our sweets. Please forgive her overeagerness. It's been difficult since Papa passed away."

He nodded. "I understand – it's no trouble at all."

Once we reached the stone wall up the hill, she released the earl's hand and found the preferred spot on the highest part of the curved wall. Anna sat down and patted the spots next to her for us to join her as she dangled her feet against the stones. She was such a dainty little thing.

I sat in the middle, between her and Lord Drake. "*Now* we may enjoy the sweets." Anna proclaimed.

The view from here was peaceful and quaint; you could see the rooftops of many homes forming patterns of various heights. Behind them lay a rolling forestry and to the left, large farms brimmed with fresh sprouts and birds taking advantage of the farmer's absences.

Anna was particularly impressed as the earl opened the parcel of goodies. "Isabel! It's as if it were Christmas! – Thank you, Lord Drake, this is *most* kind of you. There are so very many!"

She took a bite of a strawberry tart and her eyelids closed tightly as she savored the taste.

The earl shared in her smile. "You are quite welcome. It makes me very happy to see the Miss Dawsons being treated like the angels they are."

He leaned in to whisper to me with a smug smile, "Even angels with ink on their teeth!"

I could not help but roll my eyes as I reached for a piece of gyngerbrede. "Indeed."

A childlike joy crept over me as I admired the familiar brown square. In its tender center was pressed a clove for garnish – picking it out, I sniffed its woody, spiced scent before concealing it in my pocket. I inhaled the cookie's sweet aroma of cinnamon and ginger. My mouth watered as I took a bite; the sweet honey balanced so deliciously well with the spices. *Perfection.* At that moment, I conceded the awkward walk to the fair was suddenly worthwhile.

When I tore my gaze away from my little treasure, I noticed that the earl had been watching me with an almost amused expression. I felt a bit embarrassed as I had been lost in the moment without realizing I was being watched so intently.

My sister, quite forgetting herself, spoke hastily, "Lord Drake, how is it that you are unmarried? I think most girls would love to be married to someone who spoils them with sweets!"

My eyes widened. *Traitor.*

I finished swallowing my bite. "Anna! That is an impertinent thing to ask."

Far from being insulted, the earl nearly choked on the cake he had taken a bite of. Chuckling, he said, "It's quite all right little Miss Dawson! I've wondered the same." He glanced towards me. "I admit, most of that is my fault."

"Your fault, Lord Drake, why?" Anna asked, taking another bite.

"Well, you are too young to remember, but many years ago, before you were even born, I *was* married!"

Anna was intrigued. "You were? What happened?"

He continued in a drier tone, "She and my son passed away in childbirth. I was quite heartbroken."

Anna was quick to offer her sympathies, "Lord Drake! That's so sad. I'm very sorry."

The earl nodded kindly, "Thank you, Anna. Your father took the greatest compassion upon me and would often invite me to your house to try and cheer me up. Your sister must have been about seven years old when my wife died."

Immediately, my thoughts were transferred back to their funeral. Even as a small child, I remember thinking how utterly hollow and forlorn Lord Drake appeared. "I remember it; I'm so terribly sorry again."

Lord Drake offered me a kind smile before responding to my sister, "So you see Anna, when you lose a great love, it is very hard to find another that comes close to equaling it. That's why I'm afraid I don't usually spoil anyone with cookies or tarts."

Anna pondered thoughtfully for a moment, "Well...we are very honored that you chose to spoil us, aren't we, Isabel?"

I had completely lost all support from my little sister. There was no doubt she was teaming up with mother and Lord Drake now. Perhaps suggesting sweets was a poor idea on my part.

"Indeed," I said, noticing the rather large smile which Lord Drake tried and failed to contain.

Just then, a few of Anna's friends appeared and begged her to come play with them. She glanced up at me, asking for permission with a hopeful glimmer.

Inwardly, I groaned, yet I could not find sufficient reason to tell her no. "Go on then! I promise I won't let the Earl eat all your tarts."

She giggled and went off with her companions.

"Well," I said, grabbing a second gyngerbrede square, "it seems you have completely swayed my sister to your side. I am becoming quite outnumbered."

"But have I swayed her older sister? Does that remain to be seen?"

He leaned a bit closer to me with one arm resting on the stone wall. My heartbeat quickened at the close proximity; I was unprepared for how pleasing his manner was becoming.

"You are not without your charms, my Lord."

Perhaps my previous ideas were wrong? Had I been too harsh? Had my father been overprotective? The Earl was generous, flattering, and kind... Or was I letting all of his compliments spin my head about?

"Is it the gyngerbread? Perhaps you should try a bite of my cake instead?" He placed one before my face, encouraging me to eat from his hand.

Cocking my eyebrow at him, I took the cake in my own hand and had a small bite. "This is quite lovely as well, but I daresay the gyngerbrede is unparalleled." I handed the cake back to him. "You ought to try one!" I took another bite of my sweet.

"I have had them before in court, actually. They're some of Queen Elizabeth's favorites too. The ones she serves are crisp and shaped into various shapes, depending on the occasion."

"...Is that so?" Suddenly I liked them a little less. She was not exactly someone I wanted to have much, if anything, in common with. Yet, who could blame her in her choice of sweets?

He placed his hand over my left. "You really are so very beautiful, Miss Dawson. Will you not let me call you by your own name? It would give me the greatest of delights."

My blush returned with a new wave of unease as I swallowed my bite, "My Lord, I–"

The Earl interrupted, "I never thought I'd have to try *so* hard to gain this permission! – I know your name well enough! What makes you so unsure of me? You have known me for *years* – I dine with your family every month or more – I've come to every birthday and important event in your life. Your siblings too, of course. Do you not know me by now?"

I set the half-eaten sweet down on my lap as the clouds covered the heat of the sun. A memory of my father flashed before me. It was my the birthday I turned six and ten. Father was advising me of suitable romantic pursuits – those who aligned with our secret beliefs.

"My dear, I am not forbidding you to marry a Protestant. Your mama and I have been quite happy after all; however, I would spare you the hardships that come from marrying outside of the faith, especially in these dangerous times. I know Lord Drake has his eye on you, but it would please me if you would find a Catholic. Though I know it would make your mother happy as she very much approves of him. Be careful, my dear one. He is not the man I would choose for you; he could be a danger to your soul, and it would sadden me to see you with him."

"Miss Dawson? Are you quite well?"

"Oh, my apologies. It's terribly rude of me when my mind wanders on its own like that."

"Easily forgiven if you would but answer my question?"

"Why should you prefer my company? You are often invited to royal gatherings with the Queen. Surely there are more suitable ladies there for you to choose from – many of whom must be more fair than myself with all their fashions and allurements?"

The clouds moved off from the sun and let the rays shine down brightly upon us. I squinted for a moment to adjust.

He shifted himself towards me and held both my hands; my chest tightened.

"My dear Miss Dawson, I did not mean to cause you distress, and I can see that I have by how very quickly you were speaking. Please, I wish only to know you better, to call you by your name and you mine."

He sighed and caught my eyes with his saying, "I do confess that I have been irreversibly smitten with you for some time now; there is no other woman who compares to you in my mind, not even the Queen herself. No one is more fair in heart, mind, or body than you."

At this moment, flattery and a deep-seated hesitation fought for ground in my rapidly beating heart. I looked away for a moment as he continued,

"I do not wish to put undue stress or pressure upon you. Alas, I have tried to be patient – especially with the death of your father last year – yet I have felt your unease with me grow over recent years, as though my affection for you is what has been scaring you, pushing you further from me, so I have tried to refrain...but can contain it no longer."

Did he intend to be so confusing? He claims he does not wish to pressure me and yet I am drowning in it! I swallowed hard, afraid that he may propose the very next moment.

I retracted my hands from his. "It has never been my intention to offend you, in any way. I have not encouraged any romantic suitor since Papa's death."

"Rest assured, my dear, I am not offended, merely perplexed. ...Have you no interest in marriage?"

"I...yes, of course I do."

"And what is your opinion of me?"

All at once, I felt dreadfully dizzy. It became difficult to breathe; my chest hurt and I felt unseasonably warm. The very fabrics of my dress seemed to smother me.

"Isabel, are you well? You've gone quite pale!"

His words sounded muffled. My head swirled along with my belly. I didn't even correct him for using my name. "Excuse me, please, I need to get out of the sun."

Without waiting for a response, I rose, letting the gyngerbrede fall to the ground from my lap, and staggered back down the hill.

Shortly I found an obliging spot of shade beneath a shop's overhanging roof. The thatching jutted out just enough to provide a welcome cover.

I glanced around to see if anyone noticed me; however, I seemed to be lost amongst all the noise and distraction. I was *very* grateful for that.

Anna, with her sisterly intuition, saw me from a distance and hurried to my side.

I leaned against the cool stone as Lord Drake came rushing up behind me. My ears rang so loud, it drowned out the music in the streets; everything dulled and yet felt overwhelming at the same time.

Anna arrived only seconds before Lord Drake. "Isabel? Is it another spell? Are you alright?" she asked as she removed my gloves to help cool me down.

I nodded. My arms were shaking, and in a moment, the Earl wrapped his arm around my waist to keep me from falling.

He addressed Anna as I tried to steady my breathing, "Does this happen often? How can we help her?"

"She's had these breathing spells for as long as I can remember. Papa was best at relieving them. Sometimes water and lying down helps her or fresh air, but we are already outside!"

"Watch over your sister. I will be back with a carriage to take you both home."

"No – I'll be well soon." I insisted, "Only give me a moment. I do not require a fuss!"

Lord Drake and Anna exchanged looks, as though doubting my resolve.

"It will pass. The shade will help." I assured them both.

The Earl continued to hold me, now with both arms. "I will support you until you can manage yourself."

I shakily nodded in response as I silently prayed Ave Marias repeatedly as Papa always had me do until I steadied.

With his hand, the Earl eased my head to rest on his shoulder, which did not help me relax, quite the opposite in fact.

Lifting my head back up under the pretext of taking deep breaths, I was able to prove to them that I was indeed quite fine. I could breathe normally again, my hearing improved, and I could now stand well enough on my own. It had passed.

"I'm very sorry. I haven't had a spell in a few months now. I apologize for interrupting our outing."

"I assure you, you have nothing to apologize for! I'm only glad that you're feeling better. Though you do look rather tired, if you'll forgive my saying so. I'd feel better if you let me find us a carriage back to take you home?"

While I did feel better, I also felt drained and thought I could avoid any further romantic advances if I accepted the offer. "Thank you... I think I *would* appreciate that actually."

It wasn't long after Lord Drake left my sister and I, before an open carriage had been acquired and we were climbing aboard.

Anna sat up next to the driver as the Earl and I sat inside the carriage. The driver was a kind older man who allowed Anna to take turns holding the reins of the gray and white horse; this quite delighted her.

Feeling the breeze helped me feel much improved. However, I could sense Lord Drake's worried stare still burrowing into me.

I confess that his deep concern for me softened my opinion of him. When he tried for the second time to hold my hand, I decided to allow it.

"I assure you, I am well. You do not need to be worried on my account. It only happens sometimes."

"Forgive me, but I'll be as worried about you as I please! I feel terrible for causing you distress. Your mother would never forgive me if I did not bring you back in as good a condition as you were when we left!"

"It is not serious. Be at ease, Elwood." His name slipped from my lips without my meaning it to – I thought only of trying to ease his concern.

A smile spread across his face as he squeezed my hand, "You said my name!"

It was too late to take it back.

"Yes, well, you did say mine first. Do not let it go to your head...it is only a name."

"Of course." He beamed. I do not know that I have ever seen him look so happy before.

"Thank you...for taking care of me and for the cookies."

"I should like to take care of you and spoil you with things all my life, Isabel. Understand, there is no need to thank me; it was my deepest pleasure."

"Still, you have my gratitude."

"Dare I risk another fainting spell by repeating my question from earlier?"

"What question was that?"

"What is your opinion of me, Isabel?"

"Oh, yes." *Oh no.*

"What sort of man do you find me to be after all these years?"

"—I think you are a man who possesses many admirable qualities."

The corners of his lips rose, "I suppose harsher things have been said about me."

Raising my hand to his lips, he gently kissed it and lingered a moment before turning my hand over and kissing my wrist as well.

I was accustomed to gentlemen giving a quick kiss to my hand; however, this was different. His forwardness caught me quite off guard. I had never received affection from a man like this before; it sent a most peculiar sensation throughout me, making my heartbeat hasten as warmth rushed to my face.

Elwood smiled satisfactorily. "Ah, well that at least brought some color back to your cheeks. There, your mother need not even know you were unwell now."

I slipped my hand back to my lap. "Indeed." Perhaps letting him hold my hand had been a hasty notion.

Seeing the chimney tops of my home, I felt relieved. The white double story house with dark wood panels and roof always made me think of my father. He was so proud of our home: the home he oversaw and helped design himself.

When we arrived on the circular drive, Mama came to greet us with our servant George. Anna was all too quick in telling her all that had transpired. *Sisters.*

"Please, do stay for supper, my Lord! Allow us to repay your kindness." She insisted as Lord Drake's men readied his black carriage.

"Oh, thank you, Mistress Catherine, but I do think it's best for Miss Dawson to rest. Another time? I'm afraid I also have a rather early matter of business in the morning."

Mama clasped her hands together. "Yes, quite right you are! Why don't you come back in a fortnight? I shall have the cook prepare a lovely dinner in your honor!"

"I wouldn't miss it for the world!" He smiled graciously.

The Earl sauntered over to me, standing by the small garden in the center of the drive, with his hands behind his back. When I met his gaze, he handed me the parcel of baked goods that he had been concealing. "I saved these for you, in case you start forgetting that I'm not so scary after all."

Chapter Three

Later that evening...

"Isabel, are you daft?"

My brother – Jonathon – has such a way with words. Truly, it's astonishing he is still unattached.

I ran my fingers across Papa's desk in his study. "Jon, I didn't accept a marriage proposal! Don't be so dramatic, really."

I swear I could still hear my father's chuckle echoing from his leather chair. The memory was equally painful as it was inviting. I glanced around the room to distract my thoughts.

There were two bookshelves in opposite corners, mostly filled with his favorite books which he had considered invaluable treasures. Ivory drapes covered two windows behind his desk; the walls were otherwise empty, save a small tapestry of deer in a wooded clearing. The fire from the right of the room crackled greedily as my brother sighed.

Jon sat down on the sette that was next to the same end table and cloth I had hid beneath when Lord Drake discovered me as a child. He motioned for me to join him. "Isabel, you were right to trust your initial instincts *and* father's advice about him. While I truly do believe he treated you and Anna very well – that is not how he is known to the rest of England. He's an evil man."

I felt annoyed. "You do realize that I am nine and ten years of age, and it would behoove us all if you would treat me as an adult? Would this not have been helpful information to know ahead of time? I thought Papa didn't like him as a match for me solely because of...you know."

He rolled his blue eyes up to the ceiling, casting a few waves of brown hair to fall out of place. "As if that would not be enough." He leveled his head back. "Let us take this conversation elsewhere."

I grinned. I adored the secret entrance in Papa's study!

Walking over to the corner bookshelf past the fireplace, Jonathon pushed in a collection of poetry with a red binder and then turned a head bust of an angel counter clockwise. This combination set the gears within the wall to begin moving and the narrow bookshelf detached from its locked position with a subtle *clunk*.

As Jonathon carefully pushed the shelf-door open, I lit a candle from the tinderbox and handed it to him as we stepped inside.

The walls were lined with stone and the stairs were solid wood, yet narrow. Walking down to the left, we stepped onto a curved, short set of stairs and walked sideways for another ten steps. Then came a much longer stretch of stairs that continued to lead us on our descent.

The further down we walked, the colder and quieter it became. The poofs of dust escaping from the creaking of the house were traded for the smell of soil permeating between the stones. Finally, we came to a small wooden floor with one door and a latch lock. It was a wide enough space for a few people to stand comfortably next to one another.

After King Henry the VIII broke from the Church, Papa and others, were convinced that even darker times were coming. With the help of some trusted friends, he created this hiding place for priests and us, should we ever need it. Carpenters Walter Owen and his young son, Nicholas who acted as a friend and servant to renowned Father Campion, helped Papa build this priestly hideout over twenty years ago. The men, especially Papa, were very proud of their work. I believe he viewed it as his own Noah's Ark.

Some had accused him of overreacting at the time, but he paid them no heed. He knew to follow what God had placed in his heart. Praise God he did, for now, our house had become an integral part of the underground network of Catholic priests.

All three men were utterly convinced that the priest hunters would never discover such a well-hidden place. I only pray that it continues to hold true for us.

I took the candle from Jon as he opened the door with both hands.

Before us was an entry about double the width and length from where we came, with three doors. The one to the left opened to a tunnel that would take one out to the far back gardens. Unfortunately, it had collapsed in one spot, and we were unable to use it for now.

The one in front of us led to a humble chapel, and the one to the right was a small bedchamber with two cots, two chairs, a side table, and a desk. We headed into the bedchamber area.

Taking a seat on opposite little beds, we knew we could finally speak freely here. We were now safely underground.

The bedroom was very dark and cold; Jonathon lit a lantern and placed it on the table nearest the bed I sat on.

"There are things I must tell you," Jonathon started. "Lord Drake is one of the most anti-Catholic Magistrates that we know of. We do not need to give him any excuse to search our premises simply because he's hurt or mad. He has surely had other homes torn apart for less gracious transactions than that of the heart.

"The Queen and her snake of an advisor, Cecil, use him and his unique set of skills to hunt more Catholics than most. Especially priests. It's as if he is part bloodhound. He is very successful which earns him a close friendship with Queen Elizabeth. The guards, officers, and spies all bend to his will, whether it's strictly legal or not.

"I swear I would have told you more, but I thought you disliked him, so I didn't think it important to! I did not wish to add to your fears and increase your spells."

I felt a rock drop within me. "You are thicker than porridge sometimes, Jon. I can tell you're still holding back information."

He sighed. "Lord Drake is one of the wealthiest men in England, fiercely loyal to the Queen and pays handsome donations to the navy and military. He has his filthy hands in everything: trades, properties, businesses, imports, loans out his personal money to dozens of poor fools. Suffice to say, dear sister, he can do what he likes in the surrounding areas without repercussions. He is two-faced and can be unmerciful and cruel in his dealings with men. Although he has clearly been nothing but *charm itself* with my sister. Now. What occurred earlier? What did he say?"

I swallowed, trying to absorb so much weighty information at once. Had it not been so cold, I'm sure I'd have begun to perspire. My left hand gripped the rosary in my pocket; just the touch of the round beads brought me comfort – as though I were holding the Blessed Mother's own hand. Why is it that the men in my family feel the need to protect women from rather important details? All I knew previously was that he was a wealthy Protestant Lord and Magistrate who followed the queen's orders. Despite this, I held very little back as I relayed to him the particulars.

Jon's face crinkled dramatically. "*Augh*. Who kisses a lady's wrist? Is that not very strange and improper?"

"*Jon!*"

"I apologize. No doubt he will ask me for your hand when he comes back in a fortnight. He's arrogant enough to think I'll give it to him at once, too.

"–The problem is...if I deny Lord Drake your hand in marriage, he will see me as an enemy. I am less concerned if my business were to suffer losses, though I would prefer to avoid that. However, I fear that angering him may put our priests that we hide in danger, or put us under the watch of his spies and prevent us from harboring any others. He's very likely to tear the house apart, simply because he could."

"Do you have a plan?"

"Perhaps you could come down with a dreadful headache after supper and need to retire to your room?"

"You wish for me to lie? Really? When confession is already so scarce? And won't that only delay the inevitable?"

He leaned his back against the pillows, arranging them to be more comfortable. "Only a venial...but fine, you are right."

Jon pondered the situation deeply. He was a good older brother; he had taken on the role of protecting our family very seriously since Papa's death.

Jon and I had always been quite inseparable, even with nearly seven years between us. I have always looked up to him, and he has always held my best interests at heart.

At last, an idea was hatched. "I want you to tell him that Father was not for the marriage."

"Wouldn't that only anger him? What would my reasonings even be? I can't exactly say it's because we are Catholic!"

"Father and I discussed this as well. You see, Lord Drake tried asking him for your hand on your birthday before he died. Father turned him down, claiming you were far too innocent for a man as worldly as Lord Drake. Or excuse me, *Elwood* as you call him."

"Must you tease me?"

"Aren't we related?"

I rolled my eyes. "You never thought to mention this before? How many times did Mother drop you as a baby?"

"Too many, to be sure. That solves it, though? Does it not? Tell him, in so many words, that you feel obligated to respect Father's wishes and that you wish him the best and all of that sort of farewell nonsense."

I pursed my lips together a moment, envisioning how uncomfortable a conversation that would be. "Very well. Is there anything else you've been keeping from me that I ought to know?"

"Oh! Yes...in fact I shall need your help. Father Ingles is making his way through our area again."

Out of all the wonderful and brave priests we had ever harbored, Father Ingles had been my personal favorite. Jon could not have relayed better news!

"Oh, finally! We've not seen him for almost a year, and it's been over two months since we've had Mass! I've been feeling quite melancholy without it. When is he coming?"

"A fortnight from now."

My mouth dropped. "When the most anti-Catholic man alive shall be joining us for supper?"

"Good timing, is it not?"

"No, Jon! That's horrible timing! What if he comes during supper instead of late at night like he does sometimes? Isn't the garden tunnel still collapsed? He'll have to go through the house! This will be most difficult to hide from Mother this time, not to mention the Earl!"

"No argument from me on this, sister. However, I only received word about this today. Unfortunately, I do not have the time to repair the tunnel in time thanks to a rather binding business trip. Do not look so worried! This is where you will come in; you are the best distraction we could ever hope for."

The evening that the Earl and Father Ingles were due to arrive, mother had me wear a particularly beautiful gown. It was deep blue with intricate details sewn thoughtfully in. They created a swirled pattern that I very much liked. The sleeves opened wide, halfway to my wrist, making me feel more elegant than I was.

My hair in turn was twisted and braided up with curls falling partially down the back of my neck. A squared neckline was promptly covered with a string of pearls that had belonged to my grandmother; they felt cold against my skin.

I looked towards the enormous bundle of flowers that the Earl had sent yesterday along with a pair of lace gloves. I felt a tinge of guilt over what I knew I must do. It was hard to reconcile that the flattering and generous man at the fair was such a callous and evil man at heart. Part of me wondered if my brother was mistaken. It simply did not tally up.

Little Anna picked out a white dress for herself that made her look like an innocent fluffy cake. She twirled blissfully about the room as though she were at a grand ball. She adored whenever the Earl came to visit, as it was an excuse to dress up.

Hearing her delicate yet confident steps, I turned to see Mama wearing a dress of yellow and green coming through the door.

She shooed Anna and the servants out to have a private word with me. I felt the weight of her serious and eager gaze as she sat across from me on my bed. I swiveled in the chair before my mirror to better see her, knowing full well what was on her mind.

"My dear...I do believe that our friend, the Earl, will propose to you this night. You are prettier than a painting!"

I often wish mother knew her children were Catholic *and* hid priests. It would make everything so much simpler. However, for some unknown male reasoning, my father thought it best not to worry her with any of it. Perhaps he did not wish to be scolded, or merely wanted to keep the peace, but it was important to him. When he passed, it became equally important to my brother. I respect their wishes, but I have never approved of the deception.

It hurt me that my poor mama could not understand why I would reject him, if in fact he did ask for my hand. I thought of explaining that I was not in love with him, yet that did not always seem to matter.

"Mother, why did Papa not wish for me to marry the Earl?"

Her sparkling blue eyes fell to the floor as she smoothed out her dress. "Fathers sometimes cannot see their grown-up daughters as women, and instead always see the little girls they once were, giggling on their bouncing knees. I rather think this was the case for your dear papa.

"Lord Drake, as you know, has been nothing but kindness itself to our family...in particular towards you, my dear."

"Do I not have time to decide? There *are* many eligible men in England, after all."

Mama gave a small chuckle. "Time? You'll be twenty next year. Most of your friends are at least being courted, or are betrothed, if not married by now. You don't wish to become like Miss Smith, do you? Nearing thirty without a suitor in sight! Poor picky thing. Even your friend, Christine, was sent to Bath in search of a husband."

She sighed with a small smile. "Why let a good catch slip through your fingers while you wait? Who else could secure you a life of comfort better than he? *Really, Isabel!* You perplex me greatly. You would be *Countess*

Drake of Aylesbury! You could be the one to bring the Dawson family line into a higher class, my dear! We mostly have the money, simply not the title or blood. –Think of how many doors that would open for your brother, and especially your sister?"

I swallowed hard and turned to the jewelry chest to slip on the matching pearl earrings. If I did not feel pressure to become the Earl's wife before, I certainly felt the burden of it now. Was she correct?

Mama came up behind me and kissed my cheek. "Pray about it dear; remember the scriptures tell you to honor your parents – regardless of age."

I slipped on the gifted gloves that stopped just above my wrist. "Yes, Mama."

"Good girl! Come down soon, so as not to keep him waiting *again*." Mother sauntered back out to the hall. I could hear her conversing with the servants, "Now, be sure to serve the best of everything – I daresay we will have cause for celebration tonight!"

Looking around to ensure I was truly alone, I crossed myself slowly and begged Our Lady for strength to do the right thing and to please comfort my mother's disappointment. Then I prayed to St. Michael to help me distract Lord Drake long enough for Father Ingles to be safely hid away, should he arrive early again.

A deep breath later and I was walking downstairs to the grand entrance of our house. – Coincidentally, just in time for the Earl to be coming through the front door to see me descend the last few steps.

"Miss Dawson...I am speechless!" He gave a small bow. "You are a vision!"

I smiled graciously as he took my laced hand in his and wrapped it through the offered arm. "And might I add, flattered that you did not forget me tonight." He winked.

"I daresay the flowers and gloves you sent were helpful reminders."

"They look lovely on you."

"Thank you; I was rather surprised to receive them."

"Why should you be? A beautiful girl deserves to be spoiled. One day, I hope to give you many other gifts."

"I cannot imagine needing much else."

He smiled as we neared the drawing room. "Your humility confuses me, Isabel. Most women are apt to receive gifts and are even delighted about it."

"Forgive me. I did not mean to imply ingratitude, my Lord. Your gifts *did* delight me."

"*Elwood*." He whispered.

I was grateful we had reached the doors and was spared from responding. The servants exchanged knowing smiles between one another as they opened them before us.

Mother and Anna received his Lordship with enthusiasm, while my brother did not mind being the last to greet him. I could tell by Jon's stiffness that my arm being entwined with Lord Drake's made him uncomfortable, though he did well to hide his disgust from the others.

Lord Drake guided me to the empty settee, and sat beside me.

"Well!" My brother started. "How have you been faring these last weeks?"

Elwood crossed his leg over the other, relaxing into his seat. "My life goes well and I am in perfect company this evening! Has your hunting been successful? You seem to be doing more of that these days."

"Yes, I must say I find it a rather addictive pastime. In fact, we shall be enjoying a venison roast that I shot earlier this morning. You really should come out with your brother and I sometime; he's getting to be quite the shot now."

Knowing how my brother truly felt about him, I was impressed at how well he managed the pleasantries.

My mother began, "Lord Drake, was your journey a tiresome one? It's so good of you to travel to visit us for supper."

"Ah, Mistress Catherine, I assure you that a couple of hours of a carriage ride is nothing to be in such familiar and wonderful company! Truth be told, I would travel ten times that distance to behold the enchanting Miss Dawson!"

Mother giggled approvingly as the Earl gazed towards me fondly. My brother's lips pursed together as I managed the awkward situation as best I could.

"You're so very flattering, my Lord."

The Earl shifted his leg slightly which made the hilt of his sword reflect a bit of candlelight. Anna's eyes were drawn to the gold. "Your knife is *so* shiny, Lord Drake," she complimented.

The Earl smiled at her as he tapped his hand to it. "Thank you, little Miss Dawson. It was a gift from Queen Elizabeth herself! See, most Earls carry longer swords to boast their title, really. However, she felt that a hunter's blade was more appropriate for me, so she had the blade smith fashion a longer, more elegant version."

Anna tilted her head inquisitively. "Do you like hunting very much?"

The Earl cleared his throat with a smirk. "Not like your brother, no. The Queen has charged me with a...*different* sort of hunting, dear one. I hunt the vermin that would harm our great country and threaten her Majesty."

Jonathon and I exchanged glances as Anna slowly grasped his meaning. "Oh! ...You hunt *people* with that, Lord Drake?"

The Earl gave a low chuckle. "Only those who resist arrest ever meet my blade, little Miss Dawson. Papists are cowards and try to run and hide from their crimes. You needn't worry your pretty little self over that now – just know that this blade helps to keep me safe against lesser men."

Anna swallowed hard, understanding now that Lord Drake of Strawberry Tarts used that on Catholics – just like her. She nodded quietly.

Mother looked a bit uncomfortable and unsure of what to say. "–Do be safe, my Lord, we should miss your company if anything terrible were to befall you."

Lord Drake assured her he could handle himself as Anna still possessed the same unsettled expression. My brother and I echoed that feeling most keenly. *This* was who the Earl was.

I tried to change the subject for Anna's sake. "Are you staying home for long? Or does her Majesty have you traveling again shortly, my Lord?"

He smiled at my interest. "Hard to say. I should be here for at least a week so that I may handle my other business affairs, besides Queen Elizabeth's."

Just then a servant announced supper was ready, and we gathered around the dining table.

It was of no surprise to me that my seat had been arranged next to Lord Drake instead of my sister.

During the main course, amidst small talk, Elwood leaned closer towards me and whispered in my ear, "Isabel, I should very much like some time alone with you this evening...might that be possible?"

Glancing around the table, I witnessed my mother's prying eyes watching us intently. My brother, who also glanced at us, aggressively stabbed his venison while Anna was blissfully unaware of everything, eating happily.

I whispered quietly back, "I believe so...perhaps I could show you the library?"

The library was recommended by my brother – secluded and safe for Father Ingles to make it to the study.

His Lordship nodded his approval of this idea. "Yes, I should like that. I have brought you a gift that I believe you will like more than the others so far."

"I daresay, my Lord, what are you whispering so discreetly to my sister about?" Asked Jon.

Lord Drake sat up. "Oh, merely small talk, I assure you. – I must say, this is some of the best venison I have ever eaten! How large of a beast was it?"

My brother raised his brow. "He was a magnificent creature with some of the finest antlers I've seen. – He didn't suspect a thing until it was too late!"

"The mark of a true hunter, to be sure."

After supper was finished, I saw Lord Drake ask to have a private drink with my brother in Papa's study.

Without hesitation, Jonathon led the way and opened the door for our anti-Catholic guest. He exchanged a knowing look with Mama and raised his eyebrow at me before closing the door behind him.

She clasped her hands together excitedly as we walked towards the drawing room. "Oh! *Isabel*, I daresay the Earl is asking for your hand this very minute."

"Pray, excuse me."

"You wouldn't be leaving to eavesdrop, would you?"

"I might be."

"Good girl, come back quickly and tell me if my assumption is correct! I will have have some cider in the drawing room with your sister. Do *not* be caught."

"Yes, Mama."

In a moment I was outside with my ear pressed to the door. They seemed to be discussing it already....

Chapter Four

"WELL?" THE VOICE OF the Earl questioned deeply, "Do you approve or not, Jonathon?"

"My sister and I are very close, my Lord. She is more complicated than other girls her age."

"Yes... so I've noticed."

My brother chuckled. "No doubt. She has confided in me that she feels torn about you."

"Oh? – Did she say why?"

"I will not stand in the way of you marrying my sister; I think if nothing else, she would have a very comfortable life and want for nothing."

"However?"

"I do not agree with the old ways of forcing or coercing a marriage to take place; it is my sister's decision."

"A wise, albeit unorthodox approach. What is it exactly that's holding her back?"

"If my sister feels comfortable, she will confide this in you too. Come, let us rejoin the ladies now."

Dashing down the hall, and cutting through the dining room, I made it with plenty of time to sit and look innocent in the drawing room.

Mother was most impatient. "Well?"

"You were correct, Mama."

She squeezed my little sister's hand, and they both grinned the same elated expression.

The doors opened and their expressions magically transformed to that of a calm sea. Anna really was a near perfect replica of Mama.

"What were you gentlemen talking about?" Mother asked with a glint in her eye.

"What were you ladies discussing?" My brother counter-questioned.

"Oh...just feminine matters."

"Indeed? How amusing – we were speaking of *gentlemanly* matters."

Mama scoffed quietly as she sipped the cider.

Lord Drake sat besides me. "Might you give me that tour of the library now?"

My heart raced. I did not want to go through with any of this – I only felt an overwhelming need to run outside and not stop until I reached the stables. Then perhaps take my horse and ride until she could run no further.

"Miss Dawson? Have I lost you again? Please come back to me."

"Oh! — Library?" I glanced towards my brother, and he nodded that now was the correct time. He must have seen Father Ingles' sign from out the window.

"Yes, forgive me — now?"

Lord Drake smirked at my flustered responses. "If that is amenable to you, my dear?"

I could only nod in response.

We stood from the sette. "Mistress Catherine, would you mind terribly if I borrowed your daughter? She has kindly offered me a tour of the library."

Mother grinned as large as any I'd ever seen her give. "Of course! I'm afraid it is rather small, but books are what Harold spent most of his money on. We have several beautiful books from the old monks that I'm sure would be of interest to you, my Lord."

"Indeed! We shan't be too long."

"Take your time!" Mother replied melodically as we left the room.

My brother gave me a serious nod as we left, arm in arm. I knew what it meant: "*Hold your ground, Isabel!*"

Opening the door to the library, we were greeted with the familiar smell of books and a warm fireplace as we stepped in. A fire was always lit in this room as it often held a chill.

It was a modest-sized room with minimal furnishings; a cushioned settee and a chair nearer the small fireplace. There was one large bookshelf along the left wall; it was nearly filled with books. The small pieces of artwork seemed to make up for the lack of purpose on the rest of the walls.

As I closed the door, I turned around to see his Lordship directly behind me.

I gasped as he drew me in by my waist and kissed my forehead tenderly. "At last, we are alone. Ah, I have missed you these last many days. Come, sit with me; we have much to discuss."

Quite caught off guard, I followed him to the settee near the bookshelf and sat beside him.

He took my hands in his. "Isabel, by now, you must know that I love you."

I could not meet his gaze; I looked down at our entwined fingers instead. "...Yes."

"I have waited to speak to you alone for some time now."

"Oh?" I could feel my nervous heart beating up into my throat.

"Isabel, will you not look at me with those heavenly eyes of yours? I have missed their piercing gaze. Please?"

Obliging, I immediately regretted it. There was something entrancing about looking into his dark-as-night eyes. Why was I having these feelings? They were *most* unwanted!

"There…" he said, placing a finger under my chin. "That wasn't so hard now, was it?"

I was speechless.

In the next moment his lips were pressed upon mine. His fingers moved from my chin, down the side of my neck, and behind my head.

At first I tried to resist him by pushing against his chest; however my resolve weakened. I felt helpless, delightfully lost in the moment and the feelings his kiss brought.

"He would throw you in jail if he knew what you were!" A voice yelled in my head. *"He has helped to murder and imprison dozens of Catholics! What are you doing? Stop this!"*

Finally regaining my resolve, I pulled away and stood from our seat, breathing heavily, "*My Lord,* please!"

In a moment he was standing next to me with his arms wrapped around me. "Elwood… remember? Call me Elwood." He played with a curl of my hair.

Our bodies could scarcely be closer. I tried to look away from him. "…Elwood…this is *most* improper! I beg of you to keep a proper distance."

"I promise you it is not improper, not when you hear my question."

Hesitantly, I faced him.

He gently caressed the side of my face as he stared deeply into my eyes. "Isabel, will you marry me? Allow me to be your husband; I wish to love you and to be yours for the rest of my life."

Pulling away slightly, he removed a blue sapphire ring from his breast pocket. It was gold with three rows of gems. I had never seen a ring so extraordinary. The dark stones mirrored the mysterious allure of his own eyes; I struggled to turn my gaze from it.

"Accept this as an engagement gift; I have carried it with me for months now. The moment I laid eyes upon it, I knew it would be perfect for you." He sighed contentedly as I met his gaze. "Say you will be my wife, Isabel?"

My eyes fell back to the stunning ring before returning to him; my mouth hung open in a stupor. – I could scarcely remember what I had planned to say. I had not anticipated the swirl of emotions that his kiss had thrust upon me. I felt more confused than ever. His words felt so genuine, his touch was stirring. *How* could this be the same man my brother described to me and who had spoken so ill of Catholics, not two hours ago?

"Why do you not answer me? Why are you so quiet?" He pressed at last.

I pulled away. "Please forgive me, I am…conflicted. I need a moment."

I held my hand out to keep him at bay and moved swiftly towards the window and leaned my back against the wall, staring at the man before me. I steadied my breath as my thoughts ran wildly about.

Why was I suddenly attracted to someone who was so unsuitable for me – who was not even a good man? His dark features, his height, and his intensity was oddly captivating to me now. Even his scent no longer bothered me.

I relished in how much he wished me to be his wife, how deeply he seemed to love me. It was…intoxicating to be so desired. Would accepting him not be the responsible thing to do for my family? Would it be so very wrong? Would Mama not be happy?

What hellish temptation was this? I tried to clear my head and remembered exactly what a dangerous man he was, especially for my soul. How could I ever marry a man who hunted Catholics; what was I even debating?

He looked at me quizzically as he slipped the ring back into his chest pocket. "What is the matter? What is there to be conflicted about? I'm offering you my heart, my wealth, my title – the ability to travel whenever you wish. Anything you ask of me, I could never deny you. You clearly have at least *some* feelings for me – do not try to deny it after that kiss!"

I felt embarrassed at that. "Please, you must understand that I have no desire to hurt or offend you in any way, Elwood. I am keenly aware of everything you have to offer a woman."

He bridged the gap separating us in a few strides, sitting me next to him in the cushioned window seat.

Taking my hands in his, he questioned me further, "Simply say yes! Are you in any doubt of my love for you?"

My eyes kept focused on our hands. "No."

"I am not in any doubt of yours, even though you still haven't answered me. What is holding you back, my dear?"

I shifted my gaze to various areas of the room or parts of his dark-blue doublet. "It's a delicate conversation."

"Why are you diverting your eyes from me?" He smirked. "Am I hideous to you?"

I scoffed and undoubtedly turned red. "No, not at all."

He raised my chin with his fingers so my eyes had nowhere else to look but into his own. "Are you afraid I will kiss you again if you do?"

"Yes." I was surprised by my own candidness.

He smiled and began moving his face closer to mine, but this time I pulled away. "Elwood, we must talk."

He sighed and squeezed my hands. "Very well. What is it that troubles you my dear? What are these reservations you seem to have?"

"You see... about three years ago, my father expressed that he did not approve of you, as a suitor for me."

He released my hands. "What?" His once loving eyes turned to outrage. "Why? Damn it all to hell! Is that why you began to pull away from me back then and have been so standoffish since?"

I found his cursing offensive. "Yes."

"Why would your father not wish to have me as a son-in-law? He knew me for *years*; we were close! Are you quite certain you heard him rightly?"

I found it amusing that he was pretending not to know of my father's distrust of him; as if Papa himself had not been the one to turn down his request for my hand. –I played along as my brother instructed me to.

"It *was* a rather impressionable memory. I am certain. – He expressed that you were too ruthless and worldly for my innocence. He said we would be better suited with other people. Do you see why I was trying to avoid speaking of this? Now you are hurt and agitated."

Elwood rubbed his face, as though exasperated, but said nothing, save a few incoherent mumblings. Curses, from what I could only imagine.

"You must understand, Elwood, that Papa and I were very close; that he meant everything to me, and I feel bound to respect his wishes. – I simply cannot accept your proposal. I am terribly sorry; it pains me to hurt you. I do believe it's best if we part ways amicably."

He stared at me intensely. "You would let the opinions of a dead man affect your future? – *Our* future? You'd let a mere opinion of his determine your response to me?"

A rising anger of my own caused me to squint as he foolishly continued, "I loved and respected your father too, but why bother binding yourself to his words now? You *must* remember how he'd pontificate a hundred daft and ridiculous opinions in a single day! Why is this one any different? He is not here to be upset or happy or any other such thing. Why hurt *me* in this way for the sake of someone who is no longer here?"

The audacity! I walked to the middle of the room, images of slapping his arrogant face crossing my mind. I wondered if it was too soon to leave or not. Surely, Father Ingles would be safely away by now?

He walked swiftly to me. "Do the wishes of your mother count for nothing? Surely she has spoken *greatly* in favor of us being man and wife?"

"I am aware of what my mother wishes. –I do *not* appreciate the way you are speaking about Papa. He may not have been an Earl, but he was a very respectable country gentleman! Dead or alive, he does not deserve your disrespect. I am beginning to think he was completely right about you this whole time. I think it's best if we return to the drawing room. We seem to be finished here."

"Please God," I prayed, *"let Father Ingles be safely hidden away by now."*

A sort of panic began to set into his demeanor and tone. "No that would *not* be best! –Isabel, do you want the darkest truth about me?"

I was surprised by that question. I paused, curious what he would confess to.

"I *am* a bit ruthless – when it comes to things that are important to me – I daresay that is why I've been so successful in business. People know I mean what I say. They respect me. Some even fear me! I *have* been ruthless in pursuing you. I'll be damned if I'm going to let you slip through my fingers because I failed to garner the trust of *one* friend of mine. No, not after all the steps I've taken to procure your heart." He was almost talking to himself at this point.

My eyes narrowed. "What do you mean, exactly, by *steps*? The gifts?"

He smiled down at me. "Oh, you *are* so innocent; your father was very right about that. It is one of the many things that has endeared you to me over the years. Perhaps it would be good for me to disclose all I have done for the sake of winning your heart. You will understand, I am sure of it."

He guided me to sit on the settee again before he began. "Did you ever wonder why none of those young men pursued you after any dance or party you attended? Did even one of them call on you or so much as write you a letter?"

My face fell as the puzzle pieces connected before my eyes. "Did you...threaten them?"

"*Threaten* sounds a bit harsh. I had words with their fathers or the young men themselves, or both depending. I simply explained that, in a manner of speaking, I had my eyes on you and that it would be best for all parties involved if they pursued *other* young women."

My mouth dropped for a moment. "To any man I *ever* danced with? You thought this would be a *good* thing to tell me? That it would garner my affection and convince me of your good character?"

My mind reeled to the days after every dance, party, or picnic, and to the young men I was fond of. When *no one* ever came to call or write and even avoided me after... I had been so downcast and thought something was wrong with me *all* this time! So many of my friends were already married while I remained alone. Because of him.

He ignored my surging temper. "Danced with, smiled at, or any man who even thought of courting you. Do you not see it? *This* is how devoted I am to you; I will do anything for you to be my wife. Anything. Perhaps this is the kind of ruthlessness your father spoke of...and indeed it is true. But he did not think about how it can be used for good – how ardently I will defend you and our future family against anything in this world!"

He had erased any and all marriage prospects. He had made my choice for me: him or no one. I stood from the settee, hands clenched into fists. Never had I felt such ire.

"Did you not calculate how that would hurt me? You have eliminated all choices on my part. You have trapped me! What you have done is...incredulous! Unforgivable, even! *How* could you do this? I am either to marry you or never marry at all? What sort of man does this?"

He rose, coming within a few steps from me. "...Isabel, be calm. You must look at it from my perspective – I would do anything for your love, *anything*. Tell me to buy you the entire bakery you like so well and it is yours, ask me to knock down my castle and build you another, and it will be done! Shall I grovel at your feet and beg forgiveness? Do you not see all the trouble and heartbreaks I have saved you from? You have utterly bewitched me, and I could not risk losing you to anyone. Truly, any man in my position of power would have surely done the same."

I was speechless. How could this be happening?

As my mind attempted to accept my situation, he took my fist into his hands. Slowly, he flattened my fingers out and kissed my palm before meeting my eyes. "So you see, your father's approval, whereas it would have meant a great deal to me...it is not needed. I have your mother's and sibling's support, but above all, I know that I cannot live without you; I need you.

"–I *know* my affections are returned. You are upset now, but I know you care for me...that you are attracted to me, even. I have waited so long to ask you to be my wife. Please, end my suffering and accept my hand in marriage? I cannot bear for you to be angry with me."

He drew himself closer and ran his finger down my jawline. "Please, Isabel, forgive me and be my wife? I swear I will make you blissfully happy."

The Earl continued in my silence, "Do you not find any of what I've confessed to you romantic? Further proof of my love? That I would go through all this trouble to have you for my own? Are you not flattered? Tell me what you're feeling. Your silence is torturing me; I must know what goes on in that mind of yours!"

How was he still able to pull at my heartstrings with his pleadings? I have never before felt such disdain and such compassion, even partiality, all at the same time. What maddening power had he ensnared me with that I should still feel drawn to accept him? I swallowed. He must not see even a hint of my weakness.

My glare met his loving stare. "I am feeling angry, I know that much for certain. As for my thoughts, they are between me and God, but they don't favor you too kindly right now."

Bending his head down to me he said, "I know you don't *only* feel anger towards me."

"Exactly how do you *think* you know this?"

He smiled, pulling slightly away, studying me. "I believe that you *are* flattered by my actions; how willing I am to do anything at all for you to be mine. Despite your choler you desire me; I feel it. It is palpable."

He reached for my hand and held on to it as he continued, "You think it's wrong because your father would not approve and yet...despite these reasons, you *do* want to accept my proposal, don't you?" He placed the opposite arm around my waist and drew me into his arms.

Only part of that was true. Perhaps more of it than I wished to be.

I leaned back from him. "Whatever you believe to have divined from me, is irrelevant. Please let me go, for I wish to return to the drawing room now."

"Why would I ever want to let you go?"

I flinched away from his hand that had reached up to caress my face. "Stop trying to seduce me into accepting your apology and your proposal. It will not work."

Lord Drake smirked. "Really? Are you sure? Then why are you blushing and breathing so fast?"

Why must he be so exasperating?

I levied a stare into his playful eyes. "Elwood, enough of this."

He kept his arms looped around my waist, observing me intently. "It's as though I am witnessing a war within yourself, between your heart and mind. They seem to be telling two different tales."

I turned my face away as he continued, "I wonder, which is true? Who will win? Heart or head? Would it not be better if they simply agreed?"

"I've had enough of these tales. Let me go, Elwood!"

He released me with open hands and a look of surprise.

"What's the matter?" He asked with an amused tone. "I thought you enjoyed stories? Come now, Isabel, let us sit and resolve your hesitations together."

He offered me his hand, but I stepped back. "There is nothing more to discuss."

"I beg to differ! — Did you not find enjoyment in our kiss? I am not ashamed to say that I found it to be very pleasurable." He drew nearer. "Can you honestly say that you feel nothing for me?"

My throat tightened. His kiss was thrilling and alluring. How I wish it hadn't been. How was I to evade such a line of questioning?

"My father has forbidden our union. That is all either of us needs to know."

"After all I have done, do you think anything could dissuade me from taking you as my wife? And my dear, you are avoiding the question. Can you look at me and tell me you feel nothing?"

Think of something to say! I begged my thoughts to come together, but they only left me stuttering, "I...I — it's irrelevant."

"Is it?" With a sudden side step, he nearly pulled me into his arms again. I quickly stepped back, bumping into an armchair by the fireplace.

"Keep your distance!" I exclaimed, trying to regain my balance.

At that moment the door flew open and my brother burst through. "Taking an awfully long time to give a tour of this little library." He glared at the Earl fiercely.

Fortunately, I was not the only one eavesdropping today.

"Lord Drake was just leaving. It's getting late and he has a long ride home."

"Indeed." He said, turning towards me and kissing my hand. "I am not giving up on you, Isabel," he whispered, "although, I think you know that already."

I nodded cooly in response as he whisked past my brother and bade his farewells to the rest of my family.

Not wishing to be assaulted with a thousand questions, I also walked past my brother, ignoring his inquiries, and fled to my bedchamber. I had a great deal to ponder.

From my window, I watched Lord Drake, to make sure he was leaving. Ascending the black carriage's step, he paused, meeting my eyes with a wave. Annoyed at being seen, I closed the curtain until I heard the clips of horse hooves and wooden wheels beating down the road.

Chapter Five

MY MOTHER AND BROTHER were both at the entrance to my bedchamber within a few minutes, begging to be let in. I was both surprised and grateful they did not let themselves in.

I split open the blue-hued tapestry curtains briefly, "I am well, I am not betrothed, he is not giving up, I am not altogether pleased with Lord Drake, and I do not wish to discuss things further at this time."

In dramatic fashion, I threw the curtains closed and laid down on my bed, hearing the sounds of retreating footsteps. I was grateful they did not push their way in. I was in no mood for other people. My mind quickly reviewed all that happened; what was I to do?

I surely had no vocation to be a nun.

There were no other men to marry now except an anti-Catholic, manipulative, seductive, overbearing, conniving, and arrogant man.

He *was* at least generous and mostly kind to me, and I do believe he loves me very much.... But what would become of our children? How could I possibly raise them in the Catholic faith with Lord Drake, commissioned hunter of Catholics, as a husband? And if he ever found out *I* am Catholic? My whole family and I would be slaughtered. Was I to be miserable and alone all my life?

My servant Lily gently tapped against the entry of my bedchamber; I let her in to help me get ready for bed.

"Are you well, miss?" she asked, untying my dress.

"Yes. Lord Drake is simply not a man who takes no for an answer very well...or at all, really."

"Can't say I'm surprised to hear that, given the sort of man he is. It takes real fortitude to turn down a wealthy suitor like you did, to not be enamored by the title and all."

I pursed my lips. I didn't feel very strong; I felt like I barely survived and limped off the battlefield. I hated to recall how easily his magnetism clouded my judgment. "Thank you, Lily."

When she left, I curled up in bed and prayed my rosary to sleep. At least I could find peace within Our Lady's grace if not in this moment of my life.

About midnight, I was abruptly awoken by my brother's signature three knocks on the wall.

I spread open the tapestry, allowing him to storm in. "What happened? What did he do? I swear I will go and beat him until he's within an inch of his life if he did something to you!"

"Shh!" I said, closing the tapestry curtains behind him. "Save your strength, brother. My honor is still very much intact."

He seemed to loosen his shoulders. "I heard, at the doorway – you were asking him to keep his distance from you. What was all that about now?"

We sat down on my bed together. "You must not lose your temper if I tell you."

He nodded.

"I did not wish for him to hold me again."

Immediately he rose from the bed. "Hold you? *Again?* Did he kiss you?"

I opened my mouth to speak, but could not utter the embarrassing truth.

"He kissed you? You hadn't even accepted his hand in marriage!" My brother raved. "That arrogant blighter! You let him? Did he force you?"

"*Jonathon!* Calm yourself. I *did* end the kiss, thank you. This is not why I'm upset."

"What else happened?"

There was *no chance* of me disclosing everything that occurred.

"Things are more complicated than we feared. I may have no choice but to marry him, unless I want to be alone for the rest of my life. Quite frankly, I'm not sure which would be worse right now."

His concern increased, sitting back down. "What do you speak of?"

"Apparently, he has threatened and scared off every man who has so much as looked in my direction from pursuing me. Either them directly or their fathers. There is no one who would go against him and risk initiating a courtship with me. He has eliminated any other choice but himself."

I continued in a lowered voice, "either I become an old maid, or I marry the enemy. I am not sure what he would do to us if I chose to stay single over being his wife. I fear nothing good. He did not take no for an answer today, and I told him so more than once!"

Jonathon's whole face knitted furiously together, creating wrinkles like an old hound. I gave him some time to ponder in silence before I pressed, "What should I do?"

"Toss him!" he exclaimed, standing, only to pace my floor. "No sister of mine is getting forced into a marriage, especially not one with *him*. We'll take a trip to London, Dover, or Bath, even France if we have to, and find you a suitable bachelor that way! I cannot believe he has stooped to such ungentlemanly levels. You rejecting his proposal should have been the end of this all."

"As much as the sound of traveling thrills me, does his Lordship not often frequent those very destinations? What is to keep him from following me? What if my next refusal makes you his next target or he threatens Anna's opportunities? I'm not sure what lengths he will go to! And how could we simply up and leave when you are so busy with — you know. You're *needed* here. And when did your language become so guttural? You've been spending too much time with the peasants, I think, brother."

He paused his plodding to look at me with a corner smile. "When did my little sister become so logical? I'm not sure I like it! You would do well to acquaint yourself with more of our poorer brethren. We will figure something out. Stall him." He sat back next to me and tapped my knee with his hand. "Trust me, you will not be trapped, I promise."

I gave him a hug. "I do not want to be alone for the rest of my life, Jon." Sighing, I straightened up. "Please, at least tell me that Lord Drake was sufficiently distracted and our *guest* arrived safely?"

He whispered, "Safe and sound! A Mr. Porter joined him as well."

"Were we expecting him? Who is that?"

Jon rose to poke his head through the tapestries. Once he was satisfied no one lurked in the hall, he returned to his seat next to me.

"I have heard of him; however, I was unaware he was currently with Father Ingles. He's what we've dubbed a priest runner, or priest's assistant. He guides them to different safety locations. Protects them with his life, if need be. Much like Nicholas Owen did for Father Campion.

"He owns a cottage a couple hundred miles from here; I'm fairly certain he fell asleep before Father did! He's been traveling nonstop for several months now. He's also going to help escort Father to different nearby homes and towns and have our home be their base, in a manner of speaking."

"Interesting. Seems like a good idea for Father to have him as a companion then."

"Indeed. Mass tomorrow at one o'clock instead of the morning to give us time to spread the word and fix the tunnel. With Mr. Porter and Father's help, we should be able to have it done in time. I'll be leaving in the morning to do just that."

"Wonderful! Confession before, I'm assuming?"

"An hour prior."

"Very good. Shall I sneak them down some breakfast? That is terribly long in the day for them not to eat anything before Mass, especially with hard labor."

"Father Ingles said under the circumstances, a light and very early breakfast would be acceptable. They have not eaten well these past couple of weeks, and they need their strength."

"I'll make sure it's as early as possible. Before dawn should be acceptable. And yes – I will be careful, Jonathon."

He smiled at me through a yawn. "Excellent – I am off to bed now. By the way, you really must be more thoughtful about mother's feelings. You had her quite concerned."

"Oh...yes. I could see where I was a bit callous... I was overwhelmed at the time."

"I understand – just make sure you tell *her* that."

"I will."

He patted me dramatically on the head. "Good little sister. Now, go to bed."

The next morning, I rose before the servants and dressed myself simply in a lavender day dress with white ribbons that criss-crossed at my waist. The sleeves were far less dramatic and flowed down my arms in white.

Sneaking down to the kitchen, I retrieved a two mugs of breakfast ale, bread, some cheese, and fruit. I set it all upon a tray with a lit candle along with Communion bread, water, and wine. It was as heavy as it sounds.

The halls were dark, and every noise that I created caused my heart to leap; my mind chastised my clumsiness with each creak in the floor.

Making sure I was not seen, I slipped into the study and made my way down the secret entrance. Slowly, I inched my way through, careful not to spill a drop or crumb.

Reaching the main door, I knocked the secret knock: once, pause, knock twice, pause, three small taps.

I waited patiently until I heard the sound of shuffling feet approaching. The door was at last opened by whom I presumed to be a very disheveled Mr. Porter.

His face held many days' worth of stubble, and his white shirt was untucked, wrinkled, stained, and crooked. If that were not enough, his dark blond hair was in complete disarray, with random tufts sticking straight up and criss-crossing along the sides.

I tried to keep my countenance as he spoke,

"Oh!" He exclaimed with some surprise. "You must be Miss Dawson – Jonathon's sister?" He tried to clear the grogginess from his throat.

I could not help but smirk at the state of him. "I am. And you must be the priest-runner. I seem to have caught you by surprise; I apologize."

Quickly, he tried, and failed, to smooth his hair down with his hands. "–I'm afraid I didn't realize it was morning. I must confess, I was expecting one of the servants to risk bringing us food…not–"

"Me?"

"Well, yes."

"I prefer to do it myself. Not all of our servants are Catholic, so it is riskier for one of them to go missing. Though Missy was the one who baked the Communion bread. I'm merely the delivery person."

"Right, well, that's right brave of you all the same, Miss Dawson. Thank you."

I smiled awkwardly as we stood there in silence staring at the other.

I was still holding the tray when Father Ingles came through the chapel door across from us. "Ah! Miss Dawson, I am pleased to see you well!"

Father Ingles was a middle-aged man, thin and tall with short graying black hair and the warmest smile I'd ever seen on a priest. He had stayed with us several times in the past and had quickly become a dear friend of ours. I missed him and his wisdom very much.

My smile matched his. "Not as delighted as I am to see you alive and well, Father! I've brought a little breakfast for you and your travel companion."

"A *little* breakfast? I see you still have no concept of appropriate portions, my dear! This is a feast in comparison to our usual meals. Thank you very much!" He glanced at Mr. Porter, then me, and then back to his assistant. "Mr. Porter, do you plan to have poor Miss Dawson hold that tray for you all day? Surely she has better things to do with her time."

A mortified look took over his face which I found rather amusing.

He cleared his throat, "Forgive me, my mind must be half asleep still."

Taking the tray from me, our eyes met for a moment – he possessed such bright hazel eyes; the sort that danced in the candlelight. *He might be handsome if properly groomed.* I quickly tossed that notion away – I had enough troubles on my plate as it were.

"You both must be very tired from all your travels. Supper, I'm afraid, will be a rather late arrival though. Is there anything either of you need?"

"I believe the only need we shall have after breakfast is a nap." Father bowed his head appreciatively. "See you for Mass, Miss Dawson."

I gave a small curtsy, took my candle, and made my way back up the stairs as I heard the door lock behind me.

Admittedly, reader...making my way through the secret, dark, and drafty walls of my home was rather unpleasant to do alone. I always feared a ghost would scare me from behind, or a pursuivant, or spy would be around the next corner I turned.

I felt a splendid sense of relief when I reached the door to the bookcase. I peered into the peephole carved through a natural eye in the wood just above where the books filled in. No one was there.

Carefully, I pulled the lever back, *clunk*, and the door opened towards me. Placing the blown out candle on the side table, I pulled the door shut and reset the locks by turning the angel statue.

The sun was beginning to rise through the windows, and I could hear the footsteps of servants coming down the hallway. My breath stuck in my chest. Since some of our servants were Protestant; I had to be extra cautious. Being seen in unusual circumstances by the wrong person could warrant unwanted curiosity.

I did not want to put any of them in a difficult position. Not that I thought they would betray us...however, it is best to err on the side of caution. The less they knew, the better. For everyone's sake. We have heard stories of at least a few families who were betrayed by their servants. I can only imagine what was done to encourage them to tell such secrets.

I went to the desk at once and gathered my stack of parchment and dipped my feather into the inkwell. Odd writing hours would be nothing new to witness for them.

Touching the tip to the fresh sheet, I smiled at the welcome feelings this brought to me; my mind was like a dog let off his lead, and I could say anything without fear. The white and black feather danced dramatically as I scribbled away.

"Nothing tethers me here,
No person, thing, or place.
Only to Thee, I draw near.
I cling to every grace.
Thou, O Christ, hold all of my heart.

For Thee, I would die!
Run headfirst into blades!
Through arrows, I would fly!
Thy love for me never fades.
I pray my own for Thee never fails.
Though the times be wrecked with storms,
And I'm pressed with worries,
I know Thy Heart transforms
And Thy grace will appease.
Come what may, Thy will be done.
Be it loneliness,
Be it martyrdom,
'I am Thine', my lips confess
Till my body succumbs.
For all eternity, I am Thine and Thou art mine."

(I never said I was a good writer. Only that writing pleases me.)

Gently waving the page in the air to dry the ink, I opened the lid to the desk with my free hand. I pulled out a manuscript I had been working on, while tucking away my new poem on top.

I admit that it was perhaps silly for a woman to be writing. Yet, who would hinder a mother from telling stories to her children? Is it not the same? Have we not the same capacity for thought and language as men? Upon some acquaintances, I felt I possessed more. Though, in truth, that may be pride.

The footsteps receded. I decided to put away my story writing for another day. Quickly and silently, I made my way back upstairs to my bedchamber.

Taking a long exhale, I sunk into the pillows of my bed.

Hiding priests was stressful, but the most worthy of work to be done. Nothing made me feel more alive or useful. Yet... I could not help but wonder about many things.

What would it be like to celebrate feasts in the streets with processions, to cross myself without looking over my shoulder first? What must it be like to go to Mass in a real church with a choir? Perhaps I would live long enough to experience this. It has been my daily prayer since I was a little girl.

I grow extremely tired of Protestant services – but I must go, at least occasionally. Being taxed or jailed for not being present is absolute madness. I often wonder if we do the right thing by going at all...yet, if we did not attend, we would never have been able to avoid detection; we must not stand out. We would never have been able to hide so many priests through the years. I often think that's part of the reason why my father befriended Lord Drake. *Keep your enemies closer.*

Chapter Six

At breakfast, everyone was unusually quiet. I realized swiftly that this was more than likely my fault.

"I wanted to apologize for my abruptness last night, Mother. It was...selfish of me. I felt quite overwhelmed and needed to be alone. I did not take into consideration your feelings. I am sorry, Mama."

My brother smiled approvingly.

"Ah, my dear, all is forgiven," Mother replied. "May I ask what Lord Drake did or said that distressed you so?"

Exchanging looks with my brother, I decided that an edited version would be best. "When I explained how Papa had not wished me to be married to him and how I desired to respect those wishes...he spoke very unkindly about Papa."

Mama shook her head. "Fine way to ask a girl to marry you – insult her deceased father! How very rude and ill mannered of him."

Anna frowned. "Why would he talk badly about Papa?"

"Hush now, my dear." Mama placed her hand over Anna's to console her confusion. "The real question is, Isabel, whether you would accept an apology from him, should he offer one, and what you would do then?"

I turned to my brother. "This is far too heavy a conversation for breakfast, wouldn't you agree, Jonathon?"

Jon smirked. "Perhaps! Though I must be off. I have business in town today. I will be back for supper though."

Going around the table, he gave each of us a kiss on the head before departing to "town."

My siblings and I abstained from eating in preparation for Holy Communion. Fortunately, our mother was accustomed to her children occasionally not having much of an appetite in the mornings. Just as Mama finished her last piece of bread, a parcel was brought in by a servant, for me. I'm sure you know who it was from, too.

Taking it in hand, I brought it into the drawing room, followed closely by mother and Anna.

Once seated on the sette, I began to pull the string and unwrap the brown paper.

On top of a small book-sized crate was a letter. I read it in silence,

"My fairest Isabel,

I have been up all night thinking of how brutish my behavior was. I had no right to speak of your father the way I did; it was wrong. I deeply crave your pardon. I only hope you give me the opportunity to make proper amends.

Please accept this gift as the beginning of my apologies. The rest I would like to make in person, if you would permit me.

I hope to see you and your family at the Elharts the following Saturday for their spring party. I would be honored to dance with you there.

Forever yours,

Elwood Drake"

Seeing that it contained nothing untoward, I permitted Mama to read it aloud, for Anna's benefit as well.

"That is a rather well-written apology. What do you plan to do?"

Of course, Mother only had part of the story. "I'm unsure," I said.

Anna was nearly bouncing in her seat. "Why don't you open the present he sent you? Perhaps that would help you to decide!"

Mama and I chuckled. "Very well, Anna, I will see what it is at least."

Pulling away the string and paper revealed a beautifully carved wooden box – inside of which was a circular bottle of perfume.

A note had slid off the glass bottle:

"I discovered this scent in Paris. When I smelled its fragrance, my thoughts went immediately to you. I have been waiting for the appropriate moment to give this to you since.

Please accept it with my deepest apologies. Do write back to me, Isabel, that I may know your anger has cooled against me? Be sure to look in the box for something else, my dove. I beg you not to return these gifts, but keep them and consider me.

All my love and devotion,
Elwood"

Glancing down, I found the ring he tried to give me as an engagement present folded within a soft square of red cloth. It quickly caught the attention of my family.

Mama smiled. "Is that an engagement gift, Isabel?"

"Yes...he tried to give this to me yesterday; however, I did not accept it."

"Try it on!" Bounced Anna excitedly. "It is the most beautiful thing I've ever seen!"

Mother agreed. "You may as well, my dear! And try the perfume to see what it smells of!"

I sighed. At least my brother was not here to witness my weakness.

Sliding it on my finger, I felt like royalty. It was magnificent and the sort of jewelry every girl dreams about. The gold caught the light, contrasting beautifully with the dark sapphires as I moved my finger up and down; it was breathtaking.

Mama walked over to me and with her finger, applied the perfume to my neck and wrists. Bending my head down to meet my wrist, I inhaled the floral and herbal scent; it was truly lovely. I doubt I could have selected a perfume that would have pleased me more. It smelled as though I were immersed in a garden on a warm summer's day.

I stared at the ring on my finger. My entire life could be covered in jewels, flattery, love, and everything beautiful if I accepted Lord Drake's offer.

The very next moment, I felt ridiculous for even entertaining the thought; to trade a life of wealth and ease for that of the well-being of my own soul? And the souls of my future children? All his *love and devotion* was not worth that. Though, he did make it tempting.

I took off the ring, folding it back into the cloth. It was harder than I had imagined not to be swayed by it.

Anna pouted, "Aw, Isabel! You've taken it off so quickly! Have you not forgiven Lord Drake? He seems so very sorry. It made you look *so* pretty! You even *smell* like a princess!"

The servant who handed me the parcel asked if there would be a reply.

"No, not at this time, George. Thank you though."

I took the letters along with the perfume and jewelry in hand. "Things are more complicated when you are a grown lady, little one." I kissed her on the forehead, nodded to my mother, and retired to my room.

Heading straight for my oak jewelry chest, I tucked the ring safely inside. I flopped upon my bed and read both notes over again as I enjoyed the floral scent that engulfed me.

I fumed.

I felt compassion and empathy.

I fumed again.

Where was my brother when I needed him?

Seeking an escape, I walked downstairs into the study to write but did not get very far before being interrupted.

"Miss, another parcel has arrived for you."

"You cannot be serious."

"Afraid I am, miss."

"Is it from–"

She nodded. "Yes, miss. George placed it in the drawing room for you."

"Thank you, Missy."

Her red and gray curls bounced, breaking free of her black coif as she nodded her rounded face and walked briskly by with arms full of linen.

Entering the drawing room, Mother and Anna were both waiting for me while working on their needlepoints.

"Where have you been?" Mama asked. "Another gift has arrived from Lord Drake!"

"I was attempting to write. Oh dear, this seems rather excessive, does it not?"

Mother shrugged with a smirk and urged me to open it.

This was a larger package. Certainly not gloves or anything of that nature.

There was another note, but I will not bother recording it here since it only echoed the former two. "I'm sorry." – "Forgive me." – "Write back to me." – "I love you." Etc.

The package contained *many* of my favorite gyngerbrede squares, as well as an assortment of cakes and tarts. I dare say some of everything that baker had to offer. This was shortly followed by three more bundles of flowers: roses, digitalis, delphinium, lavender, tulips, dahlias, lilies, hollyhock, and more! They were so large and extravagant that only one servant could manage to carry a single bundle. I daresay even the servants were becoming irritated by his excessive gifts.

My mother suggested I write him back before we ran out of space. She also informed me I was being cruel in drawing out forgiveness. I have always felt guilt rather easily, so I obliged her, though I felt more anger now instead of less. As if he could purchase my forgiveness.

"Dear Elwood,

Mama is concerned we will run out of room should you keep sending gifts to me. Please, I feel quite overwhelmed and I daresay so too must the poor men making the deliveries. No more gifts are required.

I appreciate the flowers, sweets, and the beautiful perfume. The ring will remain inside my jewelry chest until such a time that I may return it to you, perhaps the perfume as well. I feel uneasy possessing these items; it does not feel right under the circumstances.

I have forgiven you, as that is what Christ asks of all of us to do. This does not mean that I am full of butterflies for you, however.

While the sweet gestures are not lost on me, you have placed me in a most uncomfortable and shocking situation. I strongly dislike being forced into things, and I worry that what you have done is only the beginning sort of control you would wield over me in marriage. A sampling of the entire bakery or not, that is a fearsome thought.

My mind is at odds with all of this. Is it possible you acted purely out of some sort of crazed love that you felt the need to blot out all other competition? Would that even excuse such extreme behavior? It is rather unthinkable! I cannot stop my mind from wondering why and how you could do such a deplorable thing to me. If you did this to someone you claim to love, what is the lot of those you consider your enemies?

I understand what you said about my father was done so in anger; nonetheless, it cannot be so easily forgotten. I had no idea you had such a low opinion of him.

Perhaps I am still more angry than I thought.

I had hoped you would understand my reasons for refusing your proposal. It seems as though you plan to ignore any answer that is not the one you seek, however.

We have already confirmed with the Elharts that we would attend.

Until then,

Isabel Dawson"

Once my letter was on the way, I pulled Anna aside and gave her the code word for Mass. She smiled and knew exactly what to do next.

"Mama!" she said walking into the drawing room. "I am going on a stroll with Isabel, is that alright?"

It always made my mother smile to hear us spending time together. "Of course, darling! Only be back in time for supper."

"Yes, Mama!"

And with that, we slipped into the study and met four of our servants with us. Down the secret entrance we strolled, until we knocked the password at the door.

Jonathon met us with a smile, still with some dirt in his hair and clothing from the tunnel. "Good, you're on time! Come into the chapel, Father is preparing for confessions now."

A meager room welcomed us with lanterns lighting the walls. Anna and I pulled white lacey coifs from our pockets and covered our heads as we took a seat on logs that were sawed into pieces.

We felt small wafts of heat from the candles and lanterns as we knelt to pray before Christ in the tabernacle.

The altar was very humble; no more than a table pushed up against the rock wall. A small wooden box acted as our tabernacle with gold curtains which I had sewn myself.

The dirt floor was covered by planks of wood, and the walls contained the same wood panels, with various religious pictures. We had managed to find a variety of religious statues and Stations of the Cross as well.

Confessions were held in the bedroom, as there was no room for a proper confessional. The line had already formed; Anna and I joined it once we prayed and examined our consciences.

Finally, my turn came. I knelt before Father Ingles who sat sideways in the chair, facing the wall where a crucifix was hung.

"Bless me Father, for I have sinned; it's been two months since my last confession."

"You may begin, daughter."

I confessed a series of venial sins and felt it in my heart to dive into more recent events as well. "Father, I will try to be quick as I know we do not have much time. But I desperately need your advice."

"What is troubling you? Do not worry about the time."

I exhaled as I whispered, "A man...kissed me, and I enjoyed it more than I should have considering that he is not a very good man. Among other things, he hunts Catholics. He has manipulated me into a situation where I must either marry him or no one. I do not know what would happen to me or my family if I were to reject him again, or if anything would occur from it. Father, what do I do?"

"Do you have feelings for this man?"

"More than I would care to admit, but I would not say that I'm in love with him. — Does that make me a horrible person?"

"I see. No, daughter, it means you try to see the good in people, and we cannot always control who our hearts take a fancy to. I do not know the circumstances and details surrounding this situation; however, it does not sound as though he is the sort of man God would have chosen for you to raise children up in the faith with."

"What if I have no other choice?"

Father nodded thoughtfully. "Do what you can to avoid the marriage. If you cannot, perhaps God can use you to help draw about his conversion. Pray – pray very much about this, my dear. Throw yourself into God's will for your life. Pray the rosary, every day, for guidance in what to do. Our Lady will not fail you. You must also be on guard against lust; do not let it grow in your soul – it is the most dangerous and slippery of slopes."

"Yes, Father, I will."

He then gave me my penance, absolution, and an additional blessing for strength.

Walking back into the chapel, I felt an incredible weight lift from my shoulders. I felt at peace and so light, even with everything going on around me. Upon praying my penance, I thanked God for Father Ingles and all the other brave priests serving in England.

Sitting, I pushed my hand deep into my pocket, but could not find my rosary! Had it fallen out somewhere? Perhaps under my pillow? What if Mama were to discover it?

Pulling me from my thoughts, Anna, Jonathon, Lily, Missy, Moreen and a few other of our servants filed into the chapel. Soon, a group of twenty or so Catholics from around the county crammed into the little chapel as Mass began. I made sure to offer my Mass and holy Communion for the repose of the soul of my father, should he still be in Purgatory.

Father Ingles made his appearance in humble white vestments. We stored one of each liturgical color for all our priestly visitors.

Mr. Porter assisted as his acolyte, dressed in the usual black and white alb and surplice. He had shaved and run a comb through his hair for Mass since last I saw him and looked quite different. Presentable. Handsome.

There would be no music or bells, for our safety, though I confess, I had never experienced them and therefore cannot properly miss them. Truly,

the Mass need not music or bells in order for a person to behold the deep mysteries and beauty that God has permitted us to worship Him in. I feel His presence strongly, comforting and calling me to be one with Him.

Father's homily touched on the need for perseverance in our prayer life and fortitude to keep us strong.

"We must be willing to lay our lives down for God's will in our own lives, whatever that may be. Should you be offered the crown of martyrdom, understand, brethren, that there is no higher act of love for God than this."

We all nodded in silent agreement.

"Like our Father Campion," Father continued, "no matter how they tortured him, be it months of being brought back and forth to the rack, being trapped in a tower room so small that he could not stand, deprivation of food and water. Even death itself could not sway him to give up his God-given Faith. How many of us are willing to follow him to martyrdom for the sake of Our Lord?"

His homily echoed in my soul; I felt a spiritual strength fortify my resolve. I would suffer anything for my Jesus.

Receiving Christ in the Eucharist for the first time in so long was indescribable – as though my soul welled up with tears to embrace my Lord and my God. I felt His love profoundly and no longer felt concerned for anything. Within this moment, nothing else mattered except Christ and I.

Closing my eyes, I imagined running towards Jesus with his arms opened up to me with a smile on His face. He hugged me as I held onto Him tightly, repeating how much I loved Him, over and over again. My heart swelled with the peace of His presence.

I talked with Him about everything that weighed on my heart and thanked Him for being here with me. I asked Him to watch over and protect my family, and all Catholics, and to end our persecution as soon as possible, but to give us strength in the meantime. I kissed His precious wounds and imagined myself resting within His Sacred Heart, trying to ignore the pain my knees were beginning to feel from the hard floors.

When Mass had ended, Anna and I slipped outside through the garden tunnel's exit and made sure no one else was in sight. Jonathon then ushered our friends into the woods in groups of four until everyone who was not staying with us was on their way back home.

Dangerous? Exhilarating? Worth every moment? I confess yes to all three.

Chapter Seven

Just before supper, as we were all beginning to enjoy our soup, another letter arrived from Lord Drake.

"How many has that been today?" asked my irritated brother.

"Eight! That is, if you count the notes included with the bundles of flowers he keeps sending!" Anna exclaimed with a grin.

Jon's brow furrowed. "A bit ridiculous, don't you think, Mother?"

I placed the letter on my lap and continued eating. I felt it unwise in the moment to further exasperate Jonathon by reading it directly.

"He is clearly anxious about losing your sister," Mother countered.

Jonathon mumbled under his breath.

Mama chastised him, "Really, Jon, why are you being so hard on someone you used to look up to as an uncle?"

"I assure you, Mother, I have not looked up to that man in any way – save the fact that he is a solid head taller than me – since I was a young boy, before I knew what a ruthless man he turned into."

Mama smiled. "You sound exactly like your Father. I know he would be on your side if he were still with us. I do so miss him, our disagreements and all."

A quiet sadness fell over the table; it had been a hard year learning to cope without his presence.

I reached across the table to hold her hand. "We all miss him. No doubt he is watching over and praying for us now."

She patted my hand, looking down at her food. "Of course, my dear."

My siblings and I exchanged concerned glances, spurring me to cheer her up, "Mama...tell us again how you met and fell in love with Papa?"

A small smile crept onto her face. "Oh! You children have heard it a thousand times!"

Anna wiggled in her seat. "Tell it again Mama!! It is *so* romantic!"

A bit of color flourished over my mother's cheeks; it warmed me to see that papa loved her so well, that even now, he could make her blush. *That* was love.

Jonathan encouraged her, "We will never tire of hearing it."

Mama sighed with a smile, "When I was a very young girl, oh, about six and ten, Miss Catherine Burnstead, mind you – your Father inherited his Uncle Phillip's land and house. What is our home now." She gestured around the room with her hands, "However, back then, it was a simple cottage.

"Your father was very smart, clever in a way that irritated older gentlemen sometimes, as he often had wisdom beyond his years. Aylesbury was a buzz with learning that a new bachelor had taken over Phillip's many acres of land. Rumors said that he was handsome, ambitious, and wholly uninterested in any woman who was introduced to him. This of course, only increased our curiosities.

"I would come with a friend, Mrs. Elhart now, and secretly spy on him, trying to discern what sort of man he was. He seemed to spend his entire day working out who would help farm parts of his land, raise livestock, and set about fixing up his cottage. He took a great deal of pride in seeing a job done well. I'd also see him pray and read after lunch. Not many men would do that, now would they?"

We all smiled. It was rare to see Papa without a book in hand or at least close by.

"Did he ever catch you spying on him?" Anna asked, her blue eyes wide with anticipation.

Mama grinned. "Once. However, I was able to make my escape without him knowing who my friend and I were. I did confess to it, after we were married, though."

"Was Papa very handsome?" Asked Anna again.

"Oh, yes! Looked similar to your brother, except he had light brown eyes, of course. Soon, a spring dance was being held at the Elhart's, and all the ladies were eager to see if Mr. Dawson from the North of England would make an appearance or not.

"I saw him enter the room – dressed in his finest blue and white doublet...his eyes met mine and a smile grew on both of our faces. I felt as if there was no other person in the room as he walked towards me."

Her thoughts seemed to trail off at the memory – a smile lingering upon her lips.

Anna was quick to ask another question. "What color dress were you wearing?"

"A white dress with blue ribbons. Your father asked me to dance for every dance that night! And indeed, for the rest of our time together. He asked my father for my hand a few months after that night."

Anna clasped her hands together slowly. "It's more romantic every time you tell it!"

"Yes, well, your grandfather wasn't too pleased with the idea at first. However, Harold, your papa that is, won him over, promising to provide the best life possible for me and our future children. I daresay he kept his word."

Later in the drawing room, we played a game of Whist. Even when Jon takes Anna for his partner, he still manages to beat me! It's most infuriating; I haven't won a game of cards for months.

After, Anna practiced on the harpsichord, Mama worked on her needle-point, Jonathon read a book, and I was finally able to open my letter and satisfy my curiosity.

"Dearest Isabel,

I should not wish to overflow your home with gifts and flowers to the point of bursting.

I hope you will forgive a more detailed response to your letter, now that I have the time to compose it. The flowers are from my own gardens, I pray they have at least been to your liking?

Your words are like daggers to my heart – the way you speak makes way for the fear that I have lost you. I do not know what I would do if that were ever the case.

Tell me that is not true? I assure you, when I began discouraging other suitors, it was not my intention to control your life or manipulate you.

My only intention was to give us a fighting chance, to secure your affections for myself. Admittedly, this was selfish; I suppose love makes a man do "extreme" things as you said.

I cannot bear the thought of you possibly loving another man. Do not give up on me because I was overzealous in securing your affections. I need you, Isabel. Truly, I will be most unwell should you pull away from me.

I swear on my very life, I love you even more than my late wife. That is not an easy fact to convey, yet it is the truth. You and you alone are the love of my life. I am completely yours.

As for your father, I intend to spend the rest of my life making up for the unthoughtful words I uttered against him. He was the very best of men, truly.

Do not be angry with me, my dear, for I cannot bear it.

Nor can I stop thinking about our kiss in the library. I waited years to feel the supple pull of your lips. I almost regret it for the sole reason that the memory tortures me. It seems all I can think of is how natural you felt in my arms and how much I wish to caress your face again.

Do not think of returning the perfume or the ring. I wish for them both to be yours. You would only sadden and hurt me by returning them. Keep and admire them; allow them to remind you how much I treasure you. Please, do not feel uncomfortable; I should very much enjoy knowing they have brought you pleasure after the hurt I have caused.

I hope one day you will want to wear the ring, that one day I will have secured your heart and earned the privilege to call you my betrothed.

Does the scent of the perfume please you?

I hope you will forgive my transgressions and give me the honor of dancing with you soon.

All my heart,
Elwood"

My anger somewhat diminished in the course of this letter. I admit, I even felt my heartbeat race at certain sentences he wrote. I felt guilty for causing him pain, but what else was I to do?

"What did he have to say for himself this time?" Jonathon asked, snapping me from my thoughts,

"Oh! Um, nothing very different – just that he's very sorry and how much he wishes to make it up to me, and he cares deeply for me."

Jonathon grunted in response, "I'm sure he's *quite* the romantic."

"And what would *you* know about being romantic, praytell?" chuckled Mama, "What with all the women you have bothered courting?"

Jonathon flushed as Anna and I giggled. "I'll have you all know that I can be very romantic! I have just been busy with other matters, that's all!"

"Of course, darling." Mother assured him sarcastically.

Pulling out a sheet of parchment, I decided to write a response to Lord Drake at the writing table next to me.

"Dear Elwood,

I will admit you have quite the way with words. And yes, the flowers are beautiful. Your gardens must be either very extensive or very bare at the moment.

Since you feel so strongly about it, I will keep the ring in my jewelry chest for now, until such a time when you ask for its return. The perfume is exquisite; I enjoy the fragrance very much. Thank you.

I apologize that my previous letter assaulted you so. I do not wish to cause you more pain by leading you on, however. I have no desire to see you hurt, Elwood. Though, I am greatly concerned that this may be unavoidable. I am at a loss of how to proceed with you.

While you profess such strong sentiments of love that I am momentarily tempted to be swayed; I do not feel that my answer to your offer can possibly change. After he warned me against you, I promised Papa that I would not accept your hand in marriage. I dearly wish you could understand that I cannot break my word to him.

However, I will promise you one dance at the Elharts.

Sincerely,

Isabel Dawson"

My brother eyed me curiously as I handed George the letter to send out.

Mama smiled. "My, that was a fast response. I take it you found this latest letter pleasing?"

"It was not displeasing."

Jonathon rolled his eyes.

"May I be excused?" I asked mother. She nodded her head, and I left for the study to deliver supper to Father and Mr. Porter.

Opening the door of the study, I found a man with his back facing me looking out the window. His shoulders were broad which spoke to his strength; I was unsure whether to be afraid or friendly and thus decided to be bold.

Quickly I closed the door, tray in hand, "Who are you and what are you doing in my father's study?"

The man was dressed well for a commoner with tan trunks, a matching vest and white long sleeve shirt. When he turned, I recognized Mr. Porter with relief.

"Miss Dawson! This is the second time you have caught me off guard. Please do not be alarmed, I am waiting to speak with your brother."

I walked further into the room. "Perhaps you should be a little more hidden until he arrives? Someone could easily come upon you as I have."

Walking closer, he lowered his tone, "I actually came through the entrance like someone who is not constantly on the run. On the premise of discussing business with Jonathon, of course."

"Oh, I see. That does make a difference then."

He nodded. "Indeed. It was decided that I am needed here for a spell, so I will be staying at the King's Head Inn For the time being."

I lowered my voice as well, "Oh, were our accommodations not comfortable enough, Mr. Porter?"

He smirked. "I doubt the Inn could hold a candle to your hospitality."

"Well, speaking of, I must deliver this to our guest. – Have you eaten?"

He shrugged. "Er, I had breakfast."

"Here, take what you'd like; there is plenty. You must eat."

Mr. Porter bowed his head slightly and did as told, grabbing bread, some meat, and a wedge of cheese.

"Thank you, Miss Dawson, you and your family are most generous."

"It's the least we can do, considering. – Your family must miss you, being away so long."

He folded his selected items into a napkin and held onto it. "I am the baby of the family I'm afraid, so all of my siblings are off, out, and married. My parents have both passed away…so, not as much as one might expect."

"I'm very sorry. I know how terrible it is to lose *one* parent; I cannot fathom both."

"I must say that …*traveling*… does a wonderful job at distracting the mind."

"I would imagine so!"

He smiled. "Father Ingles sings your praises often, you know."

I was surprised. "Oh, really? I suppose that's saying something considering he's heard my confession more than most priests!"

"I suppose so."

I shifted the weight from one foot to the other. "You'll have to excuse me; it's time to embrace my inner ghost and fade through the walls now."

He chuckled, "Your brother failed to mention your sense of humor, Miss Dawson."

"Hmm, shocking. — You really ought to join us for lunch or supper one day, Mr. Porter, since it seems you will be here for a while; and heaven knows it will take my brother forever to think of properly inviting you."

Just then Jonathon opened the door. "Isabel, you haven't given Father his supper yet? He must be starving!"

I walked the candle to the fireplace. Fortunately there was still a low fire crackling that I could borrow light from.

"What, praytell, does it appear I am on my way to do?"

Jonathon curved his lip, "Taking up Mr. Porter's time with incessant chatter?"

The light took and I moved to the bookshelf and turned the book and angel statue as I plotted my response. "You must excuse my brother, Mr. Porter, Mama dropped him on his head too many times as an infant, and it has made him a bit ill-mannered."

Jon rolled his eyes. "Go on!"

Mr. Porter chuckled as I closed the bookcase behind me. – I lingered a moment to listen in.

"You never told me how amusing and charming your sister is, Jonathon. I agree with the rumors; it's a wonder she isn't married already."

"If I didn't know any better, I'd say the next thing you're going to tell me is that she's the prettiest girl you've ever seen."

"I'd never be so foolish as to tell a man how attractive I did or didn't think his sister was."

My brother snickered, "You are smarter than you look, Porter!"

"Not the first or last time I will hear that! Call me Daniel; I'm not an old man nor a royal one."

"No, I suppose you're not. What do you think of what we spoke of earlier?"

I heard Mr. Porter sigh. "I must say, I'm undecided about these mad schemes of yours."

"What? Not losing your mettle are you?"

"All my valiance aside — forgive me if I don't fancy *suicide*. Though, I admit, the cause does strike me as a worthy one."

"That's all that matters then, does it not?"

At this point, the tray was getting heavy, and I moved on through the tunnel.

Father Ingles was excited to see the food, perhaps more than me. Duck was a favorite of his.

"Thank you, Miss Dawson. Why don't you come inside for a spell?"

Father must get rather lonely being cooped up down here. I happily obliged him.

He sat the tray down on a small table and grabbed two chairs from the bedroom. Sitting down with him at his makeshift dining room set, he said grace and was quick to converse. "So tell me the happenings above! Is Mr. Porter settled in all right at the Inn?"

"Yes, I believe so. He and Jonathon are talking upstairs at the moment."

He broke off a piece of bread. "Mr. Porter is a good man; I'm glad we are able to spend a longer period of time here. He hasn't been in one place longer than a few days in quite some time. He could use the rest."

I smiled as he took a few bites of food. "Yes, I imagine you could use the rest as well, Father."

"Indeed; I've been making it a retreat for myself down here. I wonder though, if you would be so kind as to bring me a couple books from your father's library?"

"Of course. Any specific one?"

"Oh, surprise me!" He broke off a piece of cheese. "I'm curious what your thoughts are of the young Mr. Porter?"

I watched him pop it into his mouth before I asked, "Why *my* opinion, Father?"

"Merely making conversation, dear. He has a rather high opinion of you." He took a long drink of water.

"Oh? What did he say of me?"

He smiled a wry grin in my direction. "Curious? I thought you might be." He took another bite of bread and swallowed it before answering. "Mr. Porter thinks you're very beautiful and clever. *'I've never met a more interesting woman'*, were his exact words."

I wondered if Father could detect my blush in the dim lighting. "However flattering that is, surely Jon has spoken to you of Lord Drake?"

The priest nodded. "Yes, yes, he has. I've been keeping that whole terrible situation in my prayers. You didn't answer me though, child."

"Um, what was your question, Father?"

He smiled. "What do *you* think of Mr. Porter?"

"Father, don't you have enough on your shoulders besides adding matchmaker to your list of responsibilities?"

He shrugged as he took a bite of duck. "Still dodging the question I see. I have all the time in the world, daughter."

"*Even* if I did think him to be handsome, and admired his faith, and maybe even found him to be a little charming, what good would it do me? You know better than I what Lord Drake is capable of. I wouldn't want to incur his wrath on anyone. And really, *Father Ingles*! I hardly know Mr. Porter at all. How could I form a proper opinion of him?"

"Ah! But I do. All I'm saying, my dear, is that I have traveled with the man for months now. Trust me when I say that he would make for a fine husband; he is a good man. Honest, patient, strong, and kind. Perhaps don't let Lord Drake control your actions through fear, eh? Perhaps you just follow the promptings of the Holy Ghost instead. Leave the details to God. He always ends up taking care of us, you know."

I opened my mouth to speak but found no words.

The priest smiled again. "Merely something to ponder, Miss Dawson!"

Making my way back up the stairs, my mind went over what Father had said. Didn't he know what was at stake? Wouldn't Mr. Porter be off again soon – galavanting bravely around the countryside with a priest in tow? Who knows what Lord Drake would do if he thought I found another man handsome. Surely Mr. Porter wouldn't wish me to put his life in danger?

When I finally made it to the top, I paused at the bookshelf to listen in again. I'd make some excuse for doing so, however, you know me better by now.

I heard Jon's voice, "Yes! You attending the Elharts' party will be a perfect way to introduce you around. Just remember: You're an old friend of mine from Oxford days. You're visiting me and we're working out a trade of goods. He won't suspect a thing!"

"Very well...except I don't own any finer clothes than what you see."

"You're about my build and height – you can borrow some of mine and we'll have Missy let out the hem in the arms and shoulders – it's brilliant. The more connected all of us are, the better. What do you say?"

"Alright, but the second he gets a whiff of this plan, I'll need to be off with you-know-who and any others I need to take with me."

"Absolutely. Theirs and your safety are top priorities. I should warn you about one more thing."

"Well?" Mr. Porter asked.

"You mentioned you heard rumors about my sister. What are they?"

I could tell by his tone that Mr. Porter felt uncomfortable answering. "Mostly gossip about how your sister keeps turning down the attentions of Lord Drake. There is much discussion over his infatuation with her. Mostly though, I hear tales of his victims and his cruelty."

"Good, you're aware of his reputation then."

"What Catholic isn't? The man is a terror."

"That terror has trapped Isabel into a life with him or no one at all. He threatened every possible suitor until there were none left. I'm tailspinning as to how to help her out of this mess."

"Scoundrel! Why can't you just tell him no and be done with it?"

"My father did that. It brought a world of scrutiny upon our family. Many of his business deals fell through, some people shunned our family – until his funeral, that is.

"If *I* should say no? I am convinced he would have our house searched and ransacked. As much as I wanted to tell him to shove off, I was forced to say that it's my sister's choice. Now he's spending all his time trying to convince her."

"Damn. I see. How can I help?"

"I appreciate the offer for help, my friend, but you definitely cannot. It will put you in his line of sight and that is not a place anyone needs you to be. I tell you this only to warn you. Even men who are too kind to Isabel become a target of the Earl's. At the party, be cordial to my sister, but that is all. Don't ask her to dance; don't even speak to her unless it cannot be avoided."

"Is she safe?"

"Let me worry about my sister, but keep away for your own good, at least whenever he is around."

"Very well. If you come up with another barmy plan of yours to help her, let me know. No woman should be forced into marrying that bloody fool."

"Appreciate that! Now, about my plans, we should discuss details somewhere else and get our stories straight."

I took this opportunity to pull the lever on the bookshelf and step out.

"Gentleman," I greeted, blowing my candle out and placing it on the table near me.

"Isabel! I half forgot you were down there!"

"How thoughtful of you, Jonathon," I teased. "Do not fret; I shan't disrupt your holy schemes and plots. I'm off to bed."

I kissed my brother on the cheek. "Good night."

Curtsying to Mr. Porter I said good night again as he bowed. "Pleasant dreams, Miss Dawson."

As I laid in bed, I thought over the conversation I heard. I hadn't realized I was the source for so much gossip. What else were they saying about me? What would they say if I married him? Would they stop then? An agitated sigh passed through my lips. I wished I knew where my rosary had gone; I was terrible at keeping track of the prayers with only my fingers. I needed the grace and peace too much to let missing beads deter me, however. I knew Our Lady would forgive my bumbling prayers; I settled into meditating on the agony in the garden, and was sleeping contentedly before reaching the third mystery.

Chapter Eight

Over the next couple of weeks, I decided it would be advantageous to take a stroll through the gardens after breakfast. For exercise and fresh air.

As I lingered in the back garden, admiring the spring flowers, the secret stone door popped open and out came Mr. Porter. Right on time.

"Good morning!" He greeted enthusiastically as he climbed out. "I wondered if I'd see you today."

"How are you, Mr. Porter?"

He brushed himself off. "Quite well! I'm taking Father to a couple of the neighboring towns; would you care to walk with us to the woods again? I know your company would be appreciated. I'm sure he grows tired of having only me to talk with."

"I find that hard to believe! Though I daresay walking with the two of you has become part of my morning routine as of late. How could I say no?"

Mr. Porter flashed a toothy grin. "I'm glad to hear it." He stared at me quietly for a moment.

He was dressed in more casual attire today with an open white shirt and brown pants, high white stockings, and walking shoes. He looked rather handsome in a rugged sort of way.

Father Ingles poked his head out and cleared his throat, "I suppose it's safe then Mr. Porter?"

"Oh! Father! –Yes, I'm sorry."

Father climbed out of the small hole with his long limbs, "Forgotten again for the sight of Miss Dawson, I see."

I tried to conceal a smile as Mr. Porter floundered a bit, "Ah... yes... I suppose that has become a regular occurrence, I'm sorry Father." He scratched the back of his head.

"Would it be best if I began walking another direction in the mornings?" I offered, knowing full well the idea would be rejected.

"Nonsense." Mr. Porter chuckled, "We both enjoy your company along the way, don't we, Father?"

"He's quite right, Miss Dawson. Although you might consider applying some mud to your face, so you are less of a distraction for Mr. Porter."

A large grin took over my face as Mr. Porter turned an amusing shade of red, "I don't think Mama would approve of that idea, Father. I am already scolded frequently enough for not being as lady-like as I ought to be."

"*You*? Not lady-like enough?" Mr. Porter questioned, "You have always struck me as a proper lady."

"I assure you, that appearance is only met with the greatest effort on my part."

"Well, your natural elegance makes it appear effortless."

Father closed the little door, "Shall we?"

Today Father donned the disguise of a farmer, and quite looked the part, as did Mr. Porter, though Father had the addition of a woolen tunic.

"The farmer's life suits you!" I teased as we made our way to the woods.

Father brushed off some dirt from his sleeves, "Who knew that being a priest would also allow me to live the life of an actor! The trunk of disguises your family has collected is very useful."

"Let's just be careful you never play on stage for *Good Queen Bess*." Mr. Porter said with a sarcastic air.

"Indeed! That name is the greatest antithesis of all. It's a wonder she doesn't have the Protestants direct all prayers to *her*."

"She very nearly does in her ridiculous oath." Mr. Porter replied.

I sighed, "I don't understand how anyone can condemn so many people to such terrible deaths. How does her conscience not utterly consume her?"

Father replied, "Queen Elizabeth has a great many distractions at court and plenty of advisors who ease any guilt she might feel. Especially that vile William Cecil — he is the snake in the courtyard. Yet, only one of many."

Mr. Porter folded his hands behind his back, "If only Queen Mary had been able to have children — I wonder if this would be a very different country now. At least one where Catholics could live freely."

"I'm afraid it does us no good to dwell on the great 'what ifs' of life. It may not seem so, however, persecutions can be a source of indescribable grace. The more they hunt us, the stronger it makes us."

I was puzzled by his words, "How do you mean, Father?"

"Think of it this way, Miss Dawson. When a prayer or act of love is offered up, it ripples throughout the Church. Does it help save a soul here on earth or rescue a soul from purgatory? Does it ease someone's suffering? How many souls do we assist in saving by fasting or offering up some small sacrifice? The same goes for sin but in the opposite way, of course. Sin weakens us, particularly a grave sin. Our daily choices affect the strength of us all.

"Now, think of how much grace must be poured through the whole of the Church from one act of love and faith made by a single martyr? History itself proves that Catholicism grows most during hardships. The blood of the martyrs is a fountain of grace to strengthen the Church Militant.

"As difficult as it is now, we were made for these very times. — Hopefully you two will live to see a happier period though."

His words touched me, but I couldn't help but wonder, "What is it like — to simply attend Mass on Sundays with music and celebrate all the feast days? What was it like being at seminary in France?"

He smiled, "As wonderful and beautiful as you might imagine it to be, Miss Dawson. It was admittedly difficult to leave behind. But I could not ignore Our Lord's call to come and help my fellow Englishmen here. It felt wrong to live such an easy life knowing what was happening back home. My dear friend Father Edmund Campion summed up my desire to return in his manifesto, "*The expense is reckoned, the enterprise is begun; it is of God; it cannot be withstood. So the faith was planted: So it must be restored.* He inspired me to leave England and become a priest."

The zeal in which he quoted his old mentor was contagious, "Everyone is grateful you made such a sacrifice, Father."

"Indeed, we are." Added Mr. Porter.

"Well, give all your gratitude to God; He's the one who saw fit to give me this vocation and the grace to return. I fear you will grow weary of my quoting Father Campion, but in the short time I knew him, he always had the gift for speaking my own heart better than I could myself!"

He smiled thoughtfully, "I miss our conversations greatly." He sighed. "Now, I hope you two won't mind, but I have a rosary to finish — I'll just walk on ahead and pray, if that suits the both of you?"

Mr. Porter replied, "Of course Father, we'll walk a ways behind you to give you privacy."

He nodded and picked up his pace a bit.

"If I didn't know any better," said Mr. Porter, "I'd say Father Ingles fancies us together."

"You noticed that too? Hmm. He's not as subtle as he likes to think he is."

"No, I should probably tell him that I'm much too young and attractive to be your sort." He winked at me. "I've heard Lord Drake will be forty come autumn."

I laughed. "I wasn't aware I had a type! How young are you, Mr. Porter?"

"Four and twenty! Does that lessen your opinion of me? Does my age make me too impetuous?" He raised his eyebrow playfully at me.

I tried to control the spread of my smile. "I'm afraid I don't know you well enough to draw any conclusions as of yet."

"How very discerning of you, Miss Dawson. I know it's not my place...but I hope you do not marry him; you deserve much better."

"That is a sweet opinion, Mr. Porter. But what of you? Have you left some girl heartbroken back home, waiting for your return?"

"No, I'm afraid I failed to meet anyone that captured my eye before I became a priest runner." He looked at me through the corner of his eyes. "There were no *Miss Dawsons* in Portsmouth. Well, between you and I...that's only for my cover. My real home is in Bridlington and my true family name is Clifton, not Porter. But please remember never to use those names as it helps keep my siblings, nieces, and nephews safe, should I ever be captured."

I felt honored to bear his secret. "I understand, I will be very careful, *Mr. Porter.*"

He nodded gratefully.

"How long have you been helping the priests move about?"

"Three years now. I've been with Father Ingles for several months, sometimes dropping him off in one place, going to help another and circling back."

"You don't ever get lost?"

"Rarely. I'm good with maps and have a decent sense of direction." He said with a small air of pride about him.

We had walked into the woods several yards by now. "I ought to head back and let you and Father Farmer go ahead and help the others."

He chuckled.

"Will you be back this evening?" I asked.

"No, but we should be back late tomorrow."

For the first time, he took my hand and kissed it. "I enjoy our morning strolls when we're able to have them. I hope you have an enjoyable rest of your day, Miss Dawson."

"As do I. Be safe and not too *impetuous* Mr. Porter."

"I'll do my best." He cracked a smile. "Keep us in your prayers today, if you'd be so kind."

"I'll be sure to." My hand dug into my pocket. I forgot I had misplaced my beads.

"Have you lost something?"

"My rosary. I must have left it in my bedchamber."

Without hesitation, Mr. Porter pulled a wooden rosary from his own pocket. "Here, I insist." He held it out for me in his palm.

"I cannot take yours! What will you pray with?"

"It's of no matter." He placed it in my hand and folded his fingers over mine. "To know you are praying for us, using my beads, would give me great joy."

Our eyes locked as a blush warmed my face. "I will be sure to return them to you soon."

"Please keep them." He gently pushed our hands towards me. "As a gift. One can't have too many rosaries, after all."

With a wink, he jogged to catch up with Father Ingles who had walked off in the wrong direction, lost in prayer.

Walking back to the house, I wondered whether getting to know Mr. Porter better was a wise idea or not. I don't know what Father Ingles thought he meant about not worrying over it. Should I not be cautious? Perhaps what Lord Drake didn't know, wouldn't hurt anyone. Recalling his suggestion, I gave the situation over to the Holy Ghost.

The beads he'd given me were smooth, and a little bigger than my own. I was touched by his gesture. I raised the wooden cross to my lips, and made the sign of the cross. It seemed to smell of him. Or was that my imagination?

For Father Ingles and Mr. Clifton. I whispered to Mary as I began to pray.

Entering the front door, Lily, my servant, handed me a letter and yet another bundle of flowers from Lord Drake. I sighed and took the letter into my father's study to read as Lily put the flowers in some water. It had been uncommonly long without a response and I thought perhaps he had begun to accept my answer. I sat down in the window seat and drew my legs up about me as I unfolded his letter,

"My dearest Isabel,

I apologize for not having written to you sooner; I have been extremely busy.

These vexing Catholics are getting more clever all the time and business has taken me on many travels. At least my efforts, though exhaustive, have proven successful.

I have only just now returned and have time to respond to your letter. You have been in my thoughts constantly. Even in my dreams, you are with me.

My dear, I do understand your hesitation in regards to your father's wishes. I knew him well though and I cannot imagine him wishing to keep you from love and happiness. Would you not agree with this?

It is not in my nature to give up, especially in matters of the heart. You are worth all the patience and persistence in the world.

You needn't concern yourself with whether or not you are misleading me. Stop over-thinking things. I gladly lift this burden from you. I wish only for you to do exactly as your feelings dictate without fear, guilt, or second guesses.

Wear the perfume daily, if you like! Should you run out, I will gladly travel to Paris to ensure you have another.

If you wish to wear the ring in the privacy of your bedchamber for now, do so. My only request is that you do not withdraw yourself from me. Write to me, speak with me, dance with me, kiss me if you desire to. I will always be here. I will always be yours.

I am entranced and captured by you, my little bird; I am utter clay in your hands. I will go to any lengths to win your heart and your, albeit, stubborn mind.

I wonder if your guard will lower enough for me to steal a kiss while no one is looking? Or will you draw out my torture? Do you ever think of our kiss?

So deeply tempted, am I, to come and surprise you at home, though, my duties are already calling me away from this letter.

I am counting down the days to the Elharts' party and am grateful I have secured at least one dance with you. (Though I hope to convince you to allow me many more.) It has been months since I've had that pleasure.

I will see you in a couple of days, my beautiful dove.

With all my love,

Elwood"

He wrote so alluringly, I nearly forgot why I was angry with him and why I could not give him what he so desired. How does he manage that? I always feel I must remind myself of the reasons why I may never marry him.

My fickle heart seemed to not care whether he hunted Catholics or not! Regardless of how his words confused my feelings, I *must* keep my guard up higher around him. I will not respond. How am I ever to turn him down in a manner he would accept?

I could not help but wonder, from time to time, whether I could manage living alone all my life or if it would be better to settle and marry a dangerous man. How many years would it be, before he convinced me to accept him in a moment of weakness, if indeed he truly would, "always be here?" I exhaled deeply.

My hand dipped into my pocket, feeling the gifted beads. I enjoy my time with Mr. Porter, but I do not wish to endanger his life or work. I confess, I will miss his company when he leaves; he's so very amusing and fun to converse with.

"Isabel!" Anna called for me. "Come and play cards with me! I shall beat you this time, I know it!"

I rose to go play with her, folding the note into my dress pocket; the distraction would be most welcome.

Chapter Nine

THE DAY OF THE Elharts' party had arrived. Every spring they put together a wonderful feast with music and dancing for their many friends. I detested that it was the first party of theirs that I was dreading.

Everyone would be whispering about me and the Earl, and he was sure to be overbearing. My only hope was that my dearest friend – Christy – would finally have returned from Bath, and I could see her again. I needed her now more than ever.

I chose a gown of blue and white that paired well with my grandmother's pearls. Mama insisted I wear the lace gloves which Lord Drake had gifted me. I obliged her, as they did match the floral pattern on my dress quite well.

Mama was endlessly prodding me to accept the Earl's proposal. Not a day had gone by without some nudging to that end.

"You could be a countess, Isabel!"

"Darling girl, can't you see how much the man loves you?"

"I daresay I agree with him! —Your father would understand!"

"Your stubbornness utterly confounds me. Forgive and forget – marry the man!"

Admittedly, had I not been a Catholic, I would have accepted his proposal – before I ever learned how devious he could be.

His kiss haunted my thoughts. How could something wrong feel...well, quite the opposite? I did my best to push the memory away, but found this exceedingly difficult.

Lily braided blue ribbons through my hair to ensure I looked my best. Waves of hair curled down my back, leaving the braids and ribbons woven through the top part of my head.

Anna pouted on my bed, sad that she was not old enough to attend as I applied the perfume Lord Drake had given me. The servants promised her she could stay up late and eat sweets, which did wonders to cheer her.

Riding in the carriage with Mother and Jon, I began to regret going at all. What if he was able to seduce me into another kiss? What if he would not relent and proposed again? I felt nauseous.

Stepping out of the carriage, I took a deep breath of cool air, and tried to control the racing thoughts in my mind. A brief prayer to my Guardian Angel offered me a bit of peace at least.

Walking up the steps to their well-lit home, we joined a small crowd of others arriving. It was good to see my acquaintances! Most were being escorted on the arms of their husbands or betrothed and absolutely glowing with excitement. My heart felt a pang, wondering if marriage would be in my future or not.

We talked for a bit with them on the way in; five asked if I was engaged to the Earl yet. – A very long night was ahead of me, indeed. The small talk which did *not* revolve around the Earl, was a welcome reprieve, however.

The lively music embraced my spirit as we entered their large home. Unlike ours, they dedicated most of their space to the intention of entertaining. Mr. and Mrs. Elhart were the most outgoing and social people I have ever known. They were always having someone over for dinner or putting together an outing for the younger people. Their home was a perfect reflection of their socialite personalities. The glow from their tasteful chandeliers was as enchanting as I remembered. Anna would have loved it.

I thought back to when my friend Christy and I had come here for the first time. We had both come of age the same year and were so excited and eager to dance. I smiled at how long ago that felt. I wished she were here now. Alas, it appeared I was to be deprived of her company.

We soon met with the Elharts — now more of an elderly couple who welcomed guests in with their married daughters, Lettice and Adeline. They dressed in nothing but the latest fashions from France and were always kind enough to share *every* detail about the lavish materials used.

My eyes drifted from Lettice's and Adeline's riveting conversation, to the crowd beyond them. Punch was passed around as sets of people talked, played cards, and danced. It *was* a wonderful gathering.

Admiring the dance taking place, I stumbled into Lord Drake's gaze. He smiled warmly at me as he made his way to us. Immediately, I felt my face flush. I despised how he had this effect upon me.

The tensions in my stomach steadily increased as we moved on from our hosts and met his Lordship a few feet away.

He greeted us with open arms. "Ah, at last! The Dawsons have arrived!"

He wore a gold and black doublet with gold trimmed collar ruffles. His black trunks cut at his knees, where the end of a black cape draped dramatically off his shoulders. I'd be lying if I said he didn't look dashing. I wished he were ugly. Perhaps then his fancy words would hold little sway over me. If only his gaze was not so pulling.

Mother was the only one genuinely happy to see him. "Ah, salutations my Lord! How lovely to see you again!"

He took her hand and kissed it. "To you as well! My, you and your daughter look absolutely ravishing tonight!"

I could feel my brother inwardly grimace. "Good to see you, my friend! – Mother, shall we?" Mama took Jon's arm and moved their way into the heart of the party. He gave me a "good luck" glance as he walked away. *Argh.* If only he realized my inner turmoil, he would not have left me alone with the Earl.

Lord Drake offered his inevitable arm to me. "Isabel?"

I nodded and accepted.

We walked slowly about, pausing here and there at his leisure. "I am so pleased to see you, Isabel. I tell you my heart felt on fire when I laid eyes upon you from across the room."

I witnessed many people turn to whisper about us; it made me wish I had stayed at home. Had they nothing better to gossip about?

"It is good to see you as well, my Lord." I replied, turning my sights away from the surrounding people to the floors.

"What a temperate response!" He chided me, "You know, for someone who is apparently uninterested in me, you have selected the most stunning gown to wear. You are utterly captivating."

I looked over my dark blue gown. The square neckline, bell sleeves, and sweeping flow were lovely. However, I would not say it was a dress to specifically attract attention. Certainly nothing in comparison to what the Elharts wore. However, had I been wearing beggar's attire, I fear it would have fetched the same attention from Lord Drake.

"You're too kind, as usual," I said, careful to avoid his gaze.

As we came to a crowded area, he placed his hand on my lower back to guide me through the narrow space. I held my breath as my skin rippled at his touch.

Remember, he is not a good man, you are disgusted by his actions. Do not be swayed by a hunter of Catholics!

"You are quiet, my dear, are you well?"

I offered a polite smile as he offered his arm again. "Yes, thank you."

"Still angry with me? I knew I should have sent you a puppy."

"You *are* amusing, my Lord."

He bent his head down to mine and slowly inhaled. "I was right in selecting this perfume," he whispered, "you smell positively rousing. – Perhaps you need another kiss to remind you that I'm not worth staying mad at?"

Despite my racing heart, my tone grew serious. "It would be better if you did not think this way."

He shifted his eyes into mine. "Would it? Shall you command my thoughts now? Come, Isabel, you cannot tell me you haven't found yourself reminiscing fondly of our time in the library together? You never did write back to answer that question."

He placed his hand firmly over mine as I tried to step away.

I glanced up at him. "You must behave yourself. I beg of you."

His smirk grew bold as we walked on, pausing by a column near the dance floor. "You are evading the question...you *have* thought about our kiss...more than you would ever admit to, isn't that right?"

I could not control the blush that I was sure was taking over my face again. "I do not make a habit of answering such indelicate questions."

His expression and tone was nearly playful. "And I suppose you didn't try the ring on either...?"

How was he so sure that I had? I met his dark eyes briefly. "You are full of questions tonight, Elwood."

The Earl bit his lip, seemingly pleased with my lack of an answer. "Did it fit to your liking?"

I swallowed, trying not to look directly at his face longer than necessary. "It's a beautiful ring; I have never seen it's equal."

"Shame it isn't on your finger tonight for me to admire myself. – Ah! Come, the *La Volta* is starting, and you did promise me a dance! What luck that it is my favorite one of all – the Queen's as well. In truth, I requested it be played."

"What luck, indeed then."

Of course he claimed the *La Volta* for our dance. It was far more intimate than any I'd ever learned. My brother was quite against it, but Mama had insisted I become familiar with such a popular dance in the hope I would marry above my station.

The dancing hall brimmed with people, music, and lively conversations. The walls held circular mirrors between tapestries and grand candelabras. The light from the candles flickered in their reflections making the walls appear to sparkle.

The musicians were set towards the back, allowing the sound to cascade and vibrate beautifully off the arched ceilings. I would have appreciated them better, had my heart not been throbbing with such disquietude.

Walking onto the dance floor, I saw Mr. Porter also had a young woman, Miss Smith, on his arm. He looked rather handsome, dressed in my brother's altered red doublet and black trunks. – I found him to be even more handsome than Lord Drake. I couldn't help but feel a tinge of jealousy that he danced with another girl...and yet, I knew the feeling was unwarranted.

We exchanged a glance and refixed our attentions to our dance partners.

The music began; I placed my hands around Lord Drake's shoulders as his hands wrapped around my waist.

He looked into my eyes with an intense fervor, giving my body a tingling, yet uncomfortable, sensation. "I have so looked forward to dancing with you, Isabel."

"We have danced together before, many times," I replied as we turned in unison to the music.

"It's different now though, isn't it? I know you feel the connection, the flame between us. – I hear it in the change of your breathing, your heartbeat, and how I feel when I am close to you; we are connected."

The tambourine began to chime the beat of the stringed instruments.

Father Ingles' words of caution about lust resounded in my mind as we changed positions. I sprang into the air as he supported me high, holding me tightly, leading me slowly back to the ground as I leaned against him.

I chided, trying to keep the conversation lighter, "You must have quite exquisite hearing to capture all of that amidst the music."

According to the dance, my back turned away as his left hand drew me back into him, with his hand resting on my hip. My hand raised behind and stayed on his back for a moment.

"One day, you will *really* forgive me and admit you have feelings for me." He said in a low voice.

Twirling me around, our eyes locked. I fought against the stutter that flitted across my tongue. "—I wasn't aware premonitions were among your aptitudes, Elwood."

The ladies hopped, circling their partners before the men twirled us into our original positions.

I continued, "And besides, I've already told you – I *have* forgiven you."

He rolled his eyes as I came into his arms again. "Yes, that was poppycock! You're still holding onto anger. It's all over your tone and face. You are much colder with me today."

While I truly had forgiven him, it seemed as good an excuse as any to help keep him from proposing again. "Forgiveness *can* be a process."

"What more must I do? Do you not think me sincere? Can a man not make mistakes in the heat of the moment?"

"They can, though yours were more of the premeditated nature. I seriously doubt your sincerity."

We changed partners for a moment before he could respond, "You think my words and actions are hollow? When have I ever lied to you?"

What a question from *him*!

He lifted me into the air again and brought me back to him as I replied, "I don't think I can trust you."

He nearly rested his forehead against mine, which was not part of the dance. "There is no soul whom you can trust more."

I slowly pulled my face away. Nearly everyone was staring at us. I had rarely felt so uncomfortable. I was grateful for the next steps of the dance as all the ladies leapt away and back again to their partners.

"You have undoubtedly tried to make certain of that, haven't you?" I said once back in his arms. "They are all staring at us! Do you know that we are the gossip of Aylesbury and beyond? Everyone is wondering if you've proposed yet or not. I was hounded with questions before I even gained entry into the house."

He twirled me around with a satisfied visage. The gossip and attention clearly did not bother him. "I cannot help their curiosity. There could be no one who matches my devotion to you, no one. I merely did you a favor in erasing the other interested men. It was no small feat either! More than eight desired you for their own. And they were so apt to spread the word around for me. Quite possibly double that amount."

I could hardly believe that he was now bragging about the very thing he was trying to apologize for! We danced behind one another and circled around before he continued,

"I made your choice clear and easy to see – that there is no love more fierce or true than mine."

My ears began to ring; I could feel a spell coming on. The noise, heat, and his Lordship were overwhelming me. The air felt too thick to inhale, and my chest began to hurt with each breath I drew.

I tried my best to complete the dance so as not to make a scene, "–Not that you gave them a chance to contest that."

"And why would I when I already knew the answer? It was not possible for any man to desire you as much as I. Nor for any to equal what I can offer you."

"Is that not presumptuous of you?"

"No. Only the simple truth of the matter. – You know, perhaps they all wag their tongues because, like me, they cannot fathom why you have not yet accepted my offer."

"Unlike them – I've told you my reason why." My breath was beginning to fail me.

At last, the dance ended. "Please excuse me, my Lord." I curtsied quickly and left to one of the doors leading out to the terrace. I tried hard to conceal my symptoms so he would not follow out of concern.

Walking down a few steps, I was immersed in the comfort of their gardens and a chilly breeze. There were many entwining paths with lush ferns and flowers growing between shapely bushes. The silence was most welcome to my rushing thoughts.

I walked for a few minutes past tall torches that lit my way. Finally, I found a more concealed bench in a circle garden where I would not be so easily found.

My hands shook, but I felt like I was beginning to regain control. I closed my eyes, took slow breaths, and prayed Ave's in my head. I felt relief slowly washing over me as I gripped the edge of the stone bench to steady my swirling world. It was so peaceful here that I would be content to hide here for the remainder of the evening. Perhaps I would.

"Isabel? Are you having another spell? I noticed your hand was shaking as the dance ended." It was the voice of the Earl. Exactly who I did not need at this moment. And alone.

Dash it.

"Yes. I only need a few moments."

He sat with me. "You can lean on me as you did before, if that would help."

"No, thank you. It is passing."

He took my hands in his and slowly pulled the gloves off.

"What are you doing?" I asked guardedly.

"I am helping you to cool down, as your sister did for you." He kissed my hands gently. "I hate to see you distressed. I am here my darling, be at ease." He caressed my face with his other hand and moved a curl of hair that had blown out of place in the wind.

I closed my eyes and tipped my face down; I could not bear to face him. I hated how weak I felt against his charisma. Perhaps it was being so desired that he'd stoop to any level to have me, to love only me, that I found so irresistible. Or could it be that my vanity enjoyed how complementary he was? – You'd think my disgust and anger over *who* he was would have been enough to make all of me reject him. Regardless of the reason, I felt such a fierce temptation to give into him.

Besides, what if he really was the only man I *could* marry? Would the marriage not be good for my whole family? What if he was my only chance at not being lonely, to have children? I would not wish to be a burden to Jonathon the rest of my days. Was marrying Elwood not the most reasonable course of action? Certainly it would be easier.

He drew in close. "Isabel, look at me my little dove, please? You have been avoiding my eyes all evening thus far. You torture me with such indifference."

With his finger he turned my chin towards him, staring into my eyes.

"Please hear me," he said. "I *am* sincere and honest in all that I say to you; I *am* sorry and I *do* love you –worship you even. I am entirely yours, and I cannot rest until you are mine. There is simply no point in resisting me."

My heart and breath raced as he cupped my face in his large hands and rested his forehead against mine. "I'm going to kiss you now."

I trembled, "Elwood, I—"

Without hesitation, he drew my lips into his. Unwanted desire spread through me. To my shame, I did not resist him, and even welcomed his touch.

His hands glided to my back and pulled me in closer to him. My hands rested on his chest as I allowed myself to feel the pleasure his kiss brought. I was completely consumed by it.

Briefly, his lips pulled away, just grazing mine. "Do you love me, Isabel?"

Oh no...what am I doing? My breath quivered as I met his eyes. "I – I cannot do this."

"Yes, you can." Immediately he kissed me again, wrapping his arms around me.

PULL AWAY! A voice in my head screamed.

Finally, I pushed back with sudden resolve. "I'm sorry! This is wrong." I turned and stood from him as I caught my breath. "I must return inside."

What fire am I playing with?

Forcefully, he pulled me back to him as he stood to block my way. "No, no, no. Not until you admit you have feelings for me." He hooked his free arm around me, "Lower your guard and let us be together – say you'll be my wife! Why *fight* this any longer? Admit it...you want me to keep kissing you; what do you think that means?"

That I'm mad? I am like a rabbit kissing a fox!

Upon my silence, Elwood tried kissing me again, but I stepped back. He was quick to grab my waist firmly with both hands so I could not move away again. "Isabel, it's what we both want; kiss me, give into your passions

– they are not wrong. Our desires are the same. Simply allow yourself to love me and be my wife. Don't make a grown man beg, little bird."

He hovered his lips just above my own, inviting me to accept him. My heart pounded as it never had before; it would be so easy to give in.

Reluctantly, I turned my face away. "I was swept away in the moment, Elwood; I am bound to the promise I made to my father, and I have no wish to hurt you further. Please let me go – I *need* to return inside."

I tried to pull away from his embrace, even pushing against his hands, but could not budge him. His grip on my sides tightened to a point where it hurt me. I grimaced from how sharp and deep it felt, but he did not seem to notice.

"Swept away, you say? What a compliment!" He smiled, "Isabel, your father would understand – no more excuses, no more running away. Look into my eyes and give me your answer – will you marry me?"

I met his endless gaze. "I cannot say what you want me to. As flattered and moved as I am by your offer, I *can't* be your wife. I will not go against my own father. Can you not understand that? *Please* stop trying to force me. –My waist, Elwood, please release me, you're truly hurting me!"

He grew as stern as he was passionate. "I will not release you until your *heart* answers me. Not your mind; I grow tired of listening to its unrelenting excuses about your father, or trust, or any other wild reason it comes up with.

"Marrying me is *exactly* what your heart wants to do; it wants to be with me. I *know* this in my very blood. If your heart were to beat any harder, it would leap out from your bosom and crash into my own!"

"There is no other response to give! – Is it not enough that I am asking you to let me go?"

His face creased with irritation. "Don't you realize our union would greatly benefit your family? And that ostracizing me would only serve as a disadvantage to them?"

I felt as though the breeze itself froze in fear at his insinuation. "You would threaten my family the way you threatened my suitors?"

He sighed. "I *want* only the best for you and your family, but I will do whatever it takes for you to come to your damned senses."

Some of my worst fears were unfolding. All at once I knew he could not be reasoned with, yet I still tried. "Elwood, please, you are going to cause me to have another spell. Let me go. – I'll dance another dance with you of your choosing if we return inside. – It is inappropriate for us to linger here alone. *Please* release my waist; you are hurting me."

I looked away from his stare that began to look more filled with rage than love. How was I to escape him? I felt disgusted with myself for giving into his kisses.

He did not budge, merely shook his head and pulled me closer still to him, squeezing me harder. "Another moment will not ruin your reputation, my dear. Put an end to this for both of our sakes. What does your heart want? Does it want what's best for you, me, *and* your family? Will you be my bride?" He became adamant, *"Look at me!"*

I gasped at the sharp change of his tone and faced him.

His eyes plunged into mine; my hands pushed against his forearms to see if he would release me. He would not. I wondered whether I should scream out for help or if that would only make matters worse. Should I accept his proposal to spare my family?

His voice softened, "Say yes, little bird, and we may begin our new life together. Don't you see? I must have you for my own."

In contrast to his voice, his grip on my sides increased, causing me to gasp sharply. I was growing increasingly afraid of his unchecked strength. I worried what he would do if I rejected him again and tried to stall.

"Elwood, *please*, you are holding me too tightly, it hurts! Do not put me so on the spot – let us return inside and dance? They will surely start to wonder where we are. Permit me time to consider this?"

He only gripped me tighter as I winced again. "You *will* give me the answer I seek *now*. No more childish games. Admit you desire me. Admit you want to become my wife. Or would you rather live alone and see your family fall into ruins? What choice do you have? Only a foolish and selfish girl would continue to reject me."

How dare he? All at once I shoved against him with all my anger and might, nearly shouting, "I do not love you – *let me go!*"

I held my breath. Had I just condemned my family with my outburst?

Chapter Ten

THE EARL STARED AT me fiercely. His features twitched as he studied my countenance in the dim light. I braced myself for all the fury I had wrought.

Suddenly, a voice shattered the intensity of the moment. "Ah, Miss Dawson! There you are."

It was Mr. Porter! Immediately I felt relief and yet also shame for being in Elwood's grasp. What would he tell my brother? What would Lord Drake do to Mr. Porter?

Once Elwood saw another pair of eyes, he released me and I was free. My sides throbbed. Breathing heavily, I took a few steps towards Mr. Porter, feeling safer in his proximity.

I tried to act normally to prevent a fight or scene from occurring. "Mr. Porter! How good to see you again; have you met Lord Drake, the Earl of Aylesbury?"

He cocked his eyebrow. "No, can't say that I have. How do you do? Not any relation to Captain Francis Drake, are you?"

Anyone could see that his Lordship was quite incensed about being interrupted, but he managed to speak somewhat civilly. "He is a cousin of mine. – How do you know Miss Dawson?"

"Oh, we only just met the other day when I arrived. Jonathon and I are old Oxford friends and I was in town for business."

"I see. How delightful."

"Miss Dawson, your brother is looking for you."

I was fearful for Mr. Porter interjecting himself – however grateful I was for it. "We were just returning inside, weren't we, Lord Drake?" I said, trying to subdue him with geniality.

"Indeed." He agreed pertly.

Possessively, he enveloped his arm around me, and we walked back through the garden with Mr. Porter trailing closely behind.

Once inside, he released me and offered his arm which I took to prevent his temper resurfacing. By this point, my waist was feeling much relieved. That or my mind was too preoccupied to notice the pain.

Mr. Porter walked around us to the left, discreetly keeping an eye on me.

Spotting my brother standing next to Mama, I pointed them out to Elwood, "Ah, there is Jon over there! Will you excuse me while I see why he was searching for me?"

"Nonsense, we will go together as a couple."

He turned, lowering himself enough to whisper above my ear, "I do not believe what you said back there – I *know* you love me. Your face seemed as shocked at what you said as I was to hear it. Why you feel the need to lie to me *and* yourself about that, I don't know, but I felt it in the way you responded to my kisses; there is no fooling me. You *deeply* enjoyed them. I will *not* take no for an answer. Nor do I think you want me to, for the sake of your family, am I correct? You did not mean to say those words to me, did you?"

Panic seized me. "I am sorry; I spoke without thinking. – We will go see them together as a couple, Elwood." *Why was I apologizing?*

He smiled smugly. "We will pick up where we left off in the garden another time."

I nodded in response.

Mother looked most pleased to see us walking in public, arm in arm.

My brother, of course, tried and failed to completely hide his discomfort. "Where had you gone, Isabel? Christina Burton arrived and was looking for you."

Lord Drake cut in, "I'm afraid she was feeling unwell, one of those...*breathing spells*. I took care of her and brought her back in as soon as it had passed, however."

My face heated at the distorted truth but felt it important to play along. "He was most kind in looking out for me. Rest assured I am feeling much better now."

Mother immediately expressed her gratitude to the Earl.

I saw Mr. Porter out of the corner of my eye walking past us with a concerned expression. My brother took note of this as well.

I continued, "Christy! I was hoping she would make it back in time for this evening! Where did you see her?"

My brother gestured to the beverage table.

"You will excuse me, Elwood?" I had never used his given name in public before; I knew this would please him and perhaps soften his disposition.

He smiled affectionately. "Of course my dear!" He kissed my hand and set me free.

I felt a lightness being out of his presence and an eagerness to see Christy. We had been the dearest of friends for years, and her going away to Bath for the last three months had been the longest we'd ever been separated for.

As soon as she saw me, she quickly bridged the gap and embraced me.

"Oh, Isabel! How I have missed you!"

"And I you!" Our smiles could not be wider or our appearances more different.

Christy had a calm demeanor exuding from her brown eyes and darker hair, and her frame was more petite than my own.

"You must tell me everything about Bath! Did you enjoy every moment?"

We both picked up a cup of punch and found a seat on a settee in the adjoining room.

"Yes, although I missed you terribly. And I was such a bad friend that I barely wrote, even in response to your letters which I so dearly appreciated."

"I daresay you were a good deal busier than I."

She smirked. "I wouldn't say that...but my, yes! I could scarcely draw breath between the dancing and parties! My aunt was insatiable in finding me a husband. I barely had a moment to myself."

"And was your aunt successful?"

Christy beamed. "Very nearly. Mr. Adam Anderson. He all but proposed on my last day! He said he would call on me in a few days. I dare say, he only refrained so that he could ask father's permission first."

"Oh, how wonderful! What is he like?"

The next several minutes were a detailed summary of how they met, what he looked like, and how greatly she fancied him. – Until she could not contain her curiosity any longer.

Christy leaned in closer with a look equally full of concern as it was interest. "The rumors. Are they true?"

I played coy. "Rumors? What rumors?"

"*Isabel!* I know you know of what I speak. Are you betrothed to Lord Drake or not?"

I looked around to ensure there was no one listening. "It is true he has asked me, and even though my answer was no, he still pursues me most ardently."

Her eyebrows arched. "I think perhaps you should visit me on Monday so we may talk more freely on the subject. – Where are your gloves?"

"That would be delightful, yes! Oh... I must have left them in the garden. It's no matter. I doubt anyone will judge me for missing them."

I had no desire to risk going outside to look for them. I never wanted to be alone with the Earl again. I now understood why people feared him so.

Soon, Christy and I rejoined the dance floor. Catching my attention, Mr. Porter walked over and bowed, raising with a gleam in his eye.

"Miss Dawson, would you honor me with a dance?"

Christy whispered as she walked behind me, *"Much better choice."*

I stifled a smirk.

Meeting his gaze, I lowered my voice, "Not that I don't wish to, Mr. Porter, however, Lord Drake is already vexed this evening. I should regret it if I put you in harm's way. I believe my brother warned you about dancing with me, did he not?"

Looking down and back up to my eyes, he held out his hand to me. "I am not afraid of the Earl. If it eases your concern, he has nothing to threaten me with. As for your brother...I know he means well, but I am my own man. It is, however, completely *your* choice, Miss Dawson, whether you would like to dance with me or not."

I felt warm all over as his eyes shimmered into mine. I liked Mr. Porter very much indeed. Glancing around the room, I did not see Lord Drake, only my brother watching curiously from afar.

A smile spread over my lips as I placed my hand in his. "I would, yes."

His expression matched my own. "As would I."

Leading me onto the floor, his presence elicited no anxiety in me, but instead, a certain delightful ease.

The music began as our right hands met above our heads; his left rested across my abdomen as we circled. Stealing another glance into his eyes filled my core with an incandescent sensation.

"So tell me, Miss Dawson, are you enjoying the party?"

"I find it is improving as the night goes on."

Lowering our hands, mine to his arms and his to my waist, he appeared intrigued by my response. "Is it presumptuous of me to be flattered by that?"

I could not control the corners of my mouth from rising. "You may be flattered, if you like."

The tempo of the music quickened as I danced around him. "How are you such an exquisite dancer when you are scarcely allowed to dance with anyone except that old tyrant?"

I giggled. "That's terrible to say, Mr. Porter!"

He sported a cheeky grin, "Is it?"

"Perhaps not *so* very."

We danced in a circle around each other before returning to our first position again as he responded, "I think you've put a spell on me, Miss Dawson; I do not typically enjoy dancing so well!"

I drew my face closer to his as I whispered playfully, "A papist and a witch? What *would* the Queen say?"

He grinned.

Twirling me around himself, he met my eyes again. "I'm sure you're keenly aware of this Miss Dawson, but I would regret not telling you how remarkably beautiful you are this evening."

"You are rather handsome tonight as well."

"At least in comparison to the first time we met?"

"You *were* an amusing sight to behold."

"I'll comfort myself with the fact that you found me amusing at least."

"An optimist? How refreshing!"

We placed opposite hands together above our heads and circled for a moment.

"Is it? Well, I suppose anyone would be refreshing compared to Lord Drake's company."

"Please do be careful, Mr. Porter; you have painted quite the target on your back. – I am not worth endangering yourself for."

He raised an eyebrow at me. "I gave you the choice of dancing with me – perhaps you should give me the choice of deciding whether you are worth *endangering* myself for or not...which by the way, I daresay that you are."

"You flatter me, Mr. Porter. You're either a very brave man or a foolish one. In all seriousness, you don't know him like I do. He suffers no moral quandary about getting what he wants."

His expression turned compassionate. "I'm sorry you've had to know him at all. There's a bit of fool in every brave man, though, don't you think?"

He twirled me in place before we rejoined with his hand on my waist.

I discovered that I very much enjoyed his touch. "I suspect you are a very brave sort of man."

"Is that a compliment, or are you trying to say I'm twice the fool?"

"I suppose that remains to be seen!"

He spun me about him before I exchanged dance partners. Looking up to see who my partner was, it was none other than Lord Drake. I felt a cold stake enter my abdomen as I tried to recover the look of surprise on my face.

"Isabel. Don't think that this counts as the second dance you promised me."

"Surely not, my Lord!"

"Were you so eager to dance that you could not wait for me?"

Sweat pricked my scalp as I danced around him, giving me time to form a reply, "—I fear I could not find you, Elwood. Please do not be cross."

"If ever I am cross with you, know that it would be impossible for me to remain that way for long."

As the music shifted, he reluctantly passed me back to Mr. Porter, locking him into a brief, but cold glare. The Earl's dance partner – Miss Smith – was oblivious to what was occurring.

"Welcome back!" Mr. Porter offered, trying to lighten the mood.

"Thank you." I whispered, "Is he staring at us?"

He nodded after checking over my head. "Yes, but let him. This is *our* dance, is it not?"

I felt a foreboding unease spread through me. "I am afraid it will have to be our last; I do not wish to poke the dragon further."

He gave a short nod. "I think you are correct about that. Shame too...I could easily have danced with you all night." He winked at me.

"Sadly, Mr. Porter, my entire situation is rather a shame." The music stopped. "Thank you for the dance, though; I enjoyed it as much as I thought I would." I smiled with a curtsy and walked to the beverage table.

Taking a sip of some punch, I turned around to see Lord Drake talking with Mr. Porter. *Oh no.*

My brother joined me. "Dancing with Mr. Porter? I'm sure *Elwood* just loved seeing that. We don't need to imagine what they're discussing, do we?"

"I am quite sure he won't be the *only* one getting an earful about that this evening."

Jonathon looked concerned. "Isabel... Mr. Porter told me that when he went to check on you that you were being placed in a difficult position. I don't like it for you one bit. Makes me angry and want to take a blade to him. I think it's time I had a conversation with him to leave my sister alone."

"And make him point the tip of his sword at our family? Ruin Anna's prospects, and perhaps make himself a nuisance in other areas of our life? No, Jon. I appreciate you wanting to protect me, I do. But this is between him and I – that is safest."

His brow furrowed. "Are you considering his offer?"

"He mentioned it would be *disadvantageous* to my family if I turn him down again. I will protect my family, Jon. Your work is too important, especially right now. I told him just this evening that I did not love him, and it did nothing to dissuade him, he only reminded me of the threat he made to our family."

I thought it best to leave out how frightened I was becoming of him and how he hurt my waist in the garden.

Jon clenched his jaw. "He's a knave, Isabel. You cannot marry him. Repercussions be damned! Our family has weathered his wrath once before, and we shall do so again! – What if I told you that Mr. Porter is interested in courting you?"

"Language, Jonathan!"

"Sorry, sister. It's only that he makes my blood boil."

"Has Mr. Porter...spoken of me?"

Jon rolled his eyes. "What do *you* think of him?"

"I rather like him. But what of Lord Drake?"

"Good – I thought you might. Mr. Porter may just be far enough removed from this area that the Earl will be unable to gain any knowledge about him. And yes, little sister. Mr. Porter seems to be taken by you. Are you part fairy that you should make men fall in love with you so easily? I should warn you, he is closer to commoner than gentleman, but something tells me you would not mind?"

Just as I was about to answer, we spotted Elwood coming towards us.

"Excuse me, Jonathon, your sister promised me another dance! You wouldn't mind my stealing her away, would you?"

Jon shifted his weight with a forced smile. "If you must!"

Curtsying, I took Lord Drake's hand to the dance floor. I scanned the room for Mr. Porter and found him in conversation with a few men from the military, occasionally glancing in my direction.

The music played. "Exactly why did you bother dancing with *Mr. Porter*?" Elwood asked, getting right to the point. "He seems to be a great no one from nowhere!"

We gently pushed our open palms together above our heads and stepped to the left and then to the right of the other. "I was being polite – he is a dear friend of my brother's. Are you really so very jealous?"

"I would like to say I'm not, but I think the truth is rather obvious. I don't want you dancing with other men! Especially when you haven't even given me an answer. It's rude to keep a man waiting for so long; don't you know that? It's driving me quite mad!"

His right hand moved to the middle of my back and guided me into a circle with the other dancers.

I turned to whisper, "Madness or not, I *did* try to tell you my answer in the garden...and in the library."

He moved his hand down and gripped my waist again, causing me to shrink. "Despite what your beautiful mouth says, I know the truth you struggle so greatly to conceal." He tried to look at me seductively, but those feelings were no longer returned.

"Your grip is hurting me, Elwood."

He loosened his grasp. "I'm sorry – I forget what a delicate flower you are."

We switched partners and rejoined. I could tell he was fighting back annoyance at my replies. "Perhaps we should excuse ourselves back outside so we may speak uninterrupted? It would be a shame if your brother's business deals all fell through, or if Anna did not have a selection of suitors when she came of age."

I realize Jon told me not to worry about the repercussions – however it was impossible not to. I looked up into his eyes; he was very serious.

"I think we've had enough time alone for one evening."

His stare smoldered. "My patience grows thin, my dove."

I swallowed hard as I looked away. "I am becoming rather famished, I hope supper will be served soon."

"I struggle to find my appetite these past days." His tone suggested that he was displeased at my changing the subject.

"Aren't you well?"

He sighed and looked down at me. "Isabel, you have my heart in utter turmoil. I'm afraid that takes its toll on a man's stomach."

"Oh...I *am* sorry for causing you distress."

"I can suffer anything for you, my dear. I forget that you are much younger than myself and not as sure of yourself as a person yet. If I have waited years, what is a day or longer to me? I know you are worth the wait."

I wasn't sure how to respond. Had he not *just* been demanding my immediate answer? I wished to turn the subject from myself.

"Have there been no other romantic interests for you besides me over the years?"

We twirled around each other and switched partners for a moment before coming together again.

"No one of consequence, no. It has always been you and you alone who lifted me from my period of mourning. The pretty little bird singing melodies to my heart."

The dance slowed; our hands formed a half circle above our heads while his other wrapped about my waist. He pulled me in closer than was customary. I confess that his words touched me. "You are sweet sometimes, Elwood."

His eyebrows curved up. "Only sometimes?"

"Other times you are intense and unrelenting; it's as though you possess two natures."

I spun around him according to the dance with my dress fanning out in unison with all the other gowns before he replied, "I suppose I'm a complicated man."

At this point, his lips hovered near my ear, "though, do not try and deny that you're very much attracted to my *intense* nature." He grazed his cheek against mine. "I have felt your breath quiver as I kiss you."

I felt my cheeks flush and turned my face away from him, mortified by the recent memories. How could I have been so weak? So foolish!

He continued, "It is not something to be ashamed of, my dear. Love *is* intense – you would not reciprocate my feelings when we kiss if you did not love me."

"Please, Elwood, may we speak of another subject?"

A corner grin played on his lips. "Why? It was *so* deeply pleasurable, I can scarcely think of anything else!"

"So I gathered."

"Your guilt-ridden nature perplexes me! Can you not simply enjoy my company without punishing yourself after? Do you think your papa shakes his head at you from heaven?"

"Yes, I imagine he does so whenever I am alone with you."

He released an airy chuckle. "What can I do to ease this burden from your mind, my dove?"

"I'm afraid I do not possess that knowledge, my Lord."

The music finally ended as the dance came to its last movement. Supper was announced. I exhaled, grateful to have been rescued from this conversation. *Thank you, God!*

Gathering around the oblong table, decorated with candles and flowers, we all took our seats. I'm sure, dear reader, that you will find the irony in the seating arrangement.

There I was with Lord Drake to my left and Mr. Porter to my right! Sometimes I wonder at God's sense of humor.

My brother sat next to Mr. Porter and mother next to him. Christy and her father were across from me – I could tell she found the irony amusing.

I smiled awkwardly at both gentlemen as supper began with soup and delicious rolls served with butter.

There were about forty guests; a mixture of Protestants and secret Catholics alike.

"Why is he seated next to you, my dear?" Lord Drake whispered pensively in my ear.

I whispered back. "I am not sure, perhaps there was a mistake? He is my brother's after all."

He "harrumphed" in response. Looking down the table, I witnessed my brother with a large grin on his face, which told me everything I needed to know. Somehow he had been responsible for Mr. Porter's seating arrangement.

Elwood was not finished complaining, "Having someone with *no* breeding whatsoever sitting so near us is certainly an oversight of the Elharts' planning."

I hoped Mrs. Elhart had not overheard Lord Drake complaining; they were the only family sitting above our placement. It would grieve me if my mother's friend was slighted after hosting so many gatherings.

I lowered my voice as I replied to him, "Do not let it ruin the evening; it is of no matter. Are you not pleased enough that I am sitting beside you?"

"How right you are, my dear. What could bother me so long as you are near?"

There was much conversation at the table, and it wasn't long before Mr. Porter added to it. "I say, Miss Dawson, those pearls are very pretty, are they an heirloom?"

"Thank you. From my grandmother, on my mother's side, yes."

Lord Drake reached for my hand that rested on my lap. It made my body rigid as he whispered again, "Do not entertain that *boy* any further. He can never offer you what I have waiting for you."

I responded quietly, "Elwood, you have made it clear that no other suitors exist but yourself. Mr. Porter is a friend, one who will be on his way back to Portsmouth shortly. Please do not be irritated by my politeness towards him."

He squeezed my hand before releasing it. "Good. I would hate to hurt someone you considered a friend." He smiled as he picked up his spoon to eat.

I feared my brother was being too optimistic about my situation. If Mr. Porter had no information that could be used against him, he would resort to violence. I stared uncomfortably at my soup as I tried to find my appetite, worry filling me anew.

The main courses were soon brought out; pheasant, ham and stuffed fish with roasted potatoes, and various vegetables. The servants went around to each person offering generous helpings and refilling wine. I myself was on my second glass. I found it very helpful for calming my thoughts. And tonight they required additional assistance.

"I did not realize you cared for wine so much, Miss Dawson." Lord Drake quietly posed to me. "You and your family should really come visit my castle and try some from my store of it – I think you'd be well pleased! I always make sure to bring back the finest from Paris whenever I visit."

"That's very generous of you. I shall discuss it with my family on the journey home."

"Wonderful! It's been many years since you were there."

I recalled the last time being the funeral of his wife and infant son. "I was just a small child then! I'm afraid I do not recall your home very well, except the enormous staircase you have inside."

"Yes, it is grand, but a real beast to climb every day. My great grandfather failed to think that through."

"I say," said an older gentleman sitting across from Lord Drake by the name of Mr. Fairway, "you never hold a party at your house anymore! You should, you've been mourning long enough. Let some life back inside those walls!"

His Lordship smiled and glanced at me before responding, "Should I ever have reason to celebrate again, I assure you there will be many, Richard."

A servant came by and refilled my glass with more wine, and Mr. Porter's.

Mr. Fairway engaged Lord Drake's attention for a few moments – long enough for me to whisper to Mr. Porter, "Is it time to leave yet?"

He smirked. "You've read my mind."

When Elwood looked back to me, my face was already poised away from Mr. Porter and smiling at him instead.

The wine was beginning to have a lovely effect on me; I felt calm, even jovial.

I noticed that despite his apparent lacking appetite that he had previously mentioned, Lord Drake had second helpings of most everything tonight.

He engaged in conversation with the military men diagonal to us. "Yes! You men deserve all the mead, wine, and beer your bellies can hold! Those dirty Papists have been making your lives hell, haven't they?"

I tried to keep my face neutral as they continued with raised glasses. "Quite right, my Lord! We'll have them flushed out before too long. Just can't fathom how more of their foul priests keep getting in. Filthy spies if you ask my opinion, sir."

There were several voices who clamored in agreement.

I glanced towards Christy – a fellow *dirty Papist,* and we exchanged many words with our eyes as only good friends can.

This evening could not end soon enough. And then I had a rather mischievous thought.

I feigned a look of concern and directed it to Lord Drake. "Spies? Do you think we are in very much danger? Should we be worried?"

"Do I think they mean us harm? Absolutely. Why else would they continuously send more and more in? And under the banner of *religion*, quite cowardly, really. But! You need not concern your feminine mind with such worries, Miss Dawson; our military does an excellent job at eradicating the vermin!"

Various exclamations of approval and glasses cheering reigned across the table, even though a few were for maintaining pretenses only. However, I noticed a couple Protestants did not join in. Not everyone agreed with the Queen's treatment of Catholics.

Christy gave me a look that suggested I stop. So of course, I continued. I blame it on the wine, really.

"That is considerate of you to be concerned for my *feminine mind*, Lord Drake. However, does the Queen herself not possess a feminine mind as well? And still manages to govern us all?"

There was a series of low chuckles, including from Mr. Porter and my family.

At first, the Earl was annoyed but when he saw my smirk, he could not help but grin himself. "A fine point, Miss Dawson. And a fine job she does!"

I raised my glass. "To Queen Elizabeth! May God bless her and bless our dear country!"

In all one voice the room echoed, "*To good Queen Bess!*" Followed by the clinking of many glasses.

Chapter Eleven

After the meal was over, I stood from the table with the rest of the guests. Lord Drake hastily offered his arm to guide me back to the dance hall. The musicians were already preparing to play again; I simply couldn't fathom dancing anymore tonight.

Lord Drake glanced down towards me as he placed his hand over mine. "You know, I had hoped to announce our engagement during supper."

I was also growing quite weary of being hounded. Perhaps more so now, that I felt I was being forced into accepting his offer; I would delay the inevitable for as long as possible. If only to spite him. "I am sorry to disappoint you."

"It is of no matter, I suppose. I'm confident that one day soon, you will permit me that honor."

I stopped and faced him. "I'm afraid I am rather tired, Elwood; it's time for me to retire for the evening."

His eyes widened. "What? Already? The party isn't half over yet! The card games and the dancing will continue for hours still!"

"And yet, I am ready to return home. You have given me much to think over, after all." I forced a small smile as I removed my hand from his arm, hoping this reason would appease him.

He nodded. "Allow me to take you back myself; let your mother and brother stay and enjoy the rest of the evening. It would be my pleasure to escort you home."

"So that you might squeeze an answer from me in your carriage? A *kind* offer, but I think it's best if I gather Mama and Jonathon and leave with them. She will no doubt be getting tired, and my brother hates to dance, so I do not think either will mind." I curtsied. "Good night, my Lord."

He gathered my hand and kissed it gently. "Are you sure I cannot entice you to stay for one more dance, if not a carriage ride? I have so looked forward to this evening with you and do not wish to see it end so abruptly."

"You are not told, *no*, very often, are you?"

"...I believe you have told me *no* more than my own parents and governess ever did...or really anyone. It's quite confounding, really."

"Well, I suppose that explains why you're so out of practice at accepting it for an answer." I curtsied again, "Good night, Elwood."

"Good night, my paramour." He kissed my hand once more. "I will call upon you in two days. I hope that will be sufficient time for you to gather your thoughts? Perhaps you would do me the honor of having my ring upon your finger when I arrive?"

His threats flashed vividly before me. I felt sick upon knowing my answer would have to be yes.

"Perhaps." I obliged with a weak smile and walked away to say my farewells. First to our hosts, Christy, and a few other friends until I came upon Mr. Porter.

"Heading out for the evening, Miss Dawson?"

I smiled with a light sigh. "Yes, it has been a long night."

"Indeed."

I glanced around me before continuing in a lower tone, "Thank you, by the way, for coming to find me earlier; I appreciate it."

His expression was very kind. "I only wish I had come to find you sooner."

I thought briefly how awkward it might have been had Mr. Porter came upon us while Lord Drake was kissing me. *Very* grateful indeed, that he came when he did...and not any sooner.

"You came when I needed you the most."

Mr. Porter turned and walked with me towards the door a bit. "You were absolutely brilliant at dinner; I nearly choked on my bite of ham!"

I giggled. "It's fun to stir things up now and then, isn't it?"

"It is." He bowed his head and kissed my hand gently. "Sleep well, Miss Dawson."

From the corner of my vision I could see Lord Drake eyeing us. I smiled and nodded towards him, hoping that my acknowledging him would appease his irritation.

The Earl's heavy stare continued to follow me as I left Mr. Porter to herd my family outside. He leaned in the doorway, watching me until I was seated inside our white carriage. He waved to me, and I nodded my head goodbye. There was something very eerie about Lord Drake as he hovered there. I was eager for the carriage to take us out of sight.

The horses finally started and we were off down the road. I exhaled a sigh of relief. Dear Mama was snoring within three minutes; a personal record.

"You just *had* to switch the seating arrangements around, didn't you?" I accused Jonathon in hushed tones.

He grinned like a mischievous little boy. "What? At least you had someone tolerable there too."

"If only *you* were tolerable!" I teased.

"And what was that stunt *you* pulled at dinner? I thought I was going to have a heart attack!"

I laughed. "It helps throw them off our scent...and it was *quite* entertaining. My only regret is that I couldn't see your reaction as I spoke!"

"I admit, I found it amusing after my heart stopped pounding."

"I thought Christy was going to leap across the table."

He chuckled and wiped the corner of his eye. "So I was thinking of inviting Mr. Porter over for supper tomorrow; what do you think?"

Under different circumstances, I'd have been excited by this. How could I be now? "I would not be opposed to his company."

Jonathon continued on, oblivious to the hesitation in my voice, "He owns a cottage near a ship's port and fishing village about a hundred or so miles from here. He also has a maid with a groundskeeper. Has some livestock too."

I pursed my lips. I needed to explain my intentions before he continued any further, "Jon...I *do* love the beach, but that is quite far. I fear Mama would not approve of trading a castle for a cottage. Yet, beyond those reservations, I must confess that I'm not convinced such optimism is warranted."

Jonathon gave me a serious look. "I will help you to win over Mother; do not fret about that. Daniel Porter is a good man and not the sort that I'd have to be worried about being alone with my sister. –Why didn't you tell me it was so bad with the Earl? Mr. Porter said when he came upon you, you were yelling at him to let you go!"

I sighed. "I do not doubt whether Mr. Porter is a good man or not, *he* is not the issue. Pragmatically, I know that I must marry Lord Drake. Truth be told, there is a part of Elwood that is very charming and generous; he is not *completely* malicious. While he is not my first choice, I feel people arrange far worse matches every day."

My brother was aghast. "Why have your thoughts changed so much? Were you not just asking me about Mr. Porter, not two hours ago?"

"Jon, please understand? I am terrified of what would happen to our family if I reject Lord Drake's offer *again*. He also made a point of threatening Mr. Porter after his...*impetuousness* tonight. I think he means to injure him. Would it not benefit and even save us all if I accept him? Knowing that your lives are at stake because of me is eating away at my heart."

Jon shifted uneasily in his seat. "While I sympathize, your logic is flawed. It's time to be bold and stop trying to play nice with the Earl. We will survive whatever he throws our way. Tell him no again. Have faith."

I shook my head. "He is not fond of *no*. In fact, he said he is coming to call upon me in two day's time and hopes my answer will be yes by then. If it is not... I am certain he will begin making his threats our realities." I played with the hem of my sleeve. "I appreciate your concern, I do, but I should accept his offer; it would be best for all involved. I feel I am only delaying something which may be fated."

Jon sighed and bent forward so his elbows rested upon his knees. "My dear sister, no one wishes for you to sacrifice your happiness or your very life for us. Not to mention what my future nieces and nephews would have to endure with that recreant as a father – could you imagine? The brutality they'd inherit alone! Do not let him make you so intimidated. Turn him down as many times as it takes. We have accumulated enough wealth that a plummet will not make us homeless. If our father survived him, we can too. Have you no trust that I can protect us? – And believe me when I say that Mr. Porter is more than capable of protecting himself."

The carriage jostled over some divets in the road; we both glanced at Mama to see if it would wake her. A prompt return of her buzzing snores confirmed her slumber.

I leaned forward. "It isn't that I don't trust you! I know you would do all you can. Yet, at what cost? What if he ransacks the house? What of the priests we hide? Shall Anna be thrown into prison with the rest of us? Do you not comprehend how much we have to lose? My marriage would be a small sacrifice when weighing the many merits."

His brow steeped. "Do you not *comprehend* how much *you* have to lose? Please, think of your children's well-being, if you will not consider your own misery.

"I *will* do what is necessary to protect us. I could not live knowing you were bound to such a man. Can you honestly tell me that you desire a life with him? That you think he would make a spiritually adequate head of the house? Is he the sort of man you'd wish to submit to?"

The questions he posed struck me hard. It made me grow in appreciation of how well he cared for me; it truly touched my heart. I'd be lying if I said I disagreed with him. Yet, I knew Lord Drake would destroy all who stood in his way of possessing me. "Of course not. But I could find ways to manage, ways to love him and be happy, ways to still be Catholic and raise my children in the Faith. Perhaps you could even use me as a spy?"

My brother reached across and held my hand. "Isabel, you are worrying me. What else has he done to you? I feel you are not disclosing everything that occurred. The sister I know would never risk the souls of her children to be for fear of a fight. You are smart enough to know how impossible imparting the Faith to them would be under those circumstances. You become depressed when you do not have the sacraments after a few weeks; how long do you think you'd have to wait being Countess of Aylesbury? Years?"

I was losing this debate. "I agree with all the points you've made...and yet, there is one undeniable fact which remains. Lord Drake will pursue me until his dying breath; he will never relent. I do not wish to see anyone I care about be harmed on my account, not when it is avoidable."

He bit the corner of his lip as he pondered what to say next. Nodding his head, he charged an earnest gaze. "I understand. You want to protect us. I admire your courage, however misguided it is. I am unmoved, however. I utterly forbid you to marry that man. You promised Papa you would not and I know Father Ingles does not support such a notion. In fact, I have it on good authority that he is quite in favor of Mr. Porter as well!"

My mouth hung open a bit. "How would you know that?"

He ignored my question. "Where you find peace is where you find God's will. Do you have *any* peace with the notion of marrying Lord Drake?"

I thought deeply for a moment as I weighed my soul, "No. None."

Jon's shoulders relaxed with a sigh. "Then you have your answer. I will be with you every step of the way, sister. Do not cave into such odious threats. With God, all things are possible, are they not?"

A faint smile bowed across my lips. "I suppose you are correct...as usual, Jonathon. We will try it your way."

He leaned back, visibly relieved. "Good! Thank you, Isabel. You'll see – all will be well, whether you decide to take an interest in Mr. Porter or not."

I nodded. My trepidations were not fully alleviated; however, I did allow hope to sprout. Maybe there was a way out from under his grasp that I could not yet see. I could not deny that submitting to Elwood as a husband for the rest of my life sounded more terrifying than prison.

"You *do* enjoy the company of Mr. Porter, do you not?" Jon asked.

"Why do you ask? Have you been encouraging him behind my back, Jonathon?"

I don't typically witness my brother squirm, but always make a point to enjoy the rare moments when it does occur. "Uh, er, I have spoken greatly to your credit...and perhaps agreed that I felt he would be a suitable replacement for Lord Drake."

My tone sang vexation while my lips buried a grin. "*Mm-hmm.* You've been playing matchmaker just as shamelessly as Father Ingles! I might have known."

Jon sighed. "Do not be cross, Isabel. Are you not attracted to his good character? I do not believe I have misread the situation...I was sure you favored him! Did you not say as much?"

"Fortunately for you, I admire many things about Mr. Porter...so I suppose I shan't be cross at yours and Father's meddling ways."

Jon breathed another sigh of relief. "I ought to warn him of how you take such a twisted delight in teasing!"

I giggled. "And ruin my joy when he discovers it for himself?"

"Perhaps wait until *after* the wedding so he does not change his mind."

"Whatever you think is best, brother."

He scoffed as a chuckle escaped a second later.

As we drew near to the house, Mama began to wake. "Oh my! Must have dozed off. It was such splendid evening, was it not?"

Jonathon and I exchanged smiles as I answered, "It always is with the Elharts."

Stepping out of the carriage, I experienced a surprisingly sharp pain wrapping around my waist.

"Are you alright, Isabel?" Mama inquired, hearing me gasp.

"I'm sure it's nothing."

Later, when Lily was helping untie my corset, I examined where the pain was coming from. Climbing the stairs had proven to be rather unpleasant, thus increasing my concern.

Spreading my nightgown's buttons, revealed a hand-sized purple bruise from where Lord Drake had squeezed me. I checked the other side and a smaller, though equally discolored, bruise was there as well.

Lily was horrified. "We must tell your mama or your brother about this." Lily said, green eyes wide like a perfect circle.

I had never seen such grotesque bruising. They were repulsive. Part of me, however, felt relieved when I saw them. What better sign from God could I ask for? I could never marry Elwood; my guilt finally began to retreat.

Then I realized if Mama saw this, she too would not wish me to marry him! Two of my prayers were being answered through these hideous contusions. Nodding, I obliged Lily's offer to go and fetch her.

With Mama, however, came Jonathon.

Mama gasped to see the marks once my nightgown's buttons were separated, "Lord Drake did this to you? *When?*"

"In the garden when I wished to go inside...but he...did not want me to until I agreed to marry him. Then again on the dance floor, to illustrate a point, I suppose."

Mama immediately asked Lily to fetch an ointment.

As Jon peered over Mama's shoulders, he made a sound that could only be described as a growl. I have never seen such rage in my brother's face. "That miserable, fatuous, prick!"

"Jon...do not be rash, please." I tied my house coat around me. "While I share those sentiments, my waist will heal."

Mother was scarlet with an anger that matched my brother's. "It seems I was deceived, and your father was right about him! He is *not* welcome in our home any longer. You will *not* see him again."

She turned to my brother. "Jon, your sister is right, though. Beating up an Earl is not the right course of action. It will only stoke the fire."

Jon's fists were clenched and shaking by his legs. "He *deserves* more than a beating! Isabel, you will write him a letter telling him no, pack up every gift he has ever given you and I will deliver it to him tomorrow myself. I *dare* him to handle me as he has you."

Mama and I exchanged looks and she nodded in agreement.

I was worried what the Earl would do to my brother. "Please don't do anything foolish, Jon, promise me?"

He loosened his collar. "I will do my best not to lay my hands around his throat. Why did you not tell us at the party he had hurt you? How could you have withheld this?"

"I- I didn't wish to alarm you or make the situation worse. Honestly, I did not realize how severe it was until I was getting out of the carriage." I felt an odd pang of guilt. Was this not partly my fault? I held my arms, "In truth, I don't think he meant to hurt me. He must not have realized his strength. – I was vexing him terribly."

Mama took a step closer to me. "Enough to leave bruises of *that* size and color? Do not make excuses for a vile man like that. Do not let him deceive you into thinking he is a better man than his actions have proven him to be. How many times have you vexed your brother, and he has never laid a hand upon you? Regardless of what some people think, a real man of God never lays a hand on a woman except to help her or love her."

Tears welled in my eyes. I sometimes forget how incredibly wise my Mother is. She wrapped me into a gentle hug; her tender embrace comforting me as it always had.

My brother came over and kissed my head sweetly as he put his arms around our shoulders. While his anger was still burning, his tone at least had cooled. "He will rue today, Isabel; I swear he will never lay a finger on you again. What a terrible brother I have been to let this go on. If *I* were not a Christian man, I would duel him as soon as the sun rose."

I turned to him. "You musn't think like that; it is not your fault anymore than it is mine. You are a wonderful brother and exactly the kind God knew I'd need. There will be *no* more talk of dueling."

Mama nodded in agreement.

"Mother, may I stay home from church tomorrow?"

"Oh! Of course my darling girl. I dare Lord Drake's men to fine us for your absence!"

Anna appeared at the door with an enormous yawn. "Why is everyone in here?" She yawned again. "You all promised to tell me about the party, remember?" Each of us took turns exchanging the yawn, and Mama took her hand and tucked her in for bed.

Jonathon sat down with me on my bed. "Will you feel safe by yourself tonight? Shall you come and sleep on the floor of my room as you did when we were children?"

I chuckled. "That feels as if it were a lifetime ago! I remember how you'd leave a spare pillow and blanket on the floor for me. Your presence was always enough to keep my nightmares at bay."

He smiled warmly and pulled me into a side-hug. "Those memories will always be some of the closest in my heart."

"Mine as well. I do appreciate you never accidentally stepping on me in the mornings."

He laughed. "Would you care to join me in the drawing room for a game of cards?"

"Tomorrow, perhaps. I'm exhausted. I think I shall fall asleep before my head reaches the pillow."

"Good. Rest." He went to stand, but I reached out for his hand. "Jon, what if he retaliates against our family in a way we cannot survive?"

"Let him bring the whole of England against us. You will never have to be subjected to another moment of that swine's presence again."

"I love you, Jon, I hope we can find our way through this."

Just then, Lily came back with the salve for my bruises.

"I love you too, little sister. Sleep, knowing you are safe."

When I was alone, I felt an incredible sense of relief; I was not going to have to marry Lord Drake or even speak with him again! I could finally put everything behind me. I had only to seal this chapter shut and pray it does not catch fire.

Chapter Twelve

Father Ingles was offering Mass at half past noon today and was in need of more communion bread, wine, and fresh water. I dressed myself quietly in a purple dress and went to gather the supplies onto a tray before the house awoke. Kneeling for morning prayers had proved quite arduous; I was moving a bit slower than normal today.

Finally making it down the hall, I wondered if Father Ingles had finished the last couple of books I brought down to him. I decided to pick a couple more from the library first, just in case.

Silently closing the library door, I crept into Papa's study, and wondered how long we would continue to call it his. Forever felt fitting.

Balancing the books, water, candle, and Mass supplies down the narrow staircases behind the wall was challenging. And heavy. My arms grew tired much faster today.

Coming to the door, I knocked the secret knock and waited for what seemed longer than usual.

A smile spread on my face when Mr. Porter opened the door to greet me. "I'm surprised to see you – good morning!" I said.

He took the tray and had me come inside.

"I felt better staying to make sure you had extra protection, if need be. Your brother rode out to see me last night and filled me in at the pub. Are you feeling any better today? I'm so sorry he did that to you. Makes me wish I had gone with my initial instinct and pummeled the man!"

My heart melted a bit. "It is nothing that will not heal with a little time. Thank you, Mr. Porter, your presence is very appreciated."

"I hoped it would be."

Father Ingles walked out of the chapel door. "Ah, Miss Dawson! I was terribly disturbed to hear what Lord Drake's idea of courting has been like." He took my hand comfortingly. "Be sure that I will be remembering you in my Masses and rosaries to ensure your safety and healing."

"Thank you very much, Father. – I've brought you more literature if you're in need?"

"Perfect timing! I'll fetch the others for you to return."

Mr. Porter set the tray inside the chapel and came back out with Father and the books.

"There we are," Father said, handing them to me. "So far you have excellent taste, what is next on Miss Dawson's reading list?"

"*Imitation of Christ* and *The Canterbury Tales*. I hope you like them as much as I did."

"Oh, most excellent! Thank you, my dear. I hope you'll both excuse me as I take some spiritual reading time with the Lord."

Father retreated back into the chapel. Something about his tone indicated additional motives. Not that I minded being left alone with Mr. Porter, however.

"I don't think I've ever met a woman who is as well-read as you, Miss Dawson."

I looked up to his face to try and decipher whether this was looked upon in a good manner or not. He seemed intrigued.

"My papa had such a great love for reading that it was impossible not to share in his passion for it. You do not think it wholly improper of me?"

"Oh, I've never had as great a care as I should for societal rules. Why should a woman not read if it suits her? I think it would make her a more interesting wife to converse with."

"I agree! Papa always felt it was unfair to keep the world of reading away from women. I am very grateful for his idealistic opinions."

"I feel your father and I would have agreed on a lot. Are you in much pain?" He asked, nearing closer.

The truth was that it hurt if I breathed too deeply or turned at all, but I did not wish to worry him. "Only now and then."

"Really? Because I've had my side bruised in fights before, and it was awful just to turn or laugh too hard! Can't fathom your discomfort in your dresses, the way they are."

"It is...uncomfortable." I admitted, "However, it's a good sacrifice to offer up for the conversion of our English Protestants."

He smiled. "Indeed it is. Admirable that you try to downplay it, Miss Dawson."

"I must be going for now; the servants will be moving about shortly."

"Oh – before you go..."

"Yes?"

"I wonder if perhaps you would take a stroll with me after Mass? – Just around your gardens, that is? So long as you're feeling up to it?"

The edge of nervousness in his voice endeared him to me. "A stroll? That sounds wonderful, Mr. Porter."

He kissed my hand with a smile. "Until later then."

His eyes had so much light in them that they seemed to glisten, maybe even more so in the candlelight. I could stare into them for hours and never feel at ill ease. The contrasts between Lord Drake and Mr. Porter were quite stark, in nearly every way. *Thanks be to God.*

Returning up through the walls and closing the bookshelf, I could hear the servants. I had spent too much time with Mr. Porter. The way up had been much more painful than the way down. Each step I took forced my corset to graze or push in on the bruises, which did not help me move swiftly.

They would be arriving to set the curtains back and tidy anything up in moments. After concealing the books in my desk, I decided to sit down and begin writing my letter to Lord Drake. It must be firm...but also kind as not to elicit avoidable rage.

"Dear Lord Drake,

After I arrived home last evening, I discovered two large bruises at my waist from where your hands had gripped me. Recalling everything that happened, even when I pleaded with you to stop repeatedly, you only squeezed me harder. You frightened me. Any trust I had in you is unequivocally broken.

I hope inflicting such injury upon me was not your intention. Nevertheless, I am suffering acutely from it today.

The bruises were brought to the attention of my mother and brother; they were both horrified and deeply concerned.

Mother wishes me to convey that you are no longer welcome here. This is echoed very strongly by my brother. Myself as well.

I'm sorry to cause pain or distress, but I must speak plainly. I am not in love with you, Lord Drake, nor do I ever see a future with you. Please do not try to change my mind anymore; it would be futile."

The doors opened. "Oh! Miss Dawson!" Grace curtsied. "How long have you been up for? Ah, writing again, I see!"

Grace was one of our Protestant servants; she had been with Mother since she was a new bride. I loved her dearly.

"Yes, Grace, although nothing as delightful as a story, I'm afraid."

Grace came closer to me and rested a hand on my shoulder. "Is that your farewell letter to Lord Drake, then?"

I was not mad nor surprised that news had already reached her. "It is. Not that I am convinced it will stop him from trying."

"I'm very sorry for what he's done to you – not one of us saw it coming! Terribly shocking. Are you feeling better today?"

She moved towards the drapes and drew them back, letting in very bright sheets of light.

"Yes," I said, squinting. "Although I could not tighten my corset as snug, I'm a bit swollen and tender at my waist."

Grace pursed her lips. "I could just smack him with an iron pan, I could!"

"A proper mess you'd make of him too, Grace! I will mend, though. Better to find out now rather than later."

"Quite right, miss! On both accounts! – Do you need anything before I take my leave? Tea?"

"I'll wait for breakfast, but thank you!"

When she left and closed the door behind her, I continued,

"My answer is and always will be no. I would rather be an old maid than be married to you. Any form of a relationship with you has been expressly forbidden by my family.

I am returning the gifts you were so generous as to give me over the years. I do not want them. I apologize that the lace gloves you gave me seemed to have gone missing.

As I'm quite certain you have noticed by now – Jonathon felt it important to deliver these to you personally. I have tried to tell him not to act rashly, however, no promises were made. I hope you'll forgive him as anything he said or did was done out of love for his sister.

I am sorry for the pain this letter has caused, however; I am not sorry for ending things between us – it is very necessary as I'm sure even you could not argue. Last night was quite telling.

I hope you find peace and happiness and respect my wishes to be left alone.
Sincerely,
Miss Dawson"

Folding the letter, I did not seal it so Mama could read it first.

I felt a strange sense of comfort writing this. I was grateful he had given me such an indisputable reason to break things off – no one who asked could question why, even Lord Drake...hopefully.

After I returned the books to the library, I made my way slowly upstairs. I gathered all the items Lord Drake had gifted me since I was a child.

A doll, coifs, small paintings, scarves, various seashells from his trips, an embroidered handkerchief, all his letters, the bottle of perfume, and of course, the sapphire ring.

I felt rather shocked at how many gifts there were. This was not including all the flowers and sweets, either. It made me wonder how long he had been trying to buy my affections.

Lily came and kindly offered to pack them up while I went down for breakfast. I thanked her and joined Jonathon, Anna, and Mama at the table, even though us siblings abstained from eating in lieu of Communion.

I brought the letter with me and placed it next to Mama. "I thought I would let you read it before I sent it off."

Putting down her buttered bread, she read the letter at once.

Anna sipped her water. "Mama told me Lord Drake was mean to you, Isabel. I'm very sorry he turned out to be such an awful person. Who would have thought a mean man could pretend so well at being kind!" She paused for a moment, no doubt thinking back to the conversation about his blade. "Though...perhaps not as surprising as it should have been."

"Thank you, Anna. I know what you mean."

Mama nodded approvingly. "I think that to be a very well-written and clear letter. There can be *no* misunderstanding of your meaning."

Jon held out his hand for the letter next. He read it with a serious expression, occasionally smirking.

"If a woman ever wrote me such a letter, I should crawl into the nearest cave and die!"

I laughed, though it hurt my waist. "Was I too harsh?"

Jon's eyes widened. "No! It's brilliant! If anything, you were too nice in some areas...yet you made up for it by being poetically brutal in other parts! If he tries to pursue you after this, he is truly unstable. I confess being quite eager to deliver this along with his gifts."

Anna asked to read the letter, and we all collectively replied, "No."

Lily brought the parcel of return items down to my brother. He thanked her with a smile and told us our goodbyes.

"Will you be back in time for church?" Mother asked.

"No, I don't believe I shall. However, I will be back for a later luncheon."

"Be careful," I told him.

"Yes, yes, sister – I will. You have nothing to worry about."

Since Mama went of her own accord, my siblings and I were apt to make many excuses for not attending. We went once a month, usually, if that. I ought to mention that we've discussed our Church of England attendance with several priests by now. They agreed for the sake of our mission in hiding priests, occasionally attending would not be sinful.

Stealing away to the library, I read one of Papa's books until it was time to help our friends arrive for Mass. Jon was still not back by the time people began arriving in the woods, so I brought them over myself in groups of four.

Finally, as I escorted the final group, I saw Jonathon and Mr. Porter returning. Eagerly, I walked over to meet them.

"Jon! Mr. Porter – that took longer than expected. What happened? Did everything go smoothly?"

Mr. Porter's expression said otherwise.

Jonathon began, "I caught him on his way out to church."

"And?"

"I had my driver unload the parcel before he even realized I was there. He immediately came over, surprised, of course. He asked what I was doing. I shoved your letter ... somewhat forcefully on his chest and told him to keep his..." he looked down to the grass for a moment. "Well, I'll tell you the *polite* version of what I said."

Mr. Porter chuckled. I knew what a proclivity my brother had for cussing, so I could only imagine what was really said.

Jonathon continued, "I told him to keep his filthy hands off my sister and to leave you alone. He actually had the audacity to act confused! I grabbed him by his collar and told him I'd seen the bruises from where he grabbed you so hard on your waist and not to play with me. Goodness, you should have *seen* his face! He didn't know what to do! As if he saw a ghost!"

We began walking towards the tunnel entrance. "Then I told him to take his gifts back because they weren't wanted in our house anymore and neither was he."

I clasped my hands together. "Well said! What did he do then?"

"He tried claiming that it was not up to me, and he wanted to speak directly to you, that it was a *misunderstanding*. So I got in the carriage and told him to read your letter – as it clearly states how you do not want him. And I drove off! Picked up Daniel here on the way back, of course."

Mr. Porter added, "I had a brilliant view of the whole thing as I hid behind one of his many shrubs. After your brother drove off – he went mad!"

"How so?" I asked.

"He started kicking the parcel of gifts until, suddenly, he opened it and began looking at everything individually. It only seemed to make him angrier. –Started raving at his servants to get it all out of his sight. Then he sat on his steps and read your letter. He shouted, he cursed, he crumpled the letter in his hands, and then stormed inside, pushing a servant out of his way!"

"Oh my... I feel sorry for his servants."

Mr. Porter chuckled. "As do I. But I confess I rather enjoyed seeing him explode!"

Jonathon exhaled satisfactorily. "Extremely satisfying!"

I wondered if they'd acted a bit too unconcerned, though I could not deny their joy in protecting me.

"Thank you very much – I appreciate you both."

Jonathon hugged me. "I'm only disappointed it didn't come to fists. I would have really enjoyed that."

"Perhaps *too* much..." I chided as we glanced around one more time before descending down the tunnel.

"Ladies first!" Mr. Porter offered.

Opening a door made to look like a rock in a wall outlining the garden, I took a lantern that hung just inside the tunnel.

"Why thank you!"

It was short and narrow; I had to duck my head down and be careful of my steps as the ground was uneven in areas. I'm afraid I moved quite a bit slower as bending over like this hurt rather keenly.

We all followed the light from my lantern for about five minutes before reaching the door. I knocked appropriately, and Christy opened it for me.

We hugged again as my brother and Mr. Porter came through. I was quick to make introductions, as Mass was starting very soon, and he had to get ready as the acolyte. I was grateful Father had made time for my confession before people began to arrive.

Christy helped me brush some dirt off my purple dress before we entered the chapel. "You absolutely *must* come to my house tomorrow; I feel there are many confidences you need to share with me!"

"Oh, Christy, you have no idea."

Chapter Thirteen

I OFFERED MY MASS in thanksgiving for being free of Lord Drake and my Holy Communion for his conversion. After all, if St. Paul can convert, that means it's possible for the Earl as well. I also offered the pain in my waist from kneeling for the same intention.

I watched Mr. Porter assist at Mass and I could not help but notice how sincere his devotion was to Our Lord in the Eucharist, and how much effort he placed into serving Christ. It deepened my admiration of him; *this* is a man who would help, not hinder, me and our children striving for heaven.

After Mass had ended, we escorted our guests back to the woods. Everyone was told of a meeting that was to be held at the Ruperts Barn in a few nights to discuss various things including a plan of my brother's. I wondered what the plan was – myself having to recall snippets about it from eavesdropping on him and Mr. Porter. All promised to be there. It was very dangerous to have a large gathering of Catholics in one place; however, when something was important...we risked it.

Standing outside with Christy and her father, I gave her a last hug before Jon took them to the woods.

Mr. Porter walked up beside me with a smirk. "Still willing to take a stroll with me?"

No longer in his alb, he wore a simple white shirt and black leather vest, trunks, and black boots.

I smiled. "Yes, let's start this way." I motioned towards the front of the house.

"Thank you," I said, "for being there for Jon in case things went poorly. I appreciate that."

"Of course. For no longer than I've known your brother, he's become one of my closest friends."

"As much as I do enjoy teasing him, he is a wonderful brother and friend to have."

"He's lucky to have you as well. Your relationship reminds me very much of the kind of bond I share with my sister, Theresa. Not a thing I do sneaks past her notice."

"She sounds like a woman of great sense and cleverness; I'm sure I would like her very much."

"Yes, I have little doubt of that!" He paused and took my hands in his, "Miss Dawson."

I encouraged him with as pleasant a tone as my voice could induce. "What is it Mr. Porter?"

"I'm not much for beating around the bush or very elegant words; I'm more of a matter-of-fact sort of man, so I hope you forgive my bluntness; I am no poet."

"Yes?"

"I realize that *romantic* sentiments may be unwanted, given your recent experience with them, however, I find that I cannot keep these desires to myself any longer."

A smile waited in the corners of my lips, hoping he would say what I wanted to hear.

He shifted his weight and took a breath. "See, Miss Dawson, I've developed a deep fondness for you over these past weeks. I should very much like the privilege of knowing you more intimately. "

Releasing one of my hands and taking a step closer, he caressed my face, sending pleasing shivers rushing over my skin. "You are *so* beautiful, brave, generous, smart, and mischievously humorous. You are wholly delight-ful."

I had to remind myself to breathe as he continued to gaze into my eyes.

"Your faith is something I deeply admire as well; I can tell you love our Lord very much, which only increases my affections for you. To speak simply, you are everything I've sought-after."

My face flushed. These compliments felt so genuine in comparison to how Lord Drake would speak. I stuttered a bit. "I – I have never been more flattered, Mr. Porter. Um, but I am far from this perfection you describe, I promise you!"

He shook his head with a smile. "I care not."

"You have yet to witness it, but I have a wretched temper." We walked while I continued to ramble, "I'm stubborn, vain, my head is always in the clouds, and I balk terribly when I disagree with something. I'm *horribly* outspoken. I fear you are viewing me in a distorted light."

As I looked up to meet his gaze again, I was surprised to see him trying not to laugh.

"Miss Dawson, I daresay that you forgot to add scrupulous to your list of faults. – I never thought you to be without imperfections. Though I *suppose* I do appreciate the warning of your temper. Surely you do not believe that *I* am without fault? I struggle with sins like any other, and I expected no less from you! Shall I confess my defects to make you feel better?"

I could not help but chuckle. "Aside from being impetuous, and perhaps a bit cocky you mean?"

"Cocky? Me? Wherever did you get such a notion?"

His sarcastic expression was pleasing to me. I enjoyed our banter more than I dared to let on.

We picked our walk back up again. "Then what, praytell, do you struggle with, Mr. Porter, if not the latter?"

He took in a large breath of air in before replying. "Oh, I struggle with pride, perhaps more than some men. My sister tells me I am overprotective and thickheaded, stubborn. *Cocky.* I'm also blunt. I *am* slower to anger, though it is formidable when deserved. I dislike large crowds. Why does everyone want to discuss the weather or repeat the same mundane questions that no one *truly* cares about? – Oh and when not in the presence of ladies or priests, I can have a sailor's mouth. Work in progress, that. Too much time on the docks." He exhaled, waiting to discern my reaction. "Are you satisfied? Have I scared you away from thoughts of me?"

I grinned. "I am satisfied by your answers, yes."

"Praise God! I was starting to ramble like some nervous child before their parent!"

I giggled and squeezed his hand tighter.

He paused us beneath a bloomed magnolia tree. "Since you aren't scared off then... what would you think of permitting me to court you?"

He held both of my hands to his chest, drawing me a little closer to him as he continued, "Of course, I can't offer you the same sort of luxury *others* can, though I hope in your goodness, you might overlook what a humble life I do have to offer?"

He gazed down at me with such hopeful, yet, confident eyes. I took in his whole face, how his thick hair curled against his brow in the wind, his broad shoulders, and those bright hazel eyes that displayed a shade of green in them today. He was strikingly handsome. Even the slight bend of his nose was attractive to me.

My breath nearly caught in my chest. "I'm not sure what you consider eloquent, Mr. Porter, but I've never heard such heartfelt accolades – even with your list of faults! I daresay, I have enough luxury for us both, but even if I had not...and you had nothing at all, I would still be happy to be courted by a man such as you. You possess all the characteristics a woman could hope for, really, at least for me."

He kissed my hands softly. "You've no idea how happy I am to hear you answer so. It's sort of miraculous how we came to meet; I have no doubt God's hand is in it."

He offered me his arm and I gladly entwined my arm into his as we continued on. "Yes! I feel that too."

"May I call you Isabel?"

The memory of walking with Lord Drake when he was pressuring me to do the same, pushed to the front of my mind. However, this time, I felt no hesitation or strangeness about it. It felt only natural that he should.

"Yes, *Daniel....*" Oh, how I liked saying his name!

Turning beyond the front of the house, we found a garden bench surrounded by gardenias and sat down. "Isabel, I wish to know all about you; what you enjoy doing most, things you despise, what you like to daydream so much about." He gathered my hands and kissed them. "Everything."

I thought for a moment. "Well, apart from my faith, family, and my friends, I suppose reading, writing, nature, and thoughts of traveling fill me with the most pleasure. Papa and I would read and look over maps when I was a young girl, and I have imagined so many faraway places. I also enjoy riding my horse and the rush of racing with her. As for things I dislike, I despise walnuts and spiders, and Lord Drake."

He laughed as I continued with a smile. "As for the daydreams...they vary greatly. Tell me about you? – I pose you the same questions."

He looked up to the sky, calling his thoughts together. "Let me see... my faith, as well, comes first, as you may have guessed. I find a deep sense of honor and gratification from serving the priesthood, though I never felt God calling me to that vocation. I've always known one day I would be a husband and a father. I enjoy spending time with my family and friends, of course, reading, I feel at home with the shore and beach. Taking my boat out on the water is something I have greatly missed. I enjoy fishing about as much as your brother fancies hunting. As far as dislikes, Lord Drake is on that list too. I'm not overly fond of mushrooms, and I will have no issue in rescuing you from any spiders."

I laughed. "You've forgotten to add your dislike of mornings!"

Grinning, he replied, "Yes, although you are already painfully aware of that."

"And what of your daydreams?"

"I would have thought you were quite aware of that answer as well?"

I blushed as he played with my fingers in his strong hands.

Holding hands with him sent a sort of butterfly reaction throughout me that made me want to be closer to him; I found myself inching nearer.

"Isabel..." he looked into my eyes again, "It's almost unfair how pretty you are – you leave me at a loss for words more often than not."

He caressed my face, "I want to show you where I'm from – I wish to take you out on the ocean on my boat and see you smile there, with your hair blowing wildly all about you!"

My heart smiled at the imagery. "I have never been on a boat before; I feel I would enjoy that immensely."

Wrapping his arm just above my waist, he leaned his forehead against mine. "Isabel...we should continue our walk, for if we remain seated here, I will not be able to keep myself from kissing you." He cradled my face."I would never wish to dishonor you by taking such liberties so soon, despite how much it consumes my thoughts."

My breath matched his own quickened pace; our lips were nearly touching as it were. I so admired how he placed my dignity above his own desires – strangely, it only made me want to kiss him more.

I slowly pulled away from him, dragging my eyes away from his, "I understand."

"Come, let us move on."

My heart pounded as I took his arm.

We spoke for a long while. Talking with him came easily with no awkward pauses – it was as though we would never run out of things to speak of. What books we liked the most, which Saints inspired us, where we most wanted to travel, and how many children we hoped for one day. About an hour later, we were interrupted for lunch by Missy, who extended the invitation to Daniel.

We walked back to the house with blissful smiles painted across our faces. *This* was what falling in love was supposed to feel like. Effortless. Peaceful. Selfless.

Mama was pleased to see me happy. Anna was curious. Jonathon appeared satisfied as we all took our seats.

"So!" Mama began, "Tell us about where you come from and what you do, Mr. Porter!"

I was nervous that Mama would not approve of his lack of connections and wealth, and, which version he would decide to tell her.

"I deal mostly in imports and exports, trades, and ensuring people in town have plenty of fresh food and supplies at reasonable prices. I live in Portsmouth, near my siblings. Being the youngest, I was left with a modest home overseeing the ocean."

"I see. How quaint. What sort of house is yours, Mr. Porter?"

"A rather charming cottage as of this moment. When I have a family to fill it, I intend on building a proper estate."

"I see. And who is taking care of business while you're away?"

"My brothers and I handle things together, so they were able to shoulder my responsibilities while I traveled looking for opportunities for us."

Her previously tight lips turned into a small smile. "You must be all quite close to work together successfully! How many siblings do you have?"

"Four brothers and a sister."

"What a blessing!"

"I did not always view it that way growing up when fighting with them – but yes, it's quite a blessing indeed."

Anna spoke up next. "Tell me, Mr. Porter, what are your thoughts on sweets?"

I smirked at the confusion on Daniel's face as he floundered to respond. "Uh, I like both very much... particularly blackberry tarts."

"Hmm, those are good as well. My sister enjoys gyngerbrede squares the most so she must be spoiled with them very frequently."

Daniel smiled. "I see! Thank you for the tip; I'll make sure to remember that."

Anna smiled approvingly as she reached for a second piece of ham. I feared Mama had not been so easily won over.

After lunch, Mr. Porter joined us for cards and to listen to Anna's newest piece on the harpsichord, which she had mastered.

"Do you sing, Isabel?" He asked as we sat on the settee together.

I wavered my hand. "A little, yes. I wouldn't say it's very impressive though."

Mama scoffed. "She's actually quite good, though she rarely performs for us anymore. Her father adored her singing."

Daniel flashed a charming smile that made his eyes shimmer. "Would you sing for me?"

As if I could say no to him...

Anna clapped excitedly as I chose a song to which she could accompany me. Scarborough Fair; we knew it well. It had been Papa's favorite.

The familiar melody played on the harpsichord as I joined in.

"Are you going to Scarborough Fair?
Parsley, sage, rosemary, and thyme
Remember me to one who lives there
She once was a true love of mine."

I always found it difficult to have my eyes open when I sang; I sang best when I gave myself to the melody and story and lost myself in them. I am well-informed that this is an oddity of mine; however, it is a formed habit now. I did open them briefly to glance towards Daniel; the way he stared at me, as though he were in a daze, made my heart flutter something fierce. I nearly forgot the next line as I felt a burning blush rise up my neck.

I smiled as I sang some of the lyrics to him, and closed my eyes for the rest so I would not forget a word or note.

At the end, he stood and clapped. "I've never heard such a beautiful voice before."

I caught Jonathon rolling his eyes.

Mama seemed proud. "Yes, she's quite talented. She and Anna make quite the musical pairing!"

I went to sit by Daniel again as he responded, "They certainly do."

"Really!" I said, "You will both make me quite vain! Jonathon, won't you give me *some* criticism?"

"You know I'd love nothing better than to oblige you, sister…but I could find no errors. Anna's playing no doubt enhances your ability."

I smiled at Anna. "Quite right indeed! You are so very gifted, my dear."

She stood and curtsied. "Thank you! Though, I am rather tired of playing now. Mama, may I be excused to go outside?"

"Of course, dear." Mama replied lovingly.

Then, I had a brilliant idea. "Daniel, do you like riding horses? We have an extra you could ride…if Jon would grace us with his presence, of course?"

"I do enjoy riding, though, would that not hurt your waist?"

"I will take it easy and won't challenge you to a race. *This* time. Let us go!"

Daniel sighed with a smile. He couldn't say no to me either.

"What do you say Jon?"

"Hmm…I suppose…. Maybe we could even ride through the woods with my musket and…perhaps shoot a deer…should one come along."

I rolled my eyes. "Bring your gun, if you must! It's been weeks since I've ridden; poor Honey must think I've abandoned her!"

Down the hill to the right of our house were our stables. Jonathon rode a dark brown Yorkshire Trotter named Champion. Walking over to Honey, she grew excited once she heard me coming near. She was a pony mixed breed and had a sandy coloring, save one white patch on her nose.

Her legs pranced and she shook her mane as though to scold me for being away so long. I fed her a slice of apple and pet her long nose as I whispered to her my apologies. Once I had sufficiently made amends to Honey, Daniel offered his assistance to help me into the saddle. I had been riding since I could remember; nonetheless, I accepted his offer graciously. Ultimately, I was grateful for it, as I felt quite tender trying to mount the saddle with my bruises.

Once he saw me confidently secured in the saddle, he mounted our other Yorkshire Trotter, Camelot.

Jon rode off ahead of us towards the woods behind our home, leaving Daniel and I walking at an easy pace. Admittedly, this hurt far more than I imagined it would. I still felt it was worthwhile, so I pushed through the discomfort.

"I have never been this happy before," Daniel said, glancing over to me. "I give all the credit to you."

"I thank you for saying so, that is very touching. I've been thinking though."

His face looked concerned for a moment. "About?"

"It might be best if we kept our courtship quiet for a while so it does not reach Lord Drake's attention."

"Are you so worried for me?"

"I can't imagine anything good would come of it. And yes, of course, I am."

"And how long do you pose that we keep it secret, aside from your family?"

"I'm unsure. Perhaps a week or longer? Let his anger cool a bit?"

Daniel sighed. "I suppose that would be the sensible thing to do, considering. I don't want you to worry, Isabel. Even if he discovers my affection for you tomorrow, what could he do to keep us apart? There is nothing he could threaten that would keep me from you. I know we haven't known one another for long, but I have never felt so strong and affectionately for someone before. I have no desire to ever leave your side."

My heartbeat quickened. "My feelings are the same, though I believe he would stoop to unheard-of levels of depravity to punish us both. We are Catholic, after all. It isn't a far stretch to imagine what he might do."

"I do not wish for you to be so concerned about Lord Drake. He is not worth your thoughts – save them all for me!"

I chuckled at his corner grin as we crossed into the borders of the woods. My brother was still far ahead, on the hunt. The shade in the woods made me glad I wore my white petticoat. Riding with Daniel amidst all the beautiful greenery and spring flowers blooming felt a bit surreal. As though we were two characters in a fairytale with birds flying above us.

"Should he attempt anything at all, your brother and I both will handle him. *You* have *nothing* to be anxious of, you hear? Those days are over."

He reached out to me and I placed my hand in his. His gaze was so reassuring and comforting. It very nearly took away my concern. Nearly.

"I do hope you're right. Besides, he must realize that there is nothing more he could do?"

"*Exactly!* He has lost. He may not be happy about it, but there's nothing else he can do except to sulk. Now. Tell me about the stories and poems you write!"

I could see this was his way of trying to get my mind off of the Earl. I obliged nonetheless and confess it quite worked.

We rode for some time when suddenly there was a gunshot.

Chapter Fourteen

I GASPED, QUITE FORGETTING my brother was even there.

"Aha! Got one!" He shouted from a distance.

"I suppose we ought to catch up to him and congratulate him?" I offered.

"Indeed."

Heading towards his direction, we were shortly staring down at his prey.

"What a lovely dead deer, Jon. *Ugh.*"

The men chuckled.

"You like eating it!" Jon retorted.

"Yes. Staring at its bloody corpse is quite another thing to a nice herbed gravy over it, isn't it?"

"How about I take your sister back and have the servants come out to help you bring it in?"

"That's probably best. She has a weak stomach. Hurry on then, as best you can."

We turned our horses around and headed back at a leisurely pace.

"Tell me more about being a priest runner. Have you had many close calls?"

"Many, in fact. I had to fight our way out of being captured just a few months ago."

"How did you manage that?"

"Father Ingles and I were being followed; a spy had given our descriptions to a local magistrate. We knew we had to get out of town as soon as possible, so we waited until it was dark and headed out in the direction of the woods. – I've always found it safest in the woods. Easier to lose someone, if you know what you're doing. Just as we reached the tree line, we heard a gun cock. We turned around slowly to see three officers rising from some shrubbery."

He had my attention wrapped as he continued,

"We raised our hands in the air. They joked crudely about Catholics, praising their superiority as they approached us. The one nearest, stuck his gun in my face to try and intimidate me. Except he didn't realize how bad of an idea that was."

"What did you do? Were you not terrified?"

He gave a half smile. "This was not my first experience being up close with the barrel of a gun. Was my heart pounding? Absolutely. But no, I was not afraid. What he did there showed he had little experience; it was easy to grab his gun from him. He panicked and fired, shooting at the ground. Next thing he knew, I had hit his head with the butt of his own gun, and he was taking a nap in the grass. Father took cover behind a few trees to look for throwing rocks. Just as the other two were telling me to put the rifle down, Father launched the rocks at them while I charged and took one gun..." he trailed off.

"Daniel?"

"Without even thinking, I aimed it at the furthest of the queen's men as he pulled the trigger on him. Shot him in the chest. Died almost immediately. I hadn't actually killed a man until that day. Only injured them, to the best of my knowledge."

From the pause he took, I could tell this was a burdensome memory. "You don't have to finish the story."

His eyes snapped back from the past as he looked at me. "His face haunts me. Every time I go to bed at night. –I knocked the other guard out with the butt of that gun and then we tied the two officers who were unconscious to a tree and made our escape into the woods."

"I cannot pretend to understand what your life has been like these past years. I'm sure you know this, but you did the right thing; you protected Father Ingles and yourself. I am sorry you had to be in that circumstance. You're even braver than I imagined you to be. "

He patted the neck of the horse. "Father assured me of the same. Didn't stop me from requesting confession the moment we found a safe place to sleep for the night."

"I'm sure I would have done the same."

"I pray for him every day on the off chance he made it to purgatory. I gather it's the least I could do."

Knowing Daniel had taken a life to protect Father Ingles, and so expertly incapacitated the other two officers, made him even more appealing. I knew he could be my own champion protector.

"You are, by far, the best man I know. I have no doubt your actions then and now have greatly pleased Our Lord. You're a fierce and brave protector of the priesthood. I admire you deeply for it."

"Oh?" His face lifted. "Have I just become even more attractive in your eyes then?"

"Would it be peculiar for me to admit that?"

"I certainly won't question it."

I gently ran my hand through Honey's mane as she pranced excitedly over a squirrel daring to cross her path. "How did you become so proficient with weapons?"

"My grandfather was an officer and he taught my father who, in turn, trained all his boys. He felt it was important, regardless of the times. Grateful he did."

"As am I. Your father sounds as though he were a good man."

"He was. Very honorable; a bit harsh and stubborn in his ways, but my mother was the gentle touch that balanced him. What was your father like, besides the fact that he enjoyed books?"

"He was very witty and clever, learned, and brave too." I smiled at the images of him that passed through me.

"Do you think bearing the loss of a parent truly gets easier with time?"

I sighed. "Surely, I would not know. Has there been any change for you yet?"

"Only that I have learned to walk this path without them."

"Perhaps that's all that changes."

Having cleared the woods, we decided to dismount and walk our horses the rest of the way to the stables. My sides were becoming sore from the ride, so I was grateful for this. Something told me that Daniel guessed as much, since it was his suggestion. As I went to dismount, Daniel was there to help me and careful to avoid assisting at my waist, which I deeply appreciated.

We stood there, pressed together, as my feet gently touched the ground. Our eyes were transfixed; I had to remind myself to breathe once more. He fixed an unruly bit of hair away from my face as his left hand found a home in the middle of my back, pulling me closer. The core of my body felt on fire – I so desired for him to kiss me. I could tell by his uneven breaths that he was struggling not to. His fingers gently outlined the shape of my face; I could taste his breath as his lips slowly approached mine.

My horse neighed and shook her mane into our faces, causing us both to step away and laugh. He grabbed the reins to his steed with a sigh as I grabbed Honey's. We met in between our horses to hold hands as we began towards the stables.

"Would it be a sorrow to you to live far from home one day?" He asked at last, breaking the enjoyable tension of our silence.

"If it were by the shore I should not mind it so much."

"Is that so?" Daniel grinned. "You fancy the beach then?"

"I do! It's been a few years since I've been able to enjoy it though. Papa used to take us to visit his cousins in Colchester before his health began to decline."

"Colchester is beautiful; I was there last year. ...And should you mind living in a smaller house, as long as it was near the shore, of course?"

"Hmm, just how far away would be the shore?" I teased.

"I can see it from my bedchamber's window."

"*My!* Then I suspect I shouldn't mind a barn if that be the case."

He brought my hand to his lips and kissed my fingers. "You are remarkable."

"And you are quite adept at flattery."

"We're just a very suitable couple, aren't we? I enjoy giving you compliments, and you have an endless amount of qualities to dote upon!"

"The envy of all couples, to be sure."

Daniel chuckled. "I am the envy of all men at least; a very blessed man."

"Hmm, perhaps. Though I feel I am far more blessed than you."

"Oh? How do you suppose that now?"

I smirked. "Well, after all, God did lead me to a rather handsome, brave, and clever man. I feel quite myself with you. As if I can speak without any pretense or concern. For that quality alone, I'd have been grateful."

Daniel stopped and drew in slowly to kiss my forehead. "Perhaps I will concede that we are tied for blessings – just so as I'm not the one to start our first fight."

I giggled. "A wise choice."

We began walking again. "I wonder," I said, "will you let me win all the fights?"

His eyebrows raised. "Do you anticipate there being many?"

"Of course not, I just need to know whether or not to have my best prepared in advance."

"I daresay you will win most, merely from beguiling me with those blue eyes of yours. What man alive could deny you anything?"

I grinned a toothy smile. "Take care, Daniel, my vanity will have no hope if you continue on like this!"

The stable master saw us coming and met us to take the horses as well as pass the word on about my brother's kill.

Anna and Mama joined Daniel and I in the drawing room where Missy served cakes and cider. We were all chatting pleasantly until George entered the drawing room, "Miss Dawson...you have a letter."

The room fell quiet as he handed it to me.

I recognized the handwriting and red seal at once. I looked uneasily between Daniel and Mother as I opened it.

"My darling Isabel,

Words cannot express the magnitude of my apologies. I never meant to hurt you, truly. I am deeply humiliated by my unintentional strength – I can only offer that I was so entranced in the moment that I did not realize I was causing injury to you.

I would never intentionally hurt the woman I so deeply love; please believe me.

You and your family have every right to be upset with me. Though we have all been friends for over a decade; I cannot help but wonder why one mistake – that you know I did not intend to make – should make me an eternal outcast? I am quite forlorn.

Have we not all been friends? Have you and I not been more?

I swear on my life, I never meant to hurt you and I certainly never would again – I should only hold you with the tender care I would a bird. Isabel...you know me; I am not a cruel man – I am not the sort to lay hands upon a woman. Please, remember how much I love you, and you will understand that this was a terrible, terrible mistake and nothing more.

You did not have to return the gifts I gave you, even from when you were a child. Say the word and I will send them back to you and tenfold more! Tell me how I may begin to make recompense? I will do anything to win your forgiveness and trust again. I will not give up on us.

Forever yours,
Elwood"

I felt the color drain from me. I handed it to Daniel.

Pacing the room, he read it in silence, save the occasional scoff. "He's a blackguard!" He handed the letter to my mother who anxiously read it.

Daniel continued. "He still thinks there's a chance! Is he in his right mind?"

I nodded quietly as I felt the foreboding premonition begin to take course.

Upon seeing my expression, he came and sat down beside me and held my hands. "He will eventually give up; do not worry. No matter how angered he is, he will realize it's over. I will protect you from him."

I met his eyes and tried my best to appear positive, though I felt the opposite, "I'm sure you're right."

Mama finished reading the letter with a grunt. "What absurdity! How dare he try to excuse such unthinkable behavior! I hope you do not intend to respond to this, Isabel?"

"No, there's nothing else to say that I did not convey in my last letter."

"Good, I think that's wise. Your brother will definitely *not* enjoy reading this."

Just then, Jon walked in. "What won't I enjoy reading? Please, Isabel, not another book of poetry, I *beseech you*."

Daniel walked over and put a hand on his shoulder. "You're going to wish it was poetry."

Jon cocked his eyebrow as Mama handed him the letter. *"No.* Did he actually write to you?"

He sat down in his chair by the corner of the entrance as Daniel returned to my side. "The man is completely daft! How can he think you would possibly agree to any of this?"

I replied, "He is determined to the point of madness. I am not responding; however, I fear that may only increase his desperation."

Upon finishing the letter, Jon folded it into his breast pocket and called for George, who promptly walked through the door. "From here on out, any letter or parcel that comes for my sister from Lord Drake is to be returned unopened, immediately. Is that understood?"

George nodded his full head of white hair. "Absolutely, Master Dawson."

My brother turned to me. "I think it's best if you stay out of town for a while; he will undoubtedly frequent the area in hopes of speaking with you. I doubt he is stupid enough to try and come here; he knows I'd turn a gun on him."

We all concurred that this was the wisest course of action.

During supper, Daniel tried his best to lighten the mood by telling us amusing stories from his childhood. Admittedly, he was successful.

"Should I take from this that you were always the instigator of these mischievous plans?" I asked him playfully.

"Well, not *always*, I was the youngest after all. However, I certainly gave my mother cause to be at her wits end more often than not. I imagine you were a perfect angel growing up?"

My brother burst with laughter. *"Angel? Isabel? Hardly."*

Mother chastised him. "Jonathon! Speak kindly about your dear sister."

Jon was quick to retort. "Do you not remember when she tried to bake a cake in the middle of the night and nearly burned down the entire house?"

Anna laughed, having no memory of this.

"It was supposed to be a surprise for Mama's birthday!" I tried to defend myself.

"Yes, quite the surprise it was…" Mother replied, shaking her head.

"Or!" Jon continued, "that time she rescued what she thought was a dog from the gardens? It was a fox. A filthy angry fox." He turned to me as the table rippled in chuckles. "How it didn't bite you when you carried it in, I still don't know. I can still hear Mama's scream as she walked in on you feeding the animal scraps in the hall!"

I could not refrain from joining in the laughter. "It was a darling little fox and she was hungry! I know had Anna been old enough to remember, she would have sided with me."

"Exactly how many stories are there like this?" Daniel asked curiously.

Jon grinned. "Quite a few. There was the time she ate all the Christmas cakes and biscuits before a party."

I protested, "It was not *all!* Only the gyngerbrede squares."

Mama was quick to recall how sick I was that evening. "We never could get the stains out of that dress."

I felt my neck turn bright red. "Surely Mr. Porter has heard enough childhood stories for one evening."

"Have I?" He teased, smirking with his whole face.

Mother took pity on me and changed the subject. "I must say, I'm sorry Jonathon has never brought you here to visit before! You fit in rather easily here as though we have known you for years. We're very happy you decided to stay in town for a while."

"As am I, Mrs. Dawson, you've been so very warm and welcoming; I appreciate your kind hospitality."

"How long do you intend to be in Aylesbury for?"

This was a good question that I had somehow failed to ask him myself. ...Daniel is rather handsome, so you can't completely blame me for being distracted.

Daniel glanced around the table. "Honestly, I am unsure of that myself! My brothers are expecting me back sometime before the end of summer."

I calculated quickly in my head. Easter was more than four weeks ago now, which meant he would be here, at most, another month and a half or two. My mind embraced a sudden rush of new questions. Would he leave me here? Would he return for me? Would he continue his life as a priest runner? Would I be joining him in Bridlington as his wife?

Mother responded, breaking my siege of queries. "Excellent! We shall be able to enjoy your company for a while longer then. You are always welcome; come whenever you are free to do so, Mr. Porter."

"You are extremely kind, Mrs. Dawson, I only hope you do not grow tired of my company!"

Chapter Fifteen

LATER THAT EVENING, I walked Mr. Porter to our carriage which we had invited him to take back to town. Jon felt it best to have Daniel keep staying at the Inn to keep an ear to the ground.

The night was chilly and dark, save the lanterns near the entrance to the house and the glow worms which flickered in nearby bushes.

We stood near the carriage together as Daniel smiled at me. "I truly enjoy your family! It reminded me of being home with my siblings. I'm eager for you to meet them."

A breeze blew against Daniel and I breathed in his scent; it was tantalizing – it nearly made my head dizzy. "I would like to meet them, if for no other reason, so that I could hear the embarrassing tales of *your* childhood! That way we would be quite even."

"Ah, I hadn't thought of that, perhaps you don't *need* to meet them."

I laughed. "No, no, it's too late! The invitation has already been accepted."

"Blast." He smiled widely. "When may I see you again, Isabel?"

"I'm visiting Christy tomorrow afternoon...would you be able to join us for supper again?"

"Yes." Gently, he kissed my forehead. "This may sound silly...but I will miss you till then."

I smiled as we held hands between us. "I will miss you as well."

He kissed my hands and bid me good night before ascending into the carriage.

As the horses moved on, he poked his head out the window and waved goodbye. His boyish charm made me chuckle as I waved back. I stood until he was out of sight, turning back towards the house just in time to see my family awkwardly dart away from the window from which they had been spying on me.

The following day, I could hardly wait to go and see Christy. As soon as I finished lunch, I left on foot. Her house was only an hour's walk from mine, and it was a beautiful sunny day with puffy white clouds scattered across the sky. My green embroidered dress swished about my legs as I walked eagerly along, sending random crickets leaping from my path. It was that time of year again when there seemed to be more of those little insects than any other.

Following the road over the bridge and passing beneath the twisted oak trees, I took a right – opposite to town and shortly reached Christy's estate. It was smaller than ours and beautifully kept with many flower gardens.

Climbing the stairs, with still some pain in my sides, I eagerly knocked on the door. Their doorman opened it promptly and led me to their quaint drawing room; it had such pleasing artwork between the furnishings. I nearly lost myself in a daydream admiring them before Christy's voice broke through my musings. "Isabel!" She exclaimed walking through the door, "Henry, would you ask Beth to bring us some cider? – Thank you!"

Her yellow dress with a bodice of bright pink and green florals flowed around us as we hugged. We sat at the card table near a large bay window.

"Now," she said as two goblets of cider were delivered, "you must tell me everything that's been going on with Lord Drake."

"You won't be able to believe half of it. It's truly shocking."

By the time I had told her everything, her mouth hung open. "How absolutely appalling...and just... I'm speechless!"

"I know! *Trust me.*" I sipped my cider; it was sweet and crisp.

"Do you think he will continue pursuing you?"

I nodded. "He does not stop until he has what he wants. If only it wasn't *me!*"

"Although..." a wry smile grew on her lips, "he isn't the only one who desires you, is he?"

I could not contain my grin. "That *is* true."

"*Please* tell me it's that Mr. Porter!"

"Yes! It's a secret for now, but he asked me if he could court me yesterday and I agreed!"

"Ohh! I *knew* it! When he asked you to dance, I knew it!"

"I feel so at ease with Daniel; I can be myself. He's brave, strong, devout...and I feel safe when I'm in his presence."

Christy squealed. "That is exactly how I feel with Adam! – Tell me though...did you have feelings for the Earl at all?"

I swallowed.

"Oh... I was right...you did?"

I placed my cider down on the table between us. "Christy, it is rather unfair how well you can read me."

She smiled a bit too smugly. "Isn't it? – Lord Drake *is* attractive and very wealthy after all. I cannot entirely blame you. He has nothing on Mr. Porter though."

"No, Mr. Porter is his superior, in every way, except in wealth, though I feel that is a fair trade. – It's only that Elwood *was* so very alluring, Christy.

So utterly devoted. As if his life depended upon me returning his love. It was hard not to be somewhat drawn in by him. His words were truly touched by silver. I'm ashamed to admit how hard it was to resist his offer at times."

"Did you love him?"

I pondered for a moment before answering. "The feelings I had for him were confusing, still are, in a way, I suppose. A mere caress from his hand caused my heart to beat so fiercely. I do not believe that I was in love with him though, no. Not as I know it now. I think I was more in love with his touch and gaze. And the way he spoke. But it went no deeper. I will admit that it cuts me deeply to know that he is heartbroken and hurting."

Christy scoffed lightly. "You're too kindhearted. He's a horrid man, whatever façade he presented to you was not the real Earl of Aylesbury. Anyone who injured my friend like that has no claim to your compassion. You made the right choice by turning him down; he would have ruined you – no matter how lovely his touch or words were. Perhaps you were more attracted to what you *shouldn't* have."

I loved her for her blunt insight and protectiveness. Never was there a truer friend.

"You are right, of course. – I was quite afraid of him that night in the garden; that fear has not left me. There was no reasoning with him. I'm not sure what would have happened if Daniel had not appeared."

Christy sipped her cider. "You were right to be afraid of such a man. Do you suspect he will try to see you again?"

"If given the chance, yes. But how long must I be a prisoner of my house for?"

"As long as it takes! Besides...you may always come for a night as you did when we were children."

I grinned at the fond memories this brought to me. "Once the threat is over, I should like that very much. I have no desire to bring him to *your* door by accident. Now! Enough about me! Has Mr. Anderson called on you yet?"

Christy sighed. "No, but we have been writing back and forth." She sighed again. "I miss him."

"I have no doubt he misses you as much, if not more. Surely he will come by this weekend and ask your papa for your hand in marriage!"

"I hope you're correct!"

"I am eager to meet the man who has captured your heart. I hope we shall all get along well."

"Of course we shall! And one day our husbands shall be as good of friends as you and I are."

"And our children will fall in love, naturally, and we shall be connected even more one day!"

We both chuckled at our future plans. They had been the same since we were children.

Christy lifted her goblet, "Oh! I'm in need of a refill it seems. Would you like more as well?"

"Thank you, but I should probably take my leave. Daniel is coming over for supper and I'd like to change before he arrives. Would you like to come over and ride horses soon?"

"Yes, you should be off then! And I would *love* to come riding! –Just as soon as Adam comes, that is. I would hate to be away when he finally arrives."

I smiled. "I understand. I had such a lovely time as always, thank you for having me. Tell your father I send my best regards."

"Likewise! And I will; he's always hiding in his study these days."

"Taking your mother's passing hard still?"

Christy nodded solemnly. "Yes, quite. It's been three years, but to him it seems to feel as raw as the day we buried her."

"Tell him he's in my prayers."

"I will, thank you. Give your family my greetings!"

We hugged and I began the walk back home, feeling much rejuvenated from my visit. The way back, I could not stop thinking about Daniel and how eager I was to see him.

I crossed over the bridge and paused to watch the stream bubble along. I prayed a few Hail Mary's for Christy and her father, and a few more for my family and Daniel.

Moving along down the road, I knew it wouldn't be long before I could see the roof of my home in the distance.

Hearing a carriage behind me, I stepped closer to the grass so that it could move past me. But then I realized that the carriage was slowing instead. Looking back, I immediately recognized the dragon's coat of arms impressed upon the black carriage door.

Lord Drake had come for me.

Chapter Sixteen

MY HEART POUNDED IN tandem with the horrid fears that flooded my thoughts. Whatever his intentions, I knew they would not be honorable or even sane.

The carriage came to a full stop as Lord Drake jumped out of the door, ignoring the steps. "*Isabel!* It's fate that I chose to come at this time! – When my letters were returned, I knew I must come at once."

Briefly, I considered retreating to Christy's house, though I did not wish to pass by Lord Drake to do so. Or endanger my friend. Deciding to ignore him, I kept walking home.

He jogged to catch up with me as his carriage followed at a distance. "Wait, please! I only wish to speak with you! At least let me offer you a ride home?"

I paused to face him with what I'm sure was an incredulous expression. "*Why* would I accept a carriage ride from you after what you've done? What about my letter to you was unclear – in *any* way? Surely if my letter was ambiguous my brother was not!" My temper bled through my tone more than I intended.

He held his hands out with open palms. "I understand your anger, I do. I merely beg for a few moments of your time?"

"To do what? To *say* what? It is over. I will not marry a man that leaves bruises upon my body, nor would my family ever permit it! I am forbidden from marrying you or spending any amount of time in your presence. Surely you must understand why?"

"I beg of you, do not be rash. You shall destroy us both in the process."

I scoffed. "Whatever threats you have planned against us, I suppose you better be off to make good on them."

"*Isabel*, please, I seek your forgiveness."

"Ah, well then, I forgive you. You may go home now, my Lord!"

With a scowl, I turned and promptly walked away again. I surprised myself by how instantly my fear had turned to irritated rage.

Lord Drake continued tailing me, close on my heels. After a full minute, I stopped and turned around. "Do you intend to follow me all the way to my house?"

"Only until you hear what I have to say." I was taken aback by how calmly he spoke.

"This is extremely improper. My whole family has asked you to leave me alone, myself included."

A smirk rose to his face. "Yes, but secretly, you've always liked me best when I'm improper, isn't that right?"

My cheeks flushed. "If you continue, my brother will have his way with you and I won't be able to restrain him. Is that what you'd like? A proper beating?"

"If that is the punishment you seek for me, yes. Would that satisfy your wrath?"

"*No!* I don't *seek any punishment* for you – I merely wish to be left alone! Is that so hard to fathom?"

He took a step closer, piercing me with his anguished eyes, "You say you don't want me to be punished, and yet you would levy a death sentence against me? – Please, do not cut me from your life. What happened was a mistake – a *terrible* mistake, I had no intention of bruising you; I swear on my life!"

His raised and emotional voice felt so heartbroken with remorse. It moved me to be softer, "You have the appearance of sincerity, and yet, why is it that I do not trust you?"

"Out of all the years I've known you, have you ever thought me to be a violent man? I've been nothing but good to you from the first moment I saw you! How could you doubt me so?"

I did not like how he was trying to confuse my thoughts, nor how easy it was for him to do so. It made remembering the facts difficult.

"Your sister," I said. "If a man had bruised her waist with both hands after she pleaded to be released, after she told him he was hurting her – more than once – and he only squeezed her harder, would you expect her to marry that man? To trust him after he could not be reasoned with?"

"I did *not* mean to do that, Isabel."

"Then why didn't you stop?" I yelled. "Why didn't you release me?"

I no longer cared whether he thought me ladylike or not.

His chest heaved as he ran his hands through his raven hair, revealing a layer of gray at his temples. "I had no idea you were hurting *so* badly! I didn't think my grasp was that firm! I thought you were only afraid of answering my questions – of admitting your feelings for me. I was so frustrated with your damned stubbornness! – I *swear*, if I could go back in time and change my actions, I would!"

I steeled myself against his gaze. "You frightened me horribly, my Lord. This is not something I can forget. Accept the '*mistake*' as you call it, for what it was. Pursue another woman. There are many to choose from. It is over between us."

His breaths grew more erratic. "Little bird, you are the only woman I long for. You must believe how remorseful I am; I did not mean to hurt or scare you. You mustn't be afraid of me. Please, allow me to make the necessary amends, whatever you deem them to be. In time, I promise you will be able to look past my transgression, if you only give us that chance."

I stood there a moment, taking in his distressed countenance. "I do believe you to be sorry and I earnestly forgive you. I do not enjoy seeing you suffer so, my Lord. However, I *cannot* submit to becoming your wife. Please, I beg you to leave me be." I turned and walked away.

He called out after me, "Will you at least admit you *did* have feelings for me?"

My heart choked as I stood in place. "Will you promise to leave if I do?"

He hesitated, stepping closer. "Yes. At least I would know I was not imagining it."

I felt I owed him this, yet, the words did not want to come out. I folded my arms and faced him. "Yes. While I doubt it was love, I did have some feelings for you, my Lord, more than I would care to admit. Whatever they might have been, those feelings are quite dead and gone now."

His expression was pleading, bordering on pitiable. "If not love then what?"

I had made a mistake in confessing this much to him. "It does not matter now."

"It matters a great deal to *me*. Isabel, please?"

I sighed and released my arms. "You possessed a talent for stirring my emotions; I will admit that. It would be lying to say otherwise, but such affections were of a fleeting nature only."

"No, I do not believe they were as fleeting as you claim. Otherwise, why would you need to fight them as hard as you have been?"

Pursing my lips, I took a step back; somehow he had managed to come closer to me than I realized. "Please understand – there are no emotions left for you to stir. You have murdered any feelings that might have been. Go to the graveyard nearest town and you will find a fresh tombstone that's marked: the Peculiar Courtship of Lord Drake and Miss Dawson. Is that explanation clearer?"

He chuckled and rubbed his face with both hands. "*Isabel!* What am I to do with you? – You just intend to become a sarcastic old spinster? – There is no one else who will love you. Your stubbornness is truly your own undoing!"

I said nothing; outrage took over the battlefield of my emotions. I stormed off as he followed, like a dog who could not sit and stay. Why do I ever bother feeling sympathy for him?

In a few quick strides, he had caught up and kept pace alongside me. "You will not enjoy the loneliness. I can barely stand it myself. You are a passionate woman; you will want a husband, a companion in this life – children! It isn't too late for that, for us."

"I'll take my chances with loneliness; I have family and friends without you. I have not one ounce of trust in you. Do you hear? Not one! I answered your question and even clarified it. You promised to return home. Please do so!"

His voice grew surly. "*Isabel!* Don't be such an obstinate fool! Can we not discuss this rationally? This would never have happened had you not been acting so mulish last night in the first place!"

I glared at him from the corners of my eyes. How dare he try to place the blame for last night upon me?

Like a swift change in the weather, he sighed and softened his tone. "Isabel, please, I am begging you to be reasonable. Come with me in my carriage so we may talk comfortably? At least let me take you back home if not for a drive about the countryside?"

"There is nothing left to discuss! *Farewell*, Lord Drake." I marched off at a faster clip.

Closing the steps between us, he grabbed my arm to pull me towards him. Without hesitation, I screamed, "Do not touch me!" – My left arm flew around and slapped his face with full force!

I gasped at the sound of the impact; it quite shocked me as did the sting that radiated throughout my hand. The side of his face flushed bright red, like a strawberry. I froze as his hand released my arm to touch his afflicted cheek, as though in disbelief.

Had I just struck an Earl?

I stepped back, nervous as to how he would retaliate; I curtsied low to the ground. "My sincerest apologies, my Lord. Forgive me."

Elwood's mouth hung open; his eyes looked as stunned as I felt. Slowly his face turned into a wide smile, which greatly confused me. "Let me guess," he said, "you *didn't mean to*?"

I stood from my curtsy, staring back at him as he continued, "Because if that were the case, good heavens, would I understand *that*."

For a moment, my mind believed the connection he was making before I chose to cling to reality. "Do you mean to compare a slap to protect myself to how you bruised me?"

"Did you mean to slap me?"

"No...it was rather instinctual."

Another smirk played across his lips. "Then you understand how *sometimes*, we make mistakes and do things we do not intend to. And to protect yourself? *Really*? I have not hit or beat you, *woman!* I grabbed your waist too firmly! I am not a monster! It is *not* the same! Shocking? Perhaps. Wrong? Yes. Intentional? No! Dammit, Isabel, it was only an accident! Why must you and your family make it out to be more than it is?"

"If I could show you how large the bruises are, you wouldn't dare say that. Do you seek praise for *not* beating me in the manner you describe?"

He threw his arms up in the air. "I am the same man who has loved you for years! I would kill for you. I would *never* intentionally hurt you." His chest heaved fitfully as he tried to steady his breathing. "Only come into the carriage with me; we'll go for a ride and talk." His face, once again changed from ire to a calm, charming, expression. "I will keep my hands to myself, I swear. I will be the perfect gentleman. – There is a beautiful trail I would love to show you. Perhaps we could even stop by that bakery for some gyngerbrede? I know how much you adore it! And afterwards, we may go anywhere you like, anywhere at all!"

Why did he wish me to ride in his carriage so desperately? I took another step back. An incredible fear stole the space inside of me — did he mean to steal me away? Every instinct told me to run.

A strong wind blew through us, rattling the green, leafy trees in the fields nearby.

He held his hand out to me. "Isabel, come with me. You are mine and I am yours – you cannot run away and hide from me. You won't survive a spinster's life."

My skirts blew violently in another gust of wind. "I wish only to return home."

"After that slap, I think the least you could do is accept my invitation. Come, Isabel. It's only a carriage ride, my dear."

I looked at his hand, extending out closer to me.

"Run!" A voice screamed within me.

With every ounce of strength, I bolted down the road. I had only to make it until someone saw me, and they would come to my aid.

I turned back to see Lord Drake chasing me and felt a flashing panic as he gained speed, shouting my name, commanding me to stop. Fighting back the pain in my waist, I tried my best to go faster.

"Mary!" I prayed, *"Please help me! – Saint Michael, protect me!"*

The carriage rattled against the road behind me, and I ran even harder, too afraid to look back again.

Suddenly, I heard Jonathon scream behind me, "Jump in the grass!"

I turned my head back to see Jon and Daniel bounding down in the driver seats of our open carriage, slicing between Lord Drake and I.

I leapt into the grass as my brother steered the carriage to where it blocked the whole road, and Lord Drake with it. I could not help but yelp and moan at the sharp pain this caused my sides. I curled around my waist, flattening the long blades of grass about me.

The Earl stopped in his tracks as his carriage slowed and paused behind him. He held his hands out. "Jonathon – your sister and I were only talking."

Daniel flew to my side to check that I was unharmed. Lord Drake's leering eyes watched intently as Daniel assisted me to our small carriage. As I took my seat, our eyes met briefly; they were full of suspicion and hurt.

Jonathon ripped off his green doublet and threw it on the road behind him as he rolled up his billowing white sleeves. Daniel followed suit as they approached the Earl who shifted his attention to my enraged brother.

"*Only talking?* Then why the hell was my sister running away from you? You knave frig! I told you to leave her alone! She is *my* sister and she is under *MY CARE!* You have *no* business here!"

All at once, Jonathon threw a punch which Lord Drake dodged. "*Jonathon!* I can understand how that must have looked but—"

Jon's next swing met his face with incredible speed and accuracy. It sent Lord Drake flying back into the grass on his rear. The sound made my slap appear as child's play. I gasped at the impact as I stood in the carriage to gain a better view.

The Earl sat up, glancing towards me before spitting blood from his mouth. Jon shook out the pain from his hand as he stepped aside.

Daniel moved forward and loomed over Elwood with contempt and fisted hands. "I'd stay down if I were you, *my Lord.*"

Lord Drake scowled and made a sudden move to stand, reaching for the gold hilt of his hunter's sword. Without hesitation, Daniel thrust the heel of his boot into the Earl's chest, laying him flat on the ground, choking for air.

Elwood's driver stood and pointed a small firearm at Jon and Daniel. "Stay back!"

"Stop this at once!" I shouted. *"All of you!* This has gone far enough!"

Daniel backed up towards me, placing himself between me and the gun as it followed his steps. I sat down, gripping the rim of the carriage turning my knuckles white.

"You only have one shot in that," Daniel addressed the middle-aged driver. "You are aiming at *two* of us. I promise, you won't have time to reload before the other gets to you."

The Earl sat up, now having some success at catching his breath. Slowly standing to his feet, Elwood unsheathed his ornate blade as he walked back onto the road. My heartbeat thundered.

Jonathon rolled his shoulders and stepped further away from Lord Drake who licked the blood from his teeth. The driver focused the gun on my brother who was now closest to him. Daniel was quick to unsheathe two daggers from his belt, but Jon motioned for him to stand down. As though disagreeing with Jon's call, he very slowly slid them back in place. His hands remained resting on their hilts.

The Earl was furious as he exchanged looks with my protectors. "You boys have made an enemy of me and I promise that is *not* something anyone wants!"

Glancing at me briefly, Lord Drake shifted his attention to Daniel, stepping closer to him. "So, you fancy Miss Dawson for yourself, do you,

Mr. Porter? I see. Things are making more sense to me now. *You're* the reason why she's been so hesitant to forgive me. The plot thickens, indeed. What sort of things have you been filling her head with?"

The Earl pointed his glistening steel inches away from Daniel's face. It reflected the sunlight as though to highlight his words. "I *did* warn you about pursuing her. She is not yours to have. You will come to rue the day you set foot in Aylesbury, *Porter*. She belongs to me and me alone! No matter how much you've poisoned her against me."

Daniel didn't flinch a muscle.

The Earl held the blade still, gritting his teeth, as though debating whether or not to stab him through. Darting his eyes to mine, his face wrinkled with vexation. With a grunt, he withdrew the blade and backed away.

"Gentleman, *Isabel*. I do believe it's best if we went our separate ways, wouldn't you say?"

Jonathon nodded. His shaking fists revealing just how hot his rage still was.

He spat blood on the road as he addressed Jon again. "Like it or not, we *will* be in-laws. You may even be happy for us by the end of all this."

The Earl cast his fierce eyes to me. "Isabel... I will return for you another time when *all* of our tempers have cooled – we are not finished here. You will *never* be his." He sheathed his blade.

Giving one last glower towards Daniel, he climbed into the carriage. His driver turned them around and drove down the road at a clipping pace.

Exhaling, and trying not to cry, a spell rushed through my body like a broken dam. Daniel sat next to me in the back and held me as I buried my face in his strong chest. Stroking my disheveled hair, he comforted me as best he could. "He's gone, we're safe. I'm here for you, your brother is here too. I told you I would protect you." He kissed my head.

Lifting my face, I tried to calm my breathing and failed.

"Shh," he said gently. "Rest on me, be still a while."

His voice was so soothing; I let my head fall back into him with my ear resting over his heart. I found the steady, albeit rapid, rhythm calming. Daniel cradled me in his arms; I could feel his warmth enveloping me like a child's favorite blanket amidst a thunderstorm. My mind, however, raced with new anxieties. Elwood knew about us. We had added fresh wood to the fire. We were all in danger now. Our plan had failed abysmally.

Jonathon encouraged the horse to hurry on. "Is she injured?" He asked.

"No, I don't think so. I think maybe one of those spells you mentioned before?"

He turned his head around to check. "Is she shaking?"

"Yes."

"He's thrown her into a spell. *That bastard!* –Just keep her comfortable. Home is only a few minutes away."

George and the stablemaster met us as Jon pulled the horse to an abrupt stop. Daniel kept me nestled in his arms, carrying me out of the carriage and into the house. I had no desire for him to set me down anywhere. Mother and Anna were very concerned; their voices were quite high-pitched and asking many questions at once. Jon entered close behind Daniel, explaining all that transpired.

Daniel laid me down on the longest settee in the drawing room and brought over a chair to sit next to me in, holding my hand. My breathing steadied some and I was not shaking as much, but I felt weaker than normal for a spell. Mama came and kissed my forehead, commenting how damp I felt. I felt chilled all over. She had Missy fetch water, an herbal tea, and smelling salts.

"Isabel," Daniel said, "can you hear me?"

I nodded.

"Can you speak? Are you feeling any better?"

I opened my eyes to see the room was speckled with black spots. That was different. While it worried me, I decided it best to keep it to myself. They were all concerned enough as it was.

"I am well enough, yes."

Anna paced the room, not knowing what to do.

Missy came back with the salts and waved them under my nose.

Ugh! So pungent! My face creased as I sat up.

They tried giving me water next. It seemed to help a little.

"The poor thing doesn't need water or tea," exclaimed Jon, "pour her a glass of mead! She's just been through hell!"

Sitting me up a little more, I sipped the mead they gave me. After some time had passed and the drink was gone, I was able to take a deep breath again without it feeling as though I had inhaled shards of glass.

"It is passing. Please do not be so alarmed."

Everyone stared at me for a moment, as though gauging how bad off I was. I felt so uncomfortable to be studied in this manner.

"I promise I am well," I managed with a smile. " I'm sitting up on my own now. I am not *dying*! It was only a bout of ill health. –Come, let's all have a glass of mead together and play cards."

"That was the most severe spell you've ever had, Isabel. Are you sure you want to play a game?" Mother questioned.

"Admittedly, it is not every day that I am chased by a madman. A game would do me good, I promise."

A distraction was what I needed most. I did not want to think about what had happened – I wanted to think of anything else. I had never felt fear like that before, not even in the Elharts' garden. I didn't want to think about what might have happened if Lord Drake had caught up to me – if Jon and Daniel had not intervened. Would he have forced me into his carriage? Or worse, what if his driver had shot one of them? Not to mention what Lord Drake would do to all of us now. I shook the thoughts from my head. They brought the card table and chairs over to where I sat on the settee. Jonathon shuffled the deck of cards while Missy poured everyone a drink.

"You don't want to talk about what happened?" Anna asked.

My voice faltered, "–No."

"Did he hurt you?" My mother pressed.

"He grabbed my arm and I slapped him. So I rather think I hurt *him*, Mama."

Anna let out a small gasp. Even children knew how unspeakable a thing I had done was. The room fell silent.

Jonathon's dropped mouth slowly turned to a concealed smirk as he resumed dealing the cards.

Daniel grinned unabashedly; a bit of pride gleamed in his eye. He cared not even a little about the etiquette of the situation.

Mama, however, went pale. "What? You *slapped* an Earl? Have I taught you absolutely nothing child? Oh, good gracious! Do you not realize what this could mean? How he could retaliate against us all? What were you *thinking*? How could you have been so reckless?"

I could feel my cheeks burn as I looked at the floor. "I did not mean to, Mama! When he grabbed me, I screamed at him not to touch me and before I knew it...I had smacked his face. – I *did* apologize right away!"

Mama sighed. "What did he say after the fact?"

"He...smiled."

Jon put his cards down. "He what?"

"He smiled. Broadly even. Then he tried comparing my rash action with his own, saying our mistakes were the same."

Mama opened her mouth to say something, but nothing came out. They all exchanged perplexed glances with one another before looking to me again in stunned silence.

Daniel broke the awkwardness. "If I may, I think her slapping Lord Drake is the least of our worries at the moment. Isn't that right, Jon?"

My brother cleared his throat. "Considering, Mama, that I punched Lord Drake and Daniel here kicked him into the ground...we have other issues to worry about."

Mama exchanged wild glances between the three of us before her head fell into her hand. "While this *also* disappoints and concerns me, you must grasp that a woman of lower class assaulting an Earl is a greater offense than what the both of you have done — reckless as it was." She stood from the table. "Have the servants let me know when supper is ready. Until then, I'm retiring to my bedchamber to ponder the insolence of my children...and their friend. I must think of how we should all move forward from this incident."

We all sheepishly nodded as she took her leave.

Chapter Seventeen

AFTER A RATHER QUIET supper, Daniel took Anna and I outside for a stroll. In part, I believe, so that Jonathon and Mama could better discuss what course of action would be wisest.

In the twilight, Anna gathered flowers from the garden for mama. In her innocence, I believe she thought it would help her to feel better.

The evening carried a chill, but sitting next to Daniel, I could hardly tell. He made me feel so warm and cared for as he held my hands on the bench below the magnolia tree once more.

"Are you sure you are well? You've been more quiet than usual."

"Yes. Tired, admittedly, but being with you is soothing."

"As is your company to me. Isabel, may I ask you a question of a more personal nature?"

I nodded.

"Your breathing spells, when did they begin?"

I withdrew my hands and eyes. It was a fair question, but uncomfortable to answer. I had been told to conceal my ill bouts of health from others since I was a child. My parents worried that it would alter future suitors' opinions of me, that I would be considered less desirable as a wife because of them.

I cleared my throat, pushing back these old concerns. Daniel was a good man, twice the man Lord Drake was. If the Earl was not put off by my spells, then surely, Daniel wouldn't be either?

"When I was eight, Papa took Jonathon out again to help bring a priest to our house. Jon was five and ten at the time and would often help Papa with priestly matters. They were due back long before dinner, but they did not come home. For over five hours, I was convinced they were caught and dragged off to prison.

"Because Papa had made me promise never to tell Mama that we were Catholics, I had no one to confide in. I was too afraid to speak to the few Catholic servants we had then for fear Mama would overhear. When my bedtime came and they still were not home, I experienced my breathing troubles for the first time."

Daniel took a hold of my hand again. "That must have been terrifying at so young an age."

"It was. I was always scared of losing them."

"So your spells – they are the result of fear or things that bring you anxiety?"

"Yes, though not always, and sometimes I feel it happens for no reason whatsoever. It's most peculiar and embarrassing."

"There is no need to feel shame; it does not seem that you can control it. I only asked that I may understand it better."

"It does not lessen your opinion of me?"

"No! Why would you ever think such a thing? I cannot imagine anything changing how elevated you are in my thoughts. Though, something does confound me."

"What is that?"

"May I ask why your father *and* Jonathon are so bent on keeping this knowledge of the Faith from your mother, even now?"

"I do *not* agree with it. But I have respected their wishes. Papa had many quarrels with Mama about religion after they were married. It apparently became so turbulent between them, that Papa led her to believe he gave

191

up the old Faith entirely. He said it kept their marriage peaceful for her to believe he had done as she wished. His secret then became ours."

Daniel blinked in disbelief. "So much deception! How did he manage to hide priests under her nose all this time?"

"With the utmost care, believe me. –It is the one thing about Papa I do not look up to. He never should have lied to her."

Daniel nodded. "Nor forced you all to keep it. It is a miracle she still does not know. May I ask you another question?"

I braced myself. "Yes?"

"What did Lord Drake do that caused you to run? I cannot express how worried I was when I saw him chasing you down the road."

I understood his wanting to know, so I tried my best to answer. "He kept trying to bait me into his carriage, trying to convince me what happened was an accident, that I was overreacting. I feared he would force me into his carriage and that he would not allow me to return. So I ran. When he began to chase me…I really did think he would steal me away. Perhaps that was silly. Maybe I *did* overreact and only made matters worse."

Daniel squeezed my hands. "That was not a silly fear. You should always listen to your instincts; God gave us those for a reason. I'm inclined to agree with you, and I'm relieved you ran when you did."

I felt consoled at his reassurance, though my body felt shaky. "Are you sure you do not wish to return home and escape this madness?" I forced a smile. "I would understand – this entire situation is nightmarish. You're his enemy now. I am deeply concerned what this means for you. It would be better if you went back home where you would be safe. I do not want to see you hurt, or worse, on my account."

He kissed my hands and looked deeply into my eyes. "I am not scared, Isabel; I'm not going away…unless you desire my absence?"

"Of course I want you here! — I *am* scared though. I don't know what he will do to you, or Jonathon...or to any of us. – He won't give me up. He could have killed you tonight."

Daniel pulled me into a tender hug, rubbing my back gently. "Do you think I would have stood by and let him stab me? Have some faith in my abilities!"

He pulled away, caressing my face, "There is nothing he could do to make me ever leave you. I will *always* protect you. We will fight whatever battle he brings to us when it arises. If I have to smuggle you back to my family in Bridlington, so be it! Maybe even have a secret wedding here before we fly off!"

"Oh?"

"This may be soon to say, but I love you, Isabel, with my whole heart. –In truth, I have loved you from the first moment I opened the door and saw you smirking up at me. I won't let anything happen to us."

He grazed my cheek with his fingers. "Perhaps one of the reasons God brought us together is because He knew you would need a strong, experienced protector for a husband."

"Are you only in love with the *damsel in distress* then?"

"I don't love you because you need my protection... I simply love you. And because of that undeniable fact, God help the poor knave who intends you the smallest hint of malice." He paused, reading my eyes. "Do your feelings reflect my own?"

"You know they do."

"And yet you withhold the words I most long to hear?"

A grin spread across my face as I replied, "Far be it from me to torture you so. I *do* love you. I love you with a tenderness unparalleled to anything I've known."

He released a sigh as he leaned forward, "Will you be my wife, Isabel Dawson? I swear to lay down my life for you, and to always protect you. Be it from spiders or Lord Drake."

I giggled. "Are you asking me to marry you so soon, Mr. Clifton?"

He drew his face near, piercing my eyes with his. "What if I was?"

"Then I might say yes."

"Only might? I must not be as charming as I thought."

"Surely that cannot be."

He ran his fingers over my hair as his breath caressed my own, taunting my desire to kiss him.

"You find me charming then?"

I could not think of anything clever to say except the truth. "Yes."

"Do you think you could tolerate me for the rest of your life then?"

"Perhaps. So long as there was a view of the ocean."

"Naturally. One could not expect to survive married life with me otherwise."

"It certainly couldn't hurt."

"Why do you delight in teasing me so?"

"Whatever do you mean?"

He exhaled slowly, trying to hide a grin. "Will you be my bride, or must I leave you to kill your own spiders?"

"Of course I will marry you! You've no idea how often I have daydreamed of being your wife."

Without hesitation, he pressed his warm smile to my own. The sensation wrapped through my body like ribbons of fire; his kisses were thoughtful and passionate. I have never known such rapturous delight.

Resting his forehead against mine, he held my face within his strong hands. "Please do not tell your family yet."

"Why ever not?"

"Because tomorrow, I am going into town to purchase you an engagement gift like a gentleman ought to – I had not planned on asking you tonight, but I couldn't help myself."

"So impetuous," I jested. "Honestly, I do not need a present, Daniel. I am quite content with you." My lips followed my gaze to his curved mouth and kissed him tenderly.

He ran his hands down my arms as we pulled away. "I could not live with myself if you did not have a proper engagement. There is so much I can not afford you, but this, you must allow me to give you. You deserve that and so much more."

"I can see that I will not be able to change your mind on this! Until tomorrow then, I will keep it a secret for you. And from the rest of the world, perhaps a bit longer."

"Considering the circumstances, perhaps. But one day, all the world will know you are mine and I am yours, for all eternity."

"Shall our vows go beyond the grave, my love?"

He wove a curl behind my ear. "*My love*. I like the sound of that. And yes. One day, when death separates us, it shall never dissolve my bond with you. I would find it wholly impossible to love any but you, or to cease for any reason. I would not rest until your arms welcomed me into the afterlife."

My cheeks hurt from smiling so long. I rested my head upon his shoulder, tilting my lips up to his ear, "I will gladly love you for an eternity. I could never love another soul but yours."

"Would it please you to be married sooner rather than later?"

I reached my hand up to his face, enjoying the strength of his silhouette at my fingertips. "Yes, that would please me exceedingly well."

He exhaled. "Thank heavens. Call me impetuous all you want, but I am ever so eager for you to be my wife. And I feel the sooner you are, the safer you will be. Even *he* cannot pursue a married woman."

"I suppose that is true. Especially since your home is so far away."

He moved his head to stare into my eyes for a moment; a peaceful glaze resting over his features.

"I swear on my life that I will spend every moment making you as deliriously happy as you have me tonight."

He moved his hand to the side of my face and drew me into a kiss. My fingers combed through his hair as he enveloped me into his arms.

I didn't notice the last light change to night, nor the cold breeze or evening sounds of creatures. There was nothing but his lips and mine, nothing but our arms, nothing but the frantic pounding of our hearts. When he released me, I felt light-headed, as though tipsy from his kiss.

I could feel a daze-filled smile soak into every contour of my being; my vision became wholly consumed by his gaze.

"I had no idea that when I became a priest runner, it would lead me to you. God enjoys holding surprises for us, does he not?"

"I'm ever so grateful He does. –Will your family be very shocked?"

"Considering I have written to my sister, Theresa, about you already... I would say not so very."

"Oh? What did you tell her of me?"

"Only that you're the most beautiful, splendid, and interesting woman I've ever met. Fairly certain she can draw her own conclusions from there."

I chuckled. "You are blinded by love, Daniel. You speak far too graciously of me."

"Certainly not; I've never seen someone as clearly and detailed as I see you."

Just as we were about to kiss again, Anna came bounding around the corner with arms overflowing with a variety of flowers. "Look at all the pretty colors I've found for Mama! Surely these shall cheer her!"

"Indeed!" I replied as Daniel rested his head against my shoulder.

"It's getting quite dark, Isabel," Anna stated. "May we go inside? I don't much care for the night or spooky owls."

The glow from the lanterns near the house and the moon held a glow over us, but I could see her meaning. "Of course, Anna, quite right." I agreed begrudgingly.

Anna bounded in ahead of us to present her offering to Mama.

Mother's eyes twinkled at the loving gesture. "Why, thank you my darling girl! How thoughtful and sweet you are."

She handed them to a servant to place in a suitable vase as Jonathon eyed Daniel and I suspiciously as we moved further into the room. "Why are you both grinning like that?"

"Like what?" I questioned him neutrally.

"Are you betrothed?" He asked with a grin of his own, "You are, are you not?"

Mama gasped, her face lifting even more. "What! Is it true?"

Daniel and I exchanged shocked expressions before he answered. "I don't know how you deduced that – but yes! She's agreed to be my wife!"

Everyone in the room shouted with excitement, even Mama! I was relieved that she appeared to be pleased. I wondered greatly at what she and Jon had spoken of in our absence. The servants were immediately called in to celebrate with toasts of wine.

Daniel explained how he had wanted to give me an engagement present before we shared the news with them. They waved their hands off at him as though he were being silly. Anna was so pleased that she hugged Daniel and placed a flower through a tie in his shirt. He bowed to her and thanked her, "I'm very pleased that I shall be gaining such a kind and splendid young sister."

Anna beamed, quite gratified by his compliment and curtsied back.

After much celebrating and discussion, Jonathon of course, brought us back to the ground from the clouds we'd been flying in. "I hate to suggest this, but I think a small, secret wedding would be wise, given the circumstances."

Mama looked utterly disappointed. "Oh…yes, I suppose that is true. How would we go about that exactly? Invite none of our friends? How long should they be hidden for?"

"Well…" Daniel offered, "we could be married where I'm from? You'd all be invited of course and our families could be introduced! –The Earl doesn't possess the knowledge of where I'm from or even of my correct name…so there would be no risk of him barging in to ruin the ceremony."

Mama squinted. "Your *correct name*? Is it not Porter?"

Without hesitation, Daniel explained. "Forgive me, Mrs. Dawson. I have not been completely forthcoming. I am so accustomed to giving my alias." He looked around the room to ensure only the family remained before he continued. "You see, I am not ashamed to tell you that I am Catholic, Mrs. Dawson. Should that be discovered on my travels, I do not want that information to be traced back to my family in Bridlington. So when I travel I am Daniel Porter from Portsmouth. When home, I am Daniel James Clifton. I hope this does not change your opinion of me, ma'am."

My siblings and I exchanged stunned expressions as we awaited Mama's reaction.

Her face fell ashen, then blustered red as she narrowed her eyes at him in silence for a moment. At last she cleared her throat. "I can see the prudence in concealing this information…Mr. Clifton. I do not begrudge you this. However, I do not know how I feel about my daughter marrying a Catholic during such times. Well, actually I do know exactly how I feel about it. I do not like or approve of this notion at all! In my opinion, being Catholic is a most imprudent and foolhardy decision."

I bit my lip and answered before anyone could stop me, "Mama...there is something I feel you should know."

Jonathon caught his face in his palm, dreading what was to come. "*Isabel...no.*"

I continued, the nod from Daniel encouraging me to end this terrible charade. "Papa raised us all in the Catholic Faith. He bound us to secrecy so as not to worry you. Please do not be angry with us – we only meant to honor Papa's wishes, but it feels wrong to continue to do so any longer. Daniel and I share the same convictions of Faith."

Mama's jaw clenched tightly together as she stood and walked to the window in silence.

Jon glared at me as he stood to comfort her. "Mama, we have been very careful."

She held her hand up abruptly to stop him, without turning her gaze from the front gardens. "Your father, may he rest in peace, I can no longer be angry with. What incredible arrogance to hide such an important matter from me for *so* long! And to force that burden upon our children. *Oh!* He is lucky indeed to be in the grave, for it is the only place he could possibly hide from my wrath!"

I suddenly realized precisely where my own temper came from. Looking at Daniel and then to my siblings, I saw we all wore the same shade of panic.

Mama sighed deeply, turning sharply to Jon. "*And you.* A grown man! You thought this was fair and right to keep from me?"

Jonathon stared at the floor before daring to meet her eyes. "It was one of father's last requests of me, Mama. I did not like the deception, none of us have. You are right to be upset. It was I who made Isabel and Anna promise to keep it secret after his death; the fault rests entirely with me. Please do not be cross with them."

She turned her head back to the window. "I suppose I ought to thank Mr. Clifton for *his* honesty, for it has inspired my own children to be truthful."

We were silent. The room was heavy and cold, no doubt engulfing us all in a cloud of guilt as we waited for her to speak again.

Turning around, she stared at each of us in turn. "Why? Why would you all choose to risk your lives in this fashion? Have you no consideration for your own existence or what I may suffer should you all be torn away from me? Have you no loyalty to England?"

Anna stepped forward, perhaps the bravest of us all. "Because Mama, Jesus is not at the church you take us to. They cast Him out. What is the point of church without Him?"

Mother exhaled, glaring at Jonathon and I. "God is everywhere, my dear. You are breaking the law for nothing."

Jonathon rested a hand on Anna's shoulder as he addressed Mama. "Can you be one with Him, Body, Blood, Soul and Divinity, just anywhere? Did Jesus Himself not begin the Catholic Church with His Apostles? The better question would be to ask why you follow a heretical religion started by a murderous man consumed with lust?"

Mama's face flushed. "As if various Popes have been better or worse!"

Jon's voice remained calm. "Some, much better, saints even. Others are surely just as hell bound as King Henry VIII was. But Christ's Church remains unchanged. What would become of the world if everyone manipulated religion to fit their own personal ideas and whims? When would it ever end? God created *one* Church, one Mystical Body. The only imperfect thing about it is the people, but He promised it would stand until the end of time despite the weaknesses of some men. Do you really think God approves of murdering wives and divorce? Or of Luther's madness? It is his opinion that a man may commit adultery and murder several times a day and be no further from God than Anna here!"

Mama sighed and pursed her lips tightly together as her only response.

I walked to her, wrapping my arms around her stiff shoulders. "We love you and we're so very sorry for deceiving you. We will never hide things from you again. But we are not sorry for being Catholic."

Jonathon cleared his throat. "Uh, there is one, *small* thing left to disclose."

Releasing Mama from the hug, she turned around. "What more could there possibly be?"

"Papa...and us...we have been harboring priests since I can remember. And Daniel is a priest runner – an assistant to them. We did not go to Oxford together. Now that *really* is everything."

I thought flames would burst from my mother's eyes; she stormed across the room and slapped my brother's face. "You have been endangering our family behind my back *all this time?* How? Where? A priest runner? What in heaven's name, is that?"

Jon clenched. I had not witnessed Mama slapping his face since he was three and ten.

His cheek crimsoned as Lord Drake's had. "Our intentions had been to spare you the worry and concern — but it was terribly incorrect and misguided. I am profoundly sorry and I take full responsibility."

Mama sighed and folded her arms. "I'm sorry. It is your father who deserves the brunt of my anger, not you, Jonathon."

She turned to Daniel. "What is a priest runner?"

We took our seats again as Daniel explained how he volunteered to protect and guide priests across the country.

Mama slowly shook her head. "And will you continue to do this when you take my daughter as your wife?"

"No. I could not, in good conscience, leave her at home alone for such extended periods of time. I will refocus on the family business and fully dedicate myself to her and our future children. Perhaps hide priests ourselves one day."

I could not have been happier to hear this response. I squeezed his hand with both of mine. He looked back into my eyes with a smile. "If that plan is amenable to you, my love?"

I nodded eagerly.

Mama sighed. "Oh good gracious. I suppose that is, at least *slightly* better." Suddenly her face fell. "Oh dear...should Lord Drake discover *any* of this...oh my!"

"And that is another reason why a secret wedding, far from here, will be best," Daniel replied.

I agreed. "Nothing he can do once we are wed!"

"Precisely!" Jonathon raised his glass, clearly eager at the change of topic.

"That is..." Daniel said, looking towards my mother. "So long as you would approve of my marrying your daughter."

The room fell silent, awaiting her response once more.

She eyed Daniel as though weighing everything she knew about him. "I'll be forthcoming with you, Mr. Clifton. You are not my first choice for a son-in-law. You have no fortune, title, or rank. You are reckless and young. However, you've displayed true integrity, at great risk to yourself, and are more honest than possibly anyone I've ever known. I respect you for it and I can see why my daughter is drawn to you." Her stern lips curved upwards. "You have my blessing, so long as you strive to provide adequately for her. She is a horrible cook, God love her. It was not a skill I thought to allow her much practice in."

"*Mama!*" I went to hug her.

Daniel grinned. "Hiring a cook will be the first order of business, ma'am! She will be well cared for!"

"Anna…" I said turning to her. "*You* must be my bridesmaid."

She squealed with excitement. "Oh, of course, Isabel! I should dearly love that!"

We stayed up so late discussing plans that my mother insisted Daniel take the guest bedroom…and this time…not the one between the walls and ground.

Intriguing how one of my worst days became one of my absolute favorites, is it not?

Chapter Eighteen

I IMAGINED NAMES FOR our future children as I laid in bed... *Edmund, Tristan, Isaac, Eloise, Sophia, Marian...* I wondered what Daniel's family was like and how well we would get on together.

I dreamt of our wedding day, in a quaint church by the shore. I was walking up to the doors of the Church in my mother's dress with a large flowy veil. I saw Daniel dressed like a gentleman, handsome and smiling at my approach.

Just as I took his hand, Lord Drake came on horseback with guardsmen to arrest us — accusing us all of being papist spies, disloyal to the crown.

I clung to Daniel.

"Good morning, Miss Dawson," greeted Lily as she drew back the curtains, "or should I say, *Mrs. Clifton!*"

My heart was still pounding from the nightmare, but I replied as cheerily as I could, "That does have rather a lovely ring to it, does it not?"

"It does, indeed!" She grinned as she handed me a small ale.

"You will come on and stay as my favorite maid, will you not, Lily?"

Lily's thin pink lips curved into a large smile, showing off the dimples in her cheeks. "Of course, I should prefer it no other way! I'm right excited about moving to the seashore!"

I giggled. "Me too!"

Lily helped me pick out what to wear; we decided on a yellow and blue dress with a gold cross necklace.

Meeting Daniel for breakfast at the table, he was all smiles. As was I.

"You look radiant," he said, standing with Jon as I took my seat.

Breakfast was full of wedding and travel plans. We decided in three days, we would all go to Bridlington and begin the arrangements with his family. After, Daniel kissed my cheek goodbye and said he would be back soon with a gift befitting me. Jon went along with him to assist.

While the men were out, Mother had us come into her bedchambers. "I thought you might like to wear this, since there isn't much time to have one made?"

She swished a beautiful, long, cream-colored gown from her closet, the bottom hem sprawling out upon the floor. I ran my fingers over the lace details. "Oh! I should love to! May I try it on now?"

Mother nodded her head excitedly, handing the gown to Lily who helped me into it. "He isn't near as wealthy as I would like. However, I think you and Daniel will be rather happy together, my dear. He reminds me of your Papa in some ways."

I was touched and relieved to hear her say so. "I think Papa would approve of Daniel too. I can't imagine being unhappy so long as I am with him."

I gasped when I saw the mirror. The way the dress draped, hugging my figure, how the combination of taffeta and lace swept here and there, I felt beautiful. The lace gloves were long and elegant; I could not help but smile imagining Daniel's reaction when he would catch sight of me in such a dress!

"Mama! It is *stunning!* It fits me perfectly!"

She placed the matching veil on top of my head; it flowed about me like an airy cloud.

"Why are you both crying? This is happy!" Anna questioned with a confused expression.

Mama and I chuckled. "They're happy tears, dear. Oh, how your father would have loved to see you in this dress, Isabel."

We hugged tenderly, wiping tears away.

After I was back in my yellow and blue dress, Missy took Mama's wedding dress...I mean *my* wedding dress to pack it safely in a chest to take with us to Bridlington. We gathered in the drawing room, waiting eagerly for Daniel to come home. Oh, and Jon too I suppose.

We waited...and waited until luncheon had been served and there was still no sign of them. I tried to quell the worrying thoughts attacking my mind and suggested we occupy ourselves with cards. Only half paying attention, my sister won four hands in a row. At last, we heard the carriage roll into the drive! My heart fluttered just at the thought of seeing him again; I smoothed my dress as I stood to greet them. However, only an exhausted Jonathon walked through the door.

"What happened?" I asked.

His tone betrayed him faster than he could utter the words. "I don't know how to say this — how to explain it. I tried everything I could, but it was all for nothing. We should never have gone to town. I gravely underestimated what he would do."

My heart felt strangled in the silence that followed. I stepped forward. "Jon...where is Daniel?"

"There is no gentle way of saying this. While we were at the jeweler's shop, Lord Drake came and pulled a rosary from his pocket and accused him of treason. — The guards took Daniel then and there. As if they had been waiting for him."

I steamed. He didn't even have his rosary — *I* did! Lord Drake had staged it all.

"The only information I was able to acquire," Jon continued, "was that he had a rushed trial. When asked to renounce his faith by taking the Oath, he refused. Good man that he is."

I felt as if the air had abandoned my lungs. I collapsed into the settee; the wood creaked loudly from the sudden pressure. *No. No this cannot be. God, please, no!*

Mother sat next to me while questioning my brother. "Is there nothing that can be done?"

Anna sat on the floor by my feet and rested her head on my knees. My hand clutched the rosary beads he'd given me in my pocket. *This is my fault.*

Jonathon shook his head. "No, I already tried everything I could. *Sometimes* people with low level offenses are released after a fortnight or so, as a warning. But the fact that Daniel was already given the oath, I would assume Lord Drake attached a few other charges besides the rosary."

Hot tears streamed down my face as Mama attempted to comfort me, wrapping her arm around me. I could not stop my body from trembling.

"When...is his execution?" I managed to ask.

Jon cleared his throat. "I'm not sure."

"How can people do this!" Mama exclaimed. "What should it matter to the Queen what religion people are? Can't Mr. Porter just lie to save his own life?"

"He could," I said, "if he were a coward and a liar. — I cannot bear this. I should have married Lord Drake in the first place!"

Mama squeezed me. "This is *not* your fault!"

It was. I knew it. This would not be happening if not for me. I needed to be alone, not be fed platitudes. Fleeing the drawing room, I raised my skirts in hand, I raced passed George as he held the door open for me. Running as fast as my own thoughts, I did not stop until I reached the stable.

"Please, ready my horse. Hurry." I told the stablemaster who did so in haste.

In a few minutes, I was racing off into the woods, tears streaming across my face and catching in the wind behind me. They blurred my vision; I had to wipe them repeatedly with my arm. The rush from going so fast felt oddly soothing to my pain. Even my waist did not concern me. I urged Honey on faster, dodging branches that would assail my face. The harder I pushed her, the further away reality seemed.

Reaching the stream that ran under the bridge, I climbed down and tied her to a low branch. Honey needed rest. Without the speed of my horse, my thoughts and crushing feelings caught up with me all at once. I fell to my knees, clutching tufts of grass between my fingers.

How could I have been so stupid?

What did I think was going to happen?

Why did I listen to anyone's advice but my own?

How will I bear to see him so brutally killed?

How will I tell his family that I'm the real reason he's dying?

Pulling out his rosary, I held it close to my heart. A fresh wave of tears poured over me; I could not stop picturing Daniel being forced into the same fate as Father Campion...being hung to within an inch of his life, with his intestines gutted from him before they chopped off his head.

My breath would not steady. A spell took me over, and I gasped for air more aggressively; my chest hurt and pounded, yet I did not care.

I laid down next to the stream and placed my hand into the cold water. Tears streamed sideways across my face, watering the patch of grass my face rested on.

I prayed Ave's, and laid there until the pain passed, and I could breathe normally again.

My God, I prayed, *how can this be Thy will? Do you want your daughter to die of heartache? There will be nothing left of me! - Is this how You felt in your Agony in the Garden? Was your heart shattering as mine is now? I unite my sufferings with yours, my loving Savior. Oh, please, please give Daniel strength and grace to go through everything he's about to. And give me the courage to be strong for him.*

The sky was darkened by the sunset and heavy clouds moving in. It seemed only fitting that it should rain. Slowly rising to my feet, I walked over to Honey who ate her weight in the long grass around her. I guided her to the stream so she could wash it down, which she did eagerly.

In the distance, I heard a horse galloping and Jon's voice shouting my name. I could just make him out in the twilight; I waved my arm and called out where I was as I put my rosary away. Racing his horse over, he jumped off and immediately embraced me. I hugged him back and rested my head on his shoulder. Just when I thought I had no more tears left, they began gushing out of me again.

"I am *so* sorry, Isabel – I should have known – I should have had us all be more cautious. I should have taken on Lord Drake myself."

I lifted my head and looked into his mournful blue eyes. "Jonathon, if it is anyone's fault, it is *mine*. I was naïve. I should have known this is exactly how it would turn out – I had hoped we could outsmart him. I truly thought we had."

"As did I, little sister. It's not your fault that you didn't want to marry a monster or that you fell in love with Daniel. You didn't do anything wrong. If anything, I should have listened to your concerns more; we should have left for Bridlngton this morning. We should have moved this very day without the preparations I once thought were so necessary."

"It is of no matter now."

209

"My sweet sister, try to take comfort in the knowledge that he will go straight to heaven – there is nothing we can do now except pray for him and all the prisoners there."

I nodded.

"You're very pale. Did you have another breathing fit?"

I nodded again.

He sighed. "We could have taken care of you! Did you have to take Honey and race out here?"

I nodded.

"Are you hungry?"

I shook my head.

Jon heaved another sigh. "Chatty aren't you? Come now, up on your horse! It's time to head home."

It poured the whole way back. We were both properly soaked by the time we came to the stables. Once inside our home, Mother made *all the fuss* about how drenched we were. Nothing mattered to me. I was empty and hollow. I walked quietly upstairs to my room while Lily dried me off near the fireplace.

I sat on a stool near my small fireplace as she wound my hair up with strips of cloth. She seemed to understand without me having to explain that I was in need of silence. I deeply appreciated this. When she was finished, she took my wet clothes and came back up with hot soup, an assortment of leftovers and a glass of mead. The thought of food made me sick. I ignored the tray and laid in bed, praying for Daniel on his beads.

Chapter Nineteen

"Up, Miss Dawson, you must eat! I brought Father his breakfast. I know you're hurting something fierce, but we both know he'd want you taking care of yourself."

Lily was back and had opened the curtains, assaulting me with sunshine. I grimaced; as soon as I had been forced awake, I felt the large stake in my heart return, reminding me of my anguish. It was similar to how I felt after Papa died, but somehow worse? Anticipatory grief? Helpless. My whole body ached as if all my joints were mourning with me. It is an awful cross to be powerless to help someone you love. I imagined this was how the Blessed Mother must have felt along the way to Calvary.

I sat up slowly in bed, feeling like I hadn't slept at all. "Thank you for helping Father."

"Of course. – Now, which dress shall it be today?"

"You may choose."

"Hmm," Lily's green eyes scanned my collection. "Let's go with this dark blue dress with the bell sleeves. Can't fathom you in something bright today."

After Lily was satisfied with my appearance, I went downstairs for breakfast. Entering the room, all conversation ceased and they watched me closely as I took my seat.

"Oh, Isabel," Mother began, "you look quite pale dear. We're here for you darling."

I gave the best smile I could muster. "I know, Mama, thank you."

Lily walked by and placed a mug of herbal tea for me. When she noticed I was not helping myself to food, she immediately piled my plate with fruit, bread, a hard boiled egg, and a piece of ham.

"Don't think I didn't notice that you didn't eat a bite last night," she said. "You need your strength."

Everyone at the table could not contain their smirks.

"Thank you, Lily."

She nodded and went about her chores.

"You had best eat some of that before she comes round again," Jon smiled. "She might scold you if you don't."

My lips curved a bit at the thought of tiny Lily scolding me like an old burly maid. Nevertheless, I did force myself to eat the bread with my tea.

My thoughts kept circling back to Daniel – I kept imagining him in prison, cold and hungry, perhaps being tortured. I wondered when his execution would be. Would he look for me in the crowd before they killed him? I would be there.

"Isabel? Are you listening to us at all?" Mother asked, placing her hand on top of mine.

I jumped at her touch. "Sorry Mama, my mind was elsewhere."

"Would you like to take a morning walk with us?"

"Oh...no thank you. I think I'll keep inside today."

I could sense them exchanging worried expressions. Yet, I could not find it within myself to ease them; I did not know how to ease my own. I felt more tears coming and excused myself from the table. I walked back upstairs to my room and laid in bed, wondering what was happening to Daniel at this very moment.

At lunch, Lily startled me from my thoughts and forced me down again to eat. I managed to eat a bit of soup and bread. I admit, this meal did make me feel stronger, but it did not alleviate my torment.

I wandered into the drawing room and curled up on the window seat. I stared out into our gardens, reliving memories of us walking together, of how pleasant his kisses were and the reality of where he was now. It was too much. Why had God allowed me to fall in love with someone – only to have him be ripped from me so brutally? My head leaned against the window pane with more tears painting my cheeks. I heard Anna playing a song on the harpsichord, so I knew my family was there too. I didn't notice their presence otherwise.

After what I assume was half an hour or more, Jon sat across from me, "Isabel, you can't keep on in this manner. We're very worried for you. Your eyes are bloodshot and you're *so* pale."

"What would you have me do? The man who would have been my husband is being tortured in a prison, awaiting a gruesome death." My lips quivered, "Especially when it is *my* fault? When I *knew* what the consequences could be. I was selfish and gambled with his life."

Jon took my hand. "I do believe Daniel had a great deal of say in the matter. He fell in love with you too, after all. You are terribly incorrect in saying the fault is yours. Especially when the blame falls entirely on the shoulders of the Earl."

"There is nothing I can do and it is consuming me."

"We're only humans, Isabel, we can't control the actions of others. It's a broken world we live in – God gave all men free will, even though sometimes I wish he'd held back that precious gift from a few people. Lord Drake will one day pay for all the hurt he's caused, if not in this life, then the next. Perhaps a bit of both. Maybe Daniel was always called to be a martyr...perhaps not. Maybe he will stay in prison or find a way out.

Perhaps the Queen will come to her senses tomorrow and put an end to our persecution. You musn't lose *all* hope. I assume you're praying for him as much as you can?"

I nodded and wiped my eyes with the backs of my hands, a quarter of my guilt somewhat alleviated.

"Then you're helping him more than you can know."

I smiled up at him and squeezed his hand. "You know, you're a rather good brother."

He opened his mouth to reply, when we were both caught off guard by the sounds of hooves and wheels. Two carriages rushed down our drive at a thundering clip. One belonged to Lord Drake, the other was only ever used for his guardsmen or searchers.

"Anna! HIDE! Now!" Jonathon sternly ordered as he leapt off the window seat. Anna glanced outside and immediately ran to the study.

Mother stood with the face of a ghost, eyes pacing the room between us. "They know you're Catholics."

A couple of our Protestant servants had been present with us in the room. Mama covered her mouth as we all exchanged tensive glances.

George was quick to speak on their behalf, "Any good Christian knows that what the Queen is doing is wrong; we will do everything we can to protect the Dawson family." The other servant, Missy, nodded her head firmly in agreement.

Jon locked arms with him. "Grateful, George." He looked behind to Missy and nodded his thanks to her. "Anyone who is uncomfortable with this can leave without hard feelings, please let them know that."

Instead of being angry or even upset, Mama was resolute. "There is no reason for Catholics to be punished this way – I will stand by my children and die with you."

My heart broke for Mama as I watched a single tear escape the corner of her eye. I went and hugged her tightly. "We will see if it comes to that. We don't yet know why they are here."

Mama ordered us to sit and act naturally. I wiped the tear from her cheek and took my spot next to her on the settee.

Lord Drake (sporting a swollen and cracked lip) walked in with two armed men behind him. They wore their full armor, helmets, chain mail and tall boots. They kept a hand on the hilts of their swords at all times. Their presence alone was extremely intimidating. There was no group of men clamoring to search the house, however. Our secret was still safe for now. I dared not venture to imagine why he came with his guardsmen.

Lord Drake himself donned a black cape and contrasting red doublet, as though dressed to impress. "Good day to you, Mistress Catherine!"

Mother's brow raised. "Is it? What is the meaning of bringing guardsmen to my home...especially when you yourself are not exactly welcome here?"

"Excellent questions, ma'am. Misunderstandings of course led to me being unwelcome here; however this is a conversation for another time. For now, Miss Dawson will need to come with me."

My brother stood, blocking them from where I sat. "Under no circumstance are you taking her with you. She's done nothing to merit such an escort, and you cannot simply take her from us."

Lord Drake sighed smugly. "Jonathon, she can either come with me willingly or by force." He motioned to the men behind him. "The choice is yours, of course."

I squeezed Mama's hand as I rose from the settee and walked to him. "Jon..." I put my hand on his arm. "Do not be concerned; I will go with Lord Drake and I will be taken care of, will I not?" I shifted my eyes to the Earl.

His face lifted. "Yes, indeed. I will ensure no harm comes to Miss Dawson."

"I'll see you both again, soon." I assured Mama and Jon with a forced smile. Grief seemed to have muted my fear.

Walking past my brother, it was difficult to watch him struggle to restrain himself from attacking the Earl. I knew how much it was in his nature to protect me. His eyes raced between us as his jaw clenched as tightly as his fists.

"Where are you taking her?" His voice rumbled like thunder.

Lord Drake extended his arm out to me and I took it as naturally as I could. "Do not fret. Her well being is my utmost concern."

Before my brother could respond, I was escorted from my home.

Chapter Twenty

Lord Drake behaved as though this were an ordinary day, as though he were taking me for a casual outing and not abducting me. I could not grasp the delusion he seemed to be living in. As though the last few days had never happened.

I stared at the prominent coat of arms displayed on his black carriage door, trying to call forth my courage. The dragon was lined in gold; it stared back at me with beady black eyes, crouching menacingly with his talons gripping onto a cliff. It resembled Elwood in more ways than it should have.

His driver opened the door, jarring my thoughts. I noticed he was careful to avoid my eyes as Lord Drake motioned for me to step inside, "My dear, do you require assistance?"

My body hesitated. Daniel's rosary was still in my pocket. What if I was searched?

"No, I can manage. Thank you." Going against every instinct, I climbed inside.

Sitting opposite me, Lord Drake settled in and ordered the driver to move on. His carriage was darkly colored with red hues and excessive cushions. He sat there, looking at me with a proud, victorious gleam.

I kept my arms folded. "What is the meaning of all of this?"

His eyes suddenly colored with concern. "You look ill, Isabel. Are you well?"

"I've had more health troubles than usual."

"I see. I'm sorry my dear, but it will all be worth it in the end."

"What will be?"

"We have much to discuss."

I tightened my arms. "Where are you taking me?"

He ignored my questions completely. "I understand that the accidental bruising caused you and your family some alarm. I imagine they fed this fear and anger of yours which caused you to slap my face and run from me."

I looked down at the floor, feeling some trepidation. "–I *did* apologize for that."

He reached across the cabin and grabbed my hands, forcing them away from my arms, "As I apologized to you...did I not?"

I realized, very clearly by his demeanor, that it would be in my best interest if I played along nicely and not argue. I lowered my eyes to the floor of the carriage once more. "You did, my Lord."

He rubbed his hands over mine. "You admit that it *was* an accident then?"

"I believe that it was not your intention to hurt me."

"Isabel, look at me, please; you need not fear me."

I raised my eyes to his own without any worry of being lost in them.

"Good," he said. "Now, do you understand there is no reason to be afraid?"

What I wanted to do was point out that he had brought armed men to my home, forced me into his carriage, thrown my betrothed in jail, chased me down a road, caused me large bruises, and blackmailed me – all within the same week. However, I bit my tongue.

"Isabel?" He prompted me again.

"Perhaps, that is difficult to say as we are being accompanied by your guards as we speak, and given recent events. However, I imagine you are still the same man who has exhibited much kindness to me over the years."

He seemed to appreciate this answer. *"Yes,* Isabel! *I am!* Your indecisiveness drove me mad...and then this *Mr. Porter* inserting himself into your life was most vexing. – You poor naïve creature; you had no idea you were *friends* with a dirty papist, did you?"

I shook my head. I felt this was a day to be filled with many lies on my part.

"And I'm quite positive my dove did nothing to encourage him to propose marriage?"

I feigned surprise and confusion. "Excuse me?"

"He was purchasing a necklace as an engagement present with your brother yesterday! That's when he was found to be carrying a *rosary,* of all things. Terribly shocking. And might I say? It was a feeble, cheap little necklace with opals." He scoffed. "You'd never have accepted such a tasteless thing."

Anger was quick to rise in me, but I managed to conceal it. "I heard he is in prison now."

"As all dirty papists should be, yes! – I know you may have been tempted to cling to him out of rebellion towards me. I daresay I even deserved that." He cocked his head abruptly. "Did you love him?"

I met his dark eyes that scrutinized my features as though to read my answers before I spoke them, "Mr. Porter became a dear friend. I *did* care for him as he was a very kind man. I feel sorry for him that he is in prison, and I wish that was not the case." Something inside urged me to keep my affections for Daniel a secret.

He paused. Once he decided he was satisfied with my response, he said, "We must never feel sorry for the papists. They've chosen this for themselves. Mr. Porter was given the opportunity to reject his treasonous religion and say the Oath and he refused; he was a danger to society, even to the Queen herself. If he wishes to save himself, he could do so easily."

I did not respond.

"I daresay," Lord Drake continued, "even though you may not have *completely* fallen for him, I believe he cares a *great* deal for you. His last words to me were to leave you alone." He laughed. "As if he were in any position to threaten or give commands!"

Breathe, Isabel, breathe; do not lose control, be calm. I felt as though he were testing me.

"Indeed." I responded calmly.

"Hmm. Back to a more agreeable topic. My dear, will you still insist upon being...indecisive?"

"Do I still intend to remain an old maid? Yes."

"I suspected as much. Your stubbornness has no limit. I am not concerned, however. In fact, I have a feeling you will change your mind this very day."

"Why is that?"

"Patience, my dove, patience."

Several minutes passed in uncomfortable silence. I could not bear it. Not when so many questions fought to be uttered. "Why did you bring those men to my house? Where are we going?"

"Would you have agreed to come with me had I come alone? Or rather, would your doorman even let me in?"

"That seems to be a lot of trouble to go through for a carriage ride."

He shrugged. "Not as much as you might think. They do anything I ask. And I would do anything for you; nothing is too much trouble for the woman who owns my heart."

I did not respond. Looking out the window, we were already well into town. "Are you taking me to your castle?"

Lord Drake smiled but said nothing. I leaned back in my seat, stewing in my irritation.

The sounds of sharp thunks from blacksmiths pounding their tools against iron told me we had passed the center of town. I became even more confused. A short way more and the carriage halted. Lord Drake got out first to help me down the steps. As my eyes adjusted to the brightness, my heart skipped a beat. We were at the prison.

"Do you know why we are here, Isabel?"

I turned sharply to him. "Do you mean to threaten to have me arrested if I do not accept your proposal?"

The Earl belly-laughed, causing a passerby to stare. "Isabel! You greatly amuse me sometimes! What a terrible beginning to a marriage that would be. – Come, take my arm and walk with me. We are going to visit a *close friend* of yours."

I felt immensely conflicted as we walked up to the side door of the impressive stone building. What was his reason for bringing me to see Daniel? To show me what happens to men I try to be with instead of him? Was he parading me through the prison to rub it in Daniel's face? I could not help but feel eager to see him, even though it would be impossible to tell him the things I truly desired to express with his Lordship present.

In the entrance were many officers, some dredges of society, a large desk on one side with a rail and seats on the other. An unpleasant smell of filth permeated the dreadful space. Everyone paused what they were doing to stare at me; it was a most uncommon place for a lady to be.

Lord Drake walked through as if he owned the building, which in a manner of speaking, he did. He motioned for one of the officers, who came towards him with urgency. I recognized him as being one of the guests at the Elharts' party.

"At your service, my Lord."

"Escort Miss Dawson and I to the cell where Mr. Porter is being kept please."

The officer looked uncomfortable at the request, "Magistrate, forgive my saying so, but it's not an appropriate place for someone like Miss Dawson."

"I will be the judge of that. Lead the way."

The officer nodded his head and led us down a hall and unlocked a door that led to the stairs.

He grabbed the two lanterns that hung on the wall; one for himself and one for Elwood. Lighting them from the flint box that was set into a carving out of the wall, he gave me an apologetic glance. I soon understood why.

The further we walked down the hall, the worse the smell became; full chamber pots, filthy men, and mildew assaulted my nose aggressively. Spiderwebs clung to the corners of the ceilings, hanging down like hellish draperies. I tried to ignore the crouching and crawling spiders waiting for their next victims. I failed. A shiver rattled through me.

"You needn't be frightened, Isabel." Lord Drake whispered. "I will keep you safe from these ruffians. There isn't another prison for many miles, so we are always on verge of bursting here."

He held out his arm, but I refused. "I am not afraid."

"My arm remains at your service and leisure, my dear."

I nodded, continuing to take in in my surroundings. There were numerous cells with iron bars. Some prisoners shouted curses that I dare not repeat. Many more slept through the racket or completely ignored us. We walked down another set of stone stairs that curved without rails; here, I confess I did hold onto Lord Drake's arm to steady my balance.

This deeper level made the previous room smell like a bottle of perfume. The webs increased dramatically, causing the Earl to duck and weave between them. There were no windows; the only light besides our lanterns, were from the torches placed in holders along the walls. Random cries coming from women and men alike echoed into my ears. My heartbeat rose higher with each scream.

A large rat scurried across the hall, causing me to shriek and push myself into Lord Drake. In a fast, smooth motion, he effortlessly swept me from the floor, and held me in his arms. He seemed to take delight in my fright.

"I have you," he said softly. I will let nothing harm you."

I battled between feelings of gratitude and disgust as I glanced between his face and the lantern he still managed to hold onto. "The rat is gone. You may put me down now."

"As my lady requests." Gently, he placed me back on my feet, his arm lingering about my waist. "Though I'd gladly carry you the rest of the way. You never know when another rat may appear."

My eyes crossed his gaze as I moved away from his grasp, "I will keep that in mind."

"I admire your bravery, but there truly *are* many rats."

I could hear their wretched little screeches from down the hall. I may have discovered a fear greater than spiders. He offered his arm to me with a smug look that I despised. I took his arm. Like a proper coward.

At last we came to a cell door towards the end of the hall, and the officer gave the order for the guard to open it. It was a thick wooden door with a small iron-barred opening at the top. It creaked heavily as it swung into the cell.

"Ladies first," the Earl offered, gesturing towards the cell with the lantern.

Lifting up some of my skirt in hand to try and avoid the random puddles of what I hoped was water, I stepped through as bravely as I could. It was very dark and cold with no windows. I could only see what the light from outside the door brought in. Some light shone too, from the guardsman who stood just on the inside of the room.

I searched for Daniel among the fifteen or so men of differing ages. The room was no bigger than my bedchamber. – I was horrified by the conditions: no beds, a couple pots for relieving themselves, and rotting straw was strewn about the floors. All the men were in varying stages of malnourishment and so very dirty. I swallowed a wave of nausea, a hand naturally resting over my belly.

One man stumbled to his feet as I drew in nearer, though I could not make out who it was.

Lord Drake came in from behind me, his lantern casting light onto the people.

"Porter!" He taunted. "I've brought a visitor!"

The same man who had stumbled to his feet limped closer. I squinted to try and see him better; his face was severely bruised and there was blood splattered all over what was once a white shirt. My heart pounded as I looked into his one eye that was not swollen shut – it was Daniel! How was he so disfigured after only two days? My legs tried to take me to him, but Lord Drake held out his arm to prevent me.

Daniel hung his head before looking back up at me and then to the Earl. "Why... why would you bring her here? She doesn't need to see me – to see any of us like this. What game are you playing at? This is no place for her; haven't you put her through enough?"

Lord Drake gave a nod to the second guard who proceeded to punch Daniel in his abdomen, causing him to buckle onto his knees. I couldn't help but shout for them to stop.

"Be calm, Isabel." Lord Drake said. "This is the only way you can get these papists to understand anything. Now, *Porter*...prisoners don't ask questions. They just exist and do as they're told, isn't that right?"

I hated how Lord Drake seemed to be enjoying this.

Daniel nodded with his fists on the ground, catching his breath.

"Why am I here?" I asked.

Lord Drake turned to me, the lantern illuminating our faces. "To demonstrate to you that I can do anything I please. You know me as a Lord well enough, but I needed you to see me as a Magistrate as well. Everyone obeys me, without question."

He reviewed my face briefly before continuing. "Imagine, for a moment, if in my generosity, I was to tell them *not* to hang, draw, and quarter Mr. Porter? Even though it's scheduled four days from now. I have the power to release him instead."

The sliver of hope he offered stunned me. "What?"

"If you agree to marry me the next time I ask, I would consider it one of your wedding gifts. Since I know this son of a nobody is a *dear friend* of yours."

I studied his eyes to discern the truth of his words. "You would do that? You would have him released for me?"

Daniel tried standing again. "NO! Isabel do not!"

Lord Drake signaled the guard to hit him again and again, causing blood to spray the floor with each blow.

He was furious. "*Isabel!* You *dare* call a lady by her first name?"

His eyes were like fire when they looked back at me. Slowly, I took a few steps away.

The Earl bellowed, "*You* are on a first name basis with him *so easily* when it took me most of your life to earn that privilege?"

My chest heaved with fear-filled breaths as my mind offered no suggestions with how I should respond.

"No," Daniel spoke again, as a line of blood drooled from his mouth, "we are not. She would not grant me that permission when I asked for it. But when I imagine her in my mind, I always address her so."

My heart melted. Even in this circumstance, Daniel was trying to protect me. In anticipation of Lord Drake's signal, the guard punched him again, this time in his chest. I turned my eyes away so I would not have to witness it anymore; my heart was breaking for him. The sounds of him gasping for air tortured me.

"Do not imagine her in your mind! *Filthy dog*. Stop making the guard hit you; can't you see the violence is distressing her?"

I shivered as the Earl stepped to me and took my face in his hand, forcing me to look him in the eyes. "It's an awful place, isn't it, my little dove?"

My voice trembled. "Yes."

He slid his hand gently down the side of my neck to the ruffle on my dress. "Do you think you could disobey your father's wishes – *if* I were to let him go?"

"If I promise to be your wife...you will promise that Mr. Porter will be released – free to return home alive and harmed no further?"

He liberated his hand from me, but not his eyes. "Yes, you'd have my word just as I'd have you. Quite the fair trade, wouldn't you agree?"

I looked at Daniel; his face pleaded with me to refuse.

How could I trust the Earl to keep his word?

I faced him, "Do you *swear* you would release him?"

"How many ways must I promise? I vow it to you. Mr. Porter *will* be freed if you agree to my terms."

The room grew thick with silence. I paused, discerning. His unwavering gaze appeared honest. I could not let Daniel die. Even if there was only a small chance the Earl wasn't lying.

"Then I promise you my heart, Elwood. Even my father could surely not protest when such a wedding gift is offered."

Tears immediately rolled down Daniel's bruised and blood-soaked face. I could not have felt more shattered, save watching him actually die.

With his hand, Lord Drake turned my face away from Daniel and back to him. "Prove it. You have never given me a kiss of your own free will. Kiss me now to prove that *you* are sincere."

My stomach sank. "Would it not hurt your lip, my Lord?"

"I assure you any pain I felt from your soft lips would be of no matter to me."

"But in a prison...this is not a place for such displays of affection, surely?"

He raised his eyebrows. "Isabel...do we have an accord or not?"

I had no choice but to hurt Daniel in this manner. I exchanged a quick glance with him to apologize before Lord Drake bent his face and I, very gently and quickly, kissed his lips. He was not satisfied with such a polite display; he forced me into a passionate kiss with his one free arm holding my body in place. He did not stop until he heard Daniel release a tortured groan.

I could not look at anyone; I felt so mortified. All the eyes of the prisoners were upon us, witnessing our nightmare unfold. I thought of asking him to release them all, but knew that would have been futile. I *hated* being used to hurt Daniel. Yet, if it meant his life would be set free? That he could return home alive in one piece? It was a sacrifice we would both have to live with.

The Earl gloated. "She's such a *passionate* woman, is she not? I'm an exceptionally fortunate man! Congratulations on your trip back home,

Mr. Porter. I sincerely hope, for your sake, that this is the last time either of us will see you. As soon as we are married, you will be released." He grinned. "Hopefully it's not a long engagement."

Chapter Twenty-One

"Why will you not free him now?" I asked incredulously.

"Let's call it leverage, little bird."

"How will I know you've kept your word?"

He paused – irritation flickering in his tone. "Is my word not trustworthy, Isabel? You'll know he's been released because it will be our wedding day."

The way his eyes darkened startled me. "–I don't mean to doubt you, of course," I said, trying to soften my voice. "Only for my own peace of mind, is all I meant."

"What would you have me do? You wish to visit the prison to inspect it in your wedding gown? Have me bring him to my castle amidst the guests as we celebrate?"

"Would you permit my brother to retrieve him? Then Jonathon could bring me word of his release."

He hesitated a moment. "Very well. It will be arranged."

"Thank you, Elwood."

His features relaxed at the sound of his name. "Come now, my siblings are visiting, and I would like you to join us for supper. Bid your farewells to Mr. Porter. We wouldn't want to be late, my darling."

Turning to Daniel, our eyes met for the last time. I swallowed hard. "Be well, Mr. Porter. – Please be safe on your journey home."

Daniel's body rocked as he gazed at me – there were so many things we wanted to say but couldn't. "I wish you every happiness, Miss Dawson."

With that, I was jerked away and led out of the prison.

I forbade every sob that threatened to break free of my throat.

I had done the right thing; I sacrificed my life for his, in a way. He could be in no doubt that I loved him deeply. He might be upset with me now, for agreeing to marry the Earl, but he would understand one day. Because he would have sacrificed himself for me without hesitating either.

When we walked out of the prison, I took the deepest breath of air I ever had.

And then it happened. Another loathsome, ill-timed spell. I leaned against the wall of a building in front of me and felt my surroundings cave in. My ears rang so loud I could barely hear the carriages rolling over the roads. My vision began to swirl, and I nearly fell head first into the wall I leaned onto for support.

Lord Drake scooped me up into his arms as if I weighed nothing. "Come, the breeze from the carriage ride will do you well. I will help you recover." His words sounded muffled and far away. My head rolled back against his shoulder; I felt such revulsion at being pressed to his chest.

Once placed into the carriage, I struggled to steady my breathing.

This time he sat next to me. "You look utterly pallid, Isabel... I'm sorry you had to go through such a trying ordeal. You do see how it was necessary, though?"

I tried my best to hide my complete and utter disdain and leaned my head nearest the window, away from him. My arm shook terribly as I reached out to the window and gripped the frame of it.

"Isabel? Are you alright?"

I nodded.

He cleared his throat. "But you do understand?"

I ignored him.

He moved me away from the window and cradled me against his broad chest. "Hear my heart beating for you and be at ease, my dove. It is over now. There will be no more cause for these troublesome spells soon, I promise. You shall be so diverted in our new life, that no distress shall ever assail you again."

I closed my burning eyes; I did not want to be here. I prayed Aves in my head and tried to ignore his hands, enfolding me into a tighter embrace. I felt as if I were being smothered by a monster.

How could anyone wield such a duplicitous nature? How could anyone delight in the agony of another as he had just demonstrated? I had never despised a person more than at that moment.

After a few minutes he tilted my face up to his. "I'm sorry I had to bring you to the prison. There was no other way I could save you from yourself."

Feeling some strength return, I lifted up from him. "From myself?" My heart still pounded hard against my chest, though it was becoming easier to breathe.

"Yes! I know you...you would have ended up marrying that filthy, rogue papist. Then you would have been married to a damn traitor! – And why? Because he's the *only* other person you could marry? The only fool who did not heed my warning?" He scoffed. "And you, *you* fell for him! Because it was the only way to rebel against me? You'd have been utterly miserable, my fair little bird. What could he possibly offer you that I could not?"

I felt it best to reply, *everything,* in my head only, yet he waited for an answer.

"Nothing, Elwood." The lie burned my tongue to utter.

"I *did* try to warn him what would happen if he pursued you; he simply didn't listen. His being in prison was not anyone's fault but his own. In all honesty, had *you* not been so stubborn, none of this would have had to happen."

I clenched my jaw as I turned to face the scenery blurring past us. I hated that part of me felt he was correct in blaming me.

He paused a moment before continuing. "*I* don't blame you though, you know? Your family filled your head with terrible thoughts about the bruises and what kind of man that must have made me. But you and I will be happy together, I *know* this. Even if you can't see it fully yet. Tell me the truth. Would you have said yes to Mr. Porter's offer of marriage?"

My anger surged. Yet, there was no point in arguing – it would only make my current situation harder. An angry Earl was a dangerous Earl, and I needed to avoid that at all costs. I *had* to control my temper. If only this was one of my strong suits.

"*Saint Joseph, help me.*" I quickly prayed.

"How could I have? You made it very clear to me that such a thing was not possible. I told Mr. Porter as much."

Taking my hands, he kissed them before pressing them to his heart. It forced me to face him as he replied. "Good girl. I think a stroll through some fine views would help bring some color back to your cheeks; what do you think?"

"Yes." I *did* like the idea of getting out of his carriage.

"Let us never speak of the prison or of Mr. Porter again, are we in agreement?"

A pang of hollow sadness filled me. "Never existed, either one." I agreed, lying once more. *God forgive me!* I wondered how many lies I would have to tell. Was it not so long ago I avoided even a slight exaggeration?

Lord Drake smiled. "I am relieved you feel the burden lifted from the promise you made to your father."

The look in his eyes softened. "We are *free* now. Free to love each other, kiss without second thoughts or your awful waves of guilt. I will make you so happy, Isabel, I swear it. Even your dear Papa will smile down approvingly at us!"

If it was up to Papa, he would ask God to strike the Earl down with a lightning bolt. In fact, perhaps he already had.

At least I could comfort myself with the knowledge that Daniel would be released soon and on his way back home. He would be surrounded by his family and continue protecting priests across England. This sacrifice would be worth it...if only I do not lose myself.

Lord Drake had good qualities too...did he not? No one was *completely* evil. He worshiped me – maybe I wouldn't be unhappy for the rest of my days. Lying to myself proved far more difficult.

"Don't you think, my dear?"

"Oh, yes...sorry, my mind drifted."

A loving smile swept over his face as he cupped mine tenderly in his hands.

"Do you know that's why I call you my little bird? Because your mind is always taking flight from the rest of your body."

"How sweet, Elwood."

He played with a curl of my hair as the carriage came to a stop. "You must sing for me tonight. I have been deprived of your talents for months. Come, I will show you a magnificent view worthy of my beautiful songbird."

The driver opened the door and assisted me outside to where he had slightly pulled off the road. In front of me was a beautiful meadow with a trail leading through the tall grass and wildflowers.

"Come, walk with me," he said, offering his arm, which I took.

I was grateful to be outside and not cooped up in his carriage any longer. The strong breezes calmed me, but being tethered to Elwood's arm sickened me. My limbs felt the impulse to run away from him, far into the woods. The only thing that grounded me was knowing that Daniel's life depended on my going through with this marriage – and making the best of it. Even if it had to all be an act; a lifelong play.

We walked in silence for a while, until we started climbing a steeper hill.

"You've witnessed the worst of me today, Isabel. It doesn't make you think less of me?"

I took a moment before I responded. "I saw the breadth and extent of what you would do for me."

I knew this was the reply he wanted and I hoped my delivery would suffice. It was hard to force a poem to page from an empty inkwell.

"Yes, my great paramour. There is no limit to what I would do for you."

"Then you will not mind, of course, apologizing to my family for stealing me the way you did this afternoon and attempt to smooth things out with them?"

He sighed. "I will do my best."

"Then I shan't think less of you." I forced a smile.

Once on top of the hill, there was a beautiful view of a river rippling through a valley before a hilly landscape. I wondered if it was here that fed the stream that bordered the property of my home. My old home. I wondered if he would ever let me visit.

"This is beautiful," I said, taking it all in, letting it bandage the parts of my soul that it could. I sat down, wishing I was alone, dreading what was coming next.

Lord Drake sat beside me. "I knew you would like it here; you have such an appreciation for nature. I wanted this to be as memorable for you as it is for me."

He pulled out the sapphire ring from his breast pocket and held it out for me. "Isabel, my ravishing little bird — you are my heart's queen and there can never be another. Will you end my torment? Will you finally consent to being my wife?"

He placed the ring on my finger as tears escaped down my face. How could he expect me to pretend everything was normal and wonderful? How could he be so delusional? How could I keep acting in this fantasy when I loathe him? What had I agreed to?

"Oh!" Elwood exclaimed. "Do not cry, my precious one, no tears!" He wiped them away with his thumbs.

I commanded a smile as the tears withdrew. "Yes. I will marry you, Elwood."

My fate is sealed.

He hugged me tightly and drew my face into what felt like an endless kiss. Slowly pulling away, he rested his forehead against mine. "*Finally!* You cannot comprehend the agony I have endured, waiting for this moment."

It is a strange thing to be kissed so passionately and yet, feel nothing at all from it. I tried to reply as sincerely as possible, "I hope I am able to make you as happy as you think I will."

His face lit up even more. "You magnificent little bird, the only way you could make me happier in this moment is if you kissed me. *Really* gave me a kiss of your own accord – not that small peck you tried to pass off back there."

I knew I had to. I knew it would be wrong, but it was the only way I could. I closed my eyes and imagined he was Daniel. Leaning in, I gave him the sort of kiss I wish I could have given him before I left him in that terrible dungeon. When I pulled away, he appeared utterly bewildered. His mouth hung open and his eyes looked far away as they slowly opened. I couldn't help but smirk at the effect it had on him. I imagined Daniel having that expression instead, and it sparked the illusion of joy in me for a brief second.

Elwood exhaled. "I have never been kissed like that – in all my life. You're no dove...you're a *phoenix!*"

"A bird set on fire for you?"

He caressed my face and softly kissed my lips. "Precisely. Wait until you see all that I have in store for you, my beautiful bride! You will never regret this. — But, come," he said, standing and offering his hand to assist me, "let us leave for my castle and celebrate with my sister and brother. I had my kitchen staff prepare a special meal in anticipation of this moment – your favorite, in fact! A beef roast."

He seemed proud that he knew I was fond of this dish. We walked down the hill, arm in arm.

"That's very thoughtful, though perhaps I could return home first and change? – I am a little untidy and casual for supper." The prison had deeply stained the hem of my dress to a murky grey, but moreover, I desperately wished for my family to know I was safe. I could only imagine the worries that had been consuming them.

Lord Drake arched his shoulders proudly. "No need! I had my servants take my third carriage to your house and request some of your belongings and explain that you were invited to stay at my home with my siblings and I. Your belongings should be there and set up in a guest bedchamber already." He stood and brushed his dark gray and black pants off.

"Oh! Thoughtful again! – And how long did your servant say that I'd be away for?"

"You may as well stay until we are married; don't you think?"

I tried to silence the panic growing in my mind. We passed by several hawthorn trees. Their pinkish blossoms began to fade; some already twirled to the ground below.

I impelled a coy smile as I took a discreet, slow breath. "Are you afraid my family will change my mind?"

He looked uneasy at the question. "Frankly...yes. Your brother did punch me just yesterday, after all. And your mother seems to have completely turned against me after years of friendship with her and your father. I rather feel it is them who owe *me* an apology."

At once I knew, he *had* to believe I would never change my mind if I was ever to see my family again. I had to manipulate him more than he ever dreamt of manipulating me. I could not sacrifice Daniel *and* my family.

I stopped him by placing my hand on his upper arm, and gazed into his eyes. "I have chosen *you*. I belong to you, Elwood. I may take time in coming to a decision, but once I do, it is resolute, however it came to be. You must trust that my love and loyalty are not so shallow that I could be persuaded now. Merely think of all you had to do to convince me that accepting you was not being disloyal to my father? That same stubborn loyalty lies with *you* now, but even more since you are to be my husband.

"They don't understand yet, but in time, they will. I will make them see that we belong together." I ran my other hand slowly up his chest. "I am yours."

Before he could reply, I bent his face to mine with my hand combing through his slick hair and kissed him again as I would have Daniel.

His breath was thready when I pulled away. "*Your love*?" He asked with a smitten tone. "You have never used that phrase with me before."

I acted bashful and retracted my arms from him. "I thought you knew that already."

He turned my face up to his with a finger under my chin. "Knowing and hearing it are different, and in my defense you *did* tell me, on more than one occasion, that you did *not* love me." He glided his free hand along the curves of my back. "Isabel, say it again."

I made sure to stare into his eyes. "You know I was only saying that to dissuade you for the sake of my father's wishes. Will you ever forgive me? – I *do* love you. I have loved you for some time. You made it so very hard to resist you."

His eyes told me that he believed the falsehoods I uttered.

"Yes," he said, sweeping me off my feet and into his arms. "I knew you loved me all along; I could see it! Your mind fought against me so hard – you are a strong woman, Isabel. Tell me when it was that you first realized that you loved me?"

I was unsure of how to answer. "I believe it began at the fair, but I knew when you kissed me in the library. I had never felt like that before. You'll never know how tempted I was to say yes to you that day."

The Earl smiled down at me. "*I knew it.*" He carried me back the rest of the way to the carriage, stealing many kisses along the way.

Chapter Twenty-Two

FOR THE REST OF the journey, I made him believe I'd fallen asleep, resting against his arm. Occasionally, he would twirl my hair around his finger, kiss my head, or run his hand up and down my arms. While uncomfortable, I felt it was at least better than being subjected to kissing or further talk of love. One thing I felt I could never doubt was that he loved me, even if obsessively so. Though it was necessary, I felt badly for deceiving him into thinking I returned his affections.

Arriving at his property, Lord Drake woke me, eager to see what I thought of the grounds, gardens, and indeed everything. It was reminiscent of a young child seeking approval from a parent.

To put things into proper perspective, my family's salary is one hundred pounds. Lord Drake makes four times that amount. His castle and grounds, though smaller than some, absolutely reflected the magnitude of wealth procured over many generations. I imagine being in such high favor with Queen Elizabeth adds to that amount significantly.

"Do you remember it? It is the only one built with red sandstone for miles around! My grandfather was obsessed with that color when he saw it on his travels. He had every stone you see here transported by horse and carriage from Stirling. Is it not unique?"

"Indeed! It is quite striking."

While modest for a castle, it was grandiose compared to any estate in the surrounding areas. Black spires topped cylinder shaped corners with a reddish hued stone. Many stairs lead up to his massive front door made of oak and iron giving it an intimidating stature. There were also many colorful gardens, trees, and shapely bushes lining the drive to his red castle with a tall stone wall lining the road. The wall, at least, was made from ordinary gray limestone.

Stepping out of the carriage, I assured him I found everything to be impressive and magnificent. We were met by twenty servants who welcomed us as we ascended at least twenty steps.

Taking Elwood's arm, we walked up them together until the oversized doors were opened. Directly in front of us was an enormously grand staircase with balconies wrapping around the top floor. It was just as I remembered it as a child. Above us dangled a large and brightly lit chandelier, circular with tiered, layered rows of candles. Light gleamed in from many oblong windows over the entrance door and cast shadows on the stone floors covered by ornate rugs. Various tapestries and art works decorated the walls and small tables placed here and there to hold a candle or statue. I felt obscure in such a large space. Once in the middle of the grand entrance, a servant, somewhat older than myself curtsied before us.

Lord Drake nodded. "Ah, good! Sylvia, this is Miss Dawson, soon to be your Mistress." He turned to me. "Sylvia has been especially trained to care for a countess; you'll have no need for your old maid now."

"How do you do, miss?" She curtsied again.

No more Lily? Did he not trust anyone from my previous life? How was I to manage without her? She had been my friend for years.

I concealed how upset I was with an amiable pretense. "Very well, thank you, Sylvia."

Things were much more formal here than I was used to. Surely I would make a fool of myself daily by missing some form of proper etiquette or another. How I wish I had Lily or Christy to confide in.

She smiled up at me with her many pretty freckles and rounded face. Her brown hair was straight, with rolling bangs.

Lord Drake continued. "Take her to her room and help Miss Dawson get ready for supper. The red dress would be appropriate. I will be in the drawing room with my family. Please escort her straight after."

She curtsied again. "Yes, my Lord."

Red dress? I did not own a red dress. Had he had one made up for me? The thought of changing made me realize a small problem. How was a Protestant servant going to react to finding a rosary in my pocket? Especially one in the employ of the Magistrate?

Despite my looming fear, we went up the grand stairs, Sylvia leading the way. The dark wood rails curved dramatically with carvings of ivy looping about the poles; the intricate details were mesmerizing.

Once at the top we went left, and she led me to the third bedchamber. Each had arched wooden doors with black latches. The Drakes did not even spare expenses in the most mundane of things. Or perhaps all castles had doors for their bedchambers? I had no other experience to compare with.

Next to mine were three more and then the hall turned left again with a set of double doors, larger than the others. This, I assumed to be Lord Drake's sleeping quarters.

I looked to my left at what appeared to be a row of even more bedchambers that circled around the entire floor.

Sylvia lifted the latch to mine and pushed the door in. "Here Miss Dawson, this is where Lord Drake has chosen your room to be."

The room itself was elaborate, large, and beautiful; the bed was framed with tall wooden poles draped extravagantly with blue curtains and a matching canopy.

Every gift I returned was displayed here. Even the letters were bundled and sitting on the vanity. A writing desk was also placed thoughtfully in front of the middle window. *That might make for a good hiding spot. Now I merely need the opportunity.*

I walked over to the third window and saw the magnificent view of his back gardens, stables, and rolling forests behind. There was a particularly large and beautiful weeping willow tree as well, which is my favorite kind of tree.

"Are you pleased, miss? Lord Drake told me to fetch you anything you requested and to make sure you felt quite at home."

"It's more than enough, Sylvia; everything is splendid."

"Oh! You haven't seen what else his Lordship has done for you! I've never seen a man more in love than he is with you. I hope you don't mind me saying so, miss. He's been preparing for your arrival for months."

Months?

"Of course, I do not mind."

Sylvia walked over to a large white wardrobe near the head of the bed. As she opened the doors, I opened the lid to the writing desk and slipped the rosary inside. She turned back to see me walking away from the desk. I hoped I'd been inconspicuous enough. Her features did not indicate she'd seen anything curious at least.

"Oh my." I said walking up to the colorful display before me. Not only did I see a few of my dresses from home, but at least *twenty* brand new ones.

Sylvia seemed pleased at my expression as I took them all in, feeling the various fabrics with my fingers. The Elharts would have died and gone to heaven at the sight of my new wardrobe.

"Lord Drake went to the dress shop your family frequents and had all these made up for you, according to the measurements the seamstress had saved for you. Though most come straight from London or Paris! Quite generous, is he not?"

I was amazed by how long he must have planned this for. Dresses from France? A single one would have taken weeks.

"Possibly *too* generous," I replied, now viewing the equally impressive variety of shoes beneath.

Here I was, being treated like a princess, and Daniel was starving and cold. *No.* I musn't let myself think of him until it is safe to cry again. He will be free soon. He *will* be free. I have to stay focused on the present.

Sylvia grabbed a deep red taffeta dress with ivory silk ties and ruffles.

"We had better hurry and get you to the drawing room, miss. Lord Drake is always punctual and expects the same."

I tried to speak kindly. "Well, then, Sylvia, I shall have to put my trust in you, for that is one of my gravest failings."

Sylvia's eyes glistened with purpose. "I'm honored that you trust me to assist you; I will do my best not to let you down."

She styled my hair in a new way. Longer ringlets instead of curls and pinned up in curves instead of braids with less hair flowing down. I felt it improved my appearance, even though I missed the way Lily took care of me. I wondered whether I'd ever see her again.

Applying the perfume, she stood back to admire her hard work. "Very beautiful, miss! You resemble those in great paintings!"

"Thanks to you, Sylvia. – This dress, though, reveals much more skin than I am accustomed to."

The neckline opened up to my shoulders with a cream-colored ruffle. While my breasts were completely covered, much of my neck, upper chest and back were exposed. I felt cold, bare, and uncomfortable.

"This was the one he requested you wear tonight. I assure you it looks very becoming on you, miss. I'm afraid we don't have time to change, and to be plain, miss, he would not appreciate me disregarding his request."

There was no arguing that. "Very well, show me to the drawing room then, please."

As we headed to the door, I asked, "I have no memory of his sister. What is Lady Clutterbuck like?"

We walked into the hall. "She rarely visits miss, so my account of her may be incomplete. What I can say though, is that she has two children; a boy and a girl. – Careful of your footing on the stairs, please, miss. – Though," she whispered, "I would say she is as she always was."

"Ah, I see."

I followed her down as quickly as I could manage with such full skirts. Once in the grand entryway, she led me to the right and soon was opening the door for me. I felt apprehensive – like an imposter who did not belong. I was a papist in enemy territory after all. Surely I could never feel at home here.

"Ah, there you are, Miss Dawson! Well met! I hear congratulations are finally in order! Welcome to the family!" greeted Elwood's brother with a gentle kiss to my hand.

I've always enjoyed Paul's company; he was quite the contrast from his brother. Lighthearted with a disdain for politics and anything he deemed too serious. He had with him a young lady about my age. They both had curly blond hair and could easily be mistaken for siblings.

I curtsied. "Paul, what cheer? – Yes, thank you so very much!" I glanced at Elwood; his mouth slightly gaped as his eyes took me in.

Paul continued, "I have never been better. You must meet Miss Sophia Longwood! We met in London a few weeks ago," he gestured to the man next to her. "This is her brother, Henry Longwood and his betrothed, Miss Marigold Williams."

Henry was stout and tall with light brown hair, and Marigold had green eyes and blonde hair.

"I'm ever so pleased to meet you all." I curtsied politely.

They all smiled primly with their perfectly crafted pleasantries.

Lord Drake came to me. "You are positively sublime, my dear." I felt his eyes take in every inch of me and could not help but feel both vulnerable and flattered at the same time.

"I fear something is amiss, though my dear."

I looked over my dress and back to him. "What is wrong?"

From behind his back he revealed a breathtaking locket; it was gold, shaped into a heart with an oval Ruby pressed into its center. Filigree curled around the gem and flourished out to the edges. The room gasped with me as the chain twirled the large shining heart back and forth.

"*Oh!* Elwood, it's stunning – I don't know what to say!"

Everyone I had just met circled about me to gain a better view. Compliments flowed faster than I could respond to.

Elwood's face glowed as he relished in the attention his gift brought. He walked behind me to clasp it around my neck. "It belonged to my grandmother; it was her favorite. Grandfather purchased it for her on their wedding journey in Italy. It is empty now, but perhaps I can have an artist sketch the two of us soon."

It felt heavy around my neck; it was the largest and most beautiful piece of jewelry I'd ever seen. "She had exquisite taste."

His sister walked over from the chair she had been resting on. "I do hope you treasure that as much as our grandmother did, Miss Dawson."

Taking Elwood's offered arm, he walked me the rest of the way to her. "Amelia, forgive me, I grew too excited to give Isabel the locket before allowing her to greet you."

Amelia was extremely graceful; she had dark features like Elwood and was very slim. Her gown was dark green and of the highest fashions.

She smiled kindly at me, though I gathered it to be more pretense than heartfelt, "Surely this is not the same Miss Dawson I last saw at my wedding? You were such a wild little girl. I see a most elegant woman before me now."

"I was glad when Elwood told me you would be here. I can promise you that your grandmother's necklace is already greatly treasured and will be well taken care of."

She tilted her head; the posh smile never leaving her thin lips. Her husband, Lord Charles Clutterbuck, came and stood beside her. He was an overweight man with more gray hair than brown. "How do you fare, Miss Dawson?"

Before I could respond, a servant came and announced that supper was ready.

We filed out in pairs, the Earl and I leading the way.

He bent his head down and whispered. "Isabel, you are irresistible in this dress — the envy of every woman. And the locket becomes you so very well."

"I fear your sister is displeased that you have gifted it to me. Though, I confess I am extremely partial to it; it's magnificent. I did not think any jewelry could rival my sapphire ring, but I stand corrected. You have spoiled me far too much, Elwood. The dresses alone left me speechless." None of this was a lie at least.

He beamed with satisfaction. "Never mind Amelia; it was mine to give, not hers. I did tell you I could be more generous if you'd let me. Are you pleased with your room as well?"

"Yes, how could I not be?"

Servants opened the doors to the opulent dining room. Two immense circular chandeliers hung over a matching wooden dining table that stretched an impossible length. Elegant candelabras etched with cherubs made of gold lined the table. The room itself was well lit by many oblong windows and lanterns, and assisted by a grand fireplace opposite the entrance.

Across from the windows on the opposite wall was a positively massive tapestry of a hunting party being welcomed back home by the women. It was difficult not to gape at the sheer magnitude and talent behind it. Lord Drake appeared pleased by how impressed I was by it.

"You seem nervous?" Elwood whispered after we had taken our seats.

"I am."

He held my hand under the table. "There is no need to be; this is *your* home, and we are all soon to be your family, well, mostly. I don't quite know how these other rakefires came to be here."

This did not help. I missed my family's dinner table and our comfortable manners. All this pomp and circumstance made it impossible to relax. At the center right side of the table sat Lord Drake and I, along with Amelia and her husband to Lord Drake's left. The other side was filled with his brother Paul, his lady friend, and her brother and his betrothed.

The first course was served promptly – blanc mange with saffron, chicken and vegetables. I was grateful it was a hearty soup for I was surprisingly hungry.

"Do tell us when *your* wedding is going to be, Miss Dawson?" asked Miss Williams.

"Oh, we haven't quite settled on a date yet. Soon, to be sure, though. When will yours take place?"

Miss Williams gushed. "*Next month!* We plan to marry in London. – Just look at what Henry has spoiled me with as an engagement gift!"

"How exciting!" I replied as she held her hand out for me to see a bracelet made of gold and pearls. "And what a remarkable piece; it quite suits you! *Very* pretty!"

"What has the Earl gifted you upon your engagement, Miss Dawson? We are *all* curious to know…was it the locket?"

My gift was much more expensive and grand – I felt hesitant about displaying it, for I knew it would outshine Miss Williams'. However she insisted, and I knew it would please Lord Drake.

Everyone around the table gasped and heavily complimented my sapphire ring. Miss Williams, however, said nothing except a comment of how heavy it must feel upon my finger. In all honesty – it *was* quite heavy.

"Elwood has been far too generous with me." I said.

Lord Drake *was* pleased. "Look at yourself Isabel! How could I not indulge the angel who has condescended to be my wife?" He kissed my hand as his eyes lingered in my gaze.

Amelia nudged her husband. "Why don't you say pretty things like that to me, Charles?"

"As if you don't *know* you're my angel! Poor Miss Dawson seems to be quite unaware and so your brother must remind her often."

"Hmm," replied his wife. "I suppose that *is* true. She blushes as though she thinks herself to be quite undeserving of all this attention. –Relish in it, dear. There are few joys in this life to rival the thrill of when a man speaks sweet things to us."

A strong French wine was served with the beef roast, and I was grateful for it. If ever I was in need of it, today was the day... Pretending to have one set of feelings while repressing several others was exhausting.

"Everyone," Lord Drake said, raising his glass. "I propose a toast to my betrothed!"

Everyone's glasses raised as he stood. "To my fairest love, my diamond among the stars, you have made me happy beyond compare. I want for nothing else in this life except to walk next to you in it."

Amidst the ooh's and aah's it was hard to comprehend that this was the same man, who, mere hours ago, dragged me through a prison and blackmailed me into marriage.

"To Elwood and Isabel!" cheered Paul.

Sitting down, Elwood kissed my hand again as his guests echoed the cheer.

After supper, we all retired back to the drawing room and played cards. The ladies took turns playing the harpsichord and or singing, as the men danced with whichever woman was free to. Finally, it became an acceptable time for me to excuse myself for the evening. Despite many protests, I insisted that I was quite tired. I could not bear acting the part of a happy woman in love any longer.

Finally conceding to my request to retire, Lord Drake offered to walk me back to my bedchamber.

"Come," he said, holding a candle. "I wish to show you something first. I know you will appreciate it as few can."

I agreed, since there was not much choice given.

Going down past the drawing room, a hall appeared. He told me to the right was a large ballroom but to the left was the library. The glow from the fireplace was blocked by a few comfortable looking chairs. He lit several candles inside from the light he carried. As the light slowly illuminated the space, I was astonished by the size. Each wall was covered with a fortune of beautiful books! Hundreds of books!

The grin on my face was so wide, it hurt my cheeks. "Oh...this is *incredible.* There are more books here than I could read in fifty lifetimes! I have never seen so many all in one place before...how?"

I went and ran my fingers along rows of books, reading different titles and admiring the binding. My father would have been amazed by this. Perhaps living with the Earl would not be *all* bad. I could spend all my time here, a million miles away.

Lord Drake took my hand and led me to the middle of the room, wrapping his arms around me. "You are not the only one who enjoys reading, my dove. My father struck a bargain with one of King Henry VIII's advisors that allowed him to take his pick of books from many of the old monasteries. Not all are in English though, some are in French or Latin. I would be happy to read them to you."

I swallowed hard. These were spoils from our persecution. "I did not realize you spoke French or Latin for that matter." I replied, trying to keep the subject neutral.

"I had tutors who taught me many things, my dear. Our children will be able to have the same advantages. Of course, attending Oxford and spending time in France helped tremendously. Does my collection please you?"

"I could not have dreamed of something more grand than this."

He smiled into my eyes. "Then it is yours. Everything I have is yours."

"Oh, Elwood...how can I ever properly thank you?"

He caressed my face and traced the chain of my locket down to the heart with his fingertips. "You may answer a question for me."

I panicked for a moment, wondering what he could want to know.

"Are you happy?" he asked, lowering his face to mine.

"Of course," I answered with relief.

He kissed me. "You smell delectable. All day, all I could think of was how much I wanted to be alone with you and kiss you. – Tell me, when do you wish our wedding to be?" He began kissing my neck down to where my exposed shoulder finally met the ruffles on my dress.

My heart pounded nervously. "—Would next Saturday be acceptable?"

All I could think of was getting Daniel out of prison as soon as possible.

He raised his face to mine. "Excellent! I should have no issues in securing the bonds for marriage on such short notice. I'm glad you are as eager as I am for our wedding."

I was grateful he did not see through my reason for wanting it so soon. "I *would* like to discuss wedding plans with my mother."

"Of course, I will allow you to speak with her about the wedding." He began kissing my neck again. His beard tickled me, but I refused to let a giggle escape.

"May we invite my family to supper tomorrow? I may even be able to wear my mother's dress, considering the short notice."

Lord Drake chuckled as he faced me, stroking my cheek. "My dear, dear Isabel. Of course we may invite them to supper tomorrow – invite them first thing in the morning. Soon you will learn to be less reliable upon them. I will be patient, as I know how close you all are. As for the dress, I have already had one designed for you, as another wedding surprise. It is elegant and beautiful, like you. From Paris!"

I hid my disappointment about my mother's dress behind a smile. "Thank you, Elwood. I am truly undone by your generosity."

"Do you see now the truth of my words? Of how much I had to offer you?"

"Yes."

He gleaned down at me with intense longing. I knew I needed to escape this room. I did not trust his self control.

Reaching up, I kissed his lips softly. "But for now, I really am so very tired, I'm about to fall over! Would you hate me if I begged to sleep now?"

He kissed me once more, a long and overdrawn kiss. "I could never hate you. Come, you *have* had a long day and tomorrow will be filled with plans."

Arm in arm, we made our way upstairs, followed at a distance by Sylvia. Once at my door, he kissed me while twirling a bit of my hair, and whispered in my ear. "Leaving you at this door is torture. Our wedding night cannot come soon enough."

My breath felt trapped. This was something I was trying to avoid thinking about at all costs. I could not hide the nervousness in my voice. "It will be here before we know it." Then, I thought of Daniel hunched over on his knees in the prison. "Unless...you wish our wedding to be sooner?"

His crooked smile grew wide as he ran his fingers over my hair. "Ah, my phoenix...I would wish it to be in the morning, if that were possible. Alas, we must allow time for people to travel here from London; I have many friends there who would feel snubbed if they were not invited."

Elwood rested his forearm against the door frame above me as my back found the side of it. "Though you tempt me something fierce to forget about the etiquette of it all...you deserve a grand and proper wedding. I wish to show you off for all the world to see."

His forehead rested against mine as his free arm drew me into another kiss.

"Soon, then, Elwood," I said shakily as he released me.

"A good night's rest to you, Isabel; you have made me very happy." He smiled as he turned to walk away.

Once in my room with Sylvia I let free a deep exhalation. I needed to find a more secure hiding place for my rosary.

"Tired, miss?"

"Yes, dreadfully. Please help me out of this dress?"

"Of course, miss."

It felt like an age, but soon I was alone. Where would be hidden from the servants?

The shoes? There certainly were enough of them. Yet...I could not guarantee what shoes I would be wearing on any given day.

A painting? I lifted them up, but none seemed to be far enough from the wall to help me.

The bed was much too obvious. Where? *Guardian Angel...show me where to hide it, please!"*

The doll! The doll that Lord Drake had given to me as a child was *here.* I went to the dresser where she stood next to my scattered seashells, a vase of flowers, and my washing bowl. Her painted wooden body was well preserved, smiling up at me. She wore a lovely dress of blue silk and white lace.

I lifted up her skirt, "Excuse me, Jane, but your assistance is required." Where her abdomen intersected with her legs, created a perfect area to wrap the rosary around. After looping the beads around the doll's waist as many as many times as I could, I fixed her skirt back down to her white painted shoes.

"You always come through for me, my holy Angel. Thank you."

With that problem taken care of, I collapsed into my oversized bed. I could hardly believe the events of today. I had become a prisoner within in a luxurious nightmare.

Daniel's words echoed through me like a blade. "*One day, when death separates us, it shall never dissolve my bond with you. I would find it wholly impossible to love any but you, or to cease for any reason. I would not rest until your arms welcomed me into the afterlife."*

Grabbing a pillow, I wept into it, muffling the sounds of my heart breaking. The day poured through my mind, wringing out my eyes. Would Daniel ever forgive me for marrying the Earl and condemning him to a life of heartache? Would he understand that I could not bear the idea of his death? Would he find happiness in another woman's arms? I pined with jealousy at the thought. Had I done the right thing?

Chapter Twenty-Three

"*Dear Mama, Jon, and Anna,*

I hope this letter finds you all well.

Lord Drake has been so kind as to invite me to his castle where some of his family are also visiting.

There is bigger news, however. Lord Drake has proposed, and I have accepted his offer! In fact, we decided to have the wedding next Saturday!

He has been kind enough to offer for me to stay here and get to know his family better until the wedding. Lord Drake has been very generous with me, even going so far as to purchase a new wardrobe and wedding gown, which are already complete.

Would you all be so kind as to come this afternoon to discuss wedding plans and to stay for supper?

I cannot wait to see you all so that we might celebrate together and put the past behind us as well.

All my love,
Isabel"

I was careful in my wording should my letter have unintended viewers. After waving it to dry, I folded and sealed the letter with hot red wax. Just as it finished drying, Sylvia opened the door.

"Oh! Good morning! You are an early riser, aren't you miss?" She said carrying in a tray with a goblet of breakfast ale and a pitcher of fresh water to wash my face with.

"How do you fare today, Sylvia?"

She looked surprised at my inquiry. "I'm very well, thank you. Did you sleep soundly?"

"Yes. Thank you for the ale, you may set it next to my bed. Would you please see that my letter is sent to my family as quickly as possible, so they have time to receive the invitation and come this afternoon?"

"I will give it to our parcel man as soon as you are set for the day." She replied as she poured the water into my basin.

I thanked her and was soon ready for the day in a pink and floral dress with small ruffles, puffy short sleeves, and drapes in the skirts. The neckline of which, thankfully, was much more modest. I would not wear that red dress again unless wholly unavoidable. What was the Drake family's obsession with red?

Sylvia clasped my locket around my neck and applied the perfume, while I slipped on my sapphire ring.

Lord Drake was waiting for me at the bottom of the stairs as Sylvia took my letter and handed it to another servant. The swelling of his lip was much improved today. "Did you sleep well, little bird?"

It was time to be on stage again.

Little bird had nightmares because of you.

"I slept quite well, and you?"

He kissed my hand and up my wrist. "Restless. I was eager for the morning so that I could be near you again."

"I wonder if you will ever run out of such sweet things to say?"

"Given the muse before me, I greatly doubt it. – Tell me, for the holiday I am taking you on after the wedding, I need your opinion. After we visit

256

London and spend some time with the Queen, where should our next stop be?"

My stomach squeezed. "Visit the Queen?"

Papa hadn't even ever taken me to Bath, let alone London to meet the Queen! I have no desire to meet her, let alone spend a great deal of time there.

"Yes, she told me if I should ever manage to capture your heart, that I was to bring you to court so she could meet you for herself."

"Oh... what did you tell her of me?"

Grinning, he continued, "I told her that your beauty was unparalleled in this world and that you were touched with fairy dust and had thus enchanted me."

"That is quite the illustration to live up to."

"I only spoke the truth, my little phoenix!" He kissed my hand again. "I'm an important man, Isabel, and therefore you must meet all the people in my circle. But now, *after* a spell in the royal court, where should you most like to visit? France? A tour around England? I have an estate on the Isle of Whight that is beautiful as well."

"I suppose France would be quite lovely?"

"It is. I would enjoy showing you Paris very much."

I entwined my arm in his, hoping for the chance to sneak off to Mass one day while we were there. "I would like that exceedingly well."

He lowered his head and kissed me before we entered the dining room for breakfast. Kissing him made me feel as though I were a traitor to Daniel and indeed to my own heart. A fresh layer of guilt was added each time, like layers of stones in a wall.

As we sat, the others slowly joined us. I helped myself to biscuits, jam, and some bacon.

"Miss Dawson, you seem much refreshed today! Did you sleep well?" asked Paul.

"Yes, thank you."

Lord Drake then shared the news of when our wedding would be and how we planned to travel to France after. Believe me when I say this filled the rest of the conversation for the whole of breakfast.

Afterwards, I decided to take a walk around the castle grounds. As though fearing his little bird would fly away from him, he insisted the whole group come with *us*. Which, of course, they did because no one says no to the Earl. I began to understand that I was not going to have any time to myself for the foreseeable future.

All us ladies wore stylish coifs and gloves as the gentleman obliged us all by offering an arm to walk on. To my chagrin, even strolls had a weight of formality to them. A lift from my disappointment was the sight of Amelia's children playing outside! They joyfully ran about us, squealing with energy; it was familiar and made me smile. "How old are they, Amelia? They're precious!"

"Fredrick is five and Daisy is eight."

"What a blessing! They're absolutely delightful."

"Yes, I suppose they are. Are you and my brother excited to have children?"

"I've always hoped for a large family. – Time will tell, of course."

Lord Drake squeezed my hand and smiled broadly at me.

I kept feeling sorry for myself; my heart ached so deeply for Daniel. I wanted to be married and have children with *him*. Still, my lot was not exactly something most people would think to pity. Meeting the Queen? Visiting Paris? A room full of books at my disposal? Endless gifts? Anything and everything I want? And, by sacrificing my life for Daniel... my love would at least still be alive. I had to keep reminding myself that being with Elwood was worth the cost.

"Honestly, I'm ever so grateful to have a governess; children can be rather a nuisance." Amelia blurted rather abruptly.

I wondered at such a statement. Her tone was so dismissive about them; I felt badly for her children to have a mother as selfish as this. I'd yet to witness any hint of love in her eyes for them, or for really anyone. What a sad existence she lives.

The stone path curved around the castle and allotted us a beautiful view of intricately placed flower beds and blooming trees. I recognized many of the flowers growing from the bouquets he had delivered to me.

Paul grew excited all a sudden. "Oh! Let's play bocci! We haven't played together since we were children ourselves, Elwood!"

Everyone agreed and latched onto his excitement. I myself was amenable to anything that helped pass the time until my family arrived. Bocci most assuredly brought out the more ambitious natures of everyone, and it was a rather feisty game. Elwood and I were admittedly the most competitive and won. I confess we made a remarkable team. Coming in second made his sister spiral into quite the sour mood. I was starting to be grateful she did *not* live close by.

Upon returning to the house we were greeted with a luncheon. A feast of various meats, cheeses and fruits were laid out for us, and I enjoyed everything I sampled. I would occasionally notice that Lord Drake would pause to stare at me while I ate, smile to himself, and continue on. I was perplexed as to why my eating made him happy? Was it simply because I was there, in his house, and from his perspective, content? He did seem to care a great deal for my comfort. Or was it that all his scheming and plans had finally come to fruition, and he was enjoying the victory?

After lunch, we all gathered in the drawing room together; I sat nearest the window so I could see my family's arrival. The ladies came over and around me on a sette and bench for the harpsichord players.

"So tell us," began Miss Marigold Williams, "is your family excited about your engagement?"

I caught Lord Drake lifting his head from the men's game of Whist across from us to listen in.

"You will see for yourself shortly," I smiled. "I am eager for them to arrive so we may truly begin planning."

Miss Sophia Longwood questioned me next, "I've heard your brother is devilishly handsome, is that true?"

I couldn't help but chuckle. "I suppose some women find him attractive."

Sophia continued, "How long have you known Lord Drake?"

"Since I was a child; he's been a family friend for many years."

"Really?" Miss Williams questioned in a high pitched cadence. "Then what's all this about him working so hard and long to pursue you?"

His sister raised an eyebrow at me as she sipped her wine, as though to warn me to respond wisely.

I tittered uncomfortably. "—I am *painfully* indecisive, Miss Williams."

"Oh please, call me Marigold! I feel as though we shall all be *such* good friends! But truly, what *was* your reservation? He's handsome and one of the richest men in England...and you've known him since you were a child?"

The way she looked at me, as if I were a blithering simpleton, made my cheeks heat. My brain hastily shuffled through possible responses.

"Well...actually, that was part of it. I grew up viewing him merely as a family friend; it took a while for me to see him in a different light. I admit, I was rather slow to that progression! Fortunately for me, he is as patient as he is persistent. Eventually, I could not deny that he was possibly the handsomest of men and certainly the most charming that I'd ever known. But more than that, he has always been so generous and kind to me. I feel rather silly for being so slow to realize what was right before me."

I had no idea what a good liar I was, dear reader. Apparently, when put on the spot, I could manage quite well! While I understand that this is not a trait to be proud of... I was grateful to possess it for this particular period of my life. Perhaps I had inherited this from my father.

His sister smiled and arched her shoulders back as if very pleased by my string of fibs. I could see Lord Drake's approval of my tale by the gentle lift in the corner of his mouth.

Marigold bounced in her seat, "That is *so* very romantic! When was it, what day, what happened that changed your mind?"

I was growing tired of the interrogation. "I think the fair was three months ago now?" I noticed Elwood continued to watch me out of the corner of his eye. "Suffice to say, not even my stubbornness could refuse his allure and chivalry."

A satisfied expression rested over Elwood. This calmed the racing of my heart; at least I had been convincing.

I smoothed out my dress. "But please, enough about me! Tell us how you and Mr. Longwood met and fell in love?"

She was not shy in disclosing details. Long, drawn-out details. To summarize, they couldn't be happier, and they met at a ball. Marigold at least succeeded in passing the time until the carriage finally came.

"They have arrived! I will go out and greet them," I said as I took my leave of the room before Lord Drake could command me to do otherwise.

While I realize it was only a day and a night, I felt we had been separated for weeks.

Descending the stairs as quickly as I could to the road, my brother met me at the bottom with a hug so tight I could not take a full breath in! Mama was quick to join in the embrace, pressing me into the middle.

I glanced behind us; Lord Drake and various servants were not far behind on the stairs.

As quickly as I could, I whispered to them, "You must play along or Daniel will die."

I pulled away with a large smile on my face. "I am so happy to see you both! Where is Anna?"

Mama tried to ease her look of concern. "She sends her love, but we thought it best she stay home."

Lord Drake hurried down the last of the stairs and offered his hand to my brother. "What do you say we let the past be in the past, Jonathon?"

I looked at him pleadingly.

Jon heaved an uncomfortable sigh. "My sister's happiness is all that matters to me."

"We have that in common; I promise you."

He turned to mother. "I must apologize for any alarm I may have caused yesterday, Mistress Catherine. I do hope there are no hard feelings between us? I should hate to get off on the wrong foot with my soon-to-be mother-in-law?"

I was genuinely curious to see how she would respond.

"I dare say you will find a way to make it up to me, won't you, Lord Drake?"

"Oh, absolutely! Say the word and it will be done!"

"Wonderful. Then you won't mind my staying here until the wedding to help with plans?"

I could not contain my grin; Mama was brilliant. "Oh! That's a wonderful idea! Surely you wouldn't mind, would you, Elwood?"

I could see him trying to hide a grimace. "Until the wedding? Of course, what an oversight on my part! You are, of course, *most* welcome to stay, Mistress Catherine."

"Thank you, Lord Drake. Please have one of your servants fetch my luggage from the carriage, would you?"

And with that, my mother placed her arm in mine, and we all climbed up the stairs together. I worried for my mother's knee with all the stairs here, but so far she seemed to be managing, or at least her pride was concealing the struggle.

Once in the drawing room, introductions were made and refreshments served. Mama was very gracious and elegant, asking thoughtful questions to everyone. Then, rather abruptly, she said, "Now, I shall require my daughter to take me to her room so that I may inspect this wedding gown before we begin with plans."

"Yes, Mama."

We exited the room and headed up the stairs together, taking them slow, for her knee was indeed troubling her after the stairs outside. Once inside my room, Sylvia brought the dress out for her inspection, and Mama asked her to fetch us some cider.

As soon as she heard Sylvia retreating, she sat down with me on the bed and spoke quietly, "What in the name of heaven is going on? Are you alright? We have been worried *sick!* And then we received that letter?"

"Lord Drake promised that if I agreed to marry him that he would have Daniel released on our wedding day. – He took me to the prison to see him there. I would do *anything* to spare Daniel another moment there and to save his life. How could I say no? Then he took me here and proposed *properly* along the way, and I accepted."

"This is why you wanted a quick wedding."

"Yes, I know... it sounds terrible. And it is. But I am taken care of; I am safe, pampered even. I could not live with myself knowing I could have saved Daniel and did not. People marry for far lesser reasons every day."

Mother's lip trembled. "I do not wish this for you, my darling girl, nor do I approve, but I *do* understand."

I hugged her tightly.

"Will you be happy with him?" she asked, pulling away and staring into my eyes to read them.

"Happy enough. He is utterly devoted, and I will never want for anything."

"Except Daniel?"

I nodded, willing my tears to stay back.

We heard Sylvia's footsteps approaching and moved over to the dress. "And have you planned a holiday for after the wedding?" Mama asked.

"London and Paris."

"I daresay you shall enjoy that immensely."

The door opened and Sylvia appeared with two glasses of cider and set them on my nightstand.

My mother viewed the dress again. "It is quite a flamboyant gown, but who could try to deny the craftsmanship of it? It's breathtaking."

Sylvia smiled and handed us each a drink, which we gratefully accepted.

"It is still not as beautiful as yours, Mama."

She gave a short smile. "What of bridesmaids?"

"I would like Anna and Christy, of course."

"Naturally. I will have your brother ask Christy on your behalf on his return home."

"I would appreciate that."

"You should also ask Lord Drake's sister and have her children be in the wedding too."

"Oh, yes...you're right."

"Come, let us return downstairs so we may include her in the plans."

Chapter Twenty-Four

WITH MY MOTHER AT the helm, the wedding was completely planned before supper. The servants were working on invitations and decorating, and I...had nothing to do but wait. Guests from out of town would begin arriving a day or two before, and we would begin the wedding procession to the church early next Saturday morning. And then it would be done.

As we were called from the drawing room to supper, my brother requested to speak to me for a moment alone. Lord Drake had little choice in the matter but to allow it. He left me with him most begrudgingly.

"What the devil is going on?" Jon whispered quickly as we stood at the furthest wall from the door.

I told him, ever so quietly, the same summary I gave to Mother.

"I don't like it," he whispered back. "You have *no* guarantee he will keep his word! And Daniel would not want this – he would rather die than see you do this to yourself! Every day of his life, he will wish he had died instead. You'd have been able to realize that had Lord Drake not heightened your emotions by forcing you into the prison with him."

His words cut me. "Perhaps. Maybe God's not done with him here on earth. I believe he *will* understand why I'm doing this. Jon, I love you, but I haven't the time to argue. — Have you thought about whether I could bear to exist knowing the power to save him was in my grasp? He would have been butchered, Jon! I will need you to be at the prison to pick Daniel up, after the ceremony. Tell me I may rely upon you."

"This is madness." He ran his hands through his hair and exhaled. "Of course you can rely on me to retrieve Daniel. – For now, I will accept this. However, your well-being is still my priority. I want you to be safe and happy. – I have an idea that may help get you out of this yet."

"I *am* safe. Do not risk anything to help me that would harm Daniel or make the Earl change his mind. Not to mention placing Anna and Mother in danger. Let things be. Now please, let's not make spectacles of ourselves and be late for supper?"

"I don't like this."

"Duly noted, brother." I whispered even lower, "You will tell Daniel that I love him...that I always will, and that I did this for his sake and not to be angry with me?"

My brother kissed the top of my head. "Yes, I will."

Hurrying to catch up with the others, we still arrived well after everyone had taken their seats. I hoped the deep embarrassment that heated my face was an overreaction. However, Lord Drake was clearly perturbed as I took my seat next to him.

"What was all of that about?" he muttered to me. "You are *late.*"

I decided it would be foolish to try and lie. "Jon needed reassurance that I was safe and happy here."

"And what did you tell him?"

I put my hand over his and looked into his eyes with another crafted smile. "That I am safe and happy here with you."

This seemed to alleviate his foul mood as he gave me a warm smile in response.

"I so appreciate you allowing me to invite them, Elwood. They mean so much to me."

"Anything for my bride."

Supper was admittedly awkward. My brother could not contain his disdain for this situation, and he was quite aloof. Mama became rather quiet too, and I realized how hard this was for them. Their hearts were broken like mine. I felt the burden of guilt for their pain; I had not once taken their feelings into account when I agreed to trade myself for Daniel.

"Dear Mr. Dawson! Why the long face?" Amelia probed.

He cleared his throat and offered a polite smile. "Lost in thought, I'm afraid. Do forgive me for being so out of sorts tonight. How have you been faring?"

"Oh, quite well! Two children and we travel whenever the opportunity presents itself! Praytell...now that both my brothers are practically off the market, you're probably the most eligible bachelor in the area!"

"I will take your word for it, Lady Clutterbuck."

"Is there an eligible young lady whose company you prefer?"

"I am keeping my options open, for now."

"My, is it possible for you to be even more indecisive than your sister?" A chortle rattled up her throat.

"Doubtful, ma'am."

"You certainly have plenty of beautiful women to choose from; what is holding you back?"

I always had a feeling my brother wished to be a priest, but I have never asked him. I knew it wouldn't be something he pursued until all of us were taken care of first. But I was curious as to how he would respond.

"Perhaps I am too picky."

"Perhaps *indeed!* These poor women, not one of them good enough for the *great* Mr. Dawson. ...Must run in the family."

"Pretentiousness is fortunately *not* a Dawson family trait," Jon retorted.

"No one would presume that from your family, surely."

"I believe that being selective in one's spouse," began Mama, "is a sign of a discerning spirit and an intelligent mind. Taking time to ensure compatibility is indeed worth its weight in gold."

Amelia pouted. "Some, I think, are simply more adept evaluators than others."

"To be sure!" Mother replied, taking a drink of mead.

"Now our Miss Dawson here, on the other hand, is an entirely different breed of discerning!" Amelia giggled as Lord Drake glared at her; she seemed wholly unaffected by the veiled threats in his eyes as she continued on, "The most eligible man in England, whom even the Queen herself tried to pair off with fine ladies of her acquaintance – and there she was, like an old lady pauper, hemming and hawing over the choice between pottage or roast."

I could sense that Jonathon was seconds away from snapping. I leapt into the conversation to distract him. "I'm impressed you even know what pottage is, Amelia. Or perhaps you enjoy gossiping with the kitchen maids too much?"

Everyone tried not to chuckle, though some failed. It was Jon. I'm not sure he even tried so very hard.

Amelia was flustered, but silent.

I continued, "To be sure, I should not liken your brother to supper, but rather a hunter instead. What matters, my dear sister-to-be, is that his hunt was successful. My heart is quite captured." I felt ill speaking such a lie before Jon and Mama who knew far better.

Lord Drake smirked and patted my knee. "Quite right my little bird, quite right."

After dinner, Jon excused himself saying that he had business in the morning to attend to. I was not surprised by his early departure.

He hugged me tightly and whispered, "I love you little sister. Keep you head down and your temper in check, yes?"

"I love you too. I will do my best."

"I will be back the day before your wedding," he said as we pulled away, "with Anna and Christy. Until then, be well dear sister."

After making the rest of his farewells to, the rest of us retired to the drawing room except Mama who went upstairs for an early rest. I offered to help her up the stairs and on my way back down, I overheard a conversation. Behind the staircase, Elwood and his sister were arguing, so, naturally, I lingered.

"What was all that about?" Elwood hissed.

"Oh, what?"

"You are meant to be making Isabel feel *welcome, not* trying to ostracize her. You just couldn't resist picking at her and her brother could you?"

"I hardly know what you're referring to. They were both perfectly able to handle themselves. I don't know what you are so upset about."

"I love her, Amelia, and I will not have you meddling."

"Yes, yes... Isabel is *perfect* and I am the devil."

"It's not a far-off comparison!"

"You disgust me. An earl like you chasing that woman around when you could have had any lady you desired! What is it about her? Is it because she reminds you of our mother? She does look quite a lot like her, even sounds like her sometimes. You always did take her death the hardest."

"Amelia... I'm not having this conversation with you. It's not my fault you married the first man who noticed you and detest everything now."

"I'd have married *anyone* to get away from here. You remember what Father was like! He became so much worse after Mother died. He didn't have *her* to beat on anymore."

"Shh, I think she's coming back. Go away."

"Of course, your *majesty*."

I retreated a few steps to make it seem like I hadn't come so far, and made the rest of the way down. Suddenly, Elwood and Amelia made more sense.

Lord Drake turned the corner and leaned on the banister looking up towards me. I will confess that I found this gesture appealing. It was also flattering to have him defend me against his own sister. I watched Amelia enter the drawing room from the corner of my eye.

"Finally, my little bird has come back to me."

He kissed my hand and offered me his arm.

"Will you always be waiting for me at the bottom of the stairs? Or will you grow tired of me someday?"

He wrapped me in a hug and kissed me. "I could never grow tired of you. And if I do, you have my full permission to push me down that oversized set of stairs."

I chuckled at the image of that. "To the drawing room?"

He sighed. "Yes... sadly."

"Why sadly?"

"I grow weary of sharing you with so many."

"Would you cage your little bird?"

"If I was in the cage with her – yes." He kissed me and let his arms travel the length of my back.

I was beginning to feel uncomfortable. "Come," I said while gently pulling away, "they will begin to wonder where we are."

"I suppose you are correct...but first, tell me you love me. Tell me, you aren't only here because I...coerced you."

I found it surprising that he required this reassurance. As if his conscience managed to take a nibble of him. Perhaps having my family here was a reminder of the truth.

I tried to be convincing and held his face in my small hands. "I love you; I can think of no one as devoted to me as you." Then I reached up and kissed him. "Are you satisfied now?"

He smiled. "Yes, let's return to the others since we must."

Walking arm in arm, my thoughts fell to Daniel. I kept adding more stones to my tower of guilt and betrayal. My mind was clouded with such contradictory thoughts and emotions.

Elwood was the enemy. Yet, I must find ways of making my life with him tolerable. Was it wrong to admire certain things about him? He was going to be my husband and the father of my children after all. But he was...deplorable, two-faced. Cruel *and* loving?

I promised Daniel another would never have my heart. While that would remain true, would I be able to continue to convince Lord Drake otherwise? Was it morally wrong to have affections for one man but still marry another?

Perhaps I could help spy for the Catholics while I'm here? I felt anxiety begin to consume me; I closed the doors to these thoughts as the drawing room opened to us.

Chapter Twenty-Five

GLIDING DOWN THE STAIRS with a candle in hand, I relished the peaceful quiet of the early hours. Not a single servant was stirring yet and all was still. The stairs did not creak and the only sounds I heard besides my own breathing, was my skirt dragging lightly behind me. I had chosen an older dress of mine to wear that was easier to put on by myself — the blue and yellow one — and braided my hair simply down the side before leaving for my little adventure. I don't know whether it was intentional or not, but I never had received a proper tour of his castle. What better time to explore when I could not fall back asleep?

I walked down the same hall where the library was, but creaked the door open to the ballroom on the right instead. The room was cold and dark, but utterly enormous! Large stone columns lined either side of the room with the largest chandelier I had ever seen in my life hanging in the center. I could make out large mirrors and exquisite paintings hanging in the room and I found myself completely lost in a daydream twirling across the ornate floors. I imagine Anna would enjoy this room best of all. My heart squeezed. I stopped twirling, lost in thought about her. Was she as sad without me as I was without her? I suppose that is part of growing up — yet, when would I see her again?

The room having lost some of its magic sway over me, I decided to explore further. I closed the door carefully behind me and found a third door down the hall. This appeared to be Lord Drake's study. It was a narrow room with an oversized desk, chairs, a few bookshelves, and tall windows. The fireplace was still smoldering with a few embers; this must be where Elwood spent much of his time in the late evenings.

Walking to the other side of his desk, I noticed a single portrait next to an empty glass. I picked up the frame and held my candle near it. It was Elwood and his siblings with his mother. I studied her face. I *did* look eerily similar to her. The only difference was that her hair was black and her eyes as dark as Elwood's. But her face, nose, and smile – even her frame – resembled me.

I felt a rooting sadness dwelling on how awful his childhood must have been. How often was he forced to witness his father hurting his mother? How often were he and Amelia beaten as well? I believe I understand his obsession with me and why he downplayed so greatly the bruises he left upon my body. He did not wish to believe he had become like his father; he desired to protect and cherish me as he had perhaps done with his mother. Placing the picture carefully back down, I decided it was best if I were not caught in here alone.

The last door in the hall was on the left; curiously, it was locked. I tried peering in through the slight cracks of the door frame. While intrigued, my curiosity would have to wait to be satiated as I saw nothing but blackness. In truth, part of me did not wish to uncover any more dark secrets of the Drake family line. I was having a difficult enough time joining it. Whatever secrets lay therein would have to wait for another time.

Walking into his grand library, I browsed for a book and found *Utopia*. It was a book my father had spoken fondly of, however, I hadn't yet read.

Nestling into an oversized chair by the vacant fireplace, my fingers admired the beautiful red binding. Releasing the book lock, I began to read by candlelight.

I am admittedly unsure over how much time passed, but I had read at least a quarter of it before I was interrupted.

The door was flung open by a very distressed earl bursting through. I was quite startled and nearly cast the book from my hands as I gasped.

He rushed towards the sound of my voice and candle burning on the side table.

"What are you doing?" he shouted angrily.

"I was reading?"

He grabbed the book from my hands and tossed it on the opposite chair. "Why the blazes would you be doing that *now?*"

Flustered, I stood from my chair. "I woke very early and could not go back to sleep. Have I done something wrong?"

His chest was heaving, as though in a panic. "You dressed and made yourself ready? You went down the stairs on your own? And you've been here all this time?"

I still failed to see the problem. "Yes?"

He rubbed his face and shouted, "You must not behave this way! You are to be a countess! Countesses do *not* dress themselves or fix their own hair! They do *not* hide away in the library for hours while your betrothed searches for you! And – more importantly – you are never, *ever* to go down the stairs without someone else present!"

I was nearly speechless; I was unaccustomed to being spoken to in this manner and it frightened me. "I apologize. I did not realize my wrongdoing."

His face still bore an anger I could not grasp as he continued, "You have no idea the fears that ran through me when Sylvia told me you were not in your room. I had her start searching for you immediately. Then it occurred to me that you might be here."

Oh.

"You thought I ran away?"

He was silent for a moment, staring at me as he shifted weight on his feet. "Yes."

I held his hand that was still balled up into a fist and tried to comfort him. "I'm sorry that I was so thoughtless – this did not occur to me. I merely couldn't fall back to sleep and did not feel comfortable leaving my room in my house robe. I agreed to marry you; I gave you my word. I am here. Did I not confess my love and loyalty to you?"

He exhaled, drawing me into his arms. "I forgive you. I understand it was not your intention."

Upon his releasing me, I asked, "Why may I not go down the stairs alone? What time is it? Surely the sun has only just recently risen?"

He walked to the windows and yanked the deep red curtains back. It was well past sunrise.

Coming back over to me he said, "The stairs are dangerous, and I do not want to risk the most precious thing in the world to me."

"Dangerous?"

He sighed and gritted his teeth before speaking. "My late wife, Beatrice, fell down the stairs when she was pregnant. The baby started to come, but it was much too early. That is how I lost them both."

"Oh, *Elwood*... I'm so very sorry. I didn't know. – This is why you are always waiting for me at the bottom stair or have ensured a servant is with me?"

"Yes."

I gave him a sincere hug. "I will respect your wishes, I promise. And I will always take extra care on the stairs."

He squeezed me back and rested his head on mine. It was the most tender and genuine gesture I had ever received from him.

"Thank you." He said.

He lowered his face to mine and kissed me lovingly. It was the first time since the Elharts' party that his kiss brought a warm and pleasant sensation throughout me. Pulling away, my breath quickened. I wasn't supposed to feel anything for him! *Not him!* Not after what he had done! No matter how much compassion his past elicited from me!

He studied my face with curiosity. "What is it?"

"–Nothing."

A grin pooled in his expression. "And to think that not so long ago you said there were no emotions left for me to stir in you."

I froze. Had he noticed the change in me? Had he known I was acting all this time? Or was it simply an offhand comment? Perhaps he only felt the shift in tenderness as I had.

Sylvia appeared in the room and curtsied. "Oh! You found her! Forgive me, my Lord, for barging in."

He released me and handed me the book he had thrown on the other chair, "Perhaps it would be wise for you to keep a book or two in your room for the next time you cannot fall back asleep."

He looked towards Sylvia. "Please fix up Miss Dawson and bring her back down for breakfast."

"Yes, of course, my Lord." She curtsied again and I followed her up the stairs as Elwood watched me from the bottom banister.

"Oh, miss, you frightened us terribly! We must hurry to get you ready – his guests have already gone down for breakfast."

Sylvia began undoing my dress and hair. I realized my old gowns were now deemed unacceptable and were brought merely as a courtesy.

"I apologize for scaring you; I will be more thoughtful in the future."

She stopped what she was doing. "Your apology is most kind, miss. Let us get you looking perfect for the day!"

I was dressed in a sky blue and purple dress with perhaps too many frills for my taste; my hair was now fixed *appropriately.* Sylvia and I walked down the stairs. Elwood was of course waiting for me.

Was I wrong to try and banish any feelings I experienced for him? What was the moral thing to do? What a peculiar dilemma to find oneself in! To fall in love with my malicious husband to be, or keep true to a man I could never be with? Was there a way to do both?

Would falling in love with Elwood not be a betrayal to everything and everyone, myself included? Yet, isn't a wife *supposed* to have feelings for her husband? Could I ever forget what he had done to Daniel and I? How cruel he truly was? My stomach churned. I didn't want to bury my feelings for Daniel; I wanted to keep them alive forever. Yet...to daydream of a man other than your spouse? Surely that must be sinful and terribly wrong.

He offered his hand out to me as I came down the last two steps, pulling me from my thoughts. "You look exquisite, my darling," he said, kissing my hand. "Come, let us join the others and decide what we are to do for the day."

Sitting at the table, the others were conversing about taking a carriage ride into town. I put some fruit and bacon on my plate with a slice of bread.

Small ales were poured for Elwood and I as Paul addressed me, "What do you think, Miss Dawson? Should we all head into town?"

Lord Drake answered for me. "I was actually thinking of us all riding on horseback? There is nothing much to do in town except to be gawked at by the commoners. I have over a hundred acres here for us to explore."

I gave a small nod to Paul who understood.

"Augh, my brother, always the one to derail a good plan! Though, I daresay, riding horses would be an acceptable diversion as well! What does everyone else think?"

Everyone, of course, agreed with the Earl.

Amelia raised her eyebrow in my direction. "You slept in rather late today, Miss Dawson. You retire from the group early and then arrive so late to breakfast? You're not of a sickly constitution, are you? Exactly how much beauty rest do you require?"

Lord Drake shot her a glare as I responded. "I am generally healthy, thank you. I confess, I lost track of my reading. Though perhaps I should have donated the time to additional rest so that your brother will have the fairest bride possible."

Elwood smiled at my response. "As if your beauty could be improved upon!"

His sister groaned. "*Reading*? Why would you waste your time in such a manner? I loathed learning it as a child and find my opinion wholly unchanged."

I swallowed a bite of bread. "Perhaps you haven't found a book you like yet. I admit that some can be tiresome. Personally, I take quite a delight in the worlds that writers have created; most are quite diverting!"

Amelia rolled her eyes. "It is *not* an attractive quality for a woman to read. It's such an arrogant, useless pastime. We have far more appropriate uses of our time, as I'm sure you'll soon discover in your new station of life."

The others at the table shifted their silent stares to me, Mama included. I was starting to look forward to the wedding, if for no other reason than to be rid of Amelia's presence.

I forced a pleasant countenance, but my tongue would not abide. "While I cannot speak for all men, it certainly hasn't made a bit of difference to your brother, has it?"

I felt his hand suddenly squeezing my knee. "I am not so easily intimidated as other men, Amelia. Her fondness for reading, while unusual, is indeed part of why I admire her."

His sister rolled her eyes and grabbed another piece of bacon from the platter.

Mama smiled. "What book were you reveling in this time?"

"*Utopia*."

Amelia's husband dropped his fork abruptly on his plate sending a clattering echo through the room. "That book is full of radical nonsense! Elwood, how could you let her head be filled with such absurdity?"

Lord Drake chewed his bite of food and swallowed. "It's only a book, Charles. What is she going to do? Deconstruct social structures because she read about one man's made up world? Miss Dawson does not have a weak mind; she knows it is an imaginary and ridiculous alternative to how the world should and does work best. Isn't that right, my dear?"

I swallowed a bite of bread. In reality, I agreed with everything I had read and wished I *did* have the power to change things. I kept these opinions to myself, however, and concurred with my betrothed.

Charles humphed. "Risky business, Lord Drake, risky business! Everyone knows women are the weaker sex, your fair bride is not excluded from the same line that ate the apple and manipulated Adam into eating it too."

My teeth gritted. I felt Elwood's hand on my knee again, as though to tell me to stand down.

Lord Drake smiled politely. "If Eve looked anything like my bride to be, I cannot fault the man! She could offer me poison straight from the vile, and I'd scarce be able to turn her down."

I placed my hand on top of his, pleased by how well he had diffused the conversation.

"Here, here!" voiced Paul.

Mama added, "I know this may not be a popular opinion, but it sounds to me that men may perhaps be the weaker sex if it took the devil to tempt Eve and *only* a woman to tempt Adam."

I giggled in chorus with the other women at the table – except Amelia. "Indeed!"

Lord Clutterbuck was quick to respond, "I see impertinence runs in the family. Good luck to you, my Lord! I believe you will have your hands full. May God give you sons instead of daughters."

Elwood sighed and looked at me with affection. "She is worth it."

Chapter Twenty-Six

THE ENTIRE CASTLE WAS in a peculiar state of organized frenzy. Servants were busy dusting, polishing, carrying various floral arrangements, decorations, tall candelabras, furniture etc. They were like ants, each with an urgent mission filing in and out of doors and halls with mathematical precision. Even if fear from his Lordship was their motivating factor, it was an impressive thing to witness. The musicians arrived earlier and set up in the ballroom while preparing for the wedding procession to the church, tuning and rehearsing with their instruments as servants made the ballroom shine.

Lord Drake decided that we would process in his carriage and have our guests follow on foot, horse, or carriages, depending. I felt pity for the poor musicians who would have to carry their instruments five miles to the Church and back. At least they were being well compensated. No matter the cost, the wedding preparations would be ready for tomorrow morning. Everyone was fluttering with excitement. Even Mama caught herself being wrapped up in the grandeur of it all. I, however, felt the opposite.

Sneaking outside by means of the back door through the ballroom, I found myself in a heavenly peace, with nothing but the sounds of nature. I sat upon the large rock beneath the great weeping willow that I could see from my room and exhaled deeply. The birds sang sweet melodies to me as I closed my eyes, reveling in blissful solitude. I felt so grateful to breathe on my own, without the eyes of guests, servants, or the Earl upon me. My marital execution was rapidly approaching. The sadness was choking me and becoming harder to conceal.

I missed Daniel fiercely and despite my efforts, I could not separate him from my thoughts; he was everywhere. I pictured his face in my mind and burned his memory there. He was worth it all. Tomorrow he would be released; tomorrow he would be free to go home. That fact brought me much comfort; he would be able to live his own life and see his family again. That would console me for the rest of my life. I knew that once vows had been exchanged, I would have to find ways to block the memories and fantasies of Daniel. ...Only, I wasn't sure how.

A strong breeze blew, waving the wistful branches about me as I gratefully inhaled the warm scent of summer's arrival. Yet my soul still felt a bitter emptiness. Attending church last week with the Earl did nothing to feed my soul. I wondered when the next time any of the Sacraments would be possible, and I felt an incredible wave of desolation.

I credit my guardian Angel for giving me the idea to make a Spiritual Communion, since I could not embrace Christ in the fullness of the Eucharist. This was the next best thing I could do. I ached for His presence even more than Daniel's.

Bowing my head in prayer I united myself to Jesus and spent several minutes with the Lord and Divine Love of my heart. He comforted me so tenderly, I had no wish to leave this moment in time. I begged Him to help me, to stay with me, to make me strong enough to bear this cross.

"Isabel!" called Lord Drake from a distance. I sighed. He truly had a knack for ruining my solitude.

I rose, walking towards him as he questioned me, "What are you doing out here? Sylvia is looking for you – you're meant to be greeting our guests that are arriving, my dear."

"Forgive me, it's so very peaceful out here."

His face softened. "Yes, my mother often found solace in that very spot. She adored that old tree."

"What was she like?"

"Not so very different from you. Kind, witty, beautiful, and warm. She had not your temper nor your tongue though! Still, I feel she would have liked you very much."

"I'm sure I would have been fond of her as well. I think I shall adopt this spot as my own. May I ask how she passed?"

Elwood stiffened, looking away from me a moment. "We don't know. She became weak and very ill one day, and the following week, she died."

I placed a hand on his arm. "I'm so sorry. How old were you and your siblings then?"

"I was ten. Amelia was eight and Paul was a baby – had just learned to walk, in fact. Father passed away a decade later." He took my hand as we walked towards the house and looped it through his arm. "Why are we speaking of such gloomy things, my dear?"

The more I learned of their family, the deeper my sympathy grew. I couldn't help but wonder if his father had something to do with his mother's death. Something nagged at me that he had.

"I only wanted to know you better, I apologize."

"It's quite alright. It was a long time ago. Now, you really must come inside so Sylvia does not burst. I fear your proclivity to wander and daydream are fuel for her nightmares."

"Perhaps my servant Lily could come and live with us and help take some of her burden?"

"My dear... *Lily* has no concept of how things are run here. I do feel that Sylvia is much better suited to your needs in your new life. You are about to become the wife of an earl – one of the most powerful and wealthy earls in all of England. There are few that have more wealth and land than I. You must rise to the occasion of being my countess, Isabel."

My heart clouded, but I knew better than to show it. "You are correct, of course; it would be tiresome to train her."

"You will need to practice holding that witty tongue of yours in check too. Not every opinion of yours must be uttered. You must be proper when the moment calls for it, and a countess knows when to stay silent. Especially one that is raised from a lower status."

My teeth clenched before answering. "I will do my best to please you."

"As I'm sure you will!" He kissed my hand as we entered back into the wedding frenzy.

It was not long before I was greeting extended family and people of import that were attending our wedding. I felt assaulted by so many conversations, and the clattering of servants echoing around me. I fought back horrid feelings of panic and spoke as joyfully and correctly as I could. The whole ordeal was draining, and I greatly feared that I would never remember their names or any details about them.

By the time supper was nearing and Sylvia was dressing me in an even more extravagant gown, a terrible sense of dread shadowed over me. My stomach swirled and my ears began to ring.

Not again.

"Leave me," I ordered her, admittedly, more harshly than I had intended to sound.

"Miss Dawson, I still need to fix your hair."

"Come back later, please."

In silence she curtsied and left the room.

I went over to the window and pushed it open. A small breeze came and attempted to relieve the beads of sweat pricking my forehead. My arms were shaking as I tried desperately to catch my breath. A war had broken out in my mind.

I can't do this!

—You must! Do you wish for Daniel to die? How could you be so selfish? His life is at stake and you're the most pampered woman you've ever met!

My wedding wasn't supposed to be like this. None of this is fair.

—Fair? You sound so childish. What will everyone think if you embarrass Lord Drake by being late? You must rise to the occasion!

I am exhausted. How can I live the rest of my life like this?

—Do not be weak! You don't have that luxury. Daniel will be spared if you just continue on, that is all you have to do. Do it for him."

My chest ached as I tried to calm myself. Each time I began to pray, my mind filled with images of Daniel and tears threatened. I desperately wanted nothing more than to be in his arms again. I blinked back the tears and refocused on my Aves.

A sharp knock on the door shattered my meditation.

"A few more minutes, Sylvia." I said as evenly as my breath would allow.

"My dear? It's Elwood, may I come in?"

I glared at the door. Sylvia must have fetched him. *Tattletale.* I was starting to lose any fondness I had for her. She was but a pawn of the Earl's.

Before I could answer, he cracked the door open and slipped in. "Sylvia said you were out of sorts. What's the matter? Surely not another spell?"

I stayed by the window. "Might I return outside for a few moments?"

He pulled me into a hug, "I'm afraid there's not time for that."

He tried to hold my face up to examine, so I rested on his chest instead; I was positive he would not try to move me from there. If he were to look at me now, I could not have concealed my pain.

"Ah, my little bird, I promise you will feel better once you have some drink and food and are surrounded by our guests. How could your troubles not be cheered away? So many have come to celebrate with us. Even the Duke of Hampshire! Are you not pleased?"

With a focused breath, I coerced the happy mask he desired to see. "Of course – it is all a bit overwhelming."

"I understand. Which is exactly why I came to comfort you. However, you really must let Sylvia come and finish preparing you for supper. It will be time soon, and you must not be late. Yes?"

"Of course."

He scrutinized his gaze. "Not even a thank you? Not every man is as understanding of women's constitutions as I, my dear. And you do seem to have a lot of these spells. They are becoming a nuisance, aren't they? Do you know most men would have never had desired to court you had they known of them? – Of course, my love for you helps me to overlook them. Hopefully once we are married, they will lessen."

I felt a deep repulsion, yet sweetness came out of my lips instead, "I am so grateful for you, Elwood." Any feelings I thought I was developing for the Earl, were now out with the pot.

Sylvia replaced the Earl's company and put the finishing touches to my hair. Just as she applied another layer of perfume, there was a knock at the door. Elwood. He took the liberty of letting himself in again. This time, carrying what seemed to be a jewelry box.

"I have one more wedding gift for you, my dear." He beamed proudly.

"Elwood, what more could you give me that you have not already?"

He opened the box before me – it was a matching sapphire necklace to my ring. The gems were encased with gold frill and went all the way around to the back clasp.

I was stunned. "Oh...my...it's so beautiful! You did not have to do this for me."

I could tell he enjoyed the way I stared at them. "Ah, but I wanted to." He took it out and placed it around my neck. "If you are to be *my* countess, you must look the part!"

The necklace matched the satin blue lace of my gown perfectly and held a decent weight to it. I felt like the Queen with such excessive jewels and gowns. I could not restrain the smile I felt as I looked at the necklace in my reflection. I sat up straighter to evaluate my new *countess* personhood in its entirety. I appeared poised, royal, and lavish. And yet? I felt homeless. This was not *me.* This was a simple girl playing dress up. I was an imposter in my own life.

I accepted Lord Drake's extended hand as I stood with a gracious smile. "It's exquisite, Elwood; thank you ever so much!"

"You are a vision of grace. Come! Let our guests see how beautiful my bride is."

My thoughts whirled. Who is this man? Do I even know him after all these years? He seems to delight in keeping my emotions and thoughts in constant fluctuation. The Earl was either tender and kind or hateful and harsh. It was as if I was marrying two different people in one.

"Have my siblings arrived yet?" I asked as we glided down the stairs.

"No, not that I have seen."

I had hoped they would have arrived early...but now not to even come for supper? I worried my brother would not show for the wedding at all. He disapproved too much. I had disappointed him. Did they not understand? Or had I been in the wrong for agreeing to this marriage?

"Mind the stairs, my dove; they are steep."

"Of course."

"Are you excited for tomorrow?"

"I feel more nervous than anything," I confessed.

We paused as he turned to look at me. "Why? You will be breathtaking and it will be a joyous day, I promise."

"I am not used to so much company. I am afraid that you have plucked a girl from obscurity! Though I assure you that I am trying my best to acclimate myself to your life."

He smiled thoughtfully. "I have no doubt that you will soon be comfortable in your new lifestyle; do not be nervous. You look the part so well already!"

I exhaled quietly. He was not capable of understanding what he had done to me or how I felt.

"Thank you, Elwood. I'm sure our wedding will be a day I shall never forget."

He kissed my hand. "Come. They have gathered in the dining room and are waiting for our entrance."

I received countless compliments as we arrived. There must have been thirty people. Lord Drake took his place at the head of the table with me sitting at his right side and my mother next to me. His siblings sat across from us.

I leaned and whispered to Mama. "Have you heard from Jon?"

She had a sheepish expression. "No, but surely they will all be here in time for your wedding, do not fear!"

My throat tightened. When would I see them again, if not at my own wedding?

The first course was served, and many conversations went on at once. Tidbits about the Queen, food, my dress and jewels, ongoings of parliament, and even the weather were all covered before the next course arrived.

"You are unusually quiet," Elwood whispered, "are you well?"

"Forgive me, I am worried something happened to Jon, Anna, and Christy. I've been waiting for them all day."

"It displeases me that you're saddened by their absence. I hope, for their sakes that they had good cause not to arrive this evening. However, my dear, do try to remember this is a happy occasion! In the morning, you are to be my wife!"

He smiled so warmly at me, I was almost tricked into feeling better.

"You're right, of course, Elwood." I put my best fake smile on. "I shall not let a sad thing overshadow the moment."

He squeezed my knee. "There you are!"

As the servants came around with the main courses, I found it exceedingly difficult to eat. I tried a few bites and spread the rest across my plate to give the illusion I had eaten more. Fortunately, no one seemed to notice, save my mother who eyed me with concern.

Towards the end of supper a letter arrived for Lord Drake. The servant whispered to him that it was urgent; he opened it there at the table. All the guests hushed as they awaited to hear its contents. To their disappointment, the earl abruptly excused himself, muttering something about business and walked in the direction of the library.

When he had not returned past the desserts, I insisted our guests head to the drawing room for games and drinks. Heading to the library to check on him, I found him in quite the state.

His black doublet was flung over a chair, and he was leaning on the hearth, staring into the large fireplace. The glow from the embers made his features look devilish. I had never seen him in only a white shirt and trunks before; it did not ease his fearsome qualities that some of his chest showed through his shirt; it made him look wild. He gripped the letter so tightly that the page wrinkled between his fingers. I hesitated to approach him.

"—Elwood? What news has there been?"

He turned to me with furious eyes. "I don't know how this is possible!"

"May I read the letter? Perhaps it would be easier than explaining it?"

"No!" He bellowed, tossing the balled up letter into the fire. After he witnessed it being consumed, he stormed over to me and grabbed me by the arms, "Just because your precious father overeducated you, doesn't mean you'll ever be able to grasp a man's business; do you understand *that?* What could you possibly do that I could not do on my own?"

I knew it would be pointless to retaliate, or tell him his grip hurt me, so I tried to placate him as best I could. "Forgive me, I sought only to comfort you."

He shoved me out of the way as he walked towards the center of the room, ranting, "Why would I need you to comfort me? Do I look like a child in need of pacifying?"

I swallowed my sarcastic responses. "I feared you had received troubling news. If I am not needed, I will attend to our guests."

"No. You will stay in my sight – at all times. At least until after the wedding."

I was confused by that statement. Trepidation began to rise. I said nothing, but took a seat in the corner of the room in an armchair, putting as much space between us as possible.

He apparently disagreed with the distance separating us. In a moment, his arms were leaning on my chair with his body hovering above me. His chest was heaving, as though he could not catch his own breath. His turbulent eyes threatened to burn through me. What had been in that letter to cause such erratic behavior?

"Elwood, you are starting to frighten me."

"You are marrying me tomorrow, Isabel. No matter what has happened. – Say yes."

"Elwood, what has happened?"

"Say YES!" He growled at me.

I trembled. "—Yes. Of course. As promised."

He stood and straightened his shirt, clearing his throat. "I just received word that Mr. Porter and several other prisoners died this afternoon from the bloody flux."

I heard his voice repeat itself in my head as the shock pierced through me. *Died. Mr. Porter died. This afternoon. The bloody flux. Died.* Each repetition cut through me deeper and deeper until I was completely gutted. My body folded over itself; I covered my face with my hands, trying to tell myself to breathe instead of cry.

Lord Drake kneeled next to me, suddenly soft in his tenor, placing an arm around my curved back. "Isabel, calm yourself."

I raised my posture, naturally forcing him to remove his hand from me. My chest drummed as I swallowed back the anguish. I could not speak, for if I did, all my emotions would flood out. I fixed my gaze on the books far across from me.

He rested his hands upon my knees. "Are you angry with me? It wasn't my fault. He was supposed to be released tomorrow. I swear it, Isabel. I didn't mean for him to die. You musn't hold this against me."

I gripped the layers of my dress into fists. I could not stand to be in his presence any longer.

"Isabel? Say something! It was *not* my fault! I forbid you to be upset with me! I know this was not what we agreed upon, but people die in prisons every day. I had no way of knowing he wasn't strong enough to survive. And really…aren't we better off without another traitorous papist running amuck? – Isabel, answer me!"

The more he prattled on, the closer my limits came to reaching a boiling point. How could he be so cold? Daniel had died on the floor of that horrible place the day before his release. Surrounded by strangers. Suffering horribly. Did he really die how he claimed, or had Lord Drake ordered him killed? And now…did he expect me to still go through with this pretense of a marriage? No wonder he sounded so worried – our deal no longer stood as a safeguard to my promise.

I could not risk Elwood witnessing how deeply my heart was bleeding. Anger and tears fought erratically within me. I needed to be alone to mourn, to scream, to figure out what to do. Stiffly, I moved his hands, stood from the chair, and walked towards the door.

"No!" He shouted, yanking my arm back to where he now stood.

He squeezed my arms tightly, so that I could not budge. "*No*, Isabel! You may not leave me. I did not plan for him to die. I did *not* lie!"

I stared away from him. I did not care what he did to me now. At least if he accidentally killed me in his rage, I would be with Daniel instead of him. Everything I had gone through had been in vain. There was no point to anything at all anymore.

He shook me, causing my head to flail. "Look at me! Damnit, Isabel! Would you have preferred I conceal this from you? I did not! I was honest! He is dead and I cannot change that!"

When he ceased, I settled my eyes upon his countenance to examine his motives. I did wonder why he told me the truth. It certainly would have been easier for him had he lied and told me tomorrow that he had been released. Had his conscience twitched for fear I'd learn the truth? Yes. He knew Jonathon would have reported the news back to me at once. He *had* to be honest with me, even if he would prefer not to be; he could never force Jonathon to keep such a secret from me.

I looked into those desperate, deep eyes of his. "No, you cannot change that now. You have failed me. You should have released him the day I accepted your proposal."

He scoffed. "And have him try to steal you away? – It was out of my hands, little bird; you must believe that."

"Must I? What reason have I to marry you when our deal is now broken? You should have moved him, or looked after him better! His well-being was *your* responsibility!" My voice faltered the higher pitched it rose.

He squeezed me hard and I winced. "Do not be cruel to me in your anger. Have I not proven my love to you over and over? Does our passion mean nothing to you? Does my own agony mean nothing? Do not break my heart in this fashion – I *need* you."

"*Me?* Cruel to you? Do you not see what you've done? You are not even half the man I once thought you to be."

There was silence. A lump lodged itself in my throat. What had I said?

The glare in his eyes told me I had spoken too harshly. The monster's cage was opened and my temper had been the key.

Before I could back away, he pushed me against a wall of books so aggressively that my jewelry chimed. Books clattered to the floor as I felt his hands dig deeper into my arms.

"*Elwood!*" I whimpered.

He froze.

Slowly, his painful grip loosened, and he readjusted his furious eyes to mine. Through gritted teeth, he calmed, and drew me into a gentle, but firm embrace.

"Forgive me. You have wounded me with that sharp beak of yours. I am no villain. I am only a man; a flawed man, who loves you beyond reason."

He pulled me away, gently holding my shoulders, trying to catch my stare. "His death was *not* my doing. I may be powerful, but I am not God, woman! How the devil was I to know he'd catch a cold? Why do you care so much that he is dead?"

My eyes burned. As I closed them, large tears spilled out the sides as my lips trembled.

Releasing my arms, he cradled my cheeks and kissed my forehead. "Mr. Porter was nothing – a mere punctuation mark in your book. *I* am your past, present, and future pages; our stories are intertwined. He is *nothing*. Why do you seek to mourn him? What was he to you but a friend? Remember everything I have done for you. Remember the fire in your veins when I touch you. Kiss me Isabel, you promised yourself to me; remember that you love *me*."

He kissed my lips.

I did not return it.

Pulling away, he struck my face with so much force that had he not been holding me with his other arm, I would have fallen. My face quivered from the burning sting of his hand. Instead of fear though, I felt only rage. I moved to strike him back with all the anger and disdain that had built up in me.

He caught my wrist in the air as he restrained the other. "There you are; *there's* the life back in your eyes!" He smiled with satisfaction and forced his kiss on me, pushing my arms down to our sides.

He breathed heavily, staring into my eyes. "Do you need motivation to love me, Isabel, is that it?" He leaned into my ear, still clasping my arms. "I'll remove the same rosary I planted in your friend's jacket from your brother's next. How does that sound? Shall that be our new deal? Jon's life for you to be my wife?"

My eyes narrowed. "Are you mad?"

"If I am mad it is because you have made me so. If you would only be reasonable, I would not have to react in this manner."

I fought to break free to no avail. The more I struggled, the harder he squeezed my wrists. As I gave up the futile endeavor, he loosened his grip and molded me into his chest. I was defeated, once more.

A few more of my tears escaped and soaked into his shirt. "Do you wish to kill your little bird, Elwood? The better I come to know you, the more brutal you reveal yourself to be. Is this how life will be? Will every argument turn to savagery?"

He kissed my head and stroked my disheveled hair. "I could never kill you, silly little bird. I don't wish to be brutal. Not with you. Not with your family or your friends. I have wanted nothing but you for years, and I alone shall possess you. I will share with no one. Not even the memory of a ghost. I know now that you cared far more for him than you let on. I had suspected your feelings for him ran deeper than you claimed, but I also knew your affections for me were stronger. Do not forget that."

I didn't know what to say; I dared not speak anymore. I had revealed too much.

He glided his fingers across my cheek. "I care not if we have a thousand such fights as these, so long as you are mine. But if you cannot love me from out of your own desire, what choice do you leave me with but to be brutal? A life without you would be as a life without water, or food. I could not survive such a thing."

My breath trembled as he continued, raising my face closer to his. "Think back to the market fair, to our first kiss in the library, all our tension-filled letters and my gifts. Recall the fire that ignited between us as we danced, to those feelings for me you fought so hard to repress – how I've always made your heart quicken. You confessed your love for me – you've kissed me with *such* passion! I'm asking you not to repress these feelings again. I know you are...upset by his death. But please do not let it cloud what we have. Perhaps it is better that he is dead; it will be easier for you to focus your attentions on me."

I remained silent as he raised my face still higher with his fingers beneath my chin. "Have you not been treated like a queen here in my home – *our* home? Do you not feel our hearts pounding together even now? Are you not the queen of my heart?"

I thought of Jonathon joining Daniel's fate and nodded.

"*Good*. I love you, Isabel, and I intend to spoil you with everything I possess for the rest of our days. We will have twenty children, if you want, and they will all be beautiful like you, and we will have a happy family without a care in the world. Nothing else matters. Simply, do not fight against us. Embrace your love for me with all of the zeal of your fiery nature that I cherish so dearly. Is love not easier and more pleasant than anger and grief?"

Our eyes locked as he continued. "Will you not forgive the one who has loved you so steadfastly?"

He moved his hands over my back until one reached my neck as the other enclosed my waist. Beginning to run his fingers over my necklace, I knew it was in my best interest to accept my situation. He would never release me until I gave him the answer he sought. This was my life now. I was to be the prisoner of a mad man, chained to his whims and fickle moods.

A thready sigh escaped me. "Of course I forgive you. Love *is* easier than anger, yes, and I choose your love. You have always brought that side out in me, for better or worse, even when I'm cross with you, even now."

He exhaled as though he had been holding his breath the whole time. "And tell me, what do I bring out in you?"

"Passion."

He lowered his lips to mine, and this time, I kissed him back with as much intensity as I could summon. I could not bear the loss of my brother as well as Daniel.

Pulling me closer, he began kissing down my neck and back up to my mouth again. He nuzzled my forehead against his. "Tell me that you love only me."

Shakily, I raised my hand to the side of his face, feeling the coarseness of his beard. He leaned into me with his hand over mine, as though savoring my touch.

"I will love only you, Elwood. And tomorrow, I will vow to be yours alone for the rest of our lives, for all to bear witness. It was always meant to be you and I."

He smiled, reveling in my ruination. It made my body ache to know that I would never experience the love I had for Daniel again. I will grieve him and the life we could have had, the rest of my cursed days, trapped with this godless earl.

Elwood kissed the palm of my hand. "Is there any love that compares to ours, little bird?"

"That would be impossible. Forgive me for causing you to doubt otherwise, I was not myself."

"Of course I forgive you. People say things they do not mean when they are angry. No quarrel could ever separate us." He kissed my lips and began traveling down my neck once more.

I was spared only from a knock at the door. A servant mentioned that our guests grew concerned over our long absence.

He held me at arms length and studied my face; he stared at every hair that had been so shaken out of place. I must have looked like a wild beast.

"My dove, why don't you retire early? We have quite the day to prepare for tomorrow haven't we? I can handle the guests tonight. Much more will join us in the morning, after all!"

"Thank you. I could use the additional rest, please excuse me to our guests."

Fetching his doublet, he put himself back together and asked the servant at the door to call for Sylvia to bring me upstairs.

"I will come to check on you in the morning." He ran his fingers over my hair. "To the world you are my dove, but to me and me alone — the phoenix who breathes fire into my soul." He kissed me deeply.

I smiled weakly, pulling away. "Until the morning then."

Chapter Twenty-Seven

SYLVIA APPLIED A COLD compress to the red mark on my cheek. She said nothing except that it should help the swelling go down. As soon as Sylvia left my room, I curled into my pillows and sobbed.

I could not fathom why God was permitting this all to happen. I felt He had abandoned me, for no wave of peace washed over me, no comfort came, only emptiness. I begged God to take me too. Only then could I be with Daniel and free of the earl.

Sitting up from my pillows, I was assailed with such a strong wave of nausea that I barely made it to my pot in time. I sat on the floor, with a shiver running through me, as I rested my head against the side of the bed. My only solace was that I knew Daniel was not suffering anymore and that he was surely praying for me now. When my tears had dried and there was nothing left but a vacant hole in my chest, I walked to the nearest window.

Through the dark, I could make out the willow tree and rock, all aglow from the stars above. I wondered about Elwood's mother — if I was about to follow in her footsteps. I wondered if his father had slowly killed her over years from harsh treatment of various forms and if Elwood's violence would escalate over time. My arms ached terribly. I worried for any children we would have together. How would I protect them?

All at once my room felt small, as if the walls were closing in upon me. My ears rang and the air became thick. Grabbing my house robe, I quickly tied it and put on my slippers. I didn't care to dress myself again — I needed to be outside, and I would take great care not to be seen going down or returning. Toss his suffocating rules! I ran across the room.

The door would not open. A fresh layer of panic pressed down upon me. I rattled the latch harder — it was locked from the outside — I was trapped inside! I ran back to the window, sweat pricking my skin, and stuck my head out to see just how far down it was. Too far. I looked at the dark reddish stones that made up the exterior and wondered if I could climb them down. My chest heaved with pain as I tried to slow my breathing.

My mind turned into a stampede of frantic thoughts, lashing away at my sanity. I had to break free of this prison. Now.

Dressing myself in one of my original gowns, (the green one so as to blend in with the trees), I began tying my bedding into a rope. A pulsating fear screamed through my core — I had to hurry. I had to escape. I would borrow a horse and run to Jonathon and warn him.

Wait.

My mother was here. What would he do to her if I ran away? He was not above using her.

Slumping into the bed, I stopped folding my sheets into knots. He had won. Again. Slowly, I dressed back into my nightgown and fixed my bedding so there would be no evidence to condemn me in the morning. I could not risk what things he might do to her if I left.

Resigning to the life I had chosen, I laid in bed for hours, trying to calm myself until exhaustion consumed me.

I awoke to the sound of Sylvia unlocking my door.

"Good morning Miss!" she said cheerfully. "Happy wedding day to you! I've brought a small ale and a light breakfast."

I sat up at once, feeling as angry as I had fallen asleep. "How challenging it must have been to carry the tray *while* unlocking my door."

My glare was undoubtedly fearsome. She cleared her throat as she sat the tray gingerly on the nightstand, avoiding my eyes. "Forgive me, miss, I was only following orders from Lord Drake, please, do not take your anger out on me. I surely did not wish to do so. He had the strangest fear you would have anxieties the night before the wedding and run off."

"I do not care what the earl has ordered or not. You will never have my trust nor my confidence. We shall never develop the kind of ~~report~~ rapport I once hoped we could have. From now on, you will leave me alone and not speak unless absolutely necessary. You may leave now. Come back when I must prepare for the wedding and not a moment sooner. And Sylvia?"

Her face was quite pale. "God help you if you *ever* lock me in *any* room ever again. Do we have an understanding?"

She curtsied and left the room with great haste.

Ignoring the tray, I moved back to the window and let the crisp morning air attempt to calm my temper. My cheeks were burning hot and the breeze felt like needles assaulting the warmth in them.

Grabbing my housecoat, I noticed an array of bruises along my arms and wrists from where Elwood had restrained and shook me.

Standing before the mirror, I examined them more closely. I could make out the shape of his fingers in the bruises on my arms. They were just as deep and discolored as they had been on my waist, if not more so.

I wondered how many more bruises were in my future. I wrapped my housecoat around me, covering the marks. There was no bruise on my face at least. I untied my hair and let it fall freely about me before I returned to the window.

My mind took me to dark places as I gazed outside. To Daniel dying on the floor of a prison, to the death of my free will and a barbaric marriage. Images of throwing myself out of the window to end it all flashed vividly in my mind. —It startled me.

Lord Drake knocked before letting himself in. I did not greet him.

"Good morning," he said tentatively. "Sylvia was nearly in tears leaving your room. What did you say to her?"

My anger swelled just upon hearing his voice. "I do not appreciate being locked up by her, *you*, or anyone else."

I turned sharply to him, before he could utter a word. "Am I your prisoner, Elwood? Is that what I am? Am I not free to move about the house or to go into the garden when I need fresh air? Is this the kind of hell you have planned for me?"

I pushed my flowy sleeves up to my shoulders, revealing the full extent of his handiwork. "Did you not promise that you would *never* hurt me again? I thought you loved me."

He stood still, fully dressed for our wedding with black and gold colors. Remorse was streaked across his face, and worry hung heavy in his eyes as he bore witness to the marks he had left.

"Oh, Isabel... *Of course* I love you! I am so sorry that I hurt you, I did not intend to. Last night was rather an exception and neither of us presented our best selves, now did we? I recall *having* to hold your hands at bay from beating *me!* We both have fiery tempers my dear. I am deeply sorry for hurting you."

I was unmoved. "That would only explain the bruising on my *wrists*, not the others."

He continued, taking a couple steps closer. "Isabel...it was *all* an accident; do not be petty. As for the lock, I can swear to you that that will *never* happen again. It was a precaution for last night alone. I greatly, and perhaps foolishly, feared that you would try to flee in your anger. Did you not attempt this? Is that not how you discovered it was locked?"

"I cannot fathom why," I said seething with sarcasm, "but I was experiencing the worst spell last night and had no way of going outside to alleviate my symptoms. Instead, being trapped only intensified it. I laid awake for *hours* trying just to breathe!" My voice raised higher and louder than I intended, but I did not care.

Elwood bit the corner of his lip as he dared to take a few more steps towards me. "*Shh...*my dear. I am *so* terribly sorry. Truly. I did not think my actions through. I give you my word that I will never do that again. I swear on my life."

I did not budge.

"Apparently I should have brought some gyngerbrede with me..." he said smiling, attempting to lighten the mood. "I had the bakery deliver hundreds for our celebration today! An entire tower of fresh gyngerbrede squares!"

There was no change in my posture or scowl.

Elwood opened his arms, "*My heart's queen!* Do not be angry with me on our wedding day! That does not seem quite right, now does it? I'm a fool for my mistakes, you have no argument from me on that point. Did you not agree last night that love is better than anger?"

He stepped closer and knelt on both knees before me. "Will you not forgive me? These mistakes were done out of fear of losing you... I will never have this fear again after today. I will not ever cage my little bird again. Would it make you feel better if I let you beat me? I promise I won't restrain you this time."

Between seeing him grovel and the image his words placed in my head, I confess I did smile, most unwillingly.

He looked hopeful at the slight lift in my countenance. "My word, that is what it's going to take, isn't it?"

I sighed. "No, I don't want to *beat you*." (Another lie...but who is counting now?)

"Well, thank God for that. My lip only recently went back to its normal size after your brother's punch!"

"Stop trying to make me smile, I am extremely cross with you and your jokes won't change that."

"Do I make you very angry?"

I threw my hands up in the air. *"Yes!"*

"Good, that means you *do* love me. Without some anger, there cannot be real love. Let go of your, admittedly *terrifying* rage, and allow me to make you happy again! There is no point in dwelling on unpleasant things. Let us bury the past and move forward with our lives."

My arms folded back, not knowing what to say in response to such idiocy.

He rose from his knees and gently placed his arms around my waist. "Will you not forgive me since it is our wedding day? Surely, it is bad luck to stay cross with your husband to be, today of all days? — You know, you look rather charming, captivating even, in your housecoat, especially with your hair flowing all about you! I look forward to seeing you this way more often."

I rolled my eyes as he kissed my forehead. "Please forgive me, little bird?" He brushed my cheek with his fingertips. "I can't promise we won't get angry with each other again over the years, but I do swear upon my life that I will never hurt you again. Not in body or heart. You have no idea the agony I am in after seeing the bruises on your delicate arms. I am disgusted with myself."

I hated that part of me still cared for Elwood after all he'd done. I felt an inexplicable compassion for him. Over the past many days, I had even found myself enjoying his company, or the way he'd look at me. A dark part of me relished in being loved so fanatically, so uncontrollably desired, even if I could not stand who he was or who I was becoming. I could not make sense of it beyond knowing he had twisted my mind into something I did not recognize anymore. I was a caged, tortured little bird, full of disfigured emotions. I did not want him, but I felt as though I was already bound to him.

He placed my hands on his chest so I could feel his heart beating. "Shall you be scouring at me as we exchange vows? Will you not forgive your Elwood?"

He pulled the sleeve of my housecoat up which made me recoil at first, but he held my hand in place. I could not control the fear that took me; my heartbeat panicked at his touch as he lowered his lips to kiss my bruises. I swallowed hard and looked away as he apologized with each kiss.

I realized there was no point in holding onto my anger, no matter how just it was. I had no choice but to marry him, for Jonathon's sake. My arguments did not matter and he knew it. — I *had* to make the best of it. As much as I hated to admit it, he was right.

"Hurt me again and I shall set my brother upon you, and you shall have more to worry about than a mere swollen lip. And since our discussion last night, I am assured no harm will *ever* come to him and so you will just take the beating, is that right, Elwood?"

He nodded with a smile, releasing my hands. "I feel that threat is only fair. I accept it. — Oh, speaking of! I have news that will surely make you happy! Your brother is finally here; he is with your mother in her bedchamber as we speak. Perhaps I should have spoken of this earlier."

I felt a renewed spirit. *"Yes, you should have! Oh! I was so worried he would not come. Are Anna and Christy here as well?"*

"Anna is sick, unfortunately. I'm sorry. Christy? I do not think she has arrived yet."

"Oh... Anna will be disappointed. I'm sure Christy will be here soon...surely."

I felt ill at the thought of her not coming. "Will you send my brother in to see me please? I have missed him most keenly."

"I have never seen a sibling's bond as close as yours and Jonathon's; it is quite touching. I will permit regular correspondence between you and your family. I ask only that you leave our marriage out of those letters and conversations. That goes for your friends too, of course."

I was confused by this strange permission. Are they not my own family and friends? Am I not allowed to speak with them on any subject I saw fit?

"As you prefer, Elwood." I didn't know what else to say.

He smiled approvingly, "Now, I can only leave if I know that I have your *full* forgiveness." He raised his eyebrows dramatically.

"Very well. I forgive you."

"And do you forgive poor Sylvia?"

I bit my bottom lip, I had been harsh with her. "Yes... I will forgive her as well."

Lord Drake drew me into a hug so tight that it lifted me off the floor and kissed me deeply before letting me go.

I looked into his eyes and wondered if happiness would be at all possible in my future with him.

No. Your happiness died with Daniel. This is merely what's left.

"Only a few more hours, my pretty little bride," he kissed my forehead. "I will fetch your brother, however, you must conceal the bruises. Be sure they do *not* see them. I have no desire for your brother to throw himself into a fit of rage on our wedding day. This remains between us. Thankfully your wedding gloves should cover what your sleeves do not. Do you swear it?"

"I have no desire for that either. — I *do* swear it." I pulled my sleeves down as far as they could go.

He lingered by the door as though not wishing to leave. "I promise that you will never regret marrying me."

"Hopefully you won't regret it either."

"That would be impossible. Now — tell me, do you think I make for a handsome groom, worthy of you, my dear?" He posed theatrically, I believe to elicit a smile from me.

I obliged him. "You know that you are quite handsome indeed, Elwood."

He came back inside to kiss my hand. "Can you imagine how beautiful our children will be? With our features combined?"

"Elwood, please! The door is open, someone may hear you."

He smirked mischievously. "Come down as soon as you can, I will be waiting for you. I wish to make an early start to the Church."

"I dare not rush Sylvia, but I will join you as soon as possible, I promise."

After kissing me once more, he closed the door behind him at last.

I paced my room, waiting for Jon. There was so much to tell him; I scarce knew where to begin.

The door opened with Mama and Jonathon walking quickly in. Mother wore a blue taffeta dress, and carried a package under arm as she closed the door behind them.

I ran to embrace Jon, who was dressed in his best blue doublet and trunks. Hushed tears soaked into the intricate needlework displayed on his shoulder as I held onto him tightly. "Daniel's dead! — I have failed him."

Jon eased me out of the hug and took my hands, leading me to the other side of the room. "*No!* He most certainly is not dead!"

"What do you mean?" I asked once we were next to my bed. "Lord Drake told me last night that he was dead! We had quite the row over it."

Jonathon shook his head, "Of course he would tell you that. As if he would confess to you that he had escaped! Do you not recall me speaking of the great scheme I had?"

My mind flooded with hope, still not fully believing what my ears had heard. "Vaguely? How?"

Jon was careful to whisper. "We broke into the prison and saved over twenty Catholics — Daniel being one of them!"

My mind could scarcely comprehend it. "He...he is well?"

"Daniel is...wounded and recovering, but yes, he is well."

Jon beamed proudly. "He is waiting for you at home, Isabel. He is *most eager* to see you. It is all he speaks of."

God had not abandoned me after all. I had only to trust Him. Joyful tears scurried from my eyes as I hugged him again. "Oh, praise God! Jon, how can I ever thank you?"

"By getting out of here!"

It was then that I remembered the other threat and pulled away. "Wait, Lord Drake threatened your life in the same manner as Daniel's last night — you will be in grave danger if I do not go through with this wedding."

"Stop fretting, sister. You, Daniel, Mother, and Anna are leaving for Daniel's hometown as soon as possible. As for me, you needn't worry because I will be going to Belgium once you all are safe."

A deep smile spread over me. "To study to be a priest, Jon?"

He nodded. "Yes. And then I hope to join the Jesuits in France or Rome, if they will accept me!"

I hugged him again. "I *knew* it! I am so very proud and happy for you! You will make God a wonderful priest, I know it!"

We looked at Mama. "I am slowly coming around to all of this — don't you worry about me now! We have more urgent things to focus on besides your brother's suicidal notions!"

"How do you propose that I escape from this castle?"

Mother presented the package in her arms. "We have it all planned, my darling girl."

Chapter Twenty-Eight

UNTYING THE STRING AND folding back the brown paper, revealed the attire of a kitchen maid. I giggled and at once began untying my house robe. Jonathon cleared his throat and turned to face the other way.

Mama gasped when she saw the grotesque blemishes covering my arms. Jon spun around to see what the matter was; his fury sparked like a fire gone out of control. He spat out a line of incoherent mutterings as Mama spoke so fast I couldn't understand a word of what anyone said.

I tried to calm them. "I'm safe *now*, that's what matters. You're both saving me from a life filled with these marks. We can discuss how horrible it all is later."

Jon gritted his teeth and turned back around while Mama helped me get dressed; her face the shade of a poppy. We were careful to tuck in every strand of my hair into the cap. The only thing that looked slightly amiss were my shoes; they were a size too large.

Before leaving, there was one last thing I needed to do.

"What are you doing?" Jon questioned.

"I'm writing a farewell note to Lord Drake."

He was immediately vexed. "*Isabel!* We do not have time for your scruples! Lord Drake does not deserve a note and time is of the essence!"

I was firm. "I know what he is, Jonathon. But he loves me. I cannot leave the man on our wedding day, without the courtesy of a letter."

Jon groaned with his hands rubbing his forehead. "I don't have time to argue — just get it over with so we can get you out of here. Hurry!"

I nodded and returned my quill pen to the inkwell.

"Elwood,

You have crafted me a beautiful cage, but it's a cage nonetheless. I won't survive such captivity. I am flying away to a place where you cannot find me; there is no point in trying.

I am truly sorry to hurt you in this way and that I must break my promise on what would have been our wedding day. However, you have brought this upon yourself.

Our relationship was more akin to madness than love. Papa was right. It's over now.

Please convey my apologies to Sylvia; I was unkind to her.

Be well, Elwood. I pray you find happiness. I wish this for you with all my heart. I hope one day you may even forgive me.

-Little Bird."

My hand shook as I placed the letter on the writing desk and set my ring on top of it.

What would become of him if I did this? I remembered how distraught he looked when he thought I had run away before — how enraged. I felt a rising panic that I shouldn't betray and abandon him like this. I could imagine all too well how hurt and furious he would be upon discovering me gone. He was going to be all the more dangerous. Would my decision to leave cost the lives of those closest to me?

Jon peaked out the doors. "Isabel, come, it's time to get you home safe."

Casting aside my doubts, I reaffirmed that Jon's plan was the only sane course of action. Daniel was waiting for me, hoping I would escape; I could not disappoint him after all he'd been through. I was in love with *him,* not the Earl. Daniel was safe, good, loving, and a true man of God. I would never be in fear of him hurting me or our family.

"Wait." I said, halting at the door. "I need Jane — the doll! Quickly!"

"It is a child's toy!" Jon snapped.

"*Jon,* I need what's under the doll." I darted over to the dresser and unraveled the rosary from her waist.

"Oh." Mama said as the look of confusion left hers and Jon's faces.

"Clever! Now, shove that in your pocket and hurry down the stairs!" Jon said as he placed a gentle arm around my shoulders.

I nodded.

Walking towards the stairs, I saw Amelia climbing up them; I held my breath. As though I were invisible, she paid me no heed whatsoever! She whisked right past me, never even glancing towards me. I smiled to myself as I continued on. *Bless her blind snobbery!*

I hurried down the stairs, tripping in my oversized shoes. — The right shoe fell off, causing me to nearly tumble. I clung to the rail as I regained my balance and chose to leave the shoe behind. Who would notice my feet?

My brother had instructed me to go into the kitchen and out their back entrance. In the meantime, he and Mama were to discreetly leave the way of the willow tree.

I weaved carefully through the entrance, amidst dozens of people dressed in their finest attire. Even people I was very familiar with did not recognize me in this disguise, like the Elharts' or Miss Smith. It humbled me that servants must feel this obscure every day of their lives.

Lord Drake stood at the door, welcoming a line of new guests, his gold lined cape blowing in the breeze. I was grateful he hadn't heard me lose my footing on the stairs.

My heart pounded up into my throat as I took a last glance at him; he appeared so relaxed and jovial as he shook hands with the newcomers. I wondered how long it would take him to realize I was gone. I was half surprised he could not sense my presence now. He would be as heartbroken as he had made me. That seemed oddly fitting. Instead of abandoning me, God was showing me just how swift He can be with His justice.

I turned my gaze and left him.

Entering the service door, at least twenty servants were scurrying about doing various tasks. My heart thundered. If I was to be discovered, it would be now.

The kitchen was warm and smelled of fresh bread, slow cooking meat, and herbs. The table before me was overflowing with food and trays of drinks. A massive tower of gyngerbrede stood proudly near the front, ready to be served. I felt the stab of remorse recalling how eager Elwood had looked when he spoke of this sweet gesture. Glancing to my wrist where the bruises crowned through my sleeves was a convincing reminder to keep going, however. I did not want this life for me or for my children. *Hurry!* A voice echoed within me.

Lifting a bucket of vegetable scraps, I went outside, unnoticed, where no one else was and closed the door behind me. I set the bucket down and breathed. The sun felt warm and bathed me with peace.

The beautiful words from psalm seventy-one: eight, flooded my thoughts as I walked to the road, feeling lighter than a sparrow,

"May my mouth be filled with your praise and with your honor all the day."

He had saved me and Daniel both. *"Forgive me heavenly Father,"* I prayed, *"for thinking you'd forsaken me. Please strengthen my trust and my faith in You. I love You for Yourself alone."*

I recognized our carriage trotting down the road. Jon opened the door as he and Mama motioned for me to get in quickly. Running and jumping onto the steps, I lost my other shoe as I climbed in. The carriage immediately raced down the road!

For the first time in two weeks; I was *free*. We all reached into the center for a group hug.

As I leaned back with Mama, Jon exhaled an enormous sigh of relief. "Isabel, I've been so worried for you." He grinned. "Never have I been more happy than I am right now!"

"Jon! How can I ever thank you?" I swallowed hard. "I was..." I could not find or express the words without tears welling up.

"Seeing you away from that miserable rogue is all the thanks I will *ever* need."

On the journey home, Jon told me all the details of how he and many others managed to break out so many Catholics from prison. Apparently, with just enough time to rescue me as well.

"We never could have done it had a few of the guards not been on our side. – We were planning to execute it during the Michaelmas celebrations; however, circumstances being what they were, everyone was eager to do their part to make it happen before the wedding."

"But how? How did you manage it?" I asked.

"We set fire to a hay cart as it was passing the prison. The driver released his horse from it and cried out for help. Most of the guards came to put the fire out before it caught the prison on fire too. While that was going on, our secret Catholic guards unlocked the two cells reserved for Catholics, and guided as many as possible out through a tunnel we had been working hard to finish in time."

"Running things a bit too tight, no?" Mama chided.

"Far closer than I was comfortable with! Nonetheless, it was a huge success; praise be to God! The tunnel spanned quite a distance into an obliging meadow. From there, various carts, horses, and carriages transported escapees near and far! Unfortunately, they discovered what was going on before we could free them all. I am deeply grieved by that. We were so close!"

I reached across to him and patted his knee. "You did what you could – and more than most have been able to before! How many Catholics are staying with us?"

"Three, including your *true* betrothed." Jonathon smiled. "Daniel is anxious to see you. He would not stop inquiring about your well-being."

"I am very eager to see him as well! Although, something worries me. When Lord Drake discovers we are all gone, any moment now, he will come for us, and he may very well throw us all in prison. I am certain he will try to kill you. Surely, he will check our house first?"

Jon shook his head. "I loosened the wheels of his carriages and threw the pins into the garden. That should slow them down enough to get us all hidden inside the house. We will hide there for many days, I'm afraid. The servants have all been briefed on what to do and say. Walter and Emma decided to leave, however, it is all set. They were well compensated for their silence. To be sure, we are not safe yet; however, we are another step closer. – Mama, do you remember the rosary?"

"Well, mostly. Your grandparents and I prayed it every evening when I was a child."

Jon smiled. "Good. I think it's best if we pray it on the way home for protection."

My very soul glowed – I never thought I'd be praying the rosary with my mother... I hoped this was the first of many to come.

Together we prayed the Joyful Mysteries, which, given the circum-stances, seemed the most appropriate. By the last decade, I caught Mama wiping tears from her eyes. I have rarely witnessed anything so touching as her slow return to the one true Faith.

Coming home had never felt more gladsome. I raced inside and imme-diately hugged Anna, kneeling down to embrace her. She cried into my shoulder, and I squeezed her tightly. "I missed you too, my sweet sister!"

Once Anna had calmed, I hugged Lily and Missy, and all the others. They laughed heartily upon seeing me dressed as one of them.

With great haste, Lily and I flew to my room and dressed me in a simple blue dress and packed me a bag of essentials. "Will you still come with me, Lily? I have missed you very much. I tried to have you sent for, but Lord Drake wouldn't hear of it."

Lily smiled. "I am relieved you're home! Of course I won't let you go to live on the seashore without me! My bag is already packed and down in the secret rooms, miss. — Oh, I found the rosary you had lost by the way, it was wedged in the floorboard under your bed. I've kept it in my pocket for safe keeping."

I hugged her, "Thank you! Keep it with you for now."

In a moment we were meeting Mama, Missy, Anna, and Jon in the study. I looked about me, taking in Pap's study for the last time, soaking in the familiar smells of books and leather.

I gasped. "I forgot my favorite book, the one Papa gave me! I cannot leave it behind! – I'll be right back! It's in my room. You all go down and I'll be right there."

Jonathon sighed. "Go quickly; I will wait for you and pick out a few of Father's books to take with us."

I nodded as the rest began their descent down the stairs.

I kept it in my dresser drawer; it was a collection of poetry that Papa gifted to me when I turned six and ten.

Grabbing it, I opened it to the inscription he wrote for me.

"For my precious Isabel. God has blessed my life so richly with you. I am so proud of the young lady my little girl has grown into. Never forget how much you are loved and cherished.

Love, your doting Papa."

My throat tightened every time I read those words. Then, out of the corner of my eye, I saw four carriages barreling towards our house. *Dashit!* Of course he would have borrowed his guests' carriages.

I slipped the book into my dress pocket and raced down the stairs. The servants panicked to get me to the study in time.

Just as the study door shut behind me, I heard the sounds of men in armor barging through our front entrance. Without hesitation, Jon and I bolted inside the bookcase's door and closed it behind us.

We were so hasty in our escape that we did not even light a candle to take with us. As the bookcase latched, I went to take off down the stairs, but Jonathon gently held me back and whispered. "The creaks. We must wait."

I tried to quiet my breathing as best I could and clasped hands with my brother.

The door to the study flung open.

"Look everywhere! I want them found!" boomed Lord Drake. "They could *not* have been *that* far ahead of us!"

We heard various books and objects crashing off of shelves and tables being overturned. Men carrying swords stabbed through bookshelves and walls, overturning everything they could. When they came to our bookcase, Jon and I made the sign of the cross – holding our breath in with a prayer. The searchers ripped several books out and one plunged his sword into the wooden panel separating us.

Just in time, Jon thrust a book in front of where the sword pushed through. We closed our eyes. It felt like a terrifying eternity until the sword was yanked backwards. Jon kept the book pressed up against the hole that the sword had made.

"Have you found something?" Lord Drake asked, stepping closer.

"No sign of them here, my Lord. We will move on to the next room."

"Hurry up then!"

Praise God! I silently exhaled.

The other men left the Earl pacing in our study. He weaved in and out of our line of sight. Pulling out the letter I wrote to him, he seemed to read it again and began talking to himself.

"Where did you fly to, little bird? How could you have wounded and humiliated me in this manner? – You found out Porter escaped. Your brother *knew.* He convinced you to leave with him...but how did he manage it? Has your family been cowardly papists this entire time? How did your family keep such a secret from *me*?

"Your wiles blinded me, little bird. Where are you? You *must* still be inside. I swear I can still smell your perfume lingering in the air. I will lock you away forever for what you have done to me. But you *will* be mine, and I will show you what a real cage is like!"

Folding the letter into his breast pocket, he looked around the room carefully. He pulled out a pair of gloves that I immediately recognized as the ones I lost at the Elharts' party! I leaned in closer to the peak hole. At first he smelled them and then began caressing his face with the tips of them.

My heart pounded so loud I was convinced he would surely hear it. I watched him fold the gloves back into his pocket and step out of view.

Suddenly, we heard a crash that sounded like he had hurled a chair into the window and a litany of curses spewed furiously from his lips. Jon covered my mouth to hide the sound of my gasp.

"My Lord," said a voice entering the study. "I have news."

"Then tell me before I throw you out the same window that vase went through!"

"The house has been sold – furnishings and all!"

"What!"

"The servants report Mr. Dawson and his youngest sister left yesterday with their bags, and there has been no sign of either Miss Dawsons or Mrs. Dawson. – We've checked each room as thoroughly as possible, they're not here, my Lord."

"He did *not* leave with Anna – he was in my castle this morning! Without her! – *Damnit!* – Search the roads in all directions! Storm Portsmouth! There will be no rest until Miss Dawson is found and brought back to me; is that clear? She has been taken against her will and is in great need of saving. Do you understand?"

"Yes, my Lord."

"And I want her brother and Daniel Porter dead! Can't risk any more escapes. Incompetent jackals running the prison like it's a damned inn. It's all their fault I'm in this situation to begin with. You *will* bring them to me! Those damn papists stole my bride! I want her family slaughtered. – I want Isabel to watch with me as their throats are slit."

"Yes, my Lord."

Lord Drake bellowed. "Get out of my sight! Go and find them, Captain! Send out your best spies!"

And with that, the captain rushed out of the room and began barking orders at his underlings. Lord Drake paced the floor again for a moment before we heard his footsteps leave the room and go down the hall towards the library.

My body shivered as Jonathon held me protectively. "Shh, it's over. We need to get downstairs now; can you manage that? Daniel is waiting for you."

Any guilt I was feeling for hurting Elwood was now quite alleviated. My heart fluttered at Daniel being mere steps away.

"Take me to him."

Making our way through the pitch blackness proved more challenging than either of us thought it would be. Though not enough to risk going back for a candle.

Slowly, silently, and clumsily, we arrived at the bottom. We felt along the cold stone walls until we found the wooden door. Jon knocked the password.

When the door opened, the lantern blinded us at first as we were embraced with hugs from Anna and Mama.

"We thought you were caught!" Mother said with tears running down her face.

"Very nearly." Jon admitted.

Father Ingles wore a large smile. "Thank God and all His saints in Heaven! You had us so worried, Miss Dawson!"

I hugged Father. "We are safe, thanks to your prayers, no doubt!"

As I pulled away, I noticed he was teary-eyed; this touched me deeply. I knew we meant as much to him as he did to us.

"Where is Daniel?" I asked.

"Come," Father said. "He is laying down, despite how much he argued to wait out here for you." Father lowered his voice. "He is in a weakened state, Miss Dawson. Do prepare yourself."

I nodded, as I eagerly went to open the door to the bedchamber. A lantern sat on the table with a chair next to his bed, shining a dull light on his still body facing the opposite direction of me.

"Isabel? Isabel! Is that you?" asked Daniel, straining to turn his head around.

I walked in quickly, closing the door behind me and knelt on the floor at his side. "Yes! It is me!"

My heart raced to see him, yet, ached simultaneously to see how disfigured they had made him.

Daniel had many bandages, some of which were leaking through, over his arms and chest. A blanket covered the bottom half of him, though I suspected his legs were bandaged as well.

He smiled at me through a purpled face full of gashes, bruises, and a swollen shut eye. It seemed only his hair was left undamaged by the guards. He was nearly unrecognizable.

He held his arms out for me. "You're really here!"

Immediately, I nestled into his bruised arms; I could not contain my tears as we embraced one another.

"I thought you were dead!" I choked out between sobs.

"And leave you? Never." He pulled back from our hug to look into my eyes as his hands held my face. "Do not *ever* trade yourself in marriage to save me again; I beg you! The thought of you being with him nearly killed me more than the executioner would have!"

"Well, you're alive, are you not? What would you have had me do? Let you be killed?"

"To spare you a lifetime of agony – YES!" He pulled me into a tender hug. "I'm so grateful you're here with me now. I have missed you more than I can express."

I brought his bandaged hand to my lips and kissed it repeatedly. "What have they done to you, my love?"

"I never thought I'd hear you call me that again. — Only beatings, that is all. It could have been worse, I promise. – You are more beautiful than I even remembered."

I chuckled as a few more tears ran down my face. "I have missed you terribly, Daniel. I dreamed and thought of you *all* the time. The idea of you being alive and free was the only thing that kept me sane...and when Lord Drake told me you had perished... I..."

"Please," Daniel said. "Do not think of it anymore. I am here and I will be perfectly well again very soon. That nightmare you lived through for me is over."

"*My* nightmare? What of yours! That prison... I'm so sorry for how much you have suffered. I can hardly bear to think of it."

"I cannot believe he dragged you down there like that. Makes me angry every time I think of it." He sighed. "All that matters is that you are here with me now. Your face was such a comfort to me when I would close my eyes and imagine you. I feel like I may be dreaming still."

I leaned forward and kissed his forehead. "I am real, and praise God, so are you!"

"I worried for you constantly." It was at this moment, as he kissed my hands, that he saw the bruises on my wrists protruding out beneath my sleeves.

He immediately struggled to sit up. "What has he done to you? Where else did he hurt you?"

"Daniel, you need to rest – I'm very well! You must lay down, please."

Ignoring my request, he pushed my sleeve gently up my arm and saw the deep discolorations that matched some of his own. "Isabel...nothing about this would suggest you are well." His chest heaved. "Where else has he hurt you?"

"Only my arms were bruised, I promise." I felt it best to omit the Earl slapping my face; Daniel was worked up enough.

"What possible reason did he have for doing this to you? What happened?"

"It does not matter, my love. There is no reason that would justify it; he lost control of his anger. They will heal much faster than all of your injuries.

"How often did they beat you? My goodness, Daniel... my heart would break at the sight of you if it were not so relieved and happy to see you here before me."

"I will mend in time. I hate that you put yourself through this for my sake. I could throttle his *Lordship*. I wish I had been there to protect you." He took on a devastated expression. "I failed you. I promised I would be there for you and I was not."

I kissed his forehead again. "You are making light of your own injuries, and they are much more serious than my own. You did not fail me; you stayed alive. After all, you *did* protect me in the prison that day."

He sighed, sinking back into the pillow. "It's not right. What man claims to love a woman and leaves such marks upon her?"

"A man that was raised by a monster only to follow in his footsteps."

"And a monster's end he shall have one day."

"Perhaps." I said.

A dream-like smile washed over Daniel's face. "Do you know when you came to the prison – with the light all about you, I thought I was dreaming! –When he dragged you away, I wished it *had* been a figment of my imagination, that you were safe at home with your family. The thought of you marrying him truly tortured me."

I squeezed his hand gently. "I could not bear to see you so hurt in there or to imagine how you would die – I'm so sorry for everything he made me do in front of you. I only wanted to save you."

"Shh. As much as I felt like I would die watching him and you... at first, I was angry that you had agreed to it, but I knew why you were going through with it. Your sacrifice only made me love you more and tripled my desire to strangle Lord Drake."

"I desperately hoped you'd understand! I'm so angry he broke his word and continued to have you tortured. Not that it should surprise me."

"I was told the guards made me their special target, courtesy of the Earl, of course. It was nothing I could not handle. Admittedly, my tongue probably got me into more trouble than I need have been in. I did not go to the rack like Father Fischer or a couple others suffered there. It could have been worse, I assure you. – It is only because of you that I'm alive at all, don't be saddened over these scrapes."

"It must have been hard to see the others suffer. Was Father Bugbee rescued too?"

He looked away. "It's my job to protect priests and there was nothing I could do. Father Bugbee met his martyrdom with incredible bravery. He heard all our confessions and lifted our spirits while he was still with us and never once complained. He saw the whole mess with Lord Drake. He was the only one who could calm the rage in my heart."

"God knows you did what you could."

He nodded as his eyes looked like his mind had gone back to the prison. Suddenly squeezing my hand, he looked at me with a serious countenance. "I will never let anything bad happen to you again."

I smiled. "I know, Daniel. Thank God it's over for the both of us! — Do you need anything? Water? Mead or food? What can I do to ease your pain?"

He kissed my hand. "I only need you."

Very gently, I kissed his swollen and split lips. "And you will always have me."

Chapter Twenty-Nine

I HELD DANIEL'S HAND, speaking about our future until he drifted to sleep.

Slipping out of the bedchamber, I found my family, servants, Father Ingles, and two other prisoners in the chapel. A young man and a woman; their injuries were not as severe, but they were extremely malnourished. It made me happy to see them eating heartily now.

Mama came to me. "Are you hungry? How is Mr. Clifton feeling?"

"He is resting...and yes, I am rather famished."

I sat down with the rescued prisoners and ate with them while they told me their story.

They were neighbors and farmers who refused to go to Anglican Church services and were repeat offenders of having articles of Catholic literature. Their names were Rachel Mitchel and Stephen Millbrook.

Rachel had soft brown eyes and a kind smile. Her family had been out while Lord Drake's men had turned her house inside out, discovering a copy of *Campion's Brag*, a rosary, and makeshift altar in their barn.

Stephen had short blond hair and a scruffy beard. His family's farm had been victims of the same raid and found equally damning evidence of Catholicism. His parents and brothers had not been so lucky in the escape; only he had made it out. You could feel the guilt he carried for that.

They had both been tortured, but said nothing, despite being there for almost a month, held in separate cells. I thought their resilience and hopeful attitudes inspiring in light of all they had suffered.

"I was there," Stephen said, "when Lord Drake dragged you into the cell to trick you into accepting his offer. We all felt so terrible for you and offered many prayers on your behalf."

I felt a bit embarrassed. "Thank you. I appreciate your prayers."

"He told me all about it," Rachel said. "I'd have done the same in your situation."

"Pfft. Don't be ridiculous." Replied young Mr. Millbrook.

Rachel chuckled, ignoring her neighbor's opinion. "I think what you did was very brave, Miss Dawson."

"Me? Brave? No, not in comparison to you and the other prisoners there. Were you even properly fed?"

Stephen scoffed, "If you call old bread and the occasional pottage 'proper', miss!"

Suddenly, my couple weeks at Lord Drake's did not sound so terrible.

Yet...that night as I lay on some bedding on the chapel floor, I kept having dreams of being back at the castle.

Elwood was calling for me.

Desperate.

Screaming.

I tried hiding in various places, but he would always find me. Beg me to stay with him. The more I refused, the more violent he became. Daniel or Jonathon would appear next to Elwood's stained blade with their throats slit, blood gushing from the opening in their necks.

Each time, I would wake, gasping, and drenched in a clammy sweat. As I leaned against the wall, wishing the room were not so dark, my thoughts pummeled me.

Had I done the right thing?

Had I placed us all in jeopardy once again?

Would we make it to Bridlington safely?

Was Elwood robbed of his sleep tonight as well?

Would he ever give up hunting us?

I tried my best to sleep, but between the hard floors and continued nightmares, I was largely unsuccessful.

In the morning, servants brought breakfast and fresh water. I took some in to Daniel.

"Good morning!"

Daniel groaned, slowly blinking his good eye open to the lantern I carried.

The state of his hair reminded me of the first time I saw him, and I couldn't help but grin. "I almost forgot what a *rare* sight you are to behold in the mornings."

"It is far too early for you to be witty." His voice was groggy and cracked; somehow I found his morning stupor to be entirely winsome.

"Surely not! I believe the birds found a way in while I was away and have made a proper nest in your hair!"

He glared at me. In a loving way of course. "I see you shall be a *delight* to wake up to every morning...for the rest of my life."

"Oh yes, it is very fortunate for you. How else would you wake up before mid-afternoon?"

"Indeed... ah! You must take care not to make me smile too broadly; my face is still a bit tender."

"I will try my best to contain my wit for as long as possible. But only for you. I see that your bandages are not soaked through yet; that's a good sign!"

"The pain is not as intense today."

After helping him to sit up, I spread some jam on a piece of bread and handed it to him. "Good – I'll be so relieved when you're fully healed."

Ignoring the bread, he held my hand. "As soon as I am strong enough again, I wish us to be married, here, in this hidden chapel...that is, if you'll still have me?"

My heart bubbled. "Yes, of course!" I kissed his lips gently and played with a bit of his blondish hair. "But first you must eat so you may gain your strength. I cannot have my groom falling over mid-vows."

"I cannot argue with that."

He took a bite and slowly chewed. I could tell even this action was painful for him.

"This must be quite different from how you were living the past couple of weeks," he said, motioning his hand about the room.

"His castle was its own sort of prison. As much as I do not enjoy living down here...it is preferable."

He took hold of both my hands. "Why do I feel you have not told me everything that occurred?"

I smiled, knowing I would never pain him with the unnecessary details. "I cannot say that it was easy. It could have been worse. Far worse. I could have married him. In truth, he was mostly kind to me."

"*Mostly*. Hmph. Was he...dishonorable?"

"No more than what you yourself witnessed."

He grimaced. "How often were you forced to kiss him?"

"Daniel... I love you, but you must stop torturing yourself over this. We are here *now*, together. Be at peace."

"*That* many times?" He squirmed. "I'm sorry – it's only that, this rather consumed my mind for what seemed like days on end. I worried for your safety constantly and what you must have been going through."

Sitting myself on the edge of his cot, I gently kissed his swollen lips. "My heart always remained yours. The greatest torment was knowing I'd never see you again and now? Now that you are before me? I cannot express my relief and happiness."

"Kiss me again."

I happily obliged.

It was several days before Daniel's injuries were sufficiently recovered. He still limped whenever he put pressure on his right knee, but otherwise, he managed to walk with a fair amount of ease. The swelling from the bruises on his face had healed as well, allowing his left eye to open again. Only some discoloration remained in his face. It was agreeable to see his handsomeness return.

One day, there came a knock at the main door. We all met in the main area, staring at the door. It was not the secret knock. Everyone stood still.

We exchanged pensive looks and quietly lined up to exit through to the garden, when we heard, "It's Christy! I can't remember the proper knock! Long live the Catholic Church!"

Opening the door to her, I rushed into her arms. "I made Jonathon promise not to tell," she said, "but he has sold your house to Mr. Anderson and I!"

I hugged her *so* tightly. "I could not be more pleased that you will be taking over our home; it is very fitting!"

Releasing her, I invited her to come inside. She held out her arm to show us a bracelet he had purchased for her as an engagement gift; it was gold with small rubies wrapping around it. "We are to be married in *two*

... He is back in Bath on business, but I am setting up the house with some of my belongings."

"Oh, Christy, I am so, *so* happy for you both! And the bracelet is beautiful, truly!"

"Yes, and we can continue the work Jonathon and you have been doing. Oh! But I do not know how I shall be able to part with you, Isabel. I shall miss you *so* very much."

"And I you. Come, let us not think of it for now – you're just in time for Mass. Confessions were just about to begin before you scared us all to death!"

She laughed as she apologized.

"Father Ingles..." my mother said as she drew closer to him, "I have not been to confession in... *many* years. A lifetime, really."

Father smiled kindly. "What better time to go then, Mrs. Dawson?"

"I'm afraid I have forgotten much of what to say or do."

"I will not scold you! Come, I'll help you wherever your memory fails."

My siblings and I traded excited glances. Papa must be crying tears of joy in heaven. As Mama unburdened her sins to Christ, the rest of us either filed in line for confession or entered the chapel and began our preparations for Mass.

Daniel still struggled to kneel, so Jon had become the acolyte. Which was fitting, since he was to become a priest. I was happy to sit next to my betrothed for the first time during Mass.

As I watched my brother go about the altar and light the candles... I realized how deeply I would miss him. At least when he had gone to Oxford to complete his studies, he would come home for holiday visits. It would be years before his studies at the seminary were complete, and after that? We would have to wait for him to be assigned to England, God willing. He would miss the birth of my children, of Anna becoming a woman, perhaps the final years of Mama's life. Even letters would be extremely scarce, as they could be intercepted. Tears threatened my eyes again.

"Are you well, my love?" Daniel asked in a whisper.

"I will miss him when he leaves."

Daniel followed my eyes to my brother bowing at the altar and squeezed my hand. "That *will* be a hard loss to bear; I shall miss him too. We must focus on being happy for him, though. God willing, by the time he is ordained, Catholics will not be fugitives here anymore; but either way – have faith that he *will* return one day."

I looked up into his reassuring eyes and smiled before resting my head on his shoulder.

When mama came out of confession, her face was glistening from what was no doubt, a tear-filled confession. Kneeling down next to Anna, she prayed her penance and when she sat, my sister and I hugged her, "Welcome home, Mama."

She returned the embrace warmly, "I only wish your Papa was here to witness my return. I'm ashamed for having turned my back for so long. I fell away so gradually with the changes that when Mass became outlawed, it was not hard to throw it all behind me. How weak I was!"

"We're all weak. Now you are stronger in your faith than ever. Papa is witnessing all of this from heaven. Surely, he will be kneeling with us during Mass in just a few moments."

Mama wiped the tears from her face. "Yes, quite right!"

After Mass, the servants brought down food and ale.

Anna, perhaps more than the rest of us, grew very tired of our secret dwellings. "Why can we not go upstairs and sit at a real table and chairs?" She asked with a frustrated pout. "It is so cold and dark and crowded down here! I do not like it at all. I want to be outside!"

Christy was the one to respond, "Because Lord Drake has men who are watching this house my dear. I saw them even today when I arrived. Should any of you be spotted through a window, even once...it would put us all in grave danger. Your family most of all."

Anna hung her head and sighed. "I understand."

I gave her a side hug. "Soon we will be living by the shore, Anna, and have a beautiful new life far away from his dreadful Lordship."

"Speaking of that..." said Daniel, "I rather think I'm recovered enough for a wedding!" He smiled down at me as I beamed in response. "Father, you must be the one to wed us, of course!"

Father Ingles beamed. "I'd let no other priest do it! When is it to be?"

"The sooner the better!" I said.

Mama chimed in, "I have just the dress! But what about acquiring the bonds for marriage?"

Father replied. "I would consider these dire circumstances, Mrs. Dawson. In Bridlington, I doubt any will ask to see it, as Daniel's family is so well-established there."

Daniel smiled. "Tomorrow then!"

I looked towards my little sister. "Anna and Christy shall be my bridesmaids."

Anna squealed with delight. I was relieved to give her something to distract her from our current living conditions.

Daniel looked to Jonathon. "Will you be my groomsman? You're the closest friend I have, aside from my own brothers."

He grinned. "You poor sod. That is...I would be honored. – After the wedding tomorrow, we should consider making a run for it, Daniel. We will need a distraction for Lord Drake's spies, of course. Are you up for traveling?"

"As long as it won't actually require running. I'm afraid my knee isn't back to normal yet. Something cracked rather unpleasantly in there a few weeks back and it's taking its time coming around."

I squeezed his hand. "We will give your knee more time to heal. We don't want to risk it."

Jonathon nodded. "Agreed. I will get our other escapees off and away then."

"I think I speak for both my neighbor and I when I say this," Stephen Milbrook began. "Not that we haven't appreciated your kindnesses, but we have relatives we can both be with now that we are properly mended."

"Though," Rachel said, "we would love to stay for your wedding! We've grown fond of all of you during our stay."

"Yes, please! That would make us very happy." I replied.

The next day, the servants snuck down mother's wedding dress along with a bouquet of flowers picked by Christy herself.

I got ready in the bed chamber with Mama, Christy, Anna, and Lily. There was only a small handheld mirror to see myself in, and very poor lighting...but I felt Daniel would approve of my appearance.

Mama placed the veil on me, with tears in her eyes. She kissed my cheek. "Your papa would love to see you now. I think he would greatly approve of Daniel, even more so now than before."

"You will make me cry, Mama! – Am I presentable?"

She smiled widely. "You are *beautiful*, my sweet daughter. – Daniel shan't be able to breathe when he lays eyes upon you."

Anna led the way in her favorite pink satin dress followed by Christy who wore a pink gown as well. As Stephen opened the chapel door for us, we walked into such a warm and glowing room! *All* the candelabras in the house had been brought down and lit! They flickered whimsically, warming the cold space decorated with flowers everywhere. Petals were strewn across the floor and floral arrangements stood wherever space permitted. They made the room smell sweet – it was more romantic than I ever could have hoped for.

Daniel stood at the altar with Father Ingles and my brother; he was so very handsome in a red doublet and black jerkin. His face was overjoyed; I even caught him rubbing a tear off his cheek as our eyes locked.

It was a short walk to him, and we eagerly professed our vows. Father blessed my parents' rings which added yet another level of tenderness to the moment. As Daniel took my hand in his, I had *never* felt such a burning joy before – it shook me, like a happiness painted gold by the sacredness of the sacrament.

After we were pronounced husband and wife, we embraced each other amongst quiet applause! We celebrated as best we could, in the secret dwellings of my childhood home.

The servants had baked a cake, and we had wine and a lovely array of duck, potatoes, ham, and vegetables.

Daniel looked lovingly into my eyes as we ate together, backs against the wall. "I have never seen you look more beautiful - I am the most blessed man in the entire world." He bent his head and kissed my smiling lips.

"You flatter me, Mr. Clifton."

"Indeed, *Mrs. Clifton*, I aim to flatter you all the days of my life."

I pulled his face to mine and kissed him.

Chapter Thirty

IT WAS NOT A usual wedding night, of course, as we could not spend it together. We were married at least, and that's all that mattered for now. After the food had been cleared away, Father Ingles had us gather round and he told us stories of his travels and of Father Edmund Campion.

"I had the pleasure of being called his friend," Father began. "Father Campion was raised Catholic of course, but was swayed by the Queen to become a deacon for her instead. She was smitten with his intellect and wit from the first moment they met at Oxford. Edmund was showing off for her and Lord Cecil, reciting a welcome speech to Queen Elizabeth in Latin. They formed a keen friendship and often held many lofty conversations."

"I thought he was a martyr?" Asked Anna.

"He was!" Father replied. "He came back to the faith when he was studying to be the queen's deacon. The more a soul studies history and the Bible, the easier it is to find the truth."

"What did he do then?" asked Rachel. "Wouldn't the Queen be furious?"

"Oh, I would have loved to be present when *Good Queen Bess* was told her precious Campion was not only Catholic...but had fled to Ireland, then Belgium to become a priest!

"After studies were complete there, he went to Rome to become a Jesuit. Nine years later, he returned home to England.

"In the year he served as a hidden priest, he stirred up more controversy in the Protestant faith than ever before with his printed manifesto! It was posted in all the churches, calling people back to their faith and challenged the Protestants. The Queen was furious, of course.

"Had it not been for that one spy, *Lyford Grange*, Father Campion may very well still be with us today."

"Do you think he was afraid of being killed, Father Ingles?" Asked Anna.

"He told me once that Our Lady had appeared to him and foretold his martyrdom; he was ready for it. I'm sure part of him was afraid, little Miss Anna. Though grace and fortitude always prevailed. Even when he was in prison and the Queen went herself to visit him. Nothing she offered could persuade him. Not torture either. The poor soul was stretched so hard on the rack, he could hardly move by the time he was executed."

"How did the Queen kill him?" Anna asked.

"He was hanged, drawn, and quartered."

"What does that mean, Father? Jon won't ever tell me."

Father exchanged a glance between Mama and Jonathon before he continued with their nod of approval. "My dear, that is a most terrible death, saved only for men who have committed high treason. His body was dragged behind a horse from the Tower of London all the way to where the executions take place, hung until within an inch of his life, disemboweled, beheaded, and then finally their bodies are quartered. To add another layer to the gruesome ordeal, the Queen ordered Father Campion's limbs be placed on tall spikes through England as warnings to other Catholics."

Anna's face was horrified. "Why? Why would they do that to someone? Were they going to do that to you, Mr. Porter?"

Daniel swallowed, as though his mind was transferred back to the prison. "Miss Anna, I insist upon you calling me Daniel now! And, yes, had your siblings not saved me, yes. — One soul died that very death while I was in prison, and another, a woman, was burned at the stake."

Stephen and Rachel nodded somberly.

Father cleared his throat. "We are witnesses to our Faith – walking testimonies to the strength of Christ and His Church. —But do you know what happened after they killed my dear friend, Miss Anna?"

She shook her head.

"Hundreds of Protestants converted back to the Catholic faith all because of Father Campion's bravery! You see, the devil thought he won a great victory by getting that priest killed, but instead, like with so many of his victories, he lost tenfold what he gained by the grace of God!

"The amusing part is the book he managed to write before his capture, *10 Reasons*. It refuted, in depth, the fallacies found in Protestantism. It too, like his manifesto, was placed in many Churches and became popular and widely spread. So he still managed to be a thorn in her side even after she killed him."

We all chuckled at yet another example of God's irony. I enjoy knowing He has a sense of humor.

Later that evening, Jon slipped Stephen and Rachel out into the woods and got them on their way to their extended families. A small group was a much easier task and only required minor planning. Stephen, Rachel, and Jon hid next to the horses as Christy and her father rode them out to the woods and back.

The following morning when Jon returned, we gathered for breakfast. He began with a serious conversation. "I received some news while I was out last night. Not only is Lord Drake still searching for us, he is exhausting the spies and military to expand his search even further. It will double within the week. Evidently we are all radical Catholics hell-bent on destroying England as we know it!"

I felt terrible. "I'm so sorry I'm the cause of *all* this trouble. I keep thinking of all the many things I might have done to avoid this."

Everyone assured me that the fault was not mine, but Lord Drake's. My heart still felt heavy.

Daniel sighed. "Jon... I believe what you're saying is that unless we want to be caught...we should be on the move *tonight*."

I was concerned. "Your knee, my love?"

"I'll make it work."

My brother smirked. "Actually... I have a rather clever idea. We only need to get to the Moore's farm. He has offered us help in hiding priests in the past, and I think we can use the same method."

Father Ingles chuckled. "Ah, that should be an entertaining sight to behold indeed."

My mother was suspicious. "What exactly *is* this plan?"

"We'll be traveling with some produce of sorts...however, on the bright side, we won't have to walk much! The Moore's are in Hitchin; once we're there we can be transported to St. Ives, Stamford, Newark, and so on until we reach Bridlington. We have many Catholic connections that can help us along the way.

"Now, the Moore's place is five miles from here if we cut through the woods. I've already sent word to them to set everything into motion."

It was apparent by Mama's facial expression that she did not fancy this idea, "Can we not travel by coach and spend the nights at various inns?"

Jon tried to comfort her and held her hand. "Mama... it is not possible. Lord Drake has spies in every town, and they are watching and waiting for us to make that very mistake. Trust me when I say that our lives are at stake – we cannot be too careful. This week we must travel like priests."

She nodded. "Very well. At least it will be all over and done within a few days time. –Where will Anna and I be living in Bridlington exactly?"

Daniel spoke up. "With Isabel and I, of course. —It will be smaller than you are accustomed to, but we will make the best of it! There are two bedrooms, so that will do for now until we can build onto the house."

Mama smiled. "I think you shall make a fine son-in-law!"

"I will do my best." Daniel replied.

The time had come.

Christy snuck down to say goodbye – this time, with the correct knocks at the door.

I hugged her tightly. "I only wish I could attend your wedding! —I shall miss you terribly. Being separated from you will be a torment to me." I realized I would likely not see her again in this life once Daniel and I left – a letter twice a year, at most.

Christy's lip quivered. "I will pray for you and Daniel every day. I will miss you too, my dearest friend. I wish this was not the way it had to be." She slowly pulled away, tears billowing in her eyes.

"I understand. Please tell your Mr. Anderson to take the best of care of my friend, or I shall have to come and steal you away with me." We hugged again, and I promised I would pray for her daily as well.

As the door shut behind her, I felt a piece of my heart leaving with her. I could not fathom never seeing her again. It felt wrong. How was I to manage without her?

I could not control the tears that flowed down my face.

Daniel came and hugged me tenderly. "I'm so sorry, my love. I know how much you shall miss her."

I was so very tired of crying. "Maybe one day, we will see each other again."

"Who knows what the future holds!"

Pulling back from the hug, he cradled my face in his hand, "One thing I'm sure of though, is how elated and grateful I am to be your husband."

I smiled; he knew how to cheer my spirits — as well as he could under the circumstances. Drawing me in for a kiss, I wrapped my arms around him bathing in the comfort his touch brought me. "I love you so."

He sighed contentedly as he rested his head on mine. "And I you, with more love than I knew existed."

As nine o'clock approached, I was extremely eager to leave our underground housing. I was ready to begin our new lives. We all were.

Lily agreed to come with us, as did Moreen, Anna's servant. However, Mama's servant decided to stay behind and help Christy and her husband get settled; she was up in age and such a journey would have been difficult on her. In all honesty, it will be hard for Mama.

We packed only one bag each and wore long cloaks that would stave off the night's chill as well as help to conceal our faces.

Christy was to be part of the distraction; Jonathon instructed her to scream and pretend that an owl was in her room – the omen of darkness, and death. The servants would all clamor and chase the creature outside in the front yard...while we left out the back. Hopefully, it would be enough time for us to go unnoticed before the man who watched our house overnight realized what had really occurred.

Father Ingles heard all our confessions once more and gave us a blessing of protection. "And may Our Lady's mantle wrap around your journey," he concluded.

"Do you ever travel to Bridlington, Father?" I asked, hopeful that this was not another forever goodbye.

He offered a kind smile. "Not as of yet, my dear Mrs. Clifton. That does not mean that I never will though! God's will is constantly full of surprises for us."

"Please be careful, Father, and please, if you can, come and see us?"

"I promise."

We filed into the tunnel, hoods up, bags in hand, ready to leave, awaiting Christy's outcry.

Jon was at the front assisting Mama in case her knee gave her trouble, with Anna behind them. Lily and Moreen were next while I was before Daniel who brought up the rear. I worried about his knee; it was not healed. He tried to put a brave face on for me, but I saw how his face clenched when he put too much pressure on it.

He grabbed my hand. "No matter what happens, do not stop. Keep going. I will manage; I have been doing this a long time, and I can take care of myself. I just may need to go slower than the rest of you."

I turned to face him. "If you want me safe, you best find a way to keep up. I know I only just made a vow to obey you, my love, but you cannot tell me to do things which are impossible. I cannot leave you behind."

He sighed. "*Isabel*, you must trust me." He kissed my hand. "I will always find a way back to you. Do you understand?"

"Yes, I do."

"Then please listen and do not worry if I fall behind or not."

"I will not worry because you will *not* fall behind."

"I will do my best not to."

As I nodded, we heard Christy's shrill scream echoing across the property. A sudden flow of vigor rushed us into the cold night air. Keeping low to the ground, we hurried our way through the tall grass in the direction of the woods.

Looking back frequently, Daniel managed to keep up which relieved me greatly.

In the distance we could hear the commotion, but mostly all I could hear was our breathing, the pounding of my own heart, and the dewy blades of grass whipping us as we scurried by.

We were halfway to the woods now, and the gap between Daniel and I began to increase. "Let me help you!" I begged.

"No! Keep going! Do *not* slow down!"

I could hear the pain in his voice. This was not a good sign. I gritted my teeth, looking back every few seconds. The distance between us kept spreading.

A loud bang echoed from the house.

Gunshot?

What happened?

Were we safe? Was Christy?

Had we been spotted?

Glancing back, we could garner no answers. We had to hope for the best and keep moving. If only Daniel was capable of moving faster.

The tree line started to become visible in the dark. I was grateful that the clouds were shielding us from the moon and most of the stars' light. It made it hard to see where we were going, but at least it helped to ensure our secrecy.

I turned back again to check on Daniel; he was quite a ways back now. I prayed to Mary to help him; we were so close.

I saw Jonathon and Mama make the trees, and we were soon to follow. At least her knee seemed to be managing for now.

Waiting at the edge, we watched Daniel struggle to catch up. I wondered how he would manage the five miles to the Moores'.

Jon bolted from the trees and ran to aide Daniel. I could not draw breath until Daniel finally made it to me. Jon and I quickly guided him to a fallen tree so he could sit and rest his knee.

Extending his leg, he winced. "I told you I would make it," he said between heavy breaths. "Just need a moment to rest and then we can be on our way. — I won't need to be low to the ground through the thick of these woods; it should be easier now."

We all exchanged concerned looks. His knee looked very swollen; the bandages dug into the surrounding skin.

Daniel sighed. "I will survive. Walking is good for it. I've nursed it long enough!"

"We can stop to rest as much as need be," I said. "Surely there will be no shortage of fallen trees."

Jonathon squatted next to my husband. "You will lean on me as we go, so you do not put as much pressure on your leg. Once morning comes we will be extremely vulnerable. We must make it to the farm before daylight. I'm afraid you'll have to set your pride aside today, my new brother, and let me assist you."

"It seems God is quite determined to rid me of that failing lately."

"Isn't He always?" He extended his arm out to him as Daniel grasped it and stood up carefully.

"What was that gunshot?" asked Mama. "Was that part of the plan?"

"No," Jon replied. "They must have needed a second distraction. I'm sure all is well."

I grabbed Daniel's bag as Lily grabbed Jon's. Shoulder to shoulder they led the way with us following quietly behind. I wanted to believe the hope in my brother's words. I couldn't afford to think the worst as I was often apt to do. I had to stay focused on making it to the Moores.

There were many sounds in the woods at night that I was unaccustomed to. Every owl hoot and rustling of leaves from creatures moving about caused my heart to pound.

I could not fathom how Jon and Daniel knew which way to go — I was quite lost in the dark until we came to the brook. Sitting Daniel on an obliging log, my brother began to dig around in the foliage.

I took a seat next to Daniel. "What is he doing?"

"He hid a bridge of sorts."

Just as I was about to question that statement, surely enough, Jon produced a bundle of large branches bound together with rope. It was about two shoes in width and plenty long enough to get across.

"There!" Jon said proudly as it fell perfectly across the brook. "Who should like to cross it first?"

All of us ladies were hesitant. The water in the stream would be bitingly cold at this hour.

Mama questioned him. "Dear, are you quite sure that's stable enough?"

"Of course! Daniel and I have tested it with great success." He walked halfway across the bridge. "See? Stable as they come!"

Jon bounced in the center, further illustrating how secure his craftsmanship was.

SNAP. *CRACK*. SPLASH!

Releasing an odd warbled shout, Jon fell straight through his handiwork! There he sat in the rushing steam, with the water soaking him from the chest down, with the most amusing look of shock on his face!

I laughed and tried so hard to contain it that I snorted. This caused everyone to lose control of their own hushed giggles as Jon stood up in the creek with the water flowing around his knees.

He cleared his throat, trying to regain a modicum of dignity. "Well, then! Wading across it is. Evidently, God is working on my own pride tonight as well, Daniel!"

We quieted our chuckles, and all of us ladies tied our skirts above our knees, removed our stockings and shoes, and waded across to the other side. It was as unpleasantly freezing as one might imagine. We were all shivering by the middle point of the rushing water. By the time I was on the other side, my feet and legs were nearly numb!

Jon, already having soaked most of himself, gave little care for removing anything as he crawled out of the creek to help Daniel.

Daniel held his boots in his hands as they made it across together.

"I daresay that water feels *fantastic* on my knee!" He sat down on the edge and dangled his whole leg in for a few minutes as we made ourselves travel-ready again.

"Come Daniel," my brother urged. "We've a long ways to go yet."

Daniel put his boots back on, and we applied a fresh bandage to his knee. In short order, we were back on our way.

Chapter Thirty-One

A BROAD-SHOULDERED MAN HELD out a lantern by his barn, scanning his fields. He had several penned in areas and enormous vegetable gardens. More than that, I could not make out as we followed a trail that appeared before us.

When he saw us approaching, he greeted us eagerly. "Praise God you have made it this far! — Come quickly to the barn; my wife, Sarah, has made it as comfortable as possible and set a basket of food and water in there for you all. Just don't feed the horses the apples unless you want an unpleasant odor as you sleep."

We all exchanged amused expressions. He opened the wooden barn doors for us as we thanked him heartily.

Inside was warm, with hay, blankets, a lantern, fresh water and the promised food. Some of their animals were stalled on the other side of the hay — horses, chickens, and a pig who snored worse than my brother.

Once we were inside, the farmer introduced himself as Henry Moore; Jonathon introduced the rest of us.

"I'm glad to help you all — it's important you get your rest. I will be back in the morning to get you loaded up for the trip. Rest well."

Jonathon returned his firm handshake. "Thank you — we owe you."

The weathered farmer assured us we owed nothing and locked us in the barn for the rest of the night. The smell was not my favorite, but it felt wonderful to feel safe.

I helped Daniel sit on a bed of hay and elevated his leg as best I could. His knee was quite swollen.

We devoured the bread, berries, and cheeses that were left out for us and nestled in for a few hours of rest. I fit perfectly into the curvature of Daniel's arm and barely remember falling asleep.

It felt as though no sooner had I closed my eyes that farmer Moore was waking us to load us into his covered wagons.

"I've never transported seven people at once before, but I daresay this is the easiest way to go about it. — I'll need to divide you into two wagons, have you lay down, and then we will cover you with the wool we just sheared from our sheep. My oldest boys, Thomas and Samuel will be driving the wagons. They know the way and will get you there safely. It isn't their first time making this sort of a delivery."

His wife Sarah came out with two bags of food and sheets. Her eyes were blue and her blond hair was braided down the side of her; she was remarkably beautiful.

"This should be enough food to last you a day or more," she said kindly. "We will lay these sheets between you and the wool — it should help to make your journey a bit more comfortable."

We thanked her and laid down between the sheets as they piled the wool over us. Daniel, myself, and Lily in the first with Mama, Anna, Moreen, and my brother in the second.

After the wool fully surrounded us, I was surprised by how heavy it felt! We sneezed a few times each as we adjusted to the smell. I was grateful to have the sheets acting as a barrier for us.

"God bless you. Say many rosaries as you travel, for there ain't else much for you to do! Stay quiet and be safe," uttered Henry before he tapped the wagon to roll on. They started out with a brisk pace which left us being bounced about quite a lot.

I could not see Daniel through all the wool; yet, all the way to St. Ives, he held my hand. Even with the sheets, it wasn't long before the wool made me feel extremely itchy; I knew better than to even begin to scratch, so I tried very hard to think of something else. I imagined what my new home would look like and what the best ways to decorate it might be.

After what felt like many hours, we heard Thomas call out for us to be extra silent. The dirt road turned to stone which made the earwax tickle my ears something fierce. We heard the sounds of many people, horses and other carts; we had made it to the town of St. Ives.

"You there!" boomed a deep voice. "What's in your carts?"

"Wool, officer, and lots of it!" replied Thomas with a smile in his voice.

"Hmph. Lift the covers so we can check for ourselves."

"You want to inspect my wool? Oi! Are ya interested in spinning it for yourselves then?" He chuckled. "Or maybe the Missus has a fancy to make her own clothes? The Queen's officers not gettin' paid what they used to be neither?"

The officer sounded exasperated. "Just lift the tarp – I've got orders to check every cart or carriage coming through."

"Whatever makes the Queen happy I suppose!"

I gripped Daniel's hand harder. My heart leaped into my throat as sweat dripped off my skin and clung to the sheets and wool around me. I slowly reached for Lily on the other side of me and found her hand eager to grip onto mine.

The officer took a long object and started pushing down on the wool in various sections. With what must have been the butt of his gun, he pushed down between mine and Daniel's legs. I held my breath and fought the urge to move.

Thomas was quick to try and distract them. "Is it fluffy enough for ya? Does it pass inspection?" He laughed at his own cleverness. I could see why Henry insisted on Thomas taking the lead. He was utterly fearless.

The officer grunted and moved on to the next cart.

"Why are you transporting all of your wool in one day?" The officer asked after finding nothing.

"I asked my Pa the same thing! He told me to shut my mouth and do as I was told. So I dunno what to tell you."

The officer groaned. "Just go."

"As you wish, Sir! Have a nice day inspecting carts!"

I don't know this for sure, of course, but I imagined the officer rolling his eyes as he walked away.

We exhaled a collective sigh of relief as we moved on, jostling about. Passing through the town, I could feel us leaving the stone roads and hitting the dirt again. I was grateful for the smoother ride. By the time we stopped a couple miles down the road, I had prayed three rosaries and drifted off to sleep. The sudden stop woke me with a frightened start.

As we were pried from the layers of wool, I looked at the sky and saw it was early evening.

Stretching and plucking bits of wool from our clothes and hair, Thomas and Samuel brought us to the barn of another farmer's accommodations.

Thomas smiled and tucked back a strand of his long brown hair. "The folks here are sympathetic Protestants; good people. They'll keep ya safe the same as my pa did. Stay here n' eat while we get the carts emptied and theirs ready to load you up for the rest of the journey." He instructed with a smile as we thanked him.

Within an hour, we were asked to lay down in Farmer Beaton's carts. This time we were covered with linens, spools of yarn, and various articles of clothing, blankets, shoes, and boots.

This driver was of a more quiet and serious nature. "I can only take you through the next town of Stamford to my in-law's farm. You'll sleep there for the night. And from there you should only have two more days of travel. Stay quiet. Keep praying. The town after that is Newark...you better hope they find a way around that or that your guardian angels have a battle mind about them. Many Catholics be gettin' captured there."

At the next farm we were covered up carefully with firewood. I could feel beetles crawling on my legs and nearly screamed upon seeing a spider in the log above me. Daniel tried calming me, but hearing the other women squirm and occasionally whimper ensured me this was as horrifying as it felt.

By the last stop...we were so filthy, sore, exhausted, bug bitten, and hungry that we could barely stand one another. The journey was brutal. I had gravely underestimated how terrible this was going to be.

This is what our poor priests had been gladly putting up with for years now. I felt humbled and grateful on an entirely new level.

The last cart ride dropped us off not at a farm, but at the rear entrance to a shop in town. I felt uneasy at leaving the safety of the cart in the most dangerous town to be caught in. This time we were to be all piled into one cart, uncovered. –We had to lay in coffins for our transport.

The panic my little sister felt at laying down in a coffin was severe. It took a great deal of coaxing and calming her before she could be successfully closed in. As I laid in mine and waited for the lid to come over me, I took the advice Daniel gave to Anna. I closed my eyes and pretended I was laying in bed. My chest heaved uneasily at first, feeling a spell threaten to break out of me. However, with my eyes closed, it was easier to fool my mind that I was elsewhere, laying down. Streaks of light broke through tiny cracks in the wood, offering small wafts of air to relieve me.

The fact that this was not my husband's first coffin ride made me have a better understanding of just what *he* had undergone as a priest runner.

I knew Anna had to be silently crying because I nearly was too. My poor mama was so terribly sore and in a great deal of pain; I felt horrible she had to go through all of this. Lily and Moreen seemed to be handling things as well as they could be. Jonathon clearly viewed it as practice for when he came back as a priest, and bore it all stoically. Daniel was the only one who treated it as a common way to travel. As we were stacked on top of each other and the cart began moving over the cobblestones, I could not help but briefly wonder if this was all worth it.

"Stop there!" bellowed a voice from a man who sounded not at all pleased. I clutched the rosary in my pocket.

"What can I do you for?" our driver replied evenly.

"I'm under orders to inspect every cart and carriage coming and going through our town."

"Well, officer, sir, as you can see, I'm carrying the remains of some poor souls out beyond the town limits."

"Why? – They didn't have the plague did they?"

"They might've, sir. I'm told they were terribly sick. The whole family dropped off like flies from a cow's arse. I was instructed to take them out and–"

"Burn them!" The officer interrupted, his tone changing to one of fear. "Get on with it, man! Get them out of here!"

"Yes, sir, of course sir. Better to be safe rather than to be sorry, I always say."

"Just leave, *undertaker*, and do not stop on the way."

With that, he whipped the horse to continue on.

What a clever idea!

As we rolled along, with small splinters from the wood stabbing my arms and legs, I tried reminding myself that this was all almost over – we were soon to be free from Lord Drake, forever. I was growing exceedingly tired and peevish; trying to endure this like a saint was proving nearly impossible. Resentment, anger, and hatred brewed within me against his Lordship. All of this was his fault. Everything we had been through was because of his evilness.

I tried to take a deep breath and released it slowly as I prayed, *"Lord, I know you love Elwood, even though he has done such deplorable things to Catholics, to me, and to my family. Help me not to hate him. May he convert one day and be holy, happy, and fully at peace. May he be higher in heaven than myself and find remission for all his transgressions. Thank you for permitting us to suffer by his hand. I offer it, in union with the sufferings of Thy Son's death and passion, for the conversion of Lord Drake."*

Oh, that was a hard prayer to pray. But the peace that came after told me it was right. The road bumped and caused my head to smack the lid of the coffin. My eyes opened at the surprise.

Suddenly my skin was crawling; I felt trapped and my ears rang. There was not enough air, and I felt I was suffocating! A spell washed over me, and I wondered how in the heavens I should sooth the panic while laying in a coffin! I closed my eyes again and prayed Aves for Lord Drake. Eventually my breathing evened out, and I fell into a deep sleep.

What must have been several hours later, I awoke and noticed the light was closer to dusk than before. Our last stop was to be at Daniel's eldest brother's house, and I wondered how far we were. Daylight was now gone and there was nothing but pitch blackness surrounding me, which made the coffin even worse. Now my mind imagined being buried alive in the ground.

A few more miles and I was distracted by the invigorating smell the ocean! My belly grumbled loudly from not having eaten often enough. Still the cart did not stop. We kept going all through the night. It was not until well after the morning that we finally arrived at his brother's home.

They unloaded us carefully and helped us out of the coffins. We were quite the sight, indeed. Covered in dirt, dust, hay, twigs, insect bites, wool, scratches, and sweat.

Daniel's leg at least got plenty of rest, and he was able to help me out of my coffin.

Anna was very quiet and very pale; I knew this journey had changed her forever. Indeed, it changed us all.

Daniel brought me over to his brother; I felt mortified to meet his family looking this way.

"Robert!" He embraced him in a hug before extending his arm out to me. "This is my wife, Isabel! Her mother, Mrs. Dawson, Miss Anna Dawson, Mr. Jonathon Dawson, and the two brave servants who traveled with us, Lily and Moreen! – It's been a journey. I have many stories to tell."

Robert was a little taller and more narrow in the shoulders than Daniel but shared the same grin. "Very glad to meet you all – especially you, Isabel. You all had us very worried. I'm grateful to see you've made it. We'll set out some food for you once you've all had a chance to clean up. You can meet my wife, Bridget, inside."

Chapter Thirty-Two

DEAR READER, WHEN I tell you that this was the most enjoyable bath I have ever taken... I do not exaggerate. I felt so rejuvenated and eager to change into clean clothing.

In my bag, I could only fit three dresses and a night gown. I brought two blue gowns, and another green and yellow dress. I selected the simpler of the blue dresses as Daniel's family did not seem to put on airs at all. I was so grateful to be clean, safe, and to show Daniel's family that my skin color was indeed white and not gray.

All of his siblings joined us for supper. They were all eager to meet us and to hear the stories firsthand.

There was the oldest, Robert and his wife Bridget. They currently had seven children, though just the eldest were present at this time. Polly had blue eyes and blond hair like her mother, and Rob mirrored his father's darker features. Both children seemed to be bordering on the cusp of adulthood. Bridget struck me as a kind, wise sort of person, while Robert seemed very business oriented. Anna and Polly got along straight away and sat next to one another. I knew at once that Bridget would become a favorite person of mine; her comments on our story were thoughtful, wise, and kind. She spoke with her heart with great ease and I admired her for it.

Eric and his lovely wife Mildred had four children – all young girls. Eric looked the most different from his siblings; he was a bit shorter with a very strong jawline and darker features. Mildred had green eyes and beautiful brown hair. They were a very quiet, reserved couple.

Then there was his sister, Theresa, and her husband, Andrew, with twin little girls. Theresa had darker features and was very petite, pretty, and wore a smile that let you know she possessed a mischievous streak. I recognize the smile well enough from my own reflection. I developed an instant connection to Theresa and felt we would grow to have a very fond friendship.

His brother Rodney was tall and stout with a pleasing sense of humor; his wife Catherine, was fair with freckles and red hair. They had an infant son, not yet one.

Robert and Bridget's home was modest, but not small by any means. We all fit comfortably around their dining table.

Thankfully, there was no scarcity in food, for we all ate a hearty amount of beef stew and fresh bread.

His whole family was really very kind and welcoming. We told as much of our story as we could, before we were all fighting to stay awake.

"We've prepared your home with a few housewarming gifts," said Bridget. "Perhaps Mrs. Dawson and your sister would enjoy staying the evening with us tonight? We have a spare bedroom and I think the young girls would enjoy themselves immensely."

Polly and Anna were very excited by this idea and looked hopefully towards my mother. "May we please?" Begged Anna, eyes big like an owl's.

Mama exchanged a knowing glance with Bridget and myself before she answered, "That is a most kind offer, we would appreciate that greatly."

I thought it was sweet of them to allow us the first night in our home to be just Daniel and I. — It was a short ride in their carriage to Daniel's home, and it felt like a glorious luxury! His home was perched upon a grassy hill overlooking the ocean – just as he said it did.

I was introduced to his two servants, William and Daisy, and was given a tour of his cottage. It was quaint and possessed a wonderful amount of charm. The dining room was half the size that ours had been, really every room was half the size, and there was no library or study, but there was a lovely drawing room. Yet, after living underground for weeks, it seemed just right. Before retiring to our first proper night as husband and wife, Daniel wished to take me on a walk along the beach. The exhausted part of me wanted to decline, but the romantic in me could not refuse.

The moon and stars illuminated the path before us, allowing us a view of the waves crashing upon the shore. The grassy hill tickled my legs; I had never walked the beach so late at night before and found myself raptured by the magic of it. I inhaled the enticing smell of the crisp ocean air; it brought a wonderful peace to me.

"The ocean, as promised!" Daniel smiled, wrapping me into his arms as our feet sunk into the sand a bit.

I leaned into him and kissed him deeply. "It's beautiful."

He caressed my face. "Are you happy, my love?"

"Immensely!"

Dipping me into his arms, Daniel kissed me so passionately that we both fell over into the sand, laughing hysterically. We laid there until we both regained our composure. "I blame my knee." He said as he leaned over me, laying an arm across me.

"Mm-hmm," I smiled. "You won't be able to blame things on your knee forever you know."

"Perhaps I should admit that I was utterly lost in my wife's kiss?"

"The truth is always best, after all." I kissed him again.

"Come," he said, helping me to my feet. "I think we ought to retire for the evening."

The next day, I woke up to Daniel with his hair all askew, and this time lightly snoring. He looked adorable and I giggled as I kissed him awake.

"Is it morning already?" He groggily asked.

"It is, and your wife should prefer you to be awake now."

His grin matched my own. "Would she? Well, what choice do I have then but to be awake? – In perhaps another hour or so?"

I shook my head and playfully smothered his face in kisses.

Later that day, we gathered in *our* drawing room; we all had much to discuss.

We agreed that Mama and Anna would have to put aside the name of Dawson and choose another. Mama reluctantly agreed and decided they would go with Broadmore, her maiden name.

Jonathon decided to stay with us a few days before he made his way to Belgium. It was strange to feel such happiness and relief, yet be full of dread as well. The day he was to leave, I found myself wholly inconsolable.

Tears welled in my eyes as the ocean breeze blew around us. "I will miss you so very much," I choked, trying not to cry. "What will I do without my big brother to keep my pride and vanity in check?"

He hugged me tightly and spoke softly into my ear. "I will miss you most of all, Isabel. I will return as soon as the good Lord permits, you have my word. Leaving you is my greatest sacrifice in becoming a priest."

I nodded as we pulled away, swallowing a sob that tried to break free. "—Do not make my cry, Jon. Why must God's will hurt so much of the time?"

"Because pain has always been the cost of love."

Clearing his throat, he bent down to grab his bag. "Daniel, this is money for Isabel and Anna's dowry, as well as plenty to help care for my mother. There is also money enough to do what you like with. I sold my business and my home; I'm entrusting the women of my life to your care. When I return, I expect to see them all blissfully content."

Daniel embraced him. "Upon my life, they will be well taken care of; I swear it to you."

Anna ran to Jon. "How will we know if you're safe?" she asked through tears. "You shall miss my birthday, Christmas, and everything!"

Jon knelt on the ground to comfort her in a hug, for Anna was quite small for her age. "I will find ways of getting messages to you. And I promise to come back. By then you will be a proper lady!"

Mama had tears streaming down her face. "I am so proud of you!" She kissed his face. "Promise me that you will be safe and take care of yourself?"

"Mama, I promise. I love you dearly. All will be well, you shall see."

He exchanged one last hug with all of us and walked down the road towards the port until he was out of sight.

***

Eight years later...

Over the years, God blessed Daniel and I with three sons: Isaac, Tristan, and Edmund. We also have another baby on the way! I hope you do not judge me for hoping it's a girl. For if it is, I plan to call her Christy.

We now have a carriage and two horses which makes me wildly excited to be able to ride again when I am not with child. We are teaching the boys to ride and to care for the horses as well.

Daniel and his brother's business does quite well. He is the sort of man who only looks more handsome as he ages. Not a day goes by that I'm not grateful to God for bringing us together. He is such a wonderful father; he plays as though he never actually quite grew up! He is constantly teaching the boys something new, playing games with them, or taking them out on the boat to fish.

As for hiding priests – we have protected over twenty so far in our home. I only wish my brother and Father Ingles were amongst them.

Jonathon occasionally manages to sneak a message to us. We know that he was ordained a priest, praise God! Also that he and a friend traveled to Italy together in hopes of being accepted as Jesuits. He has studied with them for years now though, and God has not willed for him to come back to England yet.

The last letter we received was six months ago. To say I miss him with all my heart does not properly convey the hole his absence has left in me. I often tell my children stories of their brave and silly uncle, and we pray for his return daily.

Mama is getting on in years; in truth we don't know how much longer she will be with us. She often complains of feeling weak and of pains in her hands and legs. She spends most of her time watching the ocean waves crash into the shoreline or indulging her grandchildren in any way she can.

Anna grew up to be very beautiful and well-rounded. She is recently married to a good Catholic man named Mr. Peter Walter. They live only a few miles away from us.

We have never heard from nor seen Lord Drake, God be praised. Rumors say he finally gave up looking for me a few years ago and lives the life of a recluse. Whether this is true or not, I cannot confirm. I hope it is not. I will always feel a certain sadness for him; I remember him in my daily prayers. More than that, though, he does not trouble or cross my mind any longer, of which I am grateful. During the early years here, I experienced terrible nightmares about him. Only on occasion do I dream of him still chasing and trying to find me now.

I still feel homesick for Aylesbury at times and wish that I could return to visit old friends. Of course, I miss Christy the most. I feel her absence keenly. I daydream about seeing her probably more than I should. We have all agreed, though, that it will never be worth the risk.

Through traveling priests, we are able to receive a yearly letter or so. From those I learned that she too became a mother and they have been successful with continuing to hide priests. The alarming news is that I have not received a letter from her in four years now. I worry something has befallen them.

I try to comfort myself with how much God has blessed my life here with family and friends. I am surrounded by more friends than I have a right to.

All the Clifton women are quite close. Though, as I predicted, I have formed a closer bond with Bridget and Theresa. We spend quite a lot of time with one another and our children have formed endearing friendships with all of their cousins.

As I write this from the desk in our bedchamber, I can see them all playing in our back gardens. As my husband promised, the ocean can also be seen from here. Each day when I look out this window, I am captured by its beauty all over again.

The children tend to swarm like bees, pollinating between all their aunts and uncle's houses; we all live within five miles of one another which delights the children as much as it does us. It's a heartwarming sight when not one of them is fighting over something. With such varying ages, from three all the way to seven and ten – that is quite the feat.

I often take this time to write in the afternoons, while the children wear themselves out. I love to gaze out across the ocean, watch the children, and revel in the joys of ink and paper. It's idyllic, especially when one considers what my life might have been with Lord Drake. Sometimes I wonder if I deserve such a contented life.

Resting my hand over the kicking babe in my womb, I spied Daniel with one of his brothers walking up a path from along the ocean.

Without thinking, a smile spread across my face. After all this time, just the sight of him thrills my heart. I wondered where Daniel had been off to in such a hurry this morning – I barely had the chance to kiss him goodbye. No doubt some business related notion with Rodney or Robert.

Only... I can't make out which brother it is he's walking with. He is too short to be Robert and too thin to be Andrew or Rodney...too dark to be Eric. Wait! *No!* Could that possibly be? *Jonathon?* – With a beard? He's home!

Look for the sequel, ***Priest of the Masquerade***, to follow Father Dawson's journey as an underground priest and discover what becomes of Lord Drake, Isabel, Daniel, and the others.

For further information about the sequel, other books, newsletter, and social media pages, please visit:
https://www.angelinasalvaggio.com/